DÉJÀ VU

The man means business, Quinn thought, but still she didn't move. Welles leaned closer, then closer again, bending his head until their mouths met at just the right incline.

The kiss was soft, smoky, sending a slow curl of heat through her body. Wanting to go limp in his arms, Quinn realized that in fact she wasn't being held, that he had one arm braced now on the wall above her head, the other at his side. Yet she felt as if he were touching her everywhere.

"No good-byes," he whispered against the corner of her mouth. Then, in the next breath, he let her go.

D0802679

Also by Leigh Riker

Morning Rain
Unforgettable

Available from
HarperPaperbacks

TEARS
OF
JADE

Leigh Riker

HarperPaperbacks
A Division of HarperCollinsPublishers

If you purchased this book without a cover, you should be
aware that this book is stolen property. It was reported as
"unsold and destroyed" to the publisher and neither the
author nor the publisher has received any payment for this
"stripped book."

This is a work of fiction. The characters, incidents, and
dialogues are products of the author's imagination and are not
to be construed as real. Any resemblance to actual events or
persons, living or dead, is entirely coincidental.

HarperPaperbacks *A Division of* HarperCollins*Publishers*
10 East 53rd Street, New York, N.Y. 10022

Copyright © 1993 by Leigh Riker
All rights reserved. No part of this book may be used or
reproduced in any manner whatsoever without written
permission of the publisher, except in the case of brief
quotations embodied in critical articles and reviews. For
information address HarperCollins*Publishers,*
10 East 53rd Street, New York, N.Y. 10022.

Cover illustration by Jeff Cornell

First printing: November 1993

Printed in the United States of America

HarperPaperbacks, HarperMonogram, and colophon are
trademarks of HarperCollins*Publishers*

❖ 10 9 8 7 6 5 4 3 2 1

To my agent, Emilie Jacobson, who has been there from the start and, through it all, believed. Continuing love and thanks, Emmy.

And to my editor, Carolyn Marino, a writer's dream—who guides with such skill and patience, always knows what does and doesn't belong, and gives me the freedom to grow. Thanks too to Karen Solem, Christey Bahn, and the rest of the wonderful staff at HarperPaperbacks.

Prologue

**The North Vietnam–Laos border
December 1972**

*Life is full of surprises, she always said. Like a
Cracker Jack box. And her words had always made him
smile.*

Nasty surprises, he thought now.

He thought he'd been lying in the dirt, a canopy of
tangled leaves above blocking out the sun, for more than
twenty-four hours: an estimate, because his watch had
shattered in the crash. Already he could feel fever rising in
him with all the power of his F-4 Phantom jet lifting off the
carrier deck for the last time in a scream of sound. Some
bloody hero, he told himself.

He couldn't stop crying but the tears had no sound; he
was too panicked by the thought of the passing patrols still
looking for him to permit the noise.

They'd come close the last time, much too close.

Heart pounding, he had rolled onto his belly, pushing

his face into the hot, damp earth, breathing his own vomit, trying not to whimper, promising himself he wouldn't beg for his life.

Coward.

He could hear soldiers now, thrashing through the nearby brush, grunting in Vietnamese, and he knew the statistics: a thousand pilots already killed; another thousand missing; six hundred men, guests of the North Vietnamese at the "Hanoi Hilton." Chances were, they'd kill him first. Slowly.

Hell, he thought, maybe it didn't matter. At fifty-five thousand feet, or skimming beneath the sweep of Vietcong radar at five hundred, or even on the ground, he was a murderer too. Was this how it felt to die?

Struggling onto his back, he braced himself, mind and gut, then inched his fingers down his chest to the torn leg of his flight suit. It had ripped on impact from crotch to knee. When he touched the leg, he bit down on his tongue to keep from crying out. Jesus, he could feel the bone. A compound fracture, and messy. His head swam and his stomach churned. By morning, if the patrols hadn't found him, infection might kill him.

In either case, his life would be over before it had really begun. No more than he deserved, he supposed, after yesterday and the crash, after . . .

He groaned. Jerking his hand away from the wound, he touched his breast pocket, but his fingers, sticky with blood, had gone numb. He couldn't feel, couldn't reach the picture hastily tucked inside—the only thing left of a life he'd wasted. Closing his eyes, instead he had to imagine her, snapped in some junk-store photo booth in the middle of a laugh: her hair the color of copper . . . impish green eyes . . . and those long wrap-around-you-in-the-dark legs. He even pressed his open mouth to his wrist as if to kiss her lips.

You crazy bastard! He cursed himself, shivering, uncertain whether the chills stemmed from fever or feeling scared out of his clammy skin. *Coward. Murderer. Liar.* Then he thought her name and must have groaned aloud. And this time they heard him. Footsteps rustled in the underbrush, a voice called out. They had found him but there would be no fight. His strength was gone. He'd never had a chance.

In the next instant a bunch of little men in black pajamas came crashing through the trees that had sheltered him.

"Quinn," was all he said.

Sassy, fragile Quinn.

1

Manhattan
July 1992

Sound asleep, Quinn Tyler decided, he looked almost normal. Listening to the quiet hum of the air conditioner, she stood over him, unwilling to leave, half smiling at his mostly bare body, sprawled face down on the diagonal across the bed.

"Andrew?" she whispered. "I'm nearly ready. The limo's picking me up at six-thirty. Are you awake?"

"Mmmm."

Her smile faded. "Even a little?"

He'd always been slow to waken, but in the past six years Quinn, an early riser, had come to relish that. She liked watching him drift from a peaceful sleep into consciousness, before reality dawned on him again. But it wasn't morning now; it was early evening and he hadn't bothered to get up that day. How she missed the laid-back Andrew Devlin of the laughing blue-gray eyes whom she'd first known. She drew her gaze from the long line of his back, the jagged scar. His left arm—his good one—curled around the pillow; the other lay hidden under his belly. Quinn focused instead on the sunny glint of his sandy-blond hair, one clump sticking out from his stubborn cowlick at the crown. She didn't look at his leg; as usual, he'd worn loose pajama bottoms to bed, even in the heat of New York city in July. Years ago, he would have slept naked.

"I'll call from Paris," she said. "I left your dinner in the microwave. Don't let it rot. Lotte will be here in the morning to fix breakfast. You'll be all right on your own?"

"Right as the rains of Ranjipur."

At his flat tone she shifted the strap of her leather bag to the other shoulder and frowned. "You're sure? I don't want to leave, but I'll be back before you miss me."

"Go," he muttered into the pillow; then, with grudging amusement, "It's six P.M., Ms. Tyler-Devlin. Do you know where your passport is?"

"Oh, God." Diving into the bag's cavernous depths like a spelunker, she riffled through its contents, finding wallet, tissues, a stray credit card, makeup—but no passport. "Damn. I thought I had everything."

"That'll be the day."

"Where could I have put it?"

Quinn swept from the room. She hadn't been out of the country in weeks. A long, loose stride carried her quickly through the rambling apartment toward the third and smallest bedroom, which she'd turned into an office when they moved here; when she'd taken her latest plunge and struck out on her own.

"Sheer boneheaded risk," Andrew had said, but she liked taking risks. And four years ago she'd proved him wrong about starting her own agency—though tomorrow's worrisome ad shoot in France had become the norm for Quinn, who traveled more than she would have liked now, because of Andrew. She couldn't hate the money, Quinn thought, averting her eyes as she passed the second bedroom, once planned as a nursery.

Andrew couldn't hate it either, especially since the accident. In her heart she knew he'd be able to use his right arm, his hand, again. Someday. For now, she was the family breadwinner and glad to have a salary in the low six figures. With the new account, her biggest thus far, on the line—Quinn's mission was to glorify the client's new stone-washed blue jeans—the money would get better. Provided she delivered what Priceless Sportswear expected. . . .

Further thoughts of blue jeans, of Andrew, were replaced by the unshakable feeling that she'd forgotten something important other than her passport. Quinn lost things every day and her office was the usual mess, but she barely saw the clutter. It matched her work space at the agency, and she'd long ago stopped trying to make order of that chaos either. She might not be able to put her finger on what she needed in an instant, but everything was here. Or there, Quinn thought with a smile.

She preferred her home office. Smaller, more cozy, it contained her personal mementos—wherever most of them were. She grinned at the nearest wall, at the life she'd led for the past fifteen years. Her professional life. The wall, papered with framed photographs of all her ad shoots, made an impressive statement, and there were even a few modeling shots of Quinn herself from the year or two she'd tried that. She hadn't been quite tall enough to hope for superstar status, not exotic enough to become her decade's Lauren Hutton or Iman. She'd quickly learned that she preferred the other side of the camera; to Quinn it was the more creative side. So she'd gone back to school, finished her degree—and plowed right in to the business of making her niche.

Typical Quinn, Andrew would say; if only she could learn to remember where she'd left the latest ad proofs . . . or her passport.

She rummaged on her desk, heaped with magazines opened to competitors' ads, but the navy blue folder stamped in gold wasn't among them. She glanced at the brass clock above the door and jerked open a drawer, finding paper clips, rubber bands, three ballpoint pens without tops, and a haphazard collection of note pads from hotels around the world.

Two drawers later, she began to sweat. It was a matter of planning, Andrew always told her; she could organize her life if she just tried. Allowed herself extra time. Made lists and didn't lose them. Quinn always replied that she preferred surprises.

But please, not now, she thought. Where was the damn passport? And what else had she misplaced?

In the last drawer she discovered personal memen-tos, old ones: pictures, handkerchiefs, and scarves, all gifts she never used. She flipped past a snapshot of her-self as a gawky child, then one of her mother as a young woman, the only way Quinn had known her. The third picture showed her father in his army uniform, standing by a jeep, his dark-blond hair—rather like Andrew's— cut short, his green eyes full of mischief. The father she had never known. How long before he'd died? she wondered. Quinn met the same bubbling warmth in her own gaze every time she looked in the mirror, but by now she was frowning.

There was no picture of a house, a home.

In fact, the only home she remembered was Doug

Lloyd's ranch house in Colorado, where her mother had worked as a cook. After her death, when Doug would have played surrogate father. . . .

Quinn slammed the drawer shut on a past she'd tried to forget, but something caught and she pulled it open again.

Her heart increased its rhythm as she pulled out a length of silk. Above all, she wanted to forget this memory. Jay had given her the white aviator scarf the day before he left for Vietnam. It had been a joke of sorts because Quinn, already missing him, had called him a "glamorous flyboy" so she wouldn't cry; but on their last night he'd used it to make love, drawing the smooth white silk along her bare skin, following with his mouth . . . stopping their laughter.

Quinn blinked back sudden tears. First love. They'd been so young—she not yet twenty, and he just turning twenty-five. Six months later his F-4 Phantom jet had plummeted from the sky over North Vietnam. That Christmas he'd been listed as missing in action; he still was. Quinn squeezed her eyes shut.

Dear God, what had happened to him?

And how could it still hurt? She had everything a woman could possibly want—a challenging career, an attractive man. . . . Almost everything.

She should pack up the past. Organize her personal life, as Andrew urged her to do. Instead, she sat, pulling the silk through her fingers, remembering warm dark eyes and coffee-brown hair and sleek skin, smelling like the pine trees that lined the driveway at the ranch.

She was trembling now. Nineteen years ago. . . .

Half her lifetime, she thought. It had been quite a while since she'd imagined—sheer self-indulgence—that she saw Jay in some crowd. She couldn't still love him. She had Andrew now, who had been his friend.

"Quinn, did you find—?"

She jumped. She hadn't heard Andrew's halting footsteps along the thickly carpeted hall. He shuffled into the room, his right arm cradled to his waist as if to ward off blows.

"My passport?" she said, laying the white scarf on the desktop. She could hardly hide it. "No." Then she plunged one hand into the patch pocket of her persimmon-colored jacket and flushed. "Oh, here it is. I should have remembered."

He would be shaking his head but she couldn't look up, into his eyes. She saw the dark shadows of pain there every day of her life, shadows she had caused.

"The limo's here," he said. "You'll miss your plane."

What could she say? Quinn focused miserably on the desk calendar, which for some reason showed the right date. Her housekeeper, Lotte, must have dusted, or at least shoved things around. She was as meticulous as Andrew.

She stared at the date on the calendar and realized what else she'd forgotten. Who was she kidding? For years she'd suffered a maddening depression around his birthday; she still wondered what had happened to Lieutenant William Jay Barron, U.S. Navy. More than that, after nineteen years she still believed he might come back.

It didn't surprise Quinn to find her agency's stylist already in the adjoining first-class seat on board their flight when she reached Kennedy Airport an hour later.

"New boyfriend with his own helicopter?" Quinn asked. "You can't have taken a cab. Traffic was gridlocked from East Fifty-ninth to the airport exit. You must have made record time."

Valerie Mason grinned. "I plan ahead. You should try it sometime." She shook her head. "I also look forward to flying as much as I do to a root canal. I like to get it over with."

Quinn slid her briefcase under the seat. "I hate to tell you, but this plane's not taking off any sooner just because you boarded with the mothers and nursing infants."

"It's not taking off any later just because you skidded down the jetway, late as usual."

After Andrew's white-lipped reaction to seeing Jay's silk scarf, Quinn was beginning to wish the plane wouldn't take off at all. The evening wasn't going her way. "I believe in dramatic entrances," she murmured. "Like any good creative director."

"That's what I love about you. You make good sense—then blow it all by losing your passport."

Quinn gaped. "How did you know?"

The grin widened. "Are you joined at the hip to one of the world's great hunks? Is the sky outside this window becoming as black as pitch? Of course you lost your passport." Her enormous earrings—Valerie's trademark—were still quivering. "Just as I know we're about to fly through this century's worst thunderstorm. And how is Andrew tonight?"

"Half asleep when I left."

They exchanged a look, and Quinn saw by the slight drift of Valerie's right eye—her lazy one—that she was genuinely worried, and not only about the flight. The long hours in bed meant Andrew was slipping into another of his depressions.

Quinn frowned at her small lie. He'd been wide awake when she left, and he hadn't kissed her goodbye. "Talk about sleep, what were you doing when you picked those earrings?" Two circles shot through with lightning bolts, they were as big as half dollars. Quinn shuddered. "Where did you find them?"

"My favorite boutique at Lex and Sixty-seventh."

"The place that sells herbal teas with things in them like—"

"Eye of newt and tongue of frog?" Valerie laughed.

"I don't know how you keep your job, except that I'm your boss." Quinn glanced at Valerie's purple harem pants, her black suede slippers studded with multicolored faux gems, her yellow cossack shirt. They could blind a normal person. Her friend's oversized scarlet jacket made two of Quinn's linen blazer. "That's ghastly, Val."

"Thank you. I like yours too. Properly upscale as always. That little knit dress the perfect color of Pacific coast salmon must have cost a week's pay." Quinn heard envy in her tone. "I suppose the shoes are Ferragamo. Real lizard."

"Don't make any announcements for the onboard environmentalists, will you? I need my job."

"You can have mine. I won't need a job by Christmas."

"Really," Quinn said, knowing there was more. Forget the bizarre costumes, the fun house jewelry. Behind those bright gray eyes, under that swatch of frosted hair, lurked a brilliant stylist who could find the perfect prop for a commercial on an hour's notice. In such a small agency, Valerie also wrote copy and generally filled in wherever needed. Quinn had worked with her for four years and knew just how shrewd, how organized, she was inside; but she also knew Valerie's blind spot. "I suppose you're meeting Mr. Right before New Year's."

Valerie whipped out a slender book. "See for yourself."

Quinn tried not to smile. Valerie believed in horoscopes, in portents and omens, and in precognition. Quinn supposed the self-indulgence was harmless, certainly less harmful than her own imaginings of Jay Barron, except in this instance. She handed the book back. "You don't actually think 'you will attract the man of your dreams in summer'? Again?"

"By Labor Day," Valerie said. "I'm not turning thirty and still living by myself."

"Val, you have four years to go. What's the hurry? I'd hate to see you hurt again."

"Are you referring to Memorial Day weekend? To that Japanese businessman who treated me like his dream geisha for three days? Or to taking my formerly best male friend on the Caribbean shoot last month—"

"And watching him run off to marry the Priceless cover girl on twenty-four hours' acquaintance?" Quinn smiled. "Well, now that you mention it—"

"I know that caused you headaches."

Quinn groaned. "And look what we've ended up with as the new spokesperson."

"We're all fallible. I lose men. You lost your passport, and last week your paycheck. And—"

"Is this your charming way of telling me I'm disorganized? I already know that."

Valerie grinned. "Ulterior motive. I want you settled, so that when I'm blissfully married to another of the world's great hunks, my belly at last swollen with child—"

"You'll still be wearing that Joseph's coat of many colors," Quinn teased, but unhappiness flashed through her.

Valerie's tone softened. "Don't want to think about babies?"

"Not particularly."

"Andrew will come around, Quinn."

"You think so? It's been six years." She sighed. "I'm running out of time. We hardly make love anymore. I don't think I can remember the last time. It's pretty hard to get pregnant without a partner." Her mouth twisted. "And where would I find the time these days to be a mother?" When Valerie's hand touched hers, she said, "Let's talk about something else."

"The ad shoot," Valerie suggested. "Versailles. Our new cover girl." As the plane's jet engines whined toward full throttle, she gripped Quinn's arm harder. "Do you think Ilse will wash out among our hundreds of crystal bowls of candles in the Hall of Mirrors?"

Quinn grimaced. Neither she nor Valerie had been enthusiastic about the German-born English-based megastar model, the client's choice, though the account was still Quinn's worry. "You mean, with her platinum ironed-flat-as-a-sheet hair?"

"No way. I feel it in my bones. They want sexy; she's not. Her horoscope says—" Riffling pages in her book, Valerie rattled off a long, depressing quote about disaster. "I tell you, she's not going to work."

Quinn's stomach rolled as the jet took off. "She has to work, Mason. Priceless is paying her a million bucks to sell blue jeans. By God, she'd better sell them by the carload." She grinned. "Or we'd both better get knocked up in a hurry."

Quinn and Valerie reached their hotel the next morning, a disappointment to Quinn, who had wanted to check in at the delicate time of day the French call *l'heure bleu*. The late afternoon, gauzy gray-blue with romantic shadows, the nearby Eiffel Tower illuminated as if through a soft-filter lens, was denied her. Taxi horns blared, a nattily dressed man cut her off at the revolving doors, and the air smelled damp and fishy, like New York. In the bright sun, so early in the day, she didn't even see the strolling lovers she'd been promised years ago. Yet the hotel looked endearingly familiar.

Quinn had checked into hundreds of hotels in her time, several in Paris, though never this one. Still, the lobby's lavish eighteenth-century splendor, its Flemish tapestries and genuine oil paintings, felt like home. Yawning after the long flight, she realized even the fact that she didn't speak French couldn't faze her.

The man standing by the registration desk did.

Quinn froze, one hand clutching the pen with which she had signed the register. Next to her, Valerie was busily doing the same and didn't look up.

Quinn had only a quick glimpse, but his posture— military straight, with shoulders squared—nearly stopped her heart. His hair is darker, she tried to tell herself, and he stood partially turned from her so she couldn't see his face. But her palms grew damp and she was suddenly breathing as if through water.

There were two other people between them at the desk, and he didn't pause long. Turning his back completely, he reached for a message the clerk handed him. Quinn heard him say *"Merci,"* then some rapid, softly uttered phrase in an accent she could only envy.

"Madame?"

"Thank you." Quinn took her credit card from another clerk, her eyes trained on the man who was walking toward the elevators.

Her pulse sped faster. Intent on his message, he had bent his head slightly and the overhead light brought out the gold in his dark hair. In his right hand he carried what Quinn recognized as a top-of-the-line Hartmann briefcase. Jay had never bought anything but the best. He even looked the right height, his shoulders just broad enough, his dark vented suit cut in the European style Jay had preferred, emphasizing the long line of his spine. Leaving Valerie behind, Quinn tore away from the desk, her heels clicking on the marble floor.

She was ten feet behind when he strode into the waiting elevator.

"Quinn?" Valerie's voice made her turn. "Where are you going in such a rush? I—" She stopped. "Hey, are you all right? You're as white as vanilla ice cream."

"I'm fine." Quinn felt more like an old bedsheet, and twice as limp. "I—I just thought I saw someone I knew." She circled around, but the elevator doors had closed and her heart sank. Even if she followed in the next car, she didn't know on which floor he was staying. "Val, why don't you go up with the bellman and our bags? I'll be right there."

Valerie's gray eyes looked as round as pie plates.

Without waiting for an answer, Quinn hurried back through the lobby. At the front desk she had to wait while a group of Japanese businessmen in identical gray suits massed for a group picture and a woman swathed in white mink argued about the accommodations she'd been given. When it was her turn, Quinn's brief conversation in mangled French with several clerks produced little beyond blank looks. Her English didn't seem to help either. The Japanese had managed much better.

Quinn stomped toward the concierge's desk and held up her room key. "Could you please help me? I'm looking for another guest of the hotel, William Jay Barron. Can you tell me his room number?"

The concierge's glance skimmed her from head to foot.

"Un moment," he said, soon advising her that the computer was down; as she expected, it was against hotel policy to disclose room numbers but the switchboard, now jammed, would connect her with the party she wanted at the earliest opportunity.

On the way upstairs Quinn suffered second thoughts. A good thing she hadn't caught the man before he reached the elevator. What would she have said?

Instead of chasing phantoms, like Valerie with her romantic horoscope, she should get some rest while she could. Instead, she was making a fool of herself. "Ridiculous," she muttered.

She'd simply had a random thought about Jay before leaving last night. That—plus jet lag and her own worry over the ad shoot, over leaving Andrew alone—had made her vulnerable to escapist fantasy, but unlike Valerie, she no longer gave in to dreams. Then why was she still wondering?

She'd no sooner reached the suite they shared when the telephone rang. Valerie was in the shower, and Quinn, in her own bedroom, hurried to answer.

"Madame Tyler-Devlin? The gentleman you have inquired about . . . I am sorry, but we 'ave no William Jay Barron at this 'otel."

"Thank you. I must have been mistaken," she said and hung up.

The adrenaline drained from her, leaving her weak and disappointed. The bedside alarm clock alternately winked the time and date. Quinn stared at it. July 7, she thought, and her eyes brimmed. Happy birthday, Jay. That's what she would have said.

By late afternoon the next day at Versailles, Quinn had been fighting a pounding headache for more hours than she cared to count. She hadn't slept well the night before, and, as she'd expected, the shoot was becoming a nightmare. When Ilse blew her lines for easily the tenth time, Quinn threw up her hands and left the set. She pushed out the heavy bronze doors into a sunlit courtyard and collapsed against a stone wall.

"Has anyone killed that German-English disaster yet?" she asked when Valerie joined her.

"Let's flip a coin. I'll make sure it's two-headed." Valerie groaned. "Can you believe the money that's getting blown for filming here? All she has to do is look good—which, God knows, shouldn't be hard with tits and an ass like that. And those legs. . . . All she has to do is stick out her rump, beam that bedroom look into the camera's eye, and say, 'For the girl in you who loves denim, for the woman in you who feels like silk. Priceless.'" Valerie struck a pose.

And Quinn added, "Tell me I didn't write that."

"The guys at the top—Frank Murray himself at Priceless, no less—loved it. Of course they loved Ilse too." Valerie's grin faded. "Quinn? What's wrong?"

"Nothing." The word came too quickly.

Valerie's huge Day-Glo hoops in neon pink bobbed in Quinn's face. "Are you fretting about Andrew?"

"No," she said. "I talked to him last night. He sounded okay, but he'd taken a pain pill and was already sleepy."

"Something's wrong."

Quinn sighed. "Remember when I thought I saw someone yesterday in the hotel lobby?" she began. Moments later, the story off her chest, she didn't feel better, but at least she didn't feel so solitary.

"Reality's certainly not my forte where love is concerned," Valerie said, "but you *do* realize that the likelihood of Jay Barron showing up at the same hotel on the same day after so much time doesn't seem that great."

"His family always stayed at the George Cinq," Quinn said. "When I was in college the Barrons toured Europe every summer. It irritated me because they took

Jay and I couldn't afford to join them—as if I'd be invited. He sent me postcards and little gifts, but I was still stuck at home earning money for fall semester. Strange," she added, "but yesterday seemed like checking in to a place where I'd stayed as many times as Jay did."

"He must have told you a lot about it," Valerie guessed. "Wow," she said. "I'm seeing you in a whole new light. Why didn't you ever tell me before?"

"About something that happened nineteen years ago? We were both kids. I rarely talk about it. But then again, maybe I made the reservation at the George Cinq to reward myself for the Priceless contract, to tell myself I've made it at last."

Valerie sighed. "Frankly, the whole romantic image blows me away: the dashing navy pilot, the white silk scarf. . . ."

Quinn smiled sadly. "When I drove him to Stapleton Airport in Denver for his flight back to base and on to Vietnam, he looped that scarf around my neck and kissed me. I was crying by then, clinging to him. I didn't think I could bear to let him walk out of my sight." Her eyes closed briefly. "He kissed me one last time; then his mouth stayed just short of touching mine again and when I tried to speak, the tears streaming down my face, you know what he whispered? 'No goodbyes, Quinn.'" She blinked. "*Then* he walked away. Smiling."

"Oh, God." Valerie hugged her.

"I never saw him again. I've always thought the worst part is just not knowing. If he'd died and the Navy had notified his parents and they called me—if they would have—or if his brother had . . ." She trailed off. "I'd know he was gone. Just like my father."

"He died in Korea, didn't he?"

"Yes, not long before I was born."

"That must have been awfully rough for your mother."

Quinn nodded. "I think his death hastened hers. She never really put it behind her. Not even after she started working for Doug Lloyd, who took us in and loved us both."

She smiled, recalling the happiest moments of her childhood. They hadn't lasted nearly long enough.

"It's a shame he didn't marry her," Valerie said.

"He would have," Quinn answered. "He wanted to. And he wanted to adopt me. But she died before it happened."

Quinn pushed away from the wall and hooked her arm through Valerie's. How had she gotten into this mawkish confession?

"Come on," she said. "Let's go see how Ilse's doing. If we can wrap this thing soon, I'll buy you dinner tonight."

"And tell me more about Jay Barron?"

Quinn said, "There's nothing more to tell."

In her mind Quinn had gone over seeing him a thousand times. His hair had been darker, she'd told herself, but after nineteen years it might be. She'd had only a quick glimpse, but even in profile she'd seen the remembered cheekbones, high and sculpted, the nose straight as the crease in his uniform trousers years ago. Such classic good looks weren't that common, even in Quinn's business; and she'd known him well enough, looked enough days and nights at his photograph, to remember him accurately. A girlhood spent watching other people's reactions, other people's moods—would they send her away again?—had given Quinn an observant nature. Yet she didn't trust her observation this time.

"I have to agree. It probably wasn't Barron," Valerie said at dinner, picking through her Caesar salad with a fork. "That hardly thrills me, romantic that I am. But the years, the distance . . . and where could he have been all this time? What would he be doing here now?"

Quinn shrugged. By the time they'd finished shooting at Versailles and soothed both Ilse's temper and the director's ego, Valerie and Quinn had felt too tired to explore the restaurants for which Paris was so justly famous. They'd decided on Les Princes, the hotel's equally fine dining room, and, at least on Quinn's part, a light meal.

She said, "Whatever he does, he probably travels on business. He was carrying expensive luggage, so obviously he doesn't lack for money."

"From what I've heard, Jay didn't either."

Quinn shook her head. "He came from a well-to-do San Francisco family. His father was a prominent attorney, his mother a former debutante turned college professor." She paused. "They lived on Pacific Heights, the best address in town, in a beautiful neo-Italianate house—a mansion, really." She flinched. "I was only there once."

"It doesn't sound like you had any fun."

"Let's just say his parents found a girl who lived on scholarships and county welfare handouts—in foster homes—unsuitable for their son. Jay's older brother couldn't have agreed more. I think Charles is senior partner in their father's law firm now."

"They disapproved of you." Valerie waved a julienned carrot on the end of her fork. "How could they?"

"They would have come around," Quinn said matter-of-factly. "That's what I always told Jay."

"Doesn't sound like they intimidated you. Which doesn't surprise me."

"They tried," was all Quinn said. She shoved her gold-rimmed plate of marinated shrimp aside. "I could have used a bit of their hauteur yesterday. Then maybe I wouldn't have gone flying after a total stranger."

Valerie snorted. "I saw him in the elevator as the doors closed. Believe me, that guy was worth flying after, Jay Barron or not."

Quinn picked up a wheat cracker, then put it down again. "I'm afraid chasing strange men doesn't go with my current lifestyle." She had Andrew to worry about. "Neither does playing private detective."

"Think again." Glancing up, she met Valerie's wide-eyed expression; she was staring over Quinn's shoulder. "Look behind you, Sherlock Holmes. Four tables back along the windows."

"Look at what?" Quinn's heart began to drum.

"The same man."

"You're sure?"

"That's not a face you forget."

"I can't look." She clenched her hands in her lap. "Who's he with?"

"Another man, oriental."

"Japanese?" The hotel was full of them.

"No," Valerie said. "His face doesn't look Japanese— remembering my weekend as a geisha. Korean, maybe, or Chinese." She shook her head. "I'm not very good with nationalities."

"Vietnamese," Quinn suggested. "Jay was shot down over the North somewhere." Her hand trembling, she drizzled oil and vinegar over her salad from a silver boat. "What's he doing now?"

"Probably buying a few thousand cases of shoelaces or computer microchips from the oriental guy. No, it looks like they're quarreling. They've called for the check."

Quinn's heart jumped into her throat.

Remembering the silk scarf, the memories she'd tried to repress, she set the salad dressing on the table.

Outside in the courtyard, where in summer the Georges V offered dining al fresco under red umbrellas, the July night seemed to glow softly, as Paris should. For lovers. Quinn was here on business, the only time she traveled now, with Andrew waiting at home. She had another life and must be mistaken. Worried about the new ad campaign, she'd conjured up a simpler time, a less complicated relationship. As always, when troubled, she had sought the security she'd never known as a child. Nothing, Quinn knew, was that simple.

Even Jay.

Still, what woman wouldn't want to see the man she'd first loved again? To learn what had happened to him?

"Ten o'clock high," Valerie murmured into her wineglass. "They've flashed the plastic, signed the check. They're coming this way." Her eyes intently catalogued the stranger's features. "Now's your chance. Move," she said. "Say something."

Unable to resist the challenge, Quinn tossed her napkin down with a soft plop. Her pulse thundered in her ears but in the next instant, as she started to rise, the damask tablecloth caught on her dress, and the silver boat of olive-oil-and-vinegar salad dressing poured over her lap.

Abruptly Quinn sat back down. Their voices low and intense, speaking French, the two men passed to the left of her table in the next row.

"Oh, Quinn," Valerie murmured.

A pair of energetic waiters with sponges and towels cut off her view. She had glimpsed only that high-boned profile again, dark hair edging the shirt collar, and nothing more.

When the waiters left, assuring Quinn that the hotel would pay to have her dress dry-cleaned, Valerie said, "Well? Do you think it was—?"

"I don't know. No, probably not. It doesn't matter." But she couldn't help one last glance at the restaurant's empty doorway. "You go ahead and order dessert," she said, rising. "I have to visit the ladies' room."

In the bathroom, after dabbing at her dress again, Quinn lingered. She washed her hands. She freshened her lipstick. She told herself a dozen times that she was being absurd, even schoolgirlish—and most of all, unfair to Andrew.

Then she sank down onto a plush-upholstered chair at the mirror and slowly unfolded a crumpled piece of black carbon paper. She'd filched it from the ashtray, the fourth table back, on her way to the rest room.

In the next second, her head seemed to clear as if she'd stepped out into the warm night and breathed deeply of Paris. The name on the check wasn't William Jay Barron. She'd been wrong after all. Quinn had no idea what she would have done if, instead, she'd been right.

2

From his sixteenth-floor office in the Banque Internationale de Genève, Welles Blackburn had an unrestricted view of the city's gemlike Lac Léman glittering in the distance—a view he stared at this morning without seeing. Below, on this side of the Mont Blanc bridge, a cluster of old white stone and newer glass-faced buildings sparkled in the morning sunlight. In Geneva everything sparkled, which suited Welles just fine. Switzerland was the cleanest place he'd ever seen, far cleaner than the fetid jungle on the Laotian border nearly eight thousand miles away.

Not far enough, Welles thought. The past had been very much in his mind, up close again and personal, for two days.

Removing his tortoiseshell glasses, he closed his eyes against the memory and the bright view outside his windows. If he studied his reflection, he was convinced his true self would be revealed on the glass, like Oscar Wilde's *Portrait of Dorian Gray*.

Welles squared his shoulders and, opening his eyes, turned back into the room. His office—his work—had long ago become a refuge; until a few days ago, for all but two of his nineteen years in Europe, he'd been able to escape into it. Escape, he acknowledged, being only one of his lesser talents.

He didn't bother rattling off the rest. He'd been told how self-destructive that was, and normally he could stop the negative thoughts with that one word: Stop.

He put his glasses back on and scanned his desk calendar, noting a full morning, then a luncheon meeting with the bank's vice-president in charge of international investments, who wanted Welles's projections on Third World loan repayments for the next fiscal quarter. Tickets for tonight's performance at the Grand Theatre would be delivered to his secretary by four o'clock. She had already made dinner reservations for two at L'Étoile afterward. A midday conference with his staff would end the day, except for the last notation, which immediately made Welles aware of his own heartbeat: *Call Duc Tran.* He supposed—knew—it had to do with their quarrel in Paris two nights ago. Dammit.

He jerked at the knot of his Italian silk tie. Tossing his gray Savile Row suit coat over the back of his chair, he braced both hands on his black walnut desk. Its surface, except for the calendar, a neat stack of mail, and a black onyx pen set, was bare, the way Welles liked it.

"Clutter," Tran had said, his dark eyes narrowed into slits, his slim hand smoothing back thin gray hair that wasn't out of place. "Change. I can't recommend it."

"I'm not asking you to," Welles had replied. "I'm telling you I've had enough. I've stayed with her for nineteen years, and every one of them I've thought of getting out."

"Then you are not a man of commitment."

"Jesus Christ, Tran. What more can I do?"

But the older man only murmured, "This is not a wise time to alter the course of events."

Welles, tempted to crush the crystal wineglass in his hand, had forced his voice lower. "Then it's true, I'm up for a promotion with the bank? Is this your inscrutable way of telling me—"

"Not to dishonor yourself or those I love."

Blackmail. Tran was a member of the board of directors. It was then that Welles had glanced angrily away and found himself staring at the woman's back four tables in front of him. Under the soft lights of the George V's discreet restaurant, her hair glowed like burnished copper. He'd felt the immediate kick of recognition—true or false—in his gut and signaled for the check.

More than one woman in the world had hair that shade.

Crazy to think that she . . .

He yanked open a desk drawer and took out the neatly trimmed newspaper clipping inside. The black-and-white line drawing instead of a photograph had drawn him first: the bright gleam in her eye, the satisfied smile, the look of success. And then he'd noticed the other look: unfinished, unhappy. Easy enough to recognize that, he'd thought. He had only to glance at himself in the office window.

He shoved the *Wall Street Journal* profile of the savvy female advertising executive back into the drawer.

If the woman was the same as the one in the restaurant, she hadn't seen him. He was sure of that much. He and Tran, still quarreling over his need to climb out of the tight box his life had become, had walked out of the restaurant. When they passed her table, she started to get up; then abruptly sat back down again. And Tran had urged him toward the door.

Had he only imagined she was the same woman? The coppery hair, the sassy smile?

The fragile eyes.

He might want out of his box, but not that way. Nineteen years ago, he'd promised himself that if he lived he would never lie again. Ever since, he'd been living with a generalized dread that one day he might have to. Now his dread had become specific. But surely, even if it had been the same face, she wouldn't find him. She wouldn't know where or how to look for him. For now, he was still safe.

Welles slammed the drawer shut and reached for the tidy stack of mail on the corner of his desk. When minutes later his intercom buzzed, he jumped—as he'd been jumping for the past two days. He realized he was half expecting the message that already frightened him, coward that he was; that filled him with swift, forbidden joy. As if he could risk such selfishness. Or exposure.

"Mr. Blackburn," his secretary would say, "there's a woman here to see you, but she hasn't an appointment. Her name is Quinn Tyler."

Quinn had driven herself crazy wondering about the name on the credit card carbon. The past two nights, in bed, she'd been wide-eyed, praying for sleep, seeing the same letters imprinted on her mind as they were on the carbon itself. Earlier that morning she'd finally crumpled the paper and tossed it in the wastebasket. There, she thought. Done. If only she could rid herself of the ad shoot at Versailles that easily.

Quinn sighed. The film they'd shot in the Hall of Mirrors had proved disappointing. "No contrast," Valerie had said with a groan after they viewed the footage for the sixth time. "Just silver light and that platinum hair. Both forgettable."

"Then we might as well forget our next paychecks," Quinn said, though she wasn't about to give up. She spent the rest of the morning chewing her lip and watching Ilse blow her lines. In midafternoon Quinn at last murmured the one-word solution.

"Outdoors."

"What?" Valerie said. She was plowing through a carton of props that might change the ad's overall look.

"Why don't we shoot in the courtyard where you found me the other day? We'd have masses of flowers for color. We could use the same silver gown, and Ilse's hair will glow. We'll shoot at dusk."

"You're crazy."

"Let's try it, Mason. What have we got to lose?"

"Nothing but film, the cost of keeping the crew another day, and some arm twisting to use Versailles again."

"This place is open to the public. There are people tramping all over the grounds right now. Even better, we'll have a captive audience and build interest in Priceless jeans before they're on the market."

"Sheer jean-ius," Valerie said, and with a laugh Quinn went off to confer with her director, who ultimately—if not willingly at first—agreed that the change was worth a try.

By nightfall, he was ready to tear out his balding hair and Quinn, with her full copper-colored mane, was ready to join him, when Ilse marched toward her.

"Miss Devlin-Tyler, I am exhausted," she informed Quinn.

"That's Tyler-Devlin."

Ilse waved a hand, dismissing the correction. "I am dripping wet with the perspiration." She tossed her silky platinum hair. "I do not go on with this charade. If no one has the idea what to do with this commercial—"

Quinn instantly saw red. She was tired too, still jet-lagged, and worrying about leaving Andrew at home alone. She'd reached her limit.

"Quinn?" the director called. "Can we get this shit in the can? At this rate we'll be here until midnight, and that means another damn day of paying the museum."

Quinn couldn't have agreed more but gave Ilse her sweetest smile, slipping an arm around the model's bony shoulders. "He's right, you know. We'd all like to get to bed tonight. You've been such a trouper, but please, just one more take. I know this one will be perfect."

"Well, I suppose . . . if you promise it's the last one today."

"For you, I'll write it in blood."

Ilse's toothy smile appeared like a sunrise. "You are the only person on this shoot I like, Devlin-Tyler."

Biting her tongue, Quinn swept one arm toward the waiting set. The model hadn't gotten her name right once. "Your Highness, after you."

Valerie was right behind them. "Jesus," she muttered. "Do you know your horoscope for today says, 'You will soothe tempers and thus find a solution to your problem?'"

"You're kidding."

"I'm glad I'm not. My feet are killing me, my stomach's screaming 'Feed me,' and I'm already worrying about that new athlete's foot medication commercial next week."

"I should be so lucky," Quinn said. "I have to come up with the cure for a sagging ad campaign on the worst hair spray to ever hit the market. Sales are in the basement."

"Hey, the consumer's smarter than you think."

Quinn was still smiling over Valerie's remark, and the yawn that had gone with it, when a thought struck her. Why hadn't she noticed before? As Ilse took her place once more and the camera rolled, Quinn rooted in her tote bag.

She'd retrieved the black carbon from the trash that morning just before Valerie knocked at her door to say that room service had delivered breakfast. Now she called her friend over and thrust the credit card receipt at her. Quinn's tone was triumphant. "'J. Welles Blackburn,'" she read aloud, doubting Val could decipher the name in the growing darkness.

"The sexy stranger in the restaurant?" Valerie said. "So?"

She waved the carbon. "Don't you see? J. Welles Blackburn . . . William Jay Barron." Quinn's pulse was pounding. "They're the same initials, Val. In different order, that's all."

"My God. Still, it might be a coincidence."

"Hold the fort," Quinn said, already walking away. Over her shoulder, she grinned. "If Ilse blows this take, shoot her. I have to make a phone call."

By Valerie's watch, an outrageously oversized circular face on a man's black band, she'd seen that it was just after seven o'clock Paris time. Which meant 11 A.M. in Colorado.

"Well, darlin', it's taken you hell's own time to make this call. What's the occasion? You and Andrew playin' in the bathroom with a home pregnancy test that just came up bright blue for positive, or what?"

Quinn laughed, relishing Doug Lloyd's warm, gritty tone.

"No such luck, I'm afraid," she said, not letting the sadness penetrate this time. "But I do have news. Possible news."

"You comin' to visit any time soon?"

She gave her usual excuses. "I wish I could, but work's a madhouse and I don't know when I'll be able to get away. Andrew's not good."

"Andrew gets mileage from not bein' good. No wonder you travel so much."

Quinn couldn't disagree. "Well, right now I'm calling from Paris." She swallowed. "Doug, I think I've seen Jay."

Silence.

"Now what makes you think that, darlin'?"

"You needn't sound like I've lost my mind—again." For one instant she couldn't quite block out the memory: Jay's parents on the phone one bright December morning, reluctantly advising her that he'd been shot down and was missing. Quinn remembered the disbelief she'd felt at first, then the denial, the anger. The numbness and the sorrow.

If it hadn't been for Doug. . . .

Quickly, before she lost her nerve, she told him about the man in the George V lobby and in Les Princes at dinner.

"Maybe I should have left that carbon in the ashtray," she finished, "but something wouldn't let me. Now these initials—"

He voiced Valerie's thought. "There are only so many letters in the alphabet, Quinn. So many ways to combine them. Could be coincidence."

"Doug, that man could have been Jay's double."

"Oh, sugar. Are you really that sure? A lot of years have passed, and you tell me you didn't even see his face." Doug was an ex-sheriff; Quinn could imagine him using the same gentle tone on some distraught wife whose husband had taken a walk. "And I hate to point this out, darlin', but you've 'seen' him before."

"I know, but—"

"American Express, you say? Corporate card? I do wonder where it's from—and why he'd be hidin' out somewhere under someone else's name." He paused. "'Course Barron always did have that reckless streak in him, the one his folks tried to suffocate. They put so many expectations on that boy, it was like somebody snuffin' out a candle. Can't say I'd blame him for runnin'—except where you're concerned." He hesitated again. "Still, you could be right. In my time as sheriff, I saw stranger things than a man dropping off the edge of the earth for almost twenty years, then showin' up again."

"You'll help me?"

There was no hesitation this time. "If I can, of course I will. You know I never could refuse you anything that's in my power to give."

Quinn swallowed the sudden lump in her throat. Long ago, she'd come to consider tears a weakness, but since she'd walked into the George V lobby . . .

"Can you get me an address?"

Quinn knew he had contacts not only in Denver but from San Francisco to Washington, D.C. Which was why she'd called him, as much as to hear his comforting voice.

"You sure you want me to, darlin'? Think hard now."

She couldn't blame him for questioning the search. He'd held her enough times while she cried, while she raged, while she simply huddled in his arms, wanting the hurt to end. To believe that there was life, somehow, somewhere, without Jay.

"I'm sure," Quinn said.

"Well, when we buried your mother, God rest her soul, at least we knew she was gone—and where to find her if we had to." He cleared his throat before adding, "That boy's been missing long enough. Read me the card number, darlin'. And spell the name."

She did.

"I'll see what I can do," Doug said; and after thanking him Quinn hung up, as she'd done ever since Jay Barron left for Vietnam, without saying goodbye.

Jay had taught her to hate goodbyes, just as he'd taught her about love and, without meaning to, about sorrow. But long years after her mother's death, she still remembered Doug Lloyd's grief too: the hours she'd lain in her bed, listening to his sobs from the room he'd shared across the hall with her mother; the days she'd watched him without daring to intrude, watched his shoulders sag and his steps slow each time he entered the empty, sprawling ranch house.

When her mother was alive how Quinn had loved the house and its barns and rough outbuildings, the soft-pitched lowing of cattle when Doug took her out on the range with him on his big roan gelding, and, when they rode home again, the smells from the ranch kitchen where her mother worked.

One night months after her mother died, Quinn tried to cook dinner on her own, burning both the meat and vegetables, and she and Doug had cried together. "I don't know what we'll do," he'd said, his arms tight around her. "I wish I knew, but I don't."

He hadn't meant the ruined meal, but Quinn didn't know that then. The following week, a woman had come to the ranch—a social worker, Doug told her, not meeting Quinn's eyes—and Quinn had had to pack her bags.

Doug Lloyd's petition to become her legal guardian had been denied. In the court's view then, a single man, a widower, was unsuited to be the adoptive parent of a fourteen-year-old girl. The county placed Quinn in the first of a series of foster homes.

But to this day Doug Lloyd remained the closest thing to a father she'd ever known, the only person in her world who could understand about Jay Barron—and the one person she could rely on now for help.

Forced to extend the ad shoot at Versailles for a third and final day, Quinn still found time to wish she hadn't bothered Doug. He'd earned his peaceful retirement. After her latest run-ins with Ilse, she had a new appreciation of serenity.

She was dressing for dinner with Valerie that night when the phone rang. Weary from three days of settling the constant skirmishes between her director and Ilse, she considered not answering. What could the call bring except more trouble?

Then she gave in to a broad streak of curiosity. Snatching a round gold love knot from her left ear, she picked up the receiver and heard one word.

"Geneva."

Quinn frowned. "Excuse me?"

"It's me, darlin'," Doug Lloyd said. "I've found your man."

Her heart began to thump. "In Switzerland?"

"Specifically, the Banque Internationale de Genève." Doug's slow western drawl tangled the French worse than Quinn could have herself. "Pricey stuff, I'm told. Top of the heap. International investments." After reading her bank's address and telephone number, he paused. "That's all I can tell you. No home address.

Even my contacts couldn't get past the corporation."

Quinn said nothing.

"Darlin', you there?"

"I'm here." Her voice quavered. "I owe you one."

"You don't owe me a thing, except being happy. You just take care of yourself." When Quinn didn't answer, he added, "And make damn sure I get another phone call from you or a letter before next Christmastime, you hear?"

"Yes. Thanks, Doug."

"Let me know what happens."

When Quinn hung up, she sat on the edge of her bed, shaking, the love knot clenched in a fist, until Valerie came into her bedroom without knocking.

"Ready for Le Grand Véfour?" Her teal-blue evening cloak hit Quinn in the chest as she swirled, displaying a yellow-green dress underneath. "Or Taillevent? I made reservations at both. Haut cuisine or nouvelle?"

Quinn wasn't hungry. "Nouvelle," she said.

"What's wrong? An hour ago you were starving."

"An hour ago Ilse was throwing her last—thank God—temper tantrum. The director was threatening to burn the film. The head of marketing at Priceless was on the line from New York, making ominous noises about the whole ad campaign. My head ached, and my baby ulcer was having fits. Now the film's in the can." And even her hand hurt. "For whatever that's worth."

Valerie glanced toward the phone. "Who called? Andrew having a bad day?"

Quinn shook her head. She forced her hand open, revealing a small indent in her palm from the earring's gold post. Putting the love knot back on, she told Valerie about Doug Lloyd's call.

"What could Jay Barron be doing under an alias in Geneva?"

"Running a bank, apparently." Quinn felt cold and achy. Strange, she thought; Jay couldn't balance a checkbook. Unlike her, he'd never had to. She jumped up and began to pace the room. "My God, Val. Switzerland! After all the years I've wondered what happened to him," she said, her voice trembling. "After picturing him in some prison camp, living like an animal, without proper food or clothing or shelter. Without medical care. *Tortured.*" Her voice broke.

"Don't cry, Quinn."

"I'm not crying." She blinked. "I'm furious. If he *is* Jay, why didn't he come home?"

"Why don't you find out?"

Quinn gave her a blank look.

Valerie said, "We're finished here. This is our night to celebrate, remember? That lovely cholesterol-stuffed meal? The bottle of two-hundred-dollar wine, courtesy of our Priceless expense account? We're done. Free . . . until hair spray and athlete's foot. Tomorrow morning you can fly to Geneva."

"No, I can't. I have Andrew to think about."

Valerie peered into Quinn's dresser mirror, checking her black kohl eyeliner and bright blue shadow. "Let me worry about Andrew," she said. "Take another day or two. I'll drop by your apartment on my way home from the airport tomorrow night. I'll take Andrew a carton of moo goo gai pan."

"He hates Chinese food. He'll think you're pitying him."

"I'll change his mind." When Quinn hesitated, she said, "Go, or you'll never know for sure."

"Val, what would be the point?" She'd been crazy to take things this far. Yet knowing where he was . . .

"You know that old ditty every kid sings in school?" Valerie chanted the words. "'Shave and a haircut—'"

"'Two bits,'" Quinn finished and, laughing, felt relief. "I see what you mean."

"In psychology it's called closure. You've been feeling rotten about Jay Barron—or his double—ever since you spied him in the lobby downstairs. Why else would you save a discarded carbon paper from someone's dirty ashtray?"

Quinn didn't tell her the rest. That she'd gone to the registration desk that same night, asked the second time for a guest—this time named J. Welles Blackburn. And been told that he had checked out in the ten minutes Quinn had been sitting in the ladies' lounge.

If J. Welles Blackburn really was William Jay Barron, Quinn decided, for some reason he didn't want to see her. He'd checked out, presumably to avoid her. Which of course assumed that he had seen her in the first place. Or was she becoming paranoid?

Closure, Valerie had said. Quinn, who'd also taken psychology, knew that the term meant finishing a thought, an action that, if left undone, drove you crazy. But there must be another way to learn the truth without making a fool of herself, and by midnight Quinn hoped she had found it.

Two years ago Jay's mother had gone to her grave, certain that her younger son was dead. Still sharing the same conviction, his father had died just six months ago. But Charles Barron, Jr., Jay's older brother, was very much alive—and, like it or not, the only member of his family she could call.

Twelve o'clock in Paris meant late afternoon in California. Quinn waited until Valerie went to bed to place the call. If she was going to make a fool of herself, she'd do it alone.

The pleasantries didn't take long. In their brief acquaintance, Charles, ten years older than Quinn, had seemed, like his parents, to have the opinion that she was beneath serious consideration. In nineteen years his attitude hadn't changed, but neither had Quinn's. She'd never warmed to Charles, who seemed as dull and stuffy as Jay was lively and irreverent.

When she finished telling Charles that the man in the George V dining room had checked out at the wrong end of the day, he murmured, "A man with the wrong name. If what you think is true and Jay is still alive, why would he be living under some alias in a foreign country? Why wouldn't he have come home?"

She'd had the same thought, and so had Valerie and Doug; Quinn felt as if she were on the witness stand.

"I don't know why, but I think someone should find out."

"Meaning me?" Charles asked. "I disagree." After Andrew's accident he'd sent her a brief note and obviously hadn't forgotten Quinn's tangled life. His voice was condescendingly patient. "I can understand why you wouldn't wish to be involved. You have your hands full with a busy career and an invalid husband."

"Andrew's not an invalid."

"Then I'm happy to hear of his improvement. But you must see my side. Haven't we all had enough waiting, hoping, being disappointed? Do you think I haven't spied some stranger in a crowd myself—dozens of times in the past nineteen years—and wanted, *needed*, that man to be my brother?"

"Charles, I—"

"There are still over fifteen hundred men missing from that godless war, perhaps imprisoned but certainly unaccounted for. Jay is only one of them." His tone hardened. "That war destroyed nearly everything my parents loved. Jay may never have told you, but our sister—"

"He told me," Quinn said softly. The middle child of three, she had dropped out of school, protested the war.

"She ended up dead of a drug overdose in some seedy Haight-Ashbury commune. A slum," he said, "that's all it was, filled with human vermin. They—and that damn war—eventually killed my mother and father. They both died, if you want my opinion, of broken hearts."

"I'm sorry." Quinn thought of her own mother. She'd never heard such passion from Charles.

He made a harsh sound. "I buried them, Quinn. I buried our sister, too, because they couldn't bear even to make her funeral arrangements. And when Jay—" He broke off. "No," he said, "I won't be destroyed as well. I'm sorry, but I can't help you."

"Charles, I'm sure he's alive. Please."

"I have a meeting to attend. It was . . . good to hear from you. I wish you the best, you and Andrew Devlin. He was a good friend to Jay."

He was about to hang up. "Wait," she said, her hand slipping on the sweat-dampened receiver.

"Quinn, think what you will. Think whatever comforts you. Even do what you feel you must." He paused. "But what you're really saying is that, if he *is* alive, Jay Barron—or whatever name he's going by—is not the brother I loved. He's a total stranger. A deserter, a coward, a traitor to his country—and to his family."

"Charles, no. Jay would never—" She heard the click in her ear first, then his final words.

"I'd rather see him dead."

With that, Quinn made up her mind. She was going to Geneva.

3

"Quinn!"

Sweating and shaken, Andrew jerked free of the nightmare. The other half of the king-sized bed was empty, and he took a moment to orient himself. Of course. Quinn was still in Europe, where she'd taken extra days to scout locations for the next Priceless commercial. In the midnight-dark bedroom, wishing she'd come home, he could hear his heart pound. He'd been asleep only an hour—as usual.

When his heart stopped racing quite so fast, he levered himself upright with his left arm—his good arm, according to Quinn. He grunted as he stood, fumbling by the bed for the blackthorn walking stick she'd bought him.

Shuffling into the kitchen, he groped for the switch and the fluorescent fixture turned the room into a glare of light. Blinking, he washed down a pain pill at the sink.

Why hadn't Quinn come home? Without her the apartment seemed too large, too silent, and he had no defense against the nightmare.

Rooting in the refrigerator, he saw nothing he wanted

and closed the door again. In the last six years he'd lost ten pounds, probably muscle, and couldn't seem to gain them back. He seldom felt hungry. The result of inactivity, Quinn said; when she was home, she all but force-fed him.

Andrew's pulse refused to settle. He was scrawny and out of shape. Had he lost whatever appeal he'd had? When he'd caught Quinn holding that white silk scarf, he'd seen his own loss reflected in her eyes. Andrew's vision of Jay Barron didn't please him anymore than it ever had. They'd been college friends, were the same age; but if Jay was alive, he'd stand straight, with that cocky I've-got-the-world-by-the-balls attitude—and he wouldn't walk with a limp.

Andrew groped his way back into the darkened living room, which Quinn had decorated along with the rest of the apartment. Nearly knocking over a tall cream vase stuffed with navy blue dried grasses, he used an oyster-white upholstered chair to steady himself. He'd dropped the blackthorn stick, dammit. Gritting his teeth, out of breath again as if the nightmare had followed him, he switched on the stereo, its pecan cabinet glowing in the darkness, and eased down on a slate-blue sofa. He propped his right leg on the chrome-and-glass coffee table, thinking he would have added more color to the room. He'd been known for his use of brilliant color once. Nearly famous, Andrew thought, before the accident.

With the soft piano of George Winston in the background, he stared at the white fireplace mantel, the photos of him and Quinn in happier days. Outlining the hearth opening were glazed tiles in Delft blue; Quinn had set and grouted them herself. He wasn't much with tools these days—or a paintbrush.

Andrew leaned back, his head against the sofa, and shut his eyes. Six years ago, he thought, and let the nightmare take him. That Christmas season Colorado had been awash in brightly colored lights and decorations, trees in every house window, carols playing on the FM station in the car. They'd been coming from a party at the home of Quinn's boss, and how pretty Quinn had looked, dressed in holiday red, her hair longer then, her belly newly rounded with their child.

He'd teased her about fitting behind the wheel of his car.

"Our designated driver," she'd said as he poured himself onto the passenger seat. He'd had too much to drink but could still sense that she was mildly annoyed. "Aren't you lucky I'm pregnant and drinking Perrier for the next four months? Don't fall asleep. I'll have us home in no time."

Andrew's heart thumped. He hadn't seen his home for six more months. The roads that night between Denver and Boulder were slick in patches with a treacherous veneer over dark pavement—black ice—and Quinn, probably angry, was driving too fast. The gentle but icy curve sent the car into a spin she couldn't control.

The Oldsmobile tore through the guardrail. He could feel his stomach roll now at the memory of the car going over the drop-off. Into a ravine. Into a wall of pines, headlights spraying white light over snow-laden branches and dark, resisting trunks. Long after they plowed to a stop, the car radio was still playing "Have Yourself a Merry Little Christmas."

After minutes—hours?—he heard Quinn, wedged against the steering wheel, quietly sobbing. "Andrew, are you all right?"

Moaning, he lay pinned into the passenger seat. He could still feel the pain. Cold. Terror.

"Andrew, I hurt. Andrew!"

Trapped in her seat belt, with one hand she'd tried to gauge his injuries. She roamed his good side and cried with relief—"Nothing broken"—but he kept groaning; she was wrong.

Two hours after reaching the hospital, Quinn lost their baby. By then, Andrew was in surgery.

His right leg was crushed. His right arm, his drawing hand . . . his fingers. In the darkness, sweating again, he opened his eyes and flexed the hand. He had little grip left, no strength. The muscles, nerves, and tendons . . . oh, hell.

"You'll work again," Quinn told him. Even now she urged him to try therapy, encouraged him to try new doctors. She even bought him sketch pads and all the latest children's books.

He couldn't look at them. His own illustrations, favored six years ago for the Caldecott medal, would have ensured his future. Quinn's future. And their child's.

He shifted to ease the pain in his leg, which the pill hadn't dulled. He hadn't won the award and she rarely mentioned children now, never went into the first room she'd furnished when they moved. Several years ago she'd taken down the crib and stored it, then packed away the tiny clothes she'd been collecting "just in case." He knew Quinn wanted to try again, knew how important a family was to her after growing up without one—he'd been an only child himself—but he didn't want a baby now. God help him, he didn't. How could he bear to see his own likeness, blond and sturdy, running through these rooms or throwing footballs in the park? Like Jay Barron's children, if he'd lived.

Andrew felt his breath catch, felt the wetness on his face. Leaning forward on the sofa, rocking, his right arm cradled in his lap, he stopped trying to avoid his other nightmare. Jay Barron, whom Quinn had always loved.

I shouldn't be trying to find him, Quinn told herself. I shouldn't have come here. In the reception area of Geneva's Banque Internationale, she stared at a wall of photographs: all mahogany-framed, in color, of the bank's founding fathers and current executives.

She should have flown back to New York with Valerie. Home to Andrew. She would have, except she still remembered Charles Barron's heartless rejection of his brother, and she was still Quinn Tyler, curious as a cat, so Jay had always said, persistent as a terrier.

"Miss Tyler?" The receptionist's cultured voice spun her around. "I'm sorry. Mr. Blackburn's schedule for today is full."

"Tomorrow," she suggested and received a sympathetic smile.

"According to his secretary, his appointment book is closed until next week."

After his escape from the George V, what else should she have expected?

"I'm only in the city through tomorrow. I'd need just a few minutes. I'll call," Quinn said, "in case Mr. Blackburn has a cancellation."

When she telephoned at nine the next morning, half an hour after the bank had opened, Quinn guessed what the answer would be before Welles Blackburn's secretary—at least she'd gotten that far this time—said the words. Outside her hotel room window, rain pelted the city, a dark omen Valerie would respect immediately but that Quinn didn't want to heed.

The woman's English-accented voice sounded cool, like Charles Barron's. "Mr. Blackburn has meetings all day. I couldn't possibly fit you in. I'm sorry. If you'd called before your arrival?"

Quinn ignored the faint reprimand. "I can stay an extra day," she tried. "If you could slot fifteen minutes tomorrow—"

"Tomorrow Mr. Blackburn is flying to London for the rest of the week."

In desperation, she said, "Then never mind an appointment. Perhaps we can do this by phone." She'd certainly know his voice. "I'll speak to him right now. Would you connect us?"

Having obviously underestimated the woman's loyalty, she ran into a brick wall of secretarial efficiency. Now the tone was anything but sympathetic or regretful. "Mr. Blackburn is already in conference and cannot be disturbed. I'd suggest sending a letter; then if there's a problem he might help you with—"

"If there's a problem, it's *Mr. Blackburn's.*"

Quinn's conciliatory mood had changed in a split second and she hung up, fuming. The elusive Welles Blackburn had checked out of the George V as if the hounds of hell were chasing him. With the reception she'd received thus far in Geneva, surely that hadn't been coincidence. Her spirits fell, but her resolve didn't falter. She'd never imagined he—Jay—wouldn't want to see her again, at least not until Paris. Now, after she'd come the rest of the way, she'd been given the brush-off. In business Quinn had been brushed off before. But damned if this time, with Jay, she'd settle for it.

For the rest of the day Quinn wondered what to do. Aimlessly, her thoughts spinning, she wandered around the Place du Bourg de Four, the city's Old Town, then walked uphill past chic boutiques, antique shops, and museums, to the Cathédrale-Saint-Pierre. Made austere by the reformer Calvin, it contained splendid excavations on lower levels, open to visitors; one dated back to the third century.

Welles Blackburn wouldn't see her, had refused to

talk to her. Quinn seriously doubted he had plans to fly to London in the morning. But just as there were many levels to the Cathédrale-Saint-Pierre, she realized, there was more than one way to locate Jay again. On the linen-textured walls of the bank's reception room she'd seen two dozen corporate photographs. His must be among them. She would find it. Up close, she would know. Then, if she'd been mistaken, she would fly home. She forced herself to wait until the bank's closing time. Just before four-thirty, after calling Andrew in New York to say she'd be delayed again, she rode a mahogany-lined elevator to the sixteenth floor of the Banque Internationale.

Outside the double glass doors to the reception room, she watched a parade of secretaries flow from the inner office corridors past her on their way home. Quinn had been in advertising long enough to know there wasn't a secretary in the world who would willingly stay late. She doubted Welles Blackburn's—Jay's—would be different, no matter how protective of him she might be.

When the receptionist herself, who had been on the phone, finally reached for her handbag under the free-form rosewood desk and left the area, Quinn waited for the elevator doors to close on her. Then she breezed into the reception room and headed for the wall of executive portraits.

She studied the pictures in turn. Besides the CEO and board chairman, she looked over the vice-presidents in charge of various divisions, scrutinizing them all, then jumping at the discreet chime of a walnut-and-brass grandfather's clock that graced one wall between handsome bookshelves.

A few executives drifted from the nearby hall, through the reception room. One nodded at her, asking in French if she needed help. Quinn replied in English.

"No, I'm meeting someone. Thank you. *Merci.*" She added lamely, *"Mon mari."* My husband. She'd learned the phrase the first night at the hotel in Paris, when she'd called Andrew.

The men left. Quinn, her heart still racing, forced herself not to hurry. Jonathan B. Stanhope, she read at the bottom of the next portrait. Wilhelm Victor Jansen. Then her heart began to speed. The next brass nameplate read J. Welles Blackburn, Senior Vice-President. Lifting her gaze to the picture, she felt hope die inside. Blond-haired, husky, and blue-eyed, the man in the photograph wasn't Jay Barron.

Quinn had turned away when her pulse suddenly leaped with renewed anticipation. Whirling, she stared at the wall again. After more careful study, she decided she was right: the face framed in dark wood, identified in brass, wasn't J. Welles Blackburn either.

With trembling fingers Quinn traced the lighter outline around the picture purporting to be his. A larger frame had hung there; the linen now exposed on the wall looked newer, cleaner. Whatever his reasons were, he'd been putting her off, all right. Maybe Charles was right: his brother had something to hide. Something so terrible that her presence in Geneva, her inquiries, had frightened him—enough to have his likeness removed, and recently, from the executive gallery, where an obviously larger portrait had hung than the one now in its place.

What could he fear from her? Yet he was here, and so was she. She could almost smell the expensive, woodsy scent he'd always worn, reminding her of Doug Lloyd's pine trees.

In the next second Quinn darted down the corridor that had disgorged the best-dressed secretaries and the executives. From behind closed doors, she could hear the low rumble of male voices and a few softer female ones. A telephone rang nearby, startling her heartbeat into an even faster rhythm.

Alive, she thought, not dead. Alive.

Andrew, forgive me, but I have to know.

Far down on the right-hand side of the corridor, she found the name on a door: J. WELLES BLACKBURN. A corner office. Her hand wet from nerves, Quinn pushed open the rosewood door into a large secretarial anteroom. Thankfully, the desk chair was empty.

All around she could see heavy corporate profits in the thick gray carpet into which her heels sank, in the discreet oil paintings in tones of rose and gray, in the blush-pink roses that sprayed from a silver vase on the desk. Chrome and smoked-glass tables flanked a low-slung charcoal-gray sofa. On the glass coffee table lay copies of European and American business magazines—*Forbes* chief among them—and *The Wall Street Journal.*

Her pulse thundered. Quinn smoothed a hand over her rust-and-black print skirt, tucked in the tail of her cream silk shirt. Her slim ivory envelope purse under one arm, she walked toward the double doors to the inner office, took one deep breath, and, without knocking, turned a brass handle.

Stepping into the office, at first Quinn thought she was alone. A swift glance took in the same gray carpeting from the anteroom, a more masculine black leather sofa and chairs, sheer white draperies, and starkly modern artwork in black and white slashed with red. Then she saw him.

At the wall of windows, he stood with one arm braced against the glass, his head down, studying the city view below or lost in deep thought, Quinn couldn't tell which. Her first impression surprised her: it was one of isolation, loneliness, and her heart went out to him.

Quinn forgot her own confusion, her earlier anger. How many long years had he been alone like this, with the memory of whatever had happened that had kept him from coming home?

Now he didn't move. He kept his back to her, and Quinn seized the opportunity of a suspended moment to feast her eyes. In the glare of late-afternoon sunlight through the windows, she could see that his hair—yes, darker than it used to be—was still, as it should be, tipped in gold. His navy blue pin-striped suit coat was slung over the desk chair, but a beautifully cut vest emphasized the breadth of his shoulders, their well-muscled definition, more so than she remembered, and the lean line of his spine. He wore his shirt cuffs neatly rolled back over strong wrists and forearms. He looked bigger-boned in maturity, his hands strong too, well-shaped and long-fingered, capable—capable of giving a woman pleasure, she couldn't help thinking, as her cheeks warmed; just as capable of defending himself. In obviously good shape, he didn't spend all his time at a desk. Quinn's gaze swept the trim seat of his pants, his long legs. She moistened her lips.

She felt like a woman who'd been dieting too long, and the thought made her guilty. She'd only come to find answers to her questions, to see him once more.

Yet now that she had found him, she couldn't seem to speak. Jay, she thought. Dear God. "Jay."

Quinn didn't think she'd spoken aloud, or even breathed the name, but suddenly he stiffened.

In the split second before he turned from the window, she tried to prepare herself—for the teasing warmth in his brown eyes, the color of brandy, for the quick flash of the smile she hadn't seen in nineteen years.

Then he turned, not smiling at all. And Quinn found herself staring at a perfect stranger.

4

He was the wrong man. Slumping back against the door for support, one hand behind her on the brass handle, Quinn felt the strength leave her limbs. She'd made a fool of herself after all.

She would have backed from his office, stammering apology for her mistake, but in the brief second it took him to turn from the window, she noted two things. He was one of the most strikingly handsome men she'd ever seen. And though his eyes were not brown like Jay's but a penetrating electric blue behind tortoiseshell glasses, they filled with recognition too strong, too genuine to hide. He knew who she was! Then, as quickly as it had flashed, the look disappeared as if someone had wiped a blackboard clean, and his features became a blank surface.

Quinn wasn't fooled by that, either, or by his slow, more dispassionate perusal of her. Welles Blackburn, she had already seen, was a solitary man, a cautious man, who rolled his shirtsleeves so neatly that even the

pleats stayed straight; a man, she sensed, who controlled
himself at all costs. Yet there was something just under
the surface; in those intense blue eyes she also saw
hunger, yearning. Quinn had the feeling she was looking
at a man behind bars, and if he ever broke free—

"How did you get in here?"

His eyes held hers. Quinn didn't try to break the
contact.

"I walked in," she said, "on two good legs."

His gaze dropped to her hemline, and Quinn's knees.
She watched him press his lips together to keep from
smiling. "I can't argue with that."

"Your secretary's gone home; so has the receptionist."

"So much for security."

"I wonder why you'd need it," she murmured.

With a slight frown, he took his suit coat from the
chair and slipped it on. It was like watching a man put
on armor, something in which he felt safe.

Quinn had no such defenses. When he came toward
her, once more the smooth executive, she pressed herself against the door and realized the extent of her mistake about his identity. He stood slightly taller than Jay,
not as rangy, his leanness more elegant but powerful,
like silk covering steel. The only scent he carried was his
own, not Jay's pungent evergreen but a scent, sharply
masculine, of skin and soap with a hint perhaps of male
hormones. Quinn tried not to breathe too deeply of
him. Those hard blue eyes, the straight blade of a nose,
she thought. He wouldn't be an easy man to deal with.
He would reveal only what he wanted known. But his
mouth . . . his mouth was more generous than Jay's,
even passionate.

And his voice, rich but unaccented, like a broad-
caster's, was clearly American, though she couldn't pinpoint where he came from.

"Would you care to tell me the purpose of this visit?"

"You know why I've come," she said.

He studied her face for a moment. "Do I?"

He knew who she was. Yet Quinn, with the exception of a recent profile in *The Wall Street Journal* when she'd gotten the Priceless account and an article several years back in *Advertising Age,* wasn't a public figure. There was only one way he could really know her—through Jay.

"Don't bother to deny it. You know my name too. Against my better judgment, I've chased you from Paris to Geneva. I've been stonewalled by your faithful secretary, fooled temporarily by that switch of portraits in the hall—a nice try, I have to admit, but—"

"Hell." The hard blue gaze met hers. "I should have known you wouldn't give up. But how did you know who I was?"

Quinn's tension eased a little. He'd just admitted what she already knew. "I saw you at the George Cinq. Twice," she explained. "Neither time from the front. I really thought, from the back, that you were Jay."

He looked stunned. "You mean you thought *I* was—?"

"Jay Barron."

Turning abruptly, he walked to his desk and sat down, as if his energy had suddenly been depleted. "Sure, we looked something alike. Maybe a lot alike. People always remarked on that. But I can't believe you'd spend the better part of a week looking for Jay after seeing the back of someone's head."

"I didn't. And I'd have let it go. I've thought before that I saw him—in a restaurant, a department store, on the street somewhere. It was your name," Quinn said.

"My name?" he repeated blankly.

"J. Welles Blackburn." If that really was his name, she thought. For all she knew, he might be a pathological liar. "William Jay Barron."

"Coincidence," he said.

"Maybe." She took a breath. "But the similarity kept me going—after I took the credit card carbon from your table at Les Princes."

He leaned back and folded his arms, another defensive pose, Quinn thought. "Look, lady—"

"No. You look," she said, crossing the room in quick, angry strides. "I really don't care what name you use or what combination of initials in what order. This has been a frustrating, painful time, and I want it to be over so I can pick up my life and go on." She sat on the leather chair in front of his desk. "I've wondered for almost twenty years what happened to Jay Barron. It turns out I've wondered more than his own family."

"Charles, you mean? He's the only one left."

Quinn's gaze was sharp. "I spoke with him from Paris after I saw—after I saw you at the hotel. He wasn't very sympathetic. It's his opinion that if Jay is still alive but never came home, he's a traitor and a coward."

"Not a coward," he said, leaning forward and clasping his hands on the desktop. "I can tell you that much."

"But no more?"

"Why keep on with this?" He stared at his hands as if for the answer. "The war ended a long time ago, but there's never been a war in the history of the world that tied up all the loose ends. Some people are still finding out what happened to relatives in the Nazi camps at Buchenwald and Treblinka. War's not that neat," he said quietly. "Why hurt yourself anymore?"

"Because I'm not cold and callous like Charles Barron. If he were my brother, I'd be ashamed to have the same name." She sat straighter. "Can't you understand? It tears me apart not to know where Jay is, what happened to him. No, I don't lie awake every night thinking about us nineteen years ago, but I loved him

then and—and I remember. The day I arrived in Paris
was his birthday."

"His forty-fourth. How old was he when you saw him
last?"

"Twenty-five."

"Isn't it time you stopped celebrating?"

Quinn shot out of her chair. Hands braced on his
black-walnut desk, she leaned forward, eyes blazing.
"Isn't it time you stopped lying?"

He looked her straight in the eye. "I'm not lying."

"Then where is he?"

"Maybe you'd better sit down."

Quinn leaned even closer. "I'm just fine on my feet."

He looked away, eyes focused on the desktop, where
not a single piece of paper or a file folder rested.
Quinn's pulse wouldn't level, but she wondered if
Blackburn's had ever wavered by one beat. Even his
onyx desk set looked as if it had never been used.

"Where?" she repeated.

And his blue eyes closed. "Nowhere," he murmured.

He was just like Charles Barron. "You cold bast—"

"Jay's dead."

After nineteen years of silence about Jay Barron,
Welles could have kicked himself for saying the brutal
words. And to Quinn Tyler of all people. Obviously, the
news stunned her.

His swift relief at having the confession—part of it,
anyway—off his conscience was just as quickly
replaced by guilt. She had turned ashen, all color
draining from her face, and her green eyes showed a
glaze of shock.

Coming to his feet, Welles didn't take time for
niceties. She was either going to start crying or pass out

in his office, and his money was on the latter. He'd never seen a face that white, not even in 'Nam. Striding toward her, he steered her back into her chair, clamped a hand around the nape of her neck, and pushed her head down below her knees.

"Breathe." He ignored the silky brush of her hair against the back of his hand, the shivers along his spine at the contact. "Deeper," he added.

He could understand the feeling. Despite his prior knowledge that Quinn Tyler was in Geneva, when she'd opened his office door he hadn't been able to hide his own shock. It had almost overcome his joy at seeing her for the first time in the flesh—not counting the night in Paris—and he was still shaken. He'd had a hard time denying his reaction.

Nineteen years hadn't done her any harm, physically. That copper hair, straight and sleek, bouncing on her shoulders, those fragile green eyes, the long legs in silk hose were even more breathtaking than he'd imagined years ago. And that sassy mouth, he thought. *I walked in on two good legs.*

He had to hand it to her. She had guts and the persistence Jay had always told him about. Welles frowned. And he'd thought she wouldn't be able to find him. Instead, to his chagrin, she hadn't recognized him from pictures Jay would have sent home; to the detriment of his ego, she hadn't been looking for him at all but for Jay himself.

Strange, when he'd thought of being found some day, he'd assumed Charles Barron would walk into his office, demanding answers, or ring his doorbell at home. Now, with Quinn Tyler, he'd stepped right in it, Welles thought. What else would she want to know?

Within minutes, her color started coming back. She had a clear, translucent complexion that made a man's fingers itch to stroke it. But she was still trembling, and Welles would have resisted the urge anyway.

Gently pushing her deeper into the chair, he walked to one of the black-lacquer floor-to-ceiling cabinets along the far wall and pulled down a Waterford tumbler. Cramming ice into it from the silver bucket his secretary refilled each morning, he poured two fingers of scotch. "Here."

She shuddered. With the gesture of distaste she looked half her age, but he didn't smile. "I don't need whiskey," she murmured.

"You do right now." He nudged the glass closer.

"I really don't think I should—"

"Drink, dammit."

Welles watched until she managed to swallow the last drop, then refilled her glass. At Quinn's protest he said, "Believe me, this stuff isn't going to touch what you're feeling."

"You sound like an expert."

"On occasion," Welles said and hunkered down in front of her chair. That night in Paris he'd checked out of the hotel, fearing that his past had caught up with him at last, and had gotten drunk on the plane to Geneva. "I'm sorry. I didn't mean to break it to you like that."

"Well, I pushed you."

He smiled. "That's what he always said about you. That you could hang on like a bulldog."

"A pit bull, more likely." She stared into the scotch, and her weak smile faded. "If only I could have held on tighter."

"Don't," he said.

Knuckles white around the Waterford crystal, she glanced up. "You're being terribly kind. When I barged into your office, you looked so . . . solitary, and when you turned and I saw your face, saw that you weren't . . .

him, I thought how well defended you seemed. How formidable a person you might be to approach. And yet I'd also seen that other look."

He guided the glass to her mouth again. "What look?"

Her tone still dull with shock, she said, "You seemed . . . glad to see me. That's when I knew that, since you weren't Jay, you must have known him—and, through him, knew me."

Welles focused on her trembling hand. The glass chattered against her teeth as she took another dutiful sip.

"How *did* you know him?" she asked.

His gut tightened. "We flew together for a while."

"In the Navy? In Vietnam?"

He hesitated. "Yeah."

"And he talked about me?"

"All the time. Like a marathon."

A slow flush spread across her cheekbones. Her face was surprisingly delicate but not a disappointment. His heart beating a slow, heavy cadence, Welles stood.

"Good things, I hope," she murmured.

"Nothing but." Unless Jay had downed a few beers after a mission. The uncomfortable memory surprised Welles. He hadn't thought about that in years and wanted now to push it away, just as he always had then.

"So that's how you knew about me . . . and about Charles Barron."

At the liquor cabinet Welles carefully recapped the scotch bottle. He set the lid on the ice bucket. "I heard plenty about his whole family. The cold sonofabitch father, the society princess he had for a mother, his hippie sister. Charles. He sounds like a chip off the old block."

"They had their faults, but Jay adored his family."

She didn't need any more bad news, Welles told himself. With a shrug, he dismissed the subject. What did he know of families, except the one he'd fashioned for himself?

Quinn put a shaking hand to her temple, and the glass threatened to slip from her grasp. He retrieved it before it could fall. "Why don't you put your head back for a few minutes? Don't talk, just try to rest. You must be feeling rocky."

"Two glasses of whiskey didn't help."

"Grief therapy," Welles said softly, but she didn't move.

What was he going to do with her? He could see she was fighting the shock, but soon enough the effort would fail.

"I should go back to my hotel," she said weakly.

He glanced at the ring finger of her left hand, the thin gold band encrusted with emeralds. He'd wondered if she was married. Once, she'd been Jay Barron's woman; now, apparently, she belonged to another man.

"Isn't your husband with you?"

She looked surprised. "No, he's not. I'm alone."

"You shouldn't be, after a blow like this. Is there anyone I can call to stay with you?"

Quinn started to rise, then sat back down again, reminding him of the George V and his first startled glimpse of her. She closed her eyes. "I'll be all right. I'm just a little dizzy." She tipped her head back against the chair. "I should have settled for aspirin instead of scotch. You're right, it doesn't dull the pain but it has gone straight to my head. I'm afraid I forgot breakfast this morning and skipped lunch. Andrew's right," she said, massaging her forehead. "He always tells me I need a keeper."

Wonderful. Andrew must be the husband, he

thought, and not much on tact. In Welles's opinion, she'd done too damn well on her own, tracking a man down with nothing to go on except a physical resemblance and a trio of initials in the wrong order. In almost twenty years, he'd never thought of that. Just as he hadn't thought of keeping his credit card carbons instead of throwing them away. Careless. Dangerous.

Like what he was about to say.

"I can't recommend a keeper, but I'd be happy to spring for an early dinner. You need food and a good night's sleep." He paused. "I can recommend a physician, if you'd like something more than that."

"I'm not a strong believer in crutches, Mr. Blackburn."

"Welles."

"In the last few years, I've filled more prescriptions than I ever thought I'd see. I've handed out pills to someone I love as if they were M and Ms. No, thank you. But if you could get me a cab, I'd be grateful."

"No. Sorry."

She opened her eyes and stared at him. "I beg your pardon?"

"I won't hear of packing you into a taxi. I'd wonder all night whether you got home safely, whether you—"

She surged to her feet and Welles silently cursed. "Mr. Blackburn, I'm not a child or an idiot. I'm a college graduate, a registered voter, a pretty fair businesswoman. I run my own ad agency and—"

"Hey, take it easy." Taking a deep breath, he asked, "Why so defensive?" Andrew, he supposed. "I didn't call you an idiot or a child."

His gaze strayed to the hemline of her skirt, which had hiked up while she sat, giving him a too-good view of her legs, which he'd struggled to ignore. When she stood, the skirt had slipped back into place just above her perfect knees but a two-inch strip of creamy lace was showing. Welles could have groaned. Quinn Tyler's classic style, her unnoticed dishabille—he had to ignore that combination too. It made him want to fall to his knees, to press his mouth against her skin.

"I'm a reasonably intelligent woman," she went on, "and though it's true I am inclined to lose things now and then, I have a decent grasp of reality. So I assure you that I haven't lost my mind, just suffered some rather terrible news."

He tensed. Her face had gone pale again, and when she swayed Welles caught her. Her body, all sleek curves and delicate angles, felt light as a breeze in his arms. He cursed his reaction.

"I'm feeding you," Welles muttered. "That's no longer an invitation."

"I don't want—"

"It's an order, dammit."

Pulse pounding, he set her away from him, then realized his mistake. He shouldn't keep staring at that lacy peekaboo hemline, that creamy lace. . . . Welles strode toward his coat closet, yanking out his Burberry trench coat. The conservative coat itself reminded him that he had obligations, responsibilities; and so did she. She might be a fantasy come true, but she was also an impending disaster. So he'd feed her. Then he'd see that she got on the first plane back to New York—out of his life. Before she ripped it wide open.

Nestled into the soft brown leather of Welles Blackburn's discreet bronze-colored Mercedes, Quinn tried to order her thoughts. She'd tried to refuse his offer. Yet after too much liquor, after what she'd just learned, her limbs felt weightless, her brain like mush. She needed desperately to be cared for, even for an hour or two, as she hadn't been for the past six years—or ever, when she thought about it. Right now, she didn't know whether to sleep or to cry.

Jay's dead.

With those words a nineteen-year vigil had ended. What else was there to say, to learn? She would go home to New York now and give Andrew the rest of the love she'd denied him for too long. Maybe then they could be happy together and she could stop questioning.

"How did he die?" she asked. Welles's hands tightened on the wheel.

"In the crash," he said. "You knew about that?"

With a lump in her throat, Quinn nodded. How would she be able to eat? She had expected them to stay in Geneva, to dine in some small but refined restaurant where the food was sublime—she couldn't imagine Welles Blackburn settling for less—and the waiters spoke only French or German, neither of which Quinn understood. Instead he was heading out of the city in the last stream of rush-hour traffic.

In the hushed, smoky twilight, in spite of the grief that threatened to overwhelm her, she grew fascinated by the scenery. "I've learned a lot about expectations on this trip," she said after a while. "In Paris I expected *l'heure bleu,* but I find it here instead. It seems fitting somehow." She glanced at him. "Where are we going?"

"You'll see. Somewhere quiet. Where the food's good and I can find you an aspirin if you want one."

Glad that for once someone else was making the decisions, Quinn stared out the window at the mansard-roofed mansions standing, one after the other, like a line of elegant soldiers on the bank of the Rhône River. A rich Puccini aria played on the car's tape deck, though Quinn preferred jazz. Had it been easier, or harder, to learn about Jay in such a setting? War and death seemed so far away here. Yet they were still facts she couldn't deny.

"Geneva's beautiful," she murmured, still fighting tears.

"This is a remarkably civilized place," Welles observed.

"Not like the U.S.?"

His glance looked wary. "You read the newspapers, don't you? Watch the seven o'clock news? You tell me. Geneva"—he waved a hand toward a manicured lawn edged with brilliant flowers—"or New York? That's where you live, isn't it?"

"Yes. How did you know?"

"Educated guess. Advertising's centered there."

"Actually, I began my career in an agency in Denver, Colorado. I . . . we moved to New York four years ago."

"And you haven't been mugged yet?"

"No." Quinn managed a laugh. "How long have you lived here?"

"Since my part in the war ended," he replied.

"Don't you miss the States?"

He paused. "I go there on business occasionally, but I never stay longer than I have to."

"No family?"

He shook his head. "Not there, no."

He slowed the car, turning into an arc of fine-graveled drive around a pretty stone fountain, its arching spray softly lighted from below. The car stopped at a wide flight of stone steps leading to a set of double doors, black with brass fittings.

The house amazed her. Not that it should look so grand, all white stone and leaded windows, very European country house, in style; Welles Blackburn held a high position with the bank, so he might well afford it. But it reminded Quinn of Jay's parents' home in San Francisco.

His hand lingering at her spine, Welles ushered her into a spacious, high-ceilinged foyer dominated by cold marble and fragrant flowers. Bouquets of white calla lilies in alabaster vases adorned every polished surface, their deep green leaves the only touch of color in the room. Tabletops, floor, walls—all were of white ebony-veined marble. Quinn tilted her head back. Overhead hung a chandelier of frosted crystal in a black mounting. The entire entryway was in black and white.

"Your home is beautiful," she said. But Quinn felt a chill and shivered at the stark decor, at the way her skin had heated when Welles touched her.

"You're cold. The sun's down and the temperature's dropping," he told her. "I'll have a fire lit in the drawing room."

When they stepped into the room, Quinn hesitated in the doorway. A fire already glowed in the vast marble hearth, and on the mantel she saw white tapers massed in black holders and a group of photographs framed in black onyx. Then her gaze shifted and she nearly gasped.

An exquisite petite woman stood beside the white marble fireplace. Dressed in white, her gown cut low to reveal white shoulders and a hint of small breasts, her black hair worn sleek and high, her eyes like jet beads on a splendid evening dress, she seemed like a porcelain doll. An oriental doll. Until, Quinn thought, she looked into those dark, unwelcoming eyes.

The woman stepped forward with an airy gesture. "I expected you earlier, *chéri.*" Ignoring Quinn, she raised her cheek to Welles, whose kiss didn't quite connect.

He said, "I would have called but something came up." He still had a hand on Quinn's back, and she could feel its warmth through her black jacket. Heart thumping, she took a step backward only to be stopped by

Welles, who increased the pressure of his touch.

"Don't be angry with me," he murmured, so that she wondered whether he meant her or the smaller woman. "I've brought a guest for dinner from America." He paused. "A friend of Jay Barron's."

The woman stiffened, and a clock ticked off the seconds.

"Mai, this is Quinn Tyler. Quinn, my wife, Mai-Lin."

The suspicion in Mai Blackburn's eyes hardened into dislike. Black ice, Quinn thought, and felt another shiver.

Then, as if in contrast to that hard gaze, heels clicked lightly along the hall outside the drawing room and a young girl appeared in a white batiste calf-length dress trimmed in lace, her sleek black hair like a flow of water down her back. She wore white hose and ebony patent leather shoes. She was thirteen or fourteen, Quinn guessed, a strikingly beautiful Amerasian girl.

She had her mother's dark enigmatic eyes, though softer, and her father's smile. His face lit up as the girl ran into his arms.

"And this is our daughter, Hannah," Welles said, releasing Quinn just in time for the exuberant embrace.

A daughter, a wife. Disappointment spiraled through Quinn. She had no idea why.

Dinner, as promised, was quiet—except for Hannah. Slim and long-legged, she'd done some modeling the season or so before and had an ongoing fascination with glamour; Quinn's career in advertising certainly qualified.

"Do you work with famous models?" she asked. "Like Carol Alt? Paulina Porizkova?"

Her mother intervened. "Hannah, Ms. Tyler has already answered enough questions."

"I don't mind questions," Quinn said, feeling perverse. "No, I've never worked with either of them, but we just finished a shoot outside Paris with Ilse Jansen."

"Ilse Jansen? What does her hair really look like? Is it smooth as satin? It looks like a wedding dress to me."

Quinn laughed. "She has wonderful hair—but just between you and me, the disposition of a gila monster."

Hannah giggled, drawing a disapproving stare from her mother.

"Hannah is inclined to hero worship. She has made idols of these women who devote their lives to fashion."

"It's what I want to do," Hannah murmured.

"My daughter's experience is limited and was a distraction that won't be repeated."

At the harsh words, Quinn saw the girl's mouth quiver. "It's all I want to do!"

Welles looked at his plate. "Her pictures are stunning."

"I imagine they would be." The exchange had made Quinn uncomfortable, and she toyed with her wineglass. Then, unable to temper her own enthusiasm, she said, "Your daughter has a fresh look, very unique. Charmingly youthful yet strikingly timeless. And her dramatic coloring—"

"I posed for *Elle*," Hannah put in, lifting her chin and meeting Quinn's gaze. "At the beach in a swimsuit. Would you like to see the magazine? It's right upstairs—"

"Enough." Mai's glance touched Quinn, then her daughter. "Your dinner's getting cold."

"Baby, eat," Welles urged.

"I'm on a diet."

"Not again." He grinned weakly at her, then passed Quinn the platter of beef *en croute* with steamed broccoli and carrots. "You're almost invisible. You'll have to stop turning sideways, or I'll think you've moved into the city to live at school."

"Oh, Daddy."

The love between father and daughter was gentle, Quinn thought, and as obvious as Mai Blackburn's hostility.

Mai offered Quinn a Limoges bowl of hollandaise sauce. "Why indulge her, Welles?"

He winked at Hannah. "Because she's my best girl."

Quinn felt certain she saw jealousy on Mai's exquisite face. It had become clear that the Blackburns shared little emotional intimacy; because their distance echoed her own with Andrew in the last few years, she easily recognized it.

"Hannah, please finish your dinner," Mai said. "Your homework is waiting." In Europe, summer break was not until the month of August.

Hannah objected, but her mother insisted. When the girl rose from the table, Welles scooped her close. "Hey, hot stuff, not so fast. Where's my kiss?"

It landed squarely on Welles's cheek, first one, then the other. He pointed to his nose and Hannah kissed him there.

"Welles, really," Mai murmured.

A gesture at his chin, and Hannah obliged. Then, both laughing, they looped arms around each other's necks. "Go on now," he said. "And where are your manners, mademoiselle?"

"Good night, Miss Tyler. Thank you for answering my questions. I hope there weren't too many."

"Not nearly enough. It was my pleasure."

She hesitated. "Could you send me some magazines from America? With your ads in them?"

"Hannah."

"Hannah," Welles echoed his wife. "You might offer to pay the postage."

"I'll send them first thing when I get back," Quinn promised. After Hannah had left the room, she said, "She's enchanting. You must be very proud."

Welles grinned. "She's at the top of her class in school."

"And her father spoils her outrageously," Mai said.

"I happen to love her, and I think children need spoiling now and then." He looked at Quinn. "She is my life," he said.

Quinn felt her stomach clench. If Welles had brought her to meet his family, assuming that it would be easier for Quinn to relax in a more private setting instead of a restaurant, if—as she'd begun to think—he even meant Hannah's bright chatter to ease her grief over Jay, the ploy had failed. Her nerves already raw, Quinn couldn't ignore the undercurrents between Welles and Mai-Lin Blackburn. She wanted to leave, to be alone.

But over coffee in the drawing room Mai mentioned Jay.

After explaining her trip to Geneva, Quinn said, "I've wondered for too long what really happened to Jay."

"And what has my husband told you?"

Welles held Mai's dark gaze. "I told her that he's dead, that he died in the crash of his plane."

Suddenly Quinn sensed there was more. She turned to Welles. "You said you flew together. Were you with him when he crashed?"

Welles stirred his coffee. His glance at Mai seemed pleading and it was she who answered.

"In the fall of 1972 your President Nixon ordered intensive bombing of North Vietnam, including Hanoi. Perhaps you remember."

"Yes," Quinn said.

"In December, on a mission near the North

Vietnam–Laos border, Jay Barron's plane was shot down. My husband also crashed."

"In a different plane?" Quinn said.

"Yes."

She looked at Welles, whose face seemed pale.

"I know the memory must be painful, but you survived. What happened to you after the crash?"

"Welles broke his leg, his left thigh bone. It was a nasty break, which became infected. He managed to crawl from the wreckage of the plane but didn't get far."

"Were you captured?" Quinn asked. If that were the case, she thought Jay might be better off. No wonder Welles hesitated each time she asked another question.

"My husband was found by villagers friendly toward the South—the Republic of Vietnam, for which your military fought. They took him in, and I nursed him."

"Mai was on the run herself," Welles said. "Her family were from Saigon, but the war had pushed them out. By then her mother was dead, her father had just died. Mai had come north looking for her only surviving brother—the eldest—who had joined the Communist cause years earlier, when she was still a child."

"He was my only family," Mai said, "and he had something of mine that I needed."

"What a fascinating story," Quinn murmured.

Welles raised an eyebrow. "There's more. In Mai's family there is—was—an exquisite necklace and earrings made of jade, pearls, and diamonds handed down from mother to daughter for centuries. They're called the Tears of Jade—from their teardrop shape. When her brother ran, he stole them: Mai's birthright."

"He had become a hard man, bitter and disillusioned. As soon as I found him," Mai said, "I wanted only to take what belonged to me and run myself."

"And did you?" Quinn leaned forward.

"Yes. I was staying with the villagers when Welles crashed. His fever burned for three days and he nearly lost his leg, but he is a strong man," Mai said, "and we survived."

Quinn couldn't imagine living through such pain or danger. It shone a different light on her quest for Jay.

"Such a terrible adventure," she murmured.

"Yet from such adventure we have created the future. During our escape from the North, my husband and I fell in love." Mai gestured at the softly lit drawing room, the cheerful fire.

Welles set his cup on the coffee table.

"What else is there to know?" he said, looking at Quinn, who thought he seemed more relaxed than he'd been since she opened his office door. "You must be tired."

"Yes, and I have a plane to catch in the morning."

By the time they reached her hotel entrance, Quinn's nerves were screaming. She could still see Mai Blackburn's hostile eyes when they'd said good night. Mai had urged her husband to call a taxi, but he insisted on driving Quinn.

"Thank you again for dinner," she said. "I didn't want to go, but I'm glad I did."

"I'm glad too." His gaze, dark as cobalt, met hers. "I wish we hadn't met at last under such sorrowful circumstances."

If not for Jay, Quinn thought, they wouldn't have met at all, which she supposed would have suited Mai Blackburn just fine. And of course she was right. When Welles offered to see Quinn inside, she firmly refused. He leaned over to open her door and as Quinn moved, his hand grazed her breast. Heat flashed through her.

"Sorry," he said, his gaze on her shirtfront.

Quinn ignored the apology. "Welles, could you

answer one last question for me?" She cleared her throat. The Blackburns' story had made war and death too vivid, no longer an abstraction, yet something seemed lacking. "Did you see Jay after the crash?"

Welles ran a finger around the steering wheel. "Some questions are better left unanswered."

"Meaning you can't tell me?"

"Yes," he said. "Good night, Quinn. Try to sleep well."

In her room, Quinn thought, What a strange evening; what a strange story. Reaching for the telephone to call Andrew, she stopped. That's just what it had been, she realized. A canned story, well rehearsed. Mai Blackburn had answered questions for her husband, and Welles had answered those about his wife.

Welles Blackburn hadn't taken Quinn home because he feared she'd break down in a public restaurant; he hadn't introduced her to his family so Hannah could help ease her grief about Jay. He'd taken Quinn home to protect himself. From what? she wondered.

5

Cradling his right arm and hobbling toward the door, Andrew peered through the security viewfinder and groaned. Instead of Quinn, whom he wanted to see—though she would have used her key—he saw a lens-distorted Valerie Mason, her frosted hair in spikes, her gray eyes downcast, their lashes like dark fans against her cheeks. And ten pounds too plump, he thought, as disappointment settled into the pit of his stomach.

Quinn had said she'd be home tomorrow but he'd prayed she was early. Her homecomings were often the best thing about their marriage now; for several days or a week afterward, they actually seemed to enjoy each other. Now he had Valerie Mason to contend with. Again. She'd dropped by two nights ago.

"Just a minute." Frowning, he fumbled the locks open left-handed and stared at her. Large cerulean-blue cloisonné circles studded her ears. She had a stained canvas bag looped over one shoulder, and as usual the rest of her attire similarly made him cringe. "What do you want, Valerie?"

"It might be nice—the polite thing—to ask me in."

"I was just about to go to bed." He faked a yawn.

As she took a step, he limped backward, fighting the temptation to look behind her, as if Quinn might be there.

"I'd be happy to tuck you in," Valerie murmured.

Because she smiled, Andrew couldn't take offense. Valerie had worked with Quinn long enough for him to know how outrageous she could be. She was also one of those women—like some men—who talk big but never deliver. Above all, she was Quinn's friend. He was safe.

In a swish of violent green and pink, Valerie preceded him into the living room, where a fire crackled on the hearth and the strains of Natalie Cole's Grammy-award-winning album continued to pour from the stereo. Andrew leaned in the doorway, a shoulder against the jamb, his weight off his bad leg. "What else can I do for you?" he asked.

"Dangerous question, Andrew." The bag plumped down beside the sofa. "As I told you night before last, I promised Quinn I'd look in on you."

"She's called several times since. She didn't mention you."

"Trust," Valerie murmured. "Quinn's full of it. She knew I'd keep my promise, so she didn't need to tell you."

She rummaged through the tote.

"There can't be anything good in there, or uncontaminated," he said, as she pulled out a large white carton of Chinese food, a pair of chopsticks, and a plastic fork.

"Quinn said you wouldn't like this, but I decided she was wrong. So are you." She popped the lid off, setting a fragrant stew of chicken strips, snow peas, onions, and tomatoes steeped in a thick gravy on the coffee table.

Andrew had picked earlier at the veal paprika Lotte had left for him. "I'm not hungry."

"You're much too skinny. Without your shirt your ribs must look like a broken ladder." When he winced at her bluntness, she said, "Sit. Eat. It won't kill you, and you might even like it. Better still, you could gain a few pounds."

"You should lose a few."

Good. She'd flinched too. They were even. Andrew made his way across the room to the sofa and, propping the blackthorn stick at its side, sat down. The smell of food was making his stomach growl. Valerie grinned.

"I'll bet you hate a woman who says 'I told you so.'"

Andrew dug into the heaping plateful she handed him. "Shut up and eat."

If she thought he would change his mind about her, she was in for a surprise. The first time Quinn had brought the woman home, he'd felt nothing but dislike. Vulgar, he thought, and pushy; she had none of Quinn's class, or her resistance.

"Valerie means well," Quinn always told him. But in six years he'd his bellyfull of well-wishers.

The fork she'd brought him clattered to the table. Valerie let it lie there. "Lost my grip," he mumbled. "I can't feel the damn plastic." With only a sympathetic glance, she let him limp into the kitchen for real silverware.

When he returned, she was scraping the last of the chicken from the container onto her plate. She didn't look up.

"You may fool Quinn with the helpless routine, Andrew, but don't try it on me. I come from a long line of dependent personalities, otherwise known as users. I learned to ignore them long ago. I'm afraid with me you're on your own."

"Fine. I was alone when you rang the bell."

"I suppose you wish I'd finish gorging myself and let you get back to your mood music"—she waved her

chopsticks toward the stereo—"so you can feel sorry for
yourself."

"I wish you'd leave, yes." He dragged the plate from
in front of her just as Valerie closed the chopsticks on
another bite of chicken. "I'm surviving on my own without your reverse brand of pity."

"Pity?" Chewing, she mulled that over. "I think pity's
a waste of time. Up straight or any other way."

"Then go. And don't come back."

Valerie's gray eyes sobered. "Are you serious?"

"Deadly."

She leaned over, retrieving the canvas bag, her tone
as taut as the Kelly green tights she wore. "You're not
the first man to throw me out—platonically, that is.
Probably you won't be the last." With a flick of the wrist,
she tossed something his way, and despite the urge to
cradle his arm in protection Andrew caught it.

"You're not my friend, you're Quinn's," he said, staring at it. "Let's keep it that way. I don't want food or
gifts or anything else from you, and I sure as hell don't
need a baby-sitter." Though he'd been sure she was
angry, Valerie's gaze softened and she gave him a
strange look. Empathy, he thought, which only made
him more furious. "Or a surrogate," he added. "I just
want my wife home."

"Then I hope you get her." Valerie gestured at the
package Andrew held against his chest. "Tonight's con-
solation prize," she murmured. "Enjoy." Then she left
the apartment, nearly catching her pink skirt in the
door, slamming it behind her.

Andrew looked around the empty living room as if
for comfort. After a few minutes of unbearable silence,
he ripped the brown paper from the package she'd
thrown at him. His heart hammered, his arms went
weak. All he'd wanted tonight was peace and Quinn; all

he'd gotten was more of the same war and loneliness.

Damn her. He wouldn't look at the copy of the Caldecott-medal-winning cover: bright red on a purple-brown, he glimpsed from the corner of his eye; slashes of navy blue and white. The color combination shouldn't have worked any better than Valerie Mason's green tights and pink skirt, her yellow sweater and huge blue cloisonné earrings—but it did. Oh, Christ, it did. Andrew heaved the offending book across the room.

In her room at the Beau-Rivage, the splendidly restored and elegantly expensive Victorian hotel on Geneva's waterfront, Quinn awoke the next morning to a beam of bright sunlight streaking between the closed draperies. Turning over, she flung an arm across her eyes and moaned. Normally a morning person, she felt groggy. It had been well past the middle of the night before she'd fallen into a troubled sleep.

She'd dreamed about Welles Blackburn and then, finally, of Jay. And cried.

Dead. Why couldn't she let it go at that?

Think, she ordered herself. She had to pack, check out, get to the airport for her nine-thirty flight. She had to go home to Andrew, who was alive and needed her. But before she even sat up, the phone rang. Quinn shoved her hair back from her face as she answered.

"Good morning." The already familiar male voice belonged to Welles Blackburn, and Quinn could feel her pulse thump.

"What time is it?" she asked.

"Quarter past ten."

"Ten-fifteen?" Quinn bounded out of bed, dragging the phone with her. "God, I've missed my plane!"

"Good."

Searching the carpet beside the nightstand, she found her travel alarm. He was right.

"We can have breakfast," he said. "I'm downstairs in the lobby. I'll meet you in the restaurant in fifteen minutes. I'll have your coffee poured so don't keep me waiting." His tone lowered. "Just throw on anything. You don't need makeup."

The words could have been suggestive, but Quinn wouldn't take them that way. She started to refuse, then stopped herself.

She didn't know why he wanted to see her this morning, but without Mai Blackburn for protection, he would have little choice but to answer Quinn's questions himself. One on one, she thought. She liked the odds.

Waiting for Quinn in the hotel dining room, Welles ordered fresh orange juice, flaky croissants, and coffee for two. Then he leaned back in his chair and tried to slow his heartbeat.

What the hell was he doing?

Only last night he'd felt halfway safe again. He'd driven Quinn back to her hotel, certain that was the last he'd see of her. Now he'd made a date for breakfast, and he could barely keep the silly grin off his face.

Why smile? he wondered. He hadn't slept all night. The dark circles under his eyes had attested to that in his shaving mirror this morning. Already he was keeping one eye out for anyone who knew him from the bank, who might see him with Quinn Tyler. And he felt as giddy as Hannah had looked at dinner last night, with what she'd later termed a near-celebrity in the house.

He must be out of his mind.

He must be middle-age crazy.

Yet here she was, walking toward him through the

sparsely peopled restaurant in a shaft of morning sun that turned her copper hair to bright fire and her eyes to clear emerald green. Dear God, he knew what he was doing. And he wasn't crazy.

Watching the gentle sway of her hips beneath the jade-green silk shirtwaist, the long flow of her legs, Welles came to his feet. Before Quinn Tyler walked out of his life, self-destructive bastard that he was, he'd look his fill—and make sure that when she left, she didn't have questions about Jay that might bring her back again.

Nearing the table, Quinn slowed her steps. Welles Blackburn was standing, waiting for her—as she'd meant to make him wait—but just looking at him, dark hair overlaid with gold in the morning light, his blue eyes steady on her, made her breath catch.

"You're late," he said with a smile that tripped Quinn's pulse as she sat opposite him.

"A woman's prerogative. I'm often late."

In her room, she'd decided on a quick shower, some lip gloss, and a decent dress to feel human. Let him wait, she'd thought. The delay might give her not only the right odds but a definite advantage.

"The wait was worth it. But I told you not to dress."

She laughed. "Oh, really. Can I see myself in the public rooms of the oh-so-proper Beau-Rivage in slippers and a bathrobe with a towel around my hair? I don't think so."

His eyes warmed. "Your hair's still wet."

She'd combed it sleek around her shoulders, holding it back from her face with a gold hairband. "You're not supposed to notice." To hide her discomfort at the exchange—intimate enough to sound as if they were lovers—she shook out her napkin.

The motion tipped her coffee over.

"Here, let me." Half rising, Welles dabbed at the puddle with his napkin. "Did it get your skirt?"

"No, I'm fine." Then she smiled ruefully. "I'm not usually this clumsy."

"Yes, you are—or were." He grinned. "In Paris at the George Cinq. What did you spill in your lap that night?"

She made a face. He had seen her. "Vinaigrette dressing."

"Jesus."

"An entire silver boat of it."

After meeting Welles's exquisite wife, she did feel like an idiot. She remembered his home, all black and white and elegant. Lucky she hadn't spilled anything there on the white carpet. Like red wine, she thought. "The morning's not starting well. I'll be lucky if I don't lose my airline tickets."

"I hope so."

Buttering a croissant, he spoke to the table. Quinn watched the sunlight play over his dark hair, the gold glinting through it as if gilded there. For the first time, she noticed he wasn't wearing a business suit but a navy blazer over an ivory cotton sweater.

"I thought we'd spend the day together," he said as if he'd just made up his mind. He looked up.

Tempted, Quinn shook her head. "If the airline has a seat on the next flight, I'm leaving for New York. I have an ad shoot the day after tomorrow, and Andrew—"

Welles set his knife aside. "Indulge me."

"I can't."

"Indulge yourself," he said. "When was your last vacation?"

"Six years ago," Quinn admitted.

Their eyes met, and at the dark tension in his she asked herself, What's happening here? She would have

risen from the table, escaping her own confusion, but
she didn't know whether she could stand. Dry-
mouthed, she sipped her orange juice.

"You didn't sleep last night," he pointed out.

Quinn choked. "Do I look that bad?"

"No, you look like a woman who spent more time
grieving than resting." He paused. "I didn't sleep
either. I've decided to take the day off and . . .
straighten myself out." He set his plate aside. "Why
not join me?"

Quinn took a breath. "Perhaps I should." He had
seen her in Paris, and he'd run, hidden . . . from her.
Looking away, she said, "Welles, last night I had a feeling that something wasn't . . . isn't right." She stirred her
coffee, which he had refilled. "Your wife doesn't like
me, for one thing. I wondered why."

Welles looked out the window. "She's from a different culture, Quinn. In America you make friends faster.
Mai's more reserved. She sizes people up first, sometimes for quite a while."

Quinn doubted that was it. "Still, the story she told
me about Jay, about your escape from the North, about
the jade. I can't quite put my finger on what disturbs
me, except some sense that she . . . that together you
rehearsed the story."

He shrugged. "It's the same story lots of other people
have heard. Maybe after so many tellings, it sounds
rehearsed."

"Maybe."

He looked at her, then away again. "What don't you
believe?"

Quinn couldn't say. He had a way of forcing her off
balance, which, in her job, few people could do—or
tried to do.

"Jay died, Quinn. Nineteen years ago. I crawled away

from . . . a similar crash, but he didn't. I know it's hard, but you have to accept it."

Breaking a croissant into pieces, she said, "Maybe there's only one question I need to ask." He hadn't answered last night.

"Did I see him, you mean?"

Quinn tried to draw his gaze. "Did you see his body?"

His face paled. When he poured the dregs of the coffee into his cup, his hand trembled. "No," he said at last.

Quinn felt an absurd hope spring to life inside her. "Did anyone?"

Welles shook his head. "As Mai told you, I was out of my head with fever for days. When it broke, and I could make someone understand what had happened, by the time they sent a search party to the site . . ."

Quinn placed a hand over his. "I know it's not easy for you either: dredging up so many unhappy memories, seeing me."

"Seeing you," he murmured. "That's the good part."

For a long moment, there was silence. Then Quinn said, "Because Jay talked about me? And you felt almost as if you knew me from the things he said?"

"No, because you're easy to look at, and because I—"

Quinn snatched her hand away. Perhaps Mai Blackburn had disliked her on sight for good reason. Maybe Welles cheated on his wife, and any unaccompanied female posed a threat. When Quinn tried to rise, his fingers circled her wrist.

"Please. Don't leave. I guess my lack of sleep is catching up with me. I'm sorry," he said. "That was a crazy thing to say."

"Then why—?"

He tossed his napkin onto the table and stood. "Quinn, when that search party reached the crash site, there was no plane left, just a charred shell." Pausing, he finished. "There was nothing. There was no . . . corpse. No body to see."

If there hadn't been a body, then maybe—

She started to speak, but the ashen color in his face forced the rest of what she was thinking from her mind. He'd told her all he knew of a painful experience, and the thought could have been only another dead end, but oddly enough Quinn felt it wasn't. For now, she noted that Welles looked shattered.

"No more questions," she promised. Clearly, she'd been wrong about him and Jay had been right about her; she could be too persistent. The least she owed Welles Blackburn now was an hour or two of shared, happier memories of Jay. "Let me call the airline. Then I'll call Andrew to tell him about my change of flight." She tried again. "What did you have in mind for today?"

"To clear some clouds away." His smile was slow in coming as Welles got up. "Let me show you Geneva."

By clouds, he meant grief and Jay, she supposed. Quinn had expected the memories to tumble out, to heal them both, but she soon sensed they would be slow in coming, like his smile. From her hotel on the Rive Droite, past the Mont-Blanc bridge and the view of the Jet d'Eau, its fountain of water rising almost five hundred feet into the air, Welles drove the Quai des Bergues along the waterfront.

"That's Île Rousseau," he told her, pointing at an island in the river. "The philosopher was born here." He smiled. "Hometown boy makes good."

At his rueful tone Quinn suppressed her need to talk about Jay. Instead, for the first time, she wondered about Welles's background but didn't interrupt his lecture. He seemed to be enjoying himself, and so, Quinn realized, was she. The day, sunny and warm, was the epitome of summer, and she relaxed against the soft leather seat of his car. It had been a long while since she'd felt so at ease and unencumbered—an irony that erased her smile when she remembered Jay.

Yet in Welles Blackburn's company, there would be time, she thought. Plenty of time to remember.

After showing Quinn the oldest buildings in the city, Welles took the Pont de l'Île, which crossed the Rhône to the Left Bank and deposited them not far from his office on the Place Bel-Air. Because Quinn had seen the nearby museum and theater district, he headed instead toward Carouge, a less familiar neighborhood of squares and charming houses, shuttered and arcaded, which made Quinn want to get out and explore. The area had once been a separate city, Welles explained, under the domination of the king of Sardinia.

He parked the car and, with his hip sometimes brushing hers, their arms frequently touching, they walked through the noontime crowd in the warm sunlight, stopping in various boutiques to browse. Quinn resisted the urge to buy fine Swiss linens, which she'd only have to jam into her luggage and carry, but she succumbed to the temptation to splurge on chocolates for Andrew; sinfully rich and filled with liqueur, they couldn't be purchased over candy counters in the States.

"Try to tell me you won't eat half of those yourself," Welles said with a laugh, feeding Quinn a sample from his own supply. He'd bought Hannah, who loved candy, the treat.

The motion brought them together again, his fingers lingering on Quinn's mouth until she swallowed. Their eyes held a moment too long before his smile faded.

"I rarely eat sweets," she said, pulling away to admire something—anything—in the next window. Grateful that her back was turned, Quinn immediately blushed. The store was a pharmacy and she was staring at an invalid commode.

"This place needs a new window designer," she murmured.

"Come on," Welles said, the laughter back in his tone. "You barely ate breakfast, and I could use some lunch."

Because of the warm weather, they chose an outdoor café. Welles removed his navy blazer, slinging it over an empty chair with Quinn's biscuit-colored linen jacket.

Still embarrassed, she focused on the menu, which was printed in French.

"Need help?" he asked.

"I'm not sure, but the"—she frowned—"*boudin* has a nice sound. What is that?"

He laughed. "Blood pudding. Geneva's big on organ meats and such, rich sausages." Quinn groaned. "The food can be pretty heavy, but it's great."

"Maybe I'll just have a glass of wine."

Welles shook his head. "Feeding you could become a full-time occupation. You don't take care of yourself." He recommended *omble chevalier,* the native Lac Léman salmon trout, which he was having, and Quinn agreed it sounded delicious.

Poached and chilled with a sprinkling of lemon and dill, the salmon melted in her mouth. Quinn discovered she was starving. And thirsty. Maybe from so much unaccustomed crying the night before, she'd become dehydrated. The second glass of fumé blanc went down just as smoothly as the first.

The wine made Quinn loquacious.

She talked about her job and asked Welles about his. His answer was short, telling her nothing she didn't already know. She confessed how much she liked Geneva, then compared it—making him smile—to New York. "I suppose it's closer in ambience to Denver, though," she finished. "The cleaner air, the mountains nearby. Where is home for you, originally?"

Welles toyed with his wineglass.

"Shreveport," he said. "Louisiana."

"You're kidding."

"Not as marvelous as Geneva, you're right."

"You don't have a southern accent."

"I worked hard to lose it."

She smiled. "I think Southerners sound charming. Men in particular."

Her eyes met his, dark blue and compelling, and Quinn wondered whether he thought she was flirting. Looking at him, his hair shining in the sun, his generous mouth not quite smiling, she thought perhaps she was. Even though it made her feel guilty, she couldn't deny the attraction between them; that much had been apparent the instant she stepped into his office.

Quinn worked often with male models so handsome they made women's mouths water, and she was usually unaffected by them—for various reasons. Many were conceited about their looks; others were gay; most had enormous egos that left no room for women except as admiring objects. Welles, on the other hand, seemed not so much oblivious to his appeal as comfortable with it. Women on the sidewalk had been casting glances at him all morning, which he'd mostly ignored. Quinn thought she'd have to be dead not to respond, but she looked away now.

"What about Shreveport?" she asked.

"The three *H*'s," he said. "Hot, humid, hellish." He smiled faintly. "What about Denver?"

"Clean, clear, conservationally correct."

"That's four *C*'s." He'd changed the subject quickly, Quinn noticed. "Tell me about your family."

"I'm an only child. My father died before I was born. My mother died when I was fourteen. I spent the rest of my childhood in foster homes, some good, some bad. But I survived." She didn't want to dwell on her past and smiled at the thought of Doug Lloyd. "I had a wonderful surrogate father with whom I still keep in touch. Do you have brothers and sisters?"

"No." He paused. "My mother did one thing right. She quit while she was ahead." When Quinn put a sympathetic hand on his forearm, she felt him tense. "There's nothing more to say. I made it to sixteen, then I left school and joined the Navy."

"Without your parents' consent?"

"I didn't ask her," he said. "I lied about my age."

He had deliberately avoided mention of his father. Quinn saw the restlessness in his eyes again. With an unhappy boyhood behind him, with the black-and-white life he led now, he was a handsome, cautious, complex man—and Quinn knew she was better off flying home in the next few hours. They hadn't even talked about Jay, the purpose of this time together.

"Welles?"

"They were a lousy sixteen years, but they're forgotten." He twirled the wineglass stem. "I've told two lies in my thirty-eight years—that was one of them. I want you to know I don't make a habit of it." When he looked up, the force of his stare made Quinn's whole body feel limp. Or was it the wine?

Quinn squirmed in her chair.

"It's getting late. I'd better get to the airport."

In the car, with a Pavarotti tape spiraling rich operatic melody out the open sunroof, Welles drove fast. Quinn told him that Andrew thought she kept a heavy foot on the gas herself.

"Mai thinks I'm a maniac at the wheel. She doesn't

drive," Welles said. "Hannah can't wait to get her license and try the roads between here and Zermatt, where we have a ski house." He glanced over. "Do you have kids?"

"No," Quinn murmured. She mentioned Andrew's accident but not her part in it. "He's not completely well." She forced a smile. "I suppose I could end up waiting so long that having children will cease to be an issue. Which won't bother Andrew much." She added, "Jay always wanted a dozen kids."

Welles looked surprised.

"We never talked about that," he said. "Most of our conversation revolved around flying missions, getting drunk afterward—and you. Not as a maternal figure."

"I don't know if I should be flattered."

He took his gaze from the road. "Take it from me, you should." He refocused his attention on traffic. "I'm curious. How did you meet him? Jay never said."

"At college in Boulder. It's a pretty remarkable setting, perfect for romance. Jay was in law school—from which he later dropped out to enter the Navy—and I was a puny freshman. Actually, I met Andrew first. He was the teaching assistant for my drawing course and Jay's friend. They weren't much alike, so I never understood the friendship, but it was important to Andrew."

"Jay liked friends who were his opposite."

Quinn realized that was true. At least Andrew had been, and Welles, a high school dropout from Shreveport, had come from the other side of the tracks compared to Jay's childhood in Pacific Heights.

"But you can't have been totally opposite. Look what you've done with your life. You're an accomplished man, successful, well educated—"

"Self-educated," Welles corrected. "So, after you met Jay, what happened?"

Remembering, Quinn smiled. This was why she'd spent the day with Welles, she reminded herself. "Oh, he thought at first that I was kooky and I thought he was an uptight yuppie—though we didn't use the term then—but somehow we clicked."

"Off and on," Welles said, his knuckles white on the wheel. "Jay went off to flight school, you stayed in Colorado. How many times did you see him before he left for 'Nam? It couldn't have been that many."

"Enough times to know I loved him. To miss him when he left. To wonder for nineteen years what happened to him." Quinn said, "What are you really asking? How good we were in bed together? How often we made love?"

She heard the answering edge in his tone. "I'm just wondering how a man could walk away from a woman like you."

"Men do leave in wartime, whether they want to or not. Yes," she said, "Jay walked away smiling. Because he didn't want to make me cry. I'm glad my last view of him was—"

"Smiling?"

His one word ruined Quinn's afternoon. For these few hours she'd suspended worry over Andrew and the agency. Tonight she'd face reality again, and her grief over Jay. Now Welles had implied that Jay wasn't quite what she remembered.

"He loved me," she said and turned her face to the side window, letting the warm breeze rush over her cheeks.

The volume increased on the tape player, and the lush dramatics of a Puccini aria filled the car for the remainder of the twenty-minute ride from Geneva to Cointrin. By the time Welles parked the car at the airport, "Nessun d'orma" was spiraling to its emotional climax. Quinn was surprised to find that the music itself had broken her grief, that tears were streaking her face.

Turning toward her, Welles tipped her chin with one finger. "Quinn, I'm sorry." Before she could pull away, he gathered her into his arms.

"It was the music, that's all. So powerful, romantic—"

"Sshh, it's all right. He was a great guy."

She sniffed. "I know I seem fixated, but I can't just put him out of my mind, not after so long."

Welles rubbed her back. "Neither can I."

His hands felt warm, strong, stirring, and Quinn soon realized that she wasn't thinking about Jay any longer. Settled against him, she remembered how fine, how free she'd felt for most of the day, before she pulled slowly away, dabbing at her eyes.

"What time is it?"

He glanced at the dashboard clock, in full view. "A half hour till boarding. I'll get your bags from the trunk." He smiled. "Do you have your ticket?"

Quinn plowed through her handbag, then patted down her pockets, at last holding up the Swissair folder.

Welles grinned but didn't tell her, as Andrew would have, that he was amazed she hadn't lost it.

In the terminal Quinn updated her ticket and checked her bags; then they headed through security and customs toward her gate as the airport loudspeaker system blared arrivals and departures in three languages.

Quinn didn't even try to understand. Welles couldn't forget about Jay either, she told herself. And why? Because there had been no body, no evidence that Jay was dead. Her tears hadn't been only from grief, just as Welles's touch had done more than simply soothe. In his arms, with his words, hope—like a stubborn alpine wildflower—had blossomed in her heart. She'd had the first inkling hours ago over breakfast at the Beau-Rivage.

If Welles had survived the crash, then maybe Jay had too.

"Are you okay?" Welles asked.

"I'm fine now." She wasn't taking home bad news after all. But she couldn't say so. It would only trouble Welles, who couldn't tell her anything more. From here on, whatever she learned would have to come from other sources.

Passengers pushed past them along the corridor to the other gates, and the smell of perfume, heavy and sweet, stung her nostrils as a dark-suited woman pressed by, throwing Quinn against Welles. Letting Quinn's carry-on bag drop to the floor, in the next instant he had nudged her closer to the wall.

"I don't want to put you on this plane in tears." His thumbs brushed her cheekbones. "I meant today to be cathartic for both of us. Then I meant to send you home. Now I don't want to put you on this plane at all."

"Welles, I have a husb—"

"Yes, and I have Mai and Hannah." His voice lowered. "That doesn't change this."

Turning slightly, he angled his body into hers and, when Quinn should have moved, he held her fast with one strong hand on her shoulder. Like a deer caught in the headlights of a car, she stayed still, wanting to bolt but afraid to. She watched Welles remove his glasses, slowly fold them, and carefully slip them into the breast pocket of his blazer. Without the glass screen, naked, his eyes looked softer, as soft as smoke. But in the dark rim of his irises, the steadiness of his look, she saw a purpose she couldn't seem to avoid.

This man means business, Quinn thought, but still she didn't move. Welles leaned closer, then closer again, bending his head until their mouths met at just the right incline.

The kiss was soft too, smoky, sending a slow curl of

heat through her body, and at the next drag of Welles's mouth across hers, the heat drifted up again. Quinn gasped. Wanting to go limp in his arms, she realized that in fact she wasn't being held; he had one arm braced now on the wall above her head, the other at his side. Yet she felt as if he were touching her everywhere.

The loudspeaker blared flight information, making Quinn stiffen, but she found she couldn't move except to ease her mouth from under his. His breath, ragged and quick, warmly struck her cheek as his next kiss met empty air. Quinn looked up into his darkened eyes.

"My plane," she managed. "They've called my flight."

When she tried to thank him for the day, for the shoulder to cry on, he only bracketed her head between both arms and lowered his mouth to hers again. Desire shot through Quinn, stronger than anything she'd ever known.

"Welles, I have to g—"

His thumb gently pressed her lips together.

"No goodbyes," he whispered against the corner of her mouth, then, in the next breath, let her go.

Without another word, they walked to the gate. She wasn't taking bad news home, Quinn thought, completely shaken, but she had more unanswered questions now, not all of them about Jay.

Still not speaking, Quinn started toward the plane. She didn't look back but felt his gaze upon her until the curve of the jetway must have cut off his view. She wouldn't see him again, and part of her thought, That's for the best. The rest of her wondered why Welles Blackburn had used Jay Barron's words of parting to her nearly twenty years ago.

$\overline{6}$

Subic Bay Naval Base
The Philippines

If he ever found him again, anywhere in this world, he'd kill the bastard.

It wasn't the first time the dark-haired man on the bed had had the thought, not even the first time he'd had it in pain. This time, though, he'd made it to a hospital. And this time there was no war.

Groaning, he slouched lower into the pillows on his bed—standard-issue military metal with a side that screeched every time the Filipino nurse dragged it up or down. The mattress was hard as the volcanic rock on which the base hospital itself had been built.

When he shifted, a mistake, fire flashed through his limbs and a daggerlike pain plunged through his right eyeball. *Such beautiful brown eyes*, she'd always said; *as warm as brandy.* Christ, he'd be lucky to see again. He should already feel lucky, the doctors told him, that he might one day, with sufficient therapy, be able to sign his name.

He'd sign all right, but more than that. He'd hold the 9mm Makarov automatic they'd had to pry from his bloody fingers when they found him and blow that bastard to hell.

"Commander?"

The military rank, which he'd never achieved during his stint in the Navy, didn't rouse him. He'd heard the soft, silky tone of voice before over the past weeks of lying here, but he'd been too long without a woman in his life to pay it any mind. Despite the years since Vietnam, the denial of his own existence that had become second nature, he didn't respond.

He'd been brought here under false papers; even if he hadn't, he was far too hurt to give a damn for courtesy. He made her say it twice, not caring if she guessed the lie. Here, now, no one would harm him.

"It's time for your shot," she added, and he turned his head.

"In my ass again?"

A warm hand on his hip nudged him over. "I'm afraid so."

"I've had worse," he said, trying not to flinch as the needle punched another hole in his left buttock. Trying not to sweat.

Her touch lingered, or he imagined it did. Then she turned away, hiding her smooth face in a swath of blunt-cut hair so black it showed no blue sheen at all. "Rest," she murmured, then left him in the private room—they didn't want him making friends—as if he were a prisoner in Laos, abandoned again.

Mercifully, his pain began to ebb, and with a sigh he fell back against the pillows, gingerly feeling the lump of bandage around his right eye. For the next four hours he wouldn't feel a thing. But when he closed his left eye and the rest of the world went dark, he could hear the long-ago scream of jet engines, hear himself shriek with pain that only the strongest drug had ever touched. And in spite of himself, he remembered.

When he got out of here this time, he would do the killing. No remorse.

As he drifted into sleep, he figured he had what he most needed for the task, the classic element of surprise. Quinn's favorite.

July 14

The morning after her return to New York from Geneva, Quinn, normally a morning person, woke with another headache. She rolled over for another hour's sleep—and came face to face with Andrew, whose blue-gray eyes smiled at her.

"I'm glad you're home," he said.

Guilt washed over her. Not that she could help having arrived home near midnight. After she'd boarded the plane at Cointrin, the pilot had waited for takeoff clearance for over an hour, only to fight vicious headwinds crossing the Atlantic. The jet had circled Kennedy for forty-five minutes before landing, and Quinn had been caught in Customs for another hour. Of course she'd had to fight for a cab, which was snared in traffic all the way into Manhattan. By the time she reached her apartment, Andrew had been half asleep on the sofa, his pain pill working overtime.

If he'd been awake, they would have made love, a fairly rare occurrence—unless she was getting back from a trip—and she would have felt even worse for lying to him about Geneva.

"I'll make breakfast," she said and scooted from bed.

Feeling his gaze on her, she belted her thick white terry-cloth robe, covering herself from neck to bare feet. Andrew followed her into the kitchen, leaning against the counter, using the blackthorn stick as a brace.

"How was Paris?" he asked as Quinn started the coffee maker.

She gave him a blank look.

Andrew eased into a chair. "The Eiffel Tower? The Rive Gauche? Versailles?"

"Paris was . . . fine. Beautiful."

But the shuttered houses of Carouge, the little café where she'd eaten lunch, flashed through her mind; a memory of Puccini, melody rising into the summer air above the sunroof of the Mercedes. Her tears.

Tell him, she thought. If she did, Andrew would grieve for his friend, share with her the happier memories of Jay Barron, then finally assume he had his wife all to himself. But Quinn didn't believe Jay was dead, and until she could, she'd keep looking for him. What difference would a little more time make?

"I wish you'd kept Valerie Mason with you longer," Andrew said. "She's been hanging around here, driving me crazy with her garish brand of cheer. I thought, in six years, I'd seen all the variations."

Quinn poured coffee into two mugs decorated with sunshine-yellow happy faces. "She promised to keep you company so you wouldn't miss me."

"I always miss you. She just made it worse."

"I'm sorry." When she lifted her gaze, she met Andrew's.

"Sorry for what? What's happened, Quinn?"

Her head throbbed and she raised a hand to massage her temple. "The ad shoot can't have turned out well."

He sipped his coffee. "You always think that. Then you win some award. Just as you did in Boulder at college, running your four-point-oh cumulative average but thinking every time you'd flunked a test. Every time," he said, "you were wrong. Magna cum laude, as I recall."

"When I finally graduated." Quinn hoped they were changing the subject and grinned weakly. "You can't still be jealous with that three point nine in Fine Arts for a Master's compared to a Bachelor's degree."

"What is it? Something's different."

Welles Blackburn. The name swept through her mind before she could stop it, like the lakeshore breeze in Geneva. She could all but see him reflected in her coffee, his dark hair brushed with gold at breakfast only the day before, his blue eyes sympathetic when she cried over Jay.

Quinn pushed away from the table. Perhaps she didn't want to tell Andrew about Jay because, in order to do so, she'd have to mention Welles.

"You're making me feel sneaky," she said. She couldn't look into Andrew's face, anymore than she could meet his eyes when he'd caught her holding Jay Barron's scarf. "I'm just tired from the trip. Unfortunately, I have a meeting at ten-thirty. I'd better shower and dress if I expect to function at all today."

"Quinn."

His voice stopped her in the doorway. She knew she could escape before he even struggled from his seat, but in deference to his disability she paused.

His chair scraped, the blackthorn stick thumped on the kitchen floor, then she felt his warmth at her back. Quinn bowed her head, and his good hand came up to rub the tension from her neck. "Mmmm," she murmured, trying not to pull away.

"Feel good?"

"Yes."

"Feels good to me too," he said.

She fought the urge to run down the hall, to latch the bathroom door behind her, to let the shower spray drown her guilt. It had only been breakfast and an afternoon of sightseeing while waiting for her plane. Welles was a perfect stranger, with the emphasis on *perfect*.

Andrew's fingers caressed her nape, her throat, a sensitive earlobe. Quinn shivered and his body fit itself to hers. "I know I can be a bear to live with," he whispered, "but I did miss you."

She turned and his mouth captured hers, his kiss warm and sweet, familiar, his tongue probing for entrance. Quinn felt herself growing moist. Sliding an arm around his waist, she moved slowly with him toward the bedroom, passing her office where the white silk scarf might still be on the desk, passing the spare room she'd once hoped might be a nursery. Her headache pulsed, the beat echoing low in her abdomen, desire fighting guilt.

Quinn wished she had come home with answers instead of more questions: wrong ones. In their room she untied her robe, letting the thick terry cloth fall to the carpet, and held out her arms. Until she learned about Jay, she wouldn't say a word to Andrew; for now, she could give herself.

Firmly, Quinn shut the bedroom door on all the questions. She shut it on Welles Blackburn and the memory of his kiss.

"Something missing?"

A week later, just after five o'clock, Quinn was on her hands and knees under her desk when Valerie stepped into her office. All Quinn saw were red leather shoes with turned-up toes and an expanse of royal blue tights topped, from her vantage point, by rounded knees.

Cursing, Quinn struggled to her feet. "The messenger dropped off the proofs of Versailles this morning, but now I can't find them." She kicked at a stack of papers under the desk and flopped into her chair.

Her office at Tyler & Devlin Advertising—she'd once hoped Andrew would become her new agency's art director and had whimsically made him a partner—looked no better organized than her office at home. Worse, she realized. After two years, the walls where she would have the company's print ads in stylish frames were still bare; behind her desk, two strips of grass cloth, one beige and one green shot with gold, seemed to vie for her attention. For a decision, actually; Quinn had been trying to decide which she preferred for the past six months.

Valerie braced both arms on the desktop. "Maybe we could put out an all points bulletin."

Quinn made a face. "It's here somewhere."

"Is that good or bad?"

Blowing hair from her eyes, she said, "Val, I think we'll lose the account. Tony Fisher warned me, but—"

"He's a good director."

"The best. But even he couldn't make Ilse Jansen look right." She sighed. "The light in the Hall of Mirrors glared, no matter how he lit the set or filtered things."

"What about the outdoor shots?"

Quinn shook her head. "It wasn't the place," she said. "It's the model."

"We knew that from day one."

"Well, Priceless Sportswear doesn't agree. I've spent all day on the phone, and I've come to one conclusion. Two, actually." She glanced at Valerie, experiencing another sinking feeling in the pit of her stomach. "One, I heartily dislike the entire corporate image at Priceless, particularly the head of their marketing department."

Valerie had once expressed an interest in him. "Frank Murray?"

"Don't remind me. And two, if that phone rings again, I'm going to smash it."

"Cheer up. It can't be that bad."

Quinn groaned. "You haven't seen the ad."

"Are you hungry?"

"Hell, yes," Quinn said before she realized Valerie had typically flipped the subject, as if it were a television channel. "Practically penniless. Andrew's royalties have all but dried up this year, and if this ad doesn't—"

"I mean *hungry*. For food."

"Oh. Yes," she said, belatedly hearing her stomach rumble. "I forgot lunch today. I was in the middle of an eye-popping, gut-wrenching, artery-blowing conversation with Frank when everyone else went out to the deli."

"Then let's go. We'll pick something up on the way home and work tonight at your place. There must be some way to soothe the corporate breast—or beast—and salvage all that time and money we spent in France."

"Just let me look once more." Rising, Quinn headed for the wall of shelves across the room. The view from her window tempted her to forget the ad proofs. In late afternoon the sun slanted down at the corridor of Fifth Avenue, bathing the nearby spire of St. Patrick's Cathedral in the kind of gauzy, ethereal light she had wanted for Ilse Jansen. Priceless, she thought, and rummaged among a stack of books and magazines on a shelf.

"Quinn."

"Don't rush me."

Hearing a rippling sound behind her, Quinn turned. Grinning, Valerie held up the missing proofs.

"All right, where did you find them?"

"Where I find everything else you lose," Valerie said. "In plain sight. In this case, right under your phone memo pad with all the doodles. Cute, Quinn—the blood-dripping dagger in that caricature of Jansen's body. Got her right through the heart."

"I wish," Quinn said.

On the way home, Quinn let Valerie talk her into Szechuan chicken, then a bottle of white wine, as she was pumped for information about Geneva and Welles Blackburn. Quinn had been so busy catching up at the office in the past week that she and Valerie hadn't spoken, except in passing.

"A wife, a kid, a mansion on the Rhône," Valerie said. They were walking slowly up Madison Avenue in the heat toward Quinn's apartment in the Seventies. "Lord, what a waste. That is one gorgeous man, and I for one—"

"Val, don't get any of your notions. In a nutshell: I thought he might be Jay but he isn't. That's the end of it."

"Right."

"It is," Quinn said, wiping her forehead.

"The guy spends a whole day with you, a perfect guy—you said so yourself—on a perfect summer day in a beautiful setting, buys you lunch and holds you while you cry, then kisses you senseless in full view of maybe a couple of hundred people—and you say that's the end of it?"

"What would you make of it?" In the lobby of her apartment building, Quinn fished for her key. "Don't answer that."

"It's fate."

"I suppose next you'll tell me my horoscope predicted it."

"Better than coincidence. What's his sign?"

Quinn groaned. "I don't know. Forget your book," she said, "or today's column in the *Daily News*. Concentrate on your own mission—a wedding band by Christmas—and leave me alone. I'm not looking for an affair, and neither is Welles Blackburn."

"He kisses everybody like that?"

"Don't buy a ticket to Geneva." Quinn stepped first into the elevator. "His wife is beautiful. She's also jealous. If jealousy could change a person's eye color, hers would be green, not black. Besides," she went on, overlooking the discord she'd sensed between the Blackburns, "Welles seems to be a devoted father, and I think that's wonderful."

"Oh, so do I."

Getting out of the elevator, Quinn ignored Valerie's tone. "I'm surprised that you'd endorse an extramarital fling. You've always been Andrew's staunch supporter, and since I've come back from Europe we've been getting on like newlyweds."

"Really."

At her apartment door, she turned to find Valerie frowning. "Yes," Quinn said. "Hugs and kisses. Sweet nothings in my ear. And every night—"

"Celibacy's cruel enough to live with, Quinn. If you don't mind, I'd rather not hear about anybody's second honeymoon, even yours."

She swept into the apartment, leaving Quinn to follow.

"Andrew, come out wherever you are," Valerie called. "We've brought nourishment, and it's time we called a truce."

She and Quinn had hung up their light jackets before Andrew limped from the bedroom. He sniffed the air. "I smell Szechuan."

"Very good." Valerie touched his forearm, then planted a kiss on his cheek, which made him wince.

"And what the hell is that you're wearing?"

"Foreplay," Valerie said. "It's the newest . . . perfume."

"It stinks," he told her.

"Well, I wouldn't want to spring any real surprises on you." Valerie began laying out food on the dining room table. "Make you smile or say something totally out of character, like, 'Gee, Val, you smell wonderful, and that outfit's great.'"

"Those shoes make you look like a court jester."

Valerie grinned. "Thank you so much, Andrew. You always make me feel well turned out."

"Will you stop bitching at each other? Let's eat," Quinn said and took a seat.

"I still hate Chinese," Andrew grumbled.

"Eat it anyway." Valerie dumped a plump chicken breast on his plate, and steam rose into the air. "I can't wait to see fire shoot from both your ears."

After dinner, Andrew retreated into the den while Valerie and Quinn closed themselves in her office to talk about the Priceless ad. It hadn't turned out that badly, in Valerie's opinion.

"Not if you airbrushed the shine off the seat of Ilse's pants and toned that cloud of white-blond hair, whittled it down somehow."

Frowning, Quinn tossed the proofs on her desk. She hadn't found Jay's scarf there a week ago when she looked for it, and it wasn't in the drawer. "There's no help for it," she said. "We'll have to reshoot."

"And who'll give that go-ahead?"

"Priceless. They'll have to."

"In your dreams."

"My nightmares," Quinn corrected. "I've had nightmares about these proofs ever since I got home. They always end badly, and I lose everything I've worked for in the last four years." She stared at the color prints. "We were partly right," she said at last. "It's Ilse, but something more too."

"Bankruptcy court," Valerie said.

"No, image." Quinn flipped through the proofs again. "Priceless wants to sell jeans to an already glutted market. That's one problem, and it's a big one. But they have a good product. With the right pitch, they could capture a market share next to Calvin Klein."

"But?" Valerie prompted.

"Think of our slogan. 'For the girl in you who loves denim . . . the woman in you who feels like silk.'" She slapped the proofs down again. "It's a good slogan, really. It should appeal to lots of women, from teenagers who live in jeans and dream about the prom to housewives who wish they could sometimes dress to the nines for a night out—in silk—to career people like you and me who spend too much time in suits and dresses, not enough time sprawling in pants. Women like Ilse," she added.

"Maybe the campaign's too broad."

"I don't think so. Everybody wears jeans, not only in America but all over the world. One of the greatest commodities in foreign countries is a pair of Levi's. Why not Priceless jeans? No," she said decisively, "I think the campaign hasn't gone far enough."

"So how do you appeal to the global market?"

"Ilse Jansen taps into one fantasy—the thin, willowy woman with endless legs. Every woman would like to look that way. Silky. Few do, though." Quinn frowned thoughtfully. "Maybe the idea's too narrow. What if we tried an entirely different look? One that cut across nationalities, ages, needs?"

"You mean, use a different model?"

"Or several of them."

"God, Quinn. Priceless is paying that woman seven figures to sell jeans. Why would they shell out for half a dozen more models?"

She grinned. "It's my job to convince them they should."

For the next two hours, Quinn sketched new ad ideas while Valerie pawed through magazines, looking for appropriate models. "I wish I had the agency books from work," Quinn told her, "but this will give us a start. And I have a few names in mind. I'll put someone on the search tomorrow, phone all the modeling agencies to put out a call."

"Before you convince Priceless?"

"Before they pull Ilse's ad."

"They're threatening to?"

"Oh, yes." She hadn't wanted to tell Valerie how bad

things were. "And before they throw us into review and cancel the whole contract."

"Go for it," Valerie said.

When Quinn saw her to the door, she was surprised to note from the mantel clock in the living room that it was midnight. Andrew had already gone to bed.

"Say good night to Prince Charming for me," Valerie said, packing the leftover Szechuan chicken into her tote bag.

"You know how he is," Quinn murmured. "He doesn't mean half of what he says."

"He means every word." Valerie sifted through the bag's contents, making things fit, then pulled out a small parcel wrapped in twine. "But that's okay. I'll wear him down. Give him this, will you? I almost forgot."

"Of course." Did Valerie know that Andrew had relegated her last gift, the year's Caldecott-medal-winning children's book, to the building's trash chute? "But Val—"

"Tell him I think he can use it."

He could use a drink, Welles told himself. Instead, he toed off his loafers, rested his head against the chair back in his darkened study, and closed his eyes. Recently, Mai had decided that keeping liquor with a fourteen-year-old girl in the house was too tempting, and she'd thrown out bottle after bottle from Welles's stock: his preferred single-malt scotch, his best gin, the vodka he'd brought back from a business trip to Moscow.

Not that Welles, because of his mother, was much of a drinker. But in his youth he'd done his share of partying—most often with Jay Barron—and he had always kept liquor on hand, mainly to prove to himself that he could resist its temptation. Sometimes, he also needed to dull the edges of his life.

Welles passed a hand over his closed eyes. He'd spent a miserable afternoon playing bank politics, which he deplored. In Welles's ideal world, everybody dealt fair and square with everybody else. A pipe dream, he knew, just as he recognized that wasn't the world he had come from either.

He sighed. Thornton, his rival now at the bank, could be an incomparable ass. With his English upper-crust accent, his cocky smile, he wanted a promotion as much as Welles did. Thornton reminded him of Jay Barron at his worst.

Opening his eyes, he sat up straight. For years, he'd had nothing but good memories of Jay, and the negative image surprised him now. Then he remembered a similar thought the day Quinn walked into his office—the day he'd told her Jay was dead.

What the hell was happening to him?

Driving home a week ago, after he'd seen her to her plane, with the taste of her still on his lips, he'd felt like a cheap philanderer. Mai had seen through him as soon as he walked into the house.

"What does that woman want, Welles?"

"Nothing," he'd told her. "She only wants to know about Jay Barron. There's always been a possibility that she'd turn up."

"With your name completely different now? Living another life, in another country? The possibility seems remote."

"Actually, I should feel relieved," he said. "For nineteen years, I think I've been waiting for someone to show up."

"And what did you tell her?"

Irritation made his voice tight. "Only that Jay is dead. You heard me. You were here."

Mai's dark eyes grew fierce. "I'm not a fool." Her gaze slid over him, then focused on the absence of his tie. "You didn't work today. You left home wearing a pinstripe suit and came back in this—casual jacket, casual pants—smelling of fresh air and sunshine."

And Quinn's scent, he thought, but wouldn't explain. "I'm sorry, Mai."

She'd given him a proud look, all dark eyes and high cheekbones, and left the room in a swish of ruby silk. She hadn't spoken to him in the week since.

Now Welles heard the door open almost soundlessly on well-oiled hinges—everything in Mai's house was sound-less—and he rolled his head to look at her. She stood in the doorway, wearing a long evening skirt of white crepe, a white silk tank top, a white brocade jacket. In that instant Welles knew he'd preferred her in stolen fatigue pants and T-shirt, running from Laos and certain death.

"You aren't dressed. Tonight is black tie. We're due at the Dumonds' in half an hour," she said.

Welles swore under his breath. "I had a bad day. Perhaps you could make my excuses." But of course he knew better.

"Change your clothes and say good night to Hannah, so we can leave."

"I'm staying home."

Crossing the room, she stood in front of him. Her lips, both upper and lower, were thin, a slash of anger on her exotic face, while Quinn's, he remembered from in the airport lounge at Cointrin, had looked sultry, inviting. He hadn't been able to resist.

"If I go, I'll only embarrass you. I can't make polite conversation about the ballet season when I'm still thinking of slow poison for Thornton. He'll steal that executive vice-presidency from me if he can."

In a rustle of fabric, Mai sank to her knees in front of his chair. "Poor darling," she murmured, leaning for-ward to loosen his tie. Welles didn't protest.

Her fingers worked at his shirt until it lay open; then she

pushed the expensive cotton aside, baring his chest. "You've had a bad day," she said. "We've had a terrible week."

When she raised her mouth to his, he took it. They knew which buttons to push with each other. Welles let her crawl into his arms, draping her small body across his in the chair, slanting her lips over his.

From somewhere upstairs, in Hannah's room, he supposed, he heard music. Something by Prince, or was it Sting? Mai's mouth trailed kisses along his throat; her fingers drew his hand to the slope of her small, exquisite breast. Moments later, she'd bared herself to him, ever eager for his touch, ever certain of his interest.

Welles felt himself grow and swell, straining toward her.

"I love you," Mai chanted. "I love you."

The sibilant hiss of his zipper made his head swim; the cool grasp of her fingers around him threatened to make him explode.

Now they were on the carpet, without his being aware of having moved from the chair, clothes heedlessly flung aside.

"Hannah," he murmured in weak protest.

"She's confined to her room, penance for a B-plus in Geometry." Mai held him, kneading him like warm clay.

He groaned. She could work magic with her mouth, her hands, the dark mystery of the East between her legs. Sometimes he thought that was the only reason he stayed with her, except for Hannah—which only made Welles hate himself.

"We'll stay home tonight," she whispered.

And with the long habit of years, Welles surrendered. He let the magic take him the rest of the way, knowing that after lovemaking, as he always did, he would feel empty, not only his body but his heart. That he would feel lonelier than he had since the day he'd killed Jay Barron.

7

Alone in her office, Quinn slammed down the phone, strangling the receiver as she ran through her favorite litany of curses.

Frank Murray at Priceless wouldn't budge.

Neither would Quinn.

Punching a button on her intercom, she said, "Get me some aspirin, will you, Daisy? Then try Andrew again. He hasn't answered all afternoon."

Not that she should be surprised, Quinn thought. The day after Valerie had left him a set of thick drawing pencils, the kind children might use, he'd started sleeping late again, and he seemed never to hear the phone when she called to check on him. With Lotte the housekeeper on vacation, Quinn experienced small panic attacks when no one answered.

"You and Valerie can just forget whatever diabolical plans you've hatched to get me working again," Andrew had said, his face twisted with rage. "I might excuse her ignorance, but when will *you* accept facts, Quinn?" He'd thrown the unwrapped parcel on the table, pencils scattering across the surface. "I'm never going to draw again!" Then he'd stormed into the den, the door crashing shut behind him.

Quinn sighed.

She didn't know what else she could do about Andrew, anymore than she knew how to stop the erotic dreams she kept having about Welles Blackburn. She didn't know how to find out the truth about Jay either, or how to convince the Priceless people that she was right about their ad campaign.

After her secretary brought the aspirin, Quinn washed it down with a bottle of Perrier from her office refrigerator, kicked back in her chair, and punched another number into the phone.

She caught Doug Lloyd just going out his door.

"On my way to town," he said, "for some of that tonic of Doc's that makes my calves' tongues curl up."

Quinn managed a laugh. "You used to try to push it down my throat too."

"Best stuff in Doc's little black bag," he told her. "How you been, darlin'? I've been wondering about your trip to Geneva."

Quinn's stomach tightened. "I'm sorry I didn't get back to you." The truth was, she hadn't known what to tell him. "I went," she said, hesitating before she added, "but the man isn't Jay."

She heard Doug let out a breath. "Well, I can't say I'm not glad. If he was, it just might dig up some worms."

Quinn thought of her dreams. "How true."

"Who is he, then?" Doug asked.

Someone she needed to forget, Quinn thought. She needed her sleep. Doug wouldn't be satisfied with flippancy, though; so she began by telling him about Welles's dark good looks, which she'd mistaken for Jay's, about his reluctance to see her in Geneva, and how he

and Jay had flown together. "I have to admit," she finished, having left out the kiss at Cointrin, "that Valerie's
right. Something's fishy, but it's not fate. What are the
chances of running into a man who also knows Jay and
what happened to him?"

"That depends," Doug said. "What aren't you telling
me? You got something more from Blackburn than a
half hour's chitchat in his office."

Quinn's heart thumped. She'd been able to cover up
her feelings with Andrew but never for Doug. "He said
Jay is dead."

"You don't believe him."

"No," she said.

"Now why doesn't that surprise me? Come now, my
favorite girl, this is Doug you're talkin' to." He paused.
"What makes you think Jay Barron's alive?"

Quinn mentioned the lack of evidence, of a body, her
voice stretched taut around the words.

"So his death, for you, remains circumstantial."
When she agreed, he said, "But this man flew with him.
He crashed in the same area. He saw the burned wreck-
age. What more could there be?"

"I don't know," she murmured. "Something."

"Oh, darlin', take Blackburn's word for it and let it end."

"I can't."

"Then what will you do?"

"I don't know," she said again. "Call PRISM, maybe."

"That MIA/POW group? You've already done that, a
dozen times. I took enough phone messages over the
years, even the few times you were with me."

"Maybe they have new information by now. And I
have more to tell them this time—" She broke off, realizing that she should have pinned Welles down about
the plane's location when it crashed. When she said so,
Doug made a sound of disgust.

"From Blackburn's hesitation to see you in the first place, I doubt he'd want to answer questions about something he'd rather keep buried."

"I thought he'd told me everything he knew," Quinn said, "but if I could just find out exactly where that plane went down, where the scraps of wreckage might still be, the precise area to search for—"

"What kind of man is Blackburn?"

Her impressions seemed to come automatically to her. "Self-assured, the successful corporate prince. Handsome but self-contained. Compulsively neat. Compassionate," she added. "Once I got in to see him, he treated me well. Cautious," she said.

"You can't blame him for wanting to forget, Quinn. Let the man have his peace." But he knew what she'd be thinking.

"What's one more question?" Quinn took her feet off the desk and slammed a drawer shut. "It's not as if I'm leaning on his doorbell like some pesky reporter. It's not as if he has anything to hide. Doug, you can be the most exasperating person, worse than Andrew."

"And you can be persistent as a tick on a hound." Doug, she knew, considered her persistence to be both a blessing and a flaw—depending on the subject, which he now attempted to change. "How is Andrew these days?"

"Withdrawn," Quinn admitted, after a pause to indicate her displeasure. She told him about the drawing pencils.

"He blames you for that?"

"He blames Valerie too. But I'm the handier target." She rubbed her forehead. "Doug, I don't know what to do with him. When I got back from Europe this time he seemed so sunny again, warm and loving. For a few days, a week, he was the Andrew Devlin I met at school and liked on sight."

"Not loved."

"I learned to."

"How much, Quinn?"

Her tone cooled another degree. "I don't have my yardstick handy."

"I'm not trying to berate you for your feelings. Whatever they are, they belong to you and you have a right to them. He conducted a pretty strong campaign to get you to marry him, and the time was right for you to look toward the future. I know that, darlin'. Things didn't work out the way you planned, but I'm sure you love him in some ways—just not the way that matters most."

"Which is?" Quinn could feel her teeth clenching.

"With all your heart. The way your mother and I would have, if we'd been given more time."

"Doug, don't push your fantasy of the perfect love off on me. I'm married to Andrew, and we'll work it out. Somehow."

Doug sounded hurt. "Well, I hope you do, darlin'. If that's what you want."

"What does that mean?" Quinn slammed upright in her chair. "I've tried and I'll keep on trying. It's my fault that Andrew can't work, that he has pain—"

"Bullshit."

"Doug, I'm responsible for his injuries. Nothing will change that, but if I have to spend the rest of my life making it up to him, that's what I'll do."

"He's got you brainwashed. I read all the police reports. You know damn well the road was icy, the tread on Andrew's tires worn—"

"I was driving! Too fast for conditions, on a curve—"

"Maybe so. And you had an accident. But that's what it was, darlin'. An accident. It wasn't deliberate, like Andrew's rejection of you now. How long are you going to blame yourself for something that probably couldn't be helped? I don't see Andrew Devlin making anythin' up to you because you lost your baby."

"It was his baby too."

"Then why hasn't he helped make another?" He took a breath. "After six years his infirmity isn't your fault, it's his. He won't continue therapy, won't try new doctors. He wouldn't believe the old ones, that he could make a decent recovery, with sufficient use of his hand . . . and do you know why?"

"I have to go." She couldn't talk to him when he got on his high horse about Andrew and the accident.

"Don't you hang up on me till I'm finished. In my opinion, Andrew doesn't want to get well. If he did, he'd have to be a man again, and function, and make a real life with you, instead of tying you to him with guilt. He'd have to stop feeling sorry for himself that he's not Jay Barron, and he'd have to give you those babies you want."

"Maybe someday," Quinn murmured, her throat tight.

"Maybe never. Stop thinking about Andrew's well-being and start thinking about your own. You may not recognize the need in yourself, but I can hear it—even when you talk about a stranger like Welles Blackburn. And it makes me want to cry. I love you, Quinn."

"I know you do," she whispered. "I love you too."

"Then make me happy, darlin'. By making yourself happy."

"Doug—"

She heard the empty line. This time, it was he who'd hung up without saying goodbye.

Quinn slumped in her desk chair, her chin propped on one hand. She stared at the Priceless file folder on the desktop, listened again as her secretary reported there'd been no answer from Andrew at the apartment.

Her temples pulsed and she felt a fluttering of nausea. No lunch again today, but she didn't have an appetite.

She hated feeling so distant again from Andrew, hated quarreling with Doug, who only had her best interests at heart.

If she'd lost him too . . . ?

The only security she'd ever really known had been at Doug's ranch, the rangeland beyond the house and barns so open and flat, still part of the prairie that stretched from Kansas into Colorado, but with the shocking beauty of the foothills of the Rockies thrusting up to the west. How many times had a younger Quinn ridden toward those mountains, certain that she could reach them in an hour . . . or a day?

The day the county social worker had come for her, she'd taken off like that. "I should have told you last night," Doug had said, his eyes begging forgiveness. "I couldn't bring myself to say the words. You'll have to pack, Quinn, and go with her."

"No! I won't. I'm never leaving here!"

She'd run from the house while the gray county station wagon was still barreling up Doug's drive, blowing clouds of dust up into the pines. Blinded by tears of anger, ignoring Doug's shouts, Quinn raced to the barn, threw her worn leather saddle onto her favorite Appaloosa mare, and galloped toward the mountains, with the scents of horseflesh and wildflowers wrapped around her like Doug's strong arms.

She stayed away until the sun went down and the air grew cold on her T-shirt-clad body and the wind whipped the tears dry on her cheeks. She brought the mare home blowing, spent, sure she'd given Doug one more reason—other than the fact that he must not want her—to send her away.

"That was a fool thing to do." He'd been sitting with the social worker on the porch when she climbed the steps, her coppery hair in tangles, her body exhausted. "Go inside," he said softly, "and get your clothes. I left a suitcase on your bed."

Quinn glanced at the woman, receiving an impression of brown: her hair, her eyes, the shapeless dress she wore. "I'll wait while you take a shower," the woman said, not unkindly, "and fix your hair."

"I don't need to impress anybody," Quinn replied and went into the house before either of them noticed her mouth quivering.

She didn't look at Doug when she left. If he didn't want her, she didn't want him either.

"Quinn," he said, stopping her with a hand on her arm.

"I'll be okay on my own."

Fending off his reach for her suitcase, she carried it herself. She got into the gray station wagon and never, not once in that long drive to the road, looked back.

Of the first foster home in which the county placed her, Quinn expected squalor, poor food, and no privacy. But in the big frame house in a pleasant Denver suburb Quinn had her own bedroom, and the plump middle-aged woman who was her foster mother cooked like heaven. In three months Quinn gained five pounds and learned how to sew. She made simple skirts for school, did her share of the housecleaning, and learned the pros and cons of having siblings. Bella Sharp and her husband had two boys of their own and cared for two other foster children, a boy and a girl.

The girl, a year older than Quinn, stole her best sweater the first week she was there, warning Quinn that if she told she'd be sorry. Quinn didn't care for threats, but she had nowhere else to go and in Bella

Sharp she'd found a reasonable replacement for her own mother, whom she missed.

The boy, a gangly sixteen-year-old with a detention record and a bad overbite, made her skin crawl and Quinn avoided him when she could.

After she had lived in Denver for three months, she was in her room one afternoon, changing from school, when the door eased open and a grinning face appeared.

"What do you want?" Quinn clutched a T-shirt to her chest. Half dressed, she didn't want Eddy, the foster boy, to see her. "Get out of my room."

"I got something to show you," he whispered. "I been waiting for old Sharp-nose to leave."

Bella had gone grocery shopping, and Quinn suddenly realized she was alone with Eddy in the house. The other kids were playing in the yard. "Go away," she said.

But he shut the door and came toward her. Quinn, her heart pounding, backed up but he kept coming, until she bumped into her bed. The motion buckled her knees and Quinn went down. Eddy fell on her, his superior weight holding Quinn captive.

"Scream, and I'll cut you," he warned.

Quinn saw the flash of his pocketknife but decided she'd rather have her throat slit than submit to whatever awful degradation Eddy had in mind. She bucked against him, bringing her knee up into his groin, hard.

The knife dropped onto the bed. "Oww!"

"Touch me again and I'll kill you." Quinn leaped up, shaking, her fingers in a death grip around the knife.

She had no idea what she would have done next, but while he was still rolling on the mattress, both hands cupped to his fly, she grabbed the first clothes she saw, wrenched open the door, and escaped into the hall. In T-shirt and jeans, with two dollars in her pocket, Quinn left Denver.

She'd never felt more alone in her life than she had that night, but now she had the same low-in-her-stomach panic, the same feeling of loss. *Doug.*

She reached for the phone again. But it wasn't only the quarrel with Doug that troubled her; it was Andrew too. She set the receiver back in place. She'd stop trying to wear the Priceless marketing people down and go home; she'd talk to Andrew. And everything would be all right.

"Hello?" Quinn called out, shutting the apartment door with one foot, both arms full of grocery bags. She'd stopped at the supermarket before coming home. She hadn't looked forward to opening the door and hearing only the silence she expected. "Andrew?"

The silence made her heart slam. She dropped her packages and purse, then raced through the apartment, suddenly fearing that she'd find him in the bathtub in a pool of blood; in bed with the covers to his chin and an empty bottle of pills nearby, his face pasty white and lifeless; in a living room chair, his brains blown out.

"Andrew?"

"In here."

She could barely hear him. Quinn strode down the hall to the bedroom. The sight of him lying on tangled sheets, his hair tousled, a day's growth of beard on his cheeks made her weak.

"You're still in your pajamas." Desperate for a bit of normality, she tried teasing. "It's almost seven o'clock, Mr. Devlin. Do you know where your clothes are?"

"I didn't feel like getting up today."

"Are you ill?" Alarmed, Quinn walked to the bed. Although it was still light outside, the room was very dark. "I called. Why didn't you answer?"

"I didn't feel like it."

"Why didn't you call me at the office then, later? I would have come home."

"I'm not sick," he said, his good arm flung over his eyes. "I'm tired. You kept me up all night."

"I kept you—?"

"Tossing and turning, thrashing. Muttering."

Oh, God. She never talked in her sleep. What could she have said? "I—I had some nightmares."

"You've been having them ever since you came home from the Versailles shoot."

Quinn felt a surge of defensive anger. What was he accusing her of? She stalked to the windows and yanked open the heavy draperies. Bypassing the air conditioner, she flung up the smaller side windows that flanked the large picture window. "It's stuffy in here, like a tomb, dark and airless. How can you stand it?"

"I've learned a person can stand most anything." He lowered his arm and stared at her. "Pain. Failure."

Her heart sank. How could she stay angry? He was deep in one of his moods again, which made her fear for his safety. "You haven't failed at anything."

"Oh," he said. "I see. We mustn't let the patient believe for a moment that he's any different from what he was before. Mustn't let him think he can't do what-ever he sets his mind to. Is that why you and Valerie decided to give me those clever little kindergarten pencils? To restore my confidence? Or to teach me all over again how to draw a straight line?"

"Andrew, please."

Pushing the covers down, he sat up bare-chested, thinner than he'd looked in the hospital six years ago. He followed her gaze. "What do you see, Quinn? The same Andrew you married in that charming little chapel near Doug's ranch, with him giving you away like the proud father he always wanted to be? No," he said, "I'm sure not. Or the same able-bodied Andrew who loaded the rental van single-handed when we moved from Denver to Boulder—six months before the accident?"

He stumbled from bed, ignoring the blackthorn stick propped by the dresser, dragging his bad leg until she had to look away.

"Or how about the Andrew who made you pregnant the month after that? Successful Andrew, Andrew drunk on champagne and celebration because his book was in contention for the Caldecott and the future looked rosy and he thought maybe, at last, his wife really loved him?"

"Stop it!" Quinn covered her ears.

He stood near her now, his breathing harsh, his voice a sneer. "Go on, Quinn. Give me another of your pep talks. Tell me that everything will be all right again, if only I let them carve me up a little more, if only I let them wrench my joints and muscles into a thousand contortions they call therapy. Tell me if I just pick up those lovely little pencils and *try*, I'll be able to draw again."

"I never said it would be easy."

"Well, that's something, isn't it? But not enough."

"I don't know what you want from me, Andrew." She laid a hand on his arm, but he flinched away. "I worry about you, and I feel so helpless that I can't make things better, but—"

"You just don't get it, do you?"

"What?"

"Nothing will get better." He touched his leg, his arm. "This is the way I am, the way I will always be. No wonder you're hiding things from me, whatever happened in Europe—"

"Nothing happened!"

"How could I blame you," he murmured, "if you chose someone else, someone whole and capable, over me? It wouldn't be the first time."

"There isn't anyone." Maybe she'd been wrong to stay quiet about Jay. Maybe telling him would help. "But you're right, something did happen while I was gone. I learned about Jay."

"What could you have learned about good old Jay, of the white silk scarf and promises?"

Quinn's stomach churned. "What did you do with the scarf, Andrew?"

"I burned it."

"Why?"

"Because I'm sick of being reminded of him."

"I've never thrown Jay at you."

"No?" he said.

"And I'm not hiding anything now." She looked at him. "When I was in Europe, I went to see someone." She told him about the George V and then Geneva. "I did lie to you when I came back, but not about an affair. I talked with Welles Blackburn. A man with a wife and family."

"You see some stranger in a hotel lobby—and he just happens to know Jay Barron, when you've been looking for him for half your life?"

Quinn met his gaze. "He used to fly with Jay in Vietnam and he said . . . he told me that Jay is dead."

There was a silence. Then he asked, "How?"

"In the crash. But his body wasn't found. This man assumes he burned too."

Andrew studied her for a moment. "And what do you assume?"

She wouldn't lie to him again. "I think there's a chance he's still alive."

"Someone tells you he saw proof, a fireball of proof, and you still choose to believe that Jay Barron isn't dead?"

"Maybe he's not."

He turned away. "It's always maybe. It's always been maybe. How the hell will you ever *know*?"

"I'll keep looking."

He stumped toward the door. "You're a fool, Quinn, if you really think Jay Barron's alive, an even bigger fool if you think you'll ever find better proof. Or should I say, an answer you'd believe." He faced her, his eyes bright. "I don't know if I care any longer what the answer might be. I just want him out of your head." He looked down at the carpet. "Dead or alive, hasn't he taken enough from you, from us?"

"That's not the point."

"Dammit, what *is* the point?" His blue-gray gaze shot up. "He took off for Vietnam almost twenty goddamn years ago with your heart on his sleeve like a fucking insignia! And that's what you're still looking for, not some cocky bastard you wouldn't recognize today if you fell over him." Andrew walked back to her, his steps unsteady but determined. "He's more married to you than I am. He took your heart, Quinn, just as you took my—" He broke off.

"What?" she whispered. "What did I take, Andrew?"

He thrust his hand in front of her face. "This." He brushed the scarred edge of his palm down her cheek. "My hand. It's ruined, like my leg, like the rest of my life. Like Jay Barron. I might as well be dead."

"No," she said.

Quinn reached her office the next morning, which was Friday, still feeling as if she'd been dragged for ten miles behind a horse at full gallop. Her parents, Doug, Jay . . . and now Andrew. She didn't think she could deal with another loss.

The office seemed quiet as a church after Sunday morning service. Daisy hadn't arrived yet, but when Quinn glanced at her desk clock, she quelled her irritation.

Was it really just eight o'clock? After the ugly scene with Andrew, she'd gone straight to bed but hadn't slept. She'd turned and twisted for hours, hearing Andrew pace the living room, shut cabinets in the kitchen, slam drawers in his den. At least, she'd thought in the long hours after midnight, he was on his feet and active, not lying in bed depressed and brooding. By four in the morning Quinn had realized the futility of trying to sleep.

She'd finally showered, dressed in jeans and a silk shirt, and in the still-cool morning walked the twenty-three downtown blocks to work.

The message light on her phone kept flashing. Quinn ignored it, making room on her desk for the cheese Danish and coffee she'd bought. Of course the cup had leaked through the bag and now dripped on her papers. She mopped at the puddle with the only thing at hand—two soggy napkins—but not before it spread onto the Priceless file folder.

"Dammit."

The phone rang but Quinn ignored that too.

Sipping hot caffeine, she stared out her windows at the morning light, spread over the spire of St. Patrick's like a blessing. Maybe she should take the day off. Walk to Central Park and feed pigeons like a bag lady and rent a toy boat to sail. The way things were going, she'd probably get mugged.

The thought made her remember Welles Blackburn and his concern about New York, as opposed to the more civilized Geneva. At least she hadn't dreamed about him last night. She tossed the leaky coffee cup into the trash. It was time to listen to her voice mail.

All the messages were from Priceless.

As soon as she finished listening, the phone rang again.

The unctuous voice she'd come to despise said, "Ms.

Tyler, this is Frank Murray at Priceless. Did you get my messages?"

"Yes, but I—"

"We've decided not to go with Ilse Jansen for a reshoot."

"Fine." That was the best news she'd heard in two weeks. "But I really don't think Versailles—"

"Versailles is in the trash. And Jansen's too old an image for the campaign."

Light at the end of the tunnel. "Well, that certainly agrees with our concept here at Tyler and Devlin," she began.

"But our CEO doesn't—and of course we all concur—want the shotgun approach you've suggested either."

Quinn forced the words out slowly. She had a bad feeling now. "So I'm to look for another single spokeswoman?"

"Yes."

"What did you all have in mind?"

"Obviously we've been brainstorming here, but we'll leave the rest up to you. One model. Youthful image. Something we can hang onto for a while, if you get my meaning."

"Something big."

"You've done it before," he said, then paused before the dreaded words: "Just get it to me by Monday." He hung up.

Quinn had already discovered she didn't like being hung up on. She also wasn't sure whether she'd won—or lost again.

8

Fingers poised above the green-and-yellow box on her desk, Quinn gnawed at her lip. Raw Sienna? Cerulean? She pulled out a crayon labeled Dandelion, a perfect complement to Jungle Green. It was strong and conflicting, exactly the way she felt.

Quinn squinted at the open coloring book in front of her. In the picture Belle, the heroine from the popular cartoon movie *Beauty and the Beast*, was being courted in a garden by the lecherous Gaston. She'd given him breeches in Plum, clothed Belle in Carnation Pink.

She had always loved to color and still did, especially when she had problems to avoid. She'd been holed up in her office since Friday, and it was now 3 A.M. on Monday morning.

"Blast." Her crayon slipped outside the lines. She still didn't know what to tell Frank Murray. "No bright ideas," she said to the empty office. "My ass is grass— color me Forest Green."

Pep-talk time, as Andrew would have said. She believed in herself. In Denver, at the tender age of twenty-nine, that unshakable confidence had produced the ad campaign for Sterling Tea, an ongoing serial of commercials about a young married couple that was still being seen and, what's more, added to. They'd just had their second baby in print and on television, and millions throughout America loved them like family. The Big Idea. It had single-handedly made Quinn's career, allowed her to risk coming to New York after Andrew's accident, to strike out on her own for the big time.

Shoving back from the desk, she dropped the crayon. In two days she hadn't been home or anywhere else except the corner deli for sandwiches, which she'd barely touched. She supposed Andrew wouldn't care, but Doug—even when angry with her too—would bully her to eat more. So would Welles Blackburn.

Quinn ran a finger inside the waistband of her sweatpants. She could swear they'd been tighter on Friday night when she'd sequestered herself in the empty office. Hell, maybe she'd model for Priceless jeans, pass herself off as the generation's icon after all, slightly used, slightly worn, her image just shy of being America's nineties Superwoman.

Lord.

She could almost see the moving men crating up her office, peeling her name off the door.

Models, Quinn thought, and leaned over her drafting board for the hundredth time, over the mug shots of gorgeous girls, one of whom just might put Priceless at the head of the denim pack.

None of them had the look she wanted.

She needed youth and a beauty that crossed international boundaries. A timely beauty, and somehow uncommon. Exotic. She went back to her desk, to the picture of Belle and Gaston. Colors, she thought. In the ad she'd use very few, but strong ones. Or no, maybe—

"Oh, my God," Quinn whispered.

As always, the concept emerged as a whole. She imagined a clean canvas, a set for the shoot all in white: white room, white floor, white light. Soft light. The model in a white shirt, romantic in style, barefoot—she'd have elegant feet—and wearing Priceless jeans. Young, so vulnerably young that she looked the next thing to a child while at the same time she seemed to know all the age-old mysteries of woman: she'd have a soft, pouty mouth, a long slick fall of jet-black hair, dark eyes. . . .

Hannah Blackburn.

Quinn let out a breath and glanced at her desk clock. In Geneva it was just past 9 A.M. The Banque Internationale opened at 8:30, and if she knew the man at all, he'd already be at his desk. Her heart beat faster. But as she reached for the receiver, she paused.

Would she be doing Hannah Blackburn a favor by calling, sounding her out through Welles as the new spokeswoman for Priceless? It was a plum modeling assignment. *It's what I want to do . . . it's all I want to do.* But the girl's own words didn't ease Quinn's indecision.

Because Hannah was a minor, there was Mai Blackburn to consider, and Quinn already knew her opinion. That night in Geneva at dinner, she'd made her opposition to Hannah's modeling clear.

Then there was Welles himself. Quinn recalled his pride in his daughter. Because of Mai, he might ride the fence, but she suspected he'd want Hannah to have this opportunity. He'd want her to come to America and work for Priceless. For Quinn.

The afternoon in Carouge breezed through her mind, the kiss at Cointrin. She'd never felt a personal concern for her models, but how could she ignore her concern for Hannah now? Hiring her for Priceless meant further contact with Welles Blackburn—and the possibility that

Hannah would see the attraction between them, that Quinn herself would be tempted to act on it.

Still, because Priceless wasn't just any client and because of her own persistent nature, she tightened her grip on the receiver and jabbed in numbers: Overseas 011, Switzerland's 41, the 22 code for Geneva, then the local number. The Blackburns' answer, because of Mai, would most likely be a resounding no. But what harm could there be in a long-distance phone call?

Quinn, who'd had just one more question to ask of Welles Blackburn on Friday, now had two.

"It's out of the question."

With the words, Welles took a long breath. He'd spoken to Quinn on Monday morning, when her call had buckled his knees, and was now, late on Tuesday, calling her back.

"Welles," was all she said.

The tone of reproach was well deserved. How many times in the past two weeks had he picked up the phone and half dialed her number before common sense made him hang up? In Paris again on business the week before, he'd nearly succumbed to the corny urge to send her a postcard of the George V; in the middle of composing a careful message—not too distant, not too friendly—he'd torn the card in half.

It was after 6 P.M. in Geneva. He'd hoped that having the element of surprise on his side this time would help, but as soon as he heard her voice, the same zing had gone through him as the day before.

She said his name—only that—and his blood pressure shot skyward, memory flashing through his mind and gut like the desire he'd felt when he kissed her at Cointrin.

"Don't waste your time arguing," he said, loosening his tie. "I ran this by Mai last night, and it's a flat refusal."

He heard Quinn sigh. "I expected as much, but I'm obligated to give you the hard sell. Welles, this would be the chance of a lifetime. The contract money would pay her way through college, which isn't that far off."

"Far enough. Hannah's just turned fourteen. Her mother has sometimes contradictory feelings toward her. One moment Hannah's a young lady who should behave like an adult, the next she's an impressionable child—which she is—but either way Mai doesn't want her exposed."

"Exposed?"

"Like some pinup, selling sex around the world."

Silence.

"You have to admit, Quinn, that's what Priceless Sportswear wants to do. It's no different from automobiles," he said reasonably, while his pulse pumped double time, even at her silence. "Some leggy blonde stretched across the hood of a car, wearing a provocative outfit and a smile to match. The implication being," he added, "that if some poor horny bastard buys the car, he'll also get laid."

"Are you trying to insult me?"

"I don't think so." There, he'd regained some control of things. She was obviously steaming. "Not you personally. Just telling the truth—about advertising. Mai and I don't want our daughter sending that message."

Her tone was icy. "Have you seen any of my work?"

"I don't know. Why don't you tell me what you've done and I'll tell you whether I've seen it."

Quinn reeled off a list of commercials, several of them heavy hitters, particularly the Sterling Tea ads, which Welles personally liked. They also mystified him. Warm, sexy, human, they made him want to brew a cup of strong, rich tea when he hated tea.

"Effective," he said when she finally paused, "but the answer's still no."

"What does Hannah think?"

Welles hesitated. "We didn't ask her."

Quinn made a sound, frustrated, impatient. "Your daughter is a very young woman, yes. She's innocent, and that, in today's permissive world, is refreshing. It's also perfect for the image Priceless jeans—and I—want to project."

"Sorry," he murmured, nearly smiling. She had a hell of an ego, which he had to admire.

"It's not as if she hasn't modeled before, and I think she has enormous potential. I thought so the night I met her, but I said nothing because your wife so obviously didn't approve."

"And still doesn't."

Quinn lost no momentum. "At the time I didn't have a spot in mind for Hannah anyway. Now the timing is right and so is her age. Europe may be different, but the U.S. is a relentlessly youth-oriented culture. If she wants to model and has this opportunity in America—"

"Quinn, the answer is no. Mai would never agree."

"What about you?"

Could she hear the lack of conviction in his voice? Since Quinn's brief sojourn in his life, things had been going well enough between him and Mai. Since the night in his study when they'd decided to miss the Dumonds' party to make love, he'd even had some hope for their marriage. Why risk it? Despite the lowdown heat in his body now at the mere sound of Quinn's voice, there was no need to see her again. Whatever his disappointment at Mai's refusal to spend last weekend at the ski house in Zermatt, he could deal with that.

His wife came from a warmer climate, a country of heat and humidity, of jungles and river deltas. She hated being cold. She didn't like snow and she didn't ski. When he and Hannah used the chalet, Mai did as she pleased, unable to appreciate, as he and Hannah did, the awesome splendor of the Alps.

He could understand that. He'd come from heat himself, and squalor, similar enough to that in Saigon during the war for Mai, who'd been born an aristocrat. Like Welles, she dreaded poverty, abhorred disorder. He glanced around his office, as always neat to the point of sterility.

His own need for order, he supposed, was a big reason why he'd become a banker. He liked being in control. He could understand that in Mai, too.

"I have to agree with my wife," he told Quinn. "Maybe in a couple of years, if Hannah's still interested. . . ."

He hadn't quite trailed off when Quinn blasted him.

"You've been holed up in Geneva too long. There's another world out here, you know. An exciting world, a risky world."

"I take enough risks with other people's money," he said, his tone hardening. "I won't risk my daughter's—"

"What?" Quinn said.

"Privacy."

"I can't promise you that if the ad campaign takes off—as I hope it will—she won't have the media breathing down her neck. But I can close the set when we shoot and hire an agent for her who could screen out all but the most necessary interviews, and we'd work around her school schedule, of course."

"No. I'm sorry, Quinn. There's no room for discussion."

"Are you always so closed-minded?"

He had to smile at the frustration in her tone. "Probably, yes. And you're not."

"I can't afford to be in my business." Then she sighed. "I'm sorry to push, I promised myself I wouldn't, but I've just spent the better part of seventy-two hours in this office, wringing my brain dry like a sponge for ideas." Her tone lowered, almost as if she were talking to herself. "I thought I'd had the best one in years. In fact," she said, "I still do."

"I guess that's your problem."

To his dismay, Quinn chose an entirely different tack. "Well. I'm sorry we can't do business, especially sorry for Hannah's sake." She paused. "For myself, I should thank you . . . for your hospitality. I enjoyed the tour of Geneva." He had started to unwind at her friendlier tone when Quinn said, "Which reminds me," and his gut tightened again. "I have another question—no, actually three."

Welles said nothing.

"When I saw you in Paris at the hotel, I thought at first I was hallucinating about Jay. Then you weren't Jay at all in Geneva, but you'd still been staying at the George Cinq. I wonder why."

He might have laughed at the irony, but he couldn't. "It's become something of a habit," he said. "I was with a relative of Mai's that night, an expatriate who's quite Gallic these days. He prefers the hotel." Welles paused, then admitted, "But that's not the only reason. I've stayed there on my own plenty of times. Jay used to rave about it, and I discovered he was right. The service is impeccable."

"Yes," Quinn murmured, "it is."

Her taut tone told him all he needed to know. "My God, you stayed there for the same reason, because of Jay. Didn't you?"

"Yes."

"So our meeting wasn't as much of a coincidence as it seemed?"

"No," she said. He sensed that the realization had taken the wind out of her sails. He didn't know why, but it delighted him.

"What's the other question?"

There was a brief silence. "At Cointrin, when you put me on the plane, you used the same words Jay did when he left for war."

Welles felt his smile slip. "Did I?"

"Yes. You did."

She didn't mention the kiss. "I'm not sure why," he said, frowning. He hadn't thought of it before. "Maybe the memories were just too strong that day. We'd been talking about him. . . ."

"I suppose so."

He pressed a hand to his stomach muscles. "Weird, isn't it? Jay was our link, even if I wanted—" You, he thought. He broke off, needing to change the subject. "Never mind. What other question did you have?"

After a moment Quinn said, "Forget it. Thanks again . . . for everything," and disconnected the call.

Welles slammed his fist on the desk.

She was trouble and she knew it. Knew just how to get under his skin, to make him need her. The reminder had him shaking with it, remembering not Jay but the strip of peekaboo lace when she'd stood up in his office and he couldn't look away from her legs. He couldn't seem to forget them, or anything about her.

He'd have to, Welles decided. To keep his hands busy, he plucked the black onyx pen from its holder. His pristine office suddenly offended him. Maybe she was right and he was closed-minded, but it didn't matter. The pen snapped in his hands. He wouldn't want what he couldn't have. He wouldn't see Quinn Tyler again.

An hour later, with Quinn still on his mind, Welles was halfway home when he realized he was late, that he should be driving Mai to the airport. By the time he stepped into the foyer, her black eyes were snapping.

"Sorry," he said, "I lost track of time. Can we still make your plane?"

She was one of the few people he knew in Europe, except occasionally himself, who didn't forego expensive continental jet travel for the train; they had the money, she always said, though Welles knew the truth: Mai hated the notion of any trip longer than an hour. It reminded her of the long journey north from Saigon years ago in search of her missing brother and the Tears of Jade, of her own flight with Welles from Laos and near-captivity. She stood now by the entrance to the library, petite but straight as a soldier, dressed in a white wool suit and black silk blouse, both hands clasped at her waist. Her knuckles were white too. Welles noticed her bags, packed and waiting by the door.

"I've phoned for a taxi. Assuming it arrives in the next five minutes, I'll just manage."

"I'm sorry," Welles said again, but her eyes didn't soften and he wondered immediately whether she'd seen something in his that gave away his earlier thoughts. "I had to make a call."

"To that woman from New York?"

"I couldn't phone earlier," he said. "She had meetings all morning, and with the time difference going the wrong way—"

"You should have faxed a simple 'no' to her proposal."

"Mai, don't be like this."

"I will not have her in our lives, Welles."

"You're being ridiculous." He knew the signs. Every time they went to dinner with friends, or attended a party like the Dumonds', he had only to send another woman an appreciative glance—he might be faithful to his wife but he wasn't dead—and Mai's normal possessiveness went into high gear. "I won't be rude to Quinn

Tyler. Her suggestion wasn't out of line. She's right; Hannah has modeled before."

"She will not do so again. Do I make myself clear?"

Welles frowned. His tolerance for Mai's rules of order went only so far. "I've told her the answer is no. I've told her your feelings on the matter. They won't change. What more would you have me do?"

"Tell her not to call again."

Shaking his head, he said, "I can't do that."

"American women," Mai murmured and turned to the foyer mirror above the Sheraton table, peering at her image over a spray of white gladioli in a black vase. "You tell me she has a husband." Mai smoothed a finger over a perfectly arched brow.

"For God's sake, it was a business call. A preliminary one, at that. There's been no formal contract offer, no negotiations, no money mentioned. It was nothing but a feeler."

Her gaze, meeting his in the mirror, looked uncertain. It never took much to destroy her precarious sangfroid.

"You're certain? There'll be no more questions about Hannah—or Jay Barron?"

Welles felt his heart skip. "None."

"I won't share you, Welles."

His own anger took control, all the more because in spite of his resolve, he'd been thinking of Quinn on the way home and felt guilty. "There's no romantic subterfuge here, dammit. The woman's a stranger and will stay a stranger. I wonder that you can't summon an ounce of gratitude for her consideration in even asking about Hannah. The opportunity for a young girl to make her fortune, to become a household word in America—"

"By peddling blue jeans?"

Mai didn't even own a pair with a designer label. Welles sighed.

"My daughter will never debase herself for the masses in such a disgusting manner. Do you think I haven't seen the magazines? The billboards?"

"So it's not your way of life," he said. "It's not mine either. But Quinn Tyler makes a damn good living at it, I'd expect, and she's good at what she does. Hannah worshiped her the night she came to dinner, but you wouldn't even let your daughter know about the idea—"

"What idea, Daddy?"

He could have groaned when Hannah appeared on the stairs. Welles's heart turned over. In the jeans her mother despised, in a school sweater, and loafers, she could have been a second-generation all-American girl like the ice skater Kristi Yamaguchi. He hadn't been fair to her.

Mai turned from the mirror. "Is my taxi here?"

"Yes, Mother. But—"

"Welles, you'll take my bags to the car?"

"I would have driven you."

"Stay and enjoy your dinner. Make sure Hannah remembers to finish her English theme tonight. She has finals soon." She swept to the door. "You know the number where I can be reached."

She was going to Florence for the week. Several years before, Mai had grown bored at home and become a volunteer with the World Refugee Foundation. Now, as a salaried fund-raiser, she traveled frequently. Welles despised himself for being glad to see her leave. He could sense Hannah, hovering on the bottom step, frozen at the conversation she'd overheard.

Mai kissed neither of them before she left. Welles busied himself, helping the cabdriver stow her luggage in the trunk so he wouldn't wring her neck. He didn't care about himself, but she had no right to hurt Hannah. By the time he came back into the house, the foyer was empty.

Rubbing his neck, Welles walked through the house, shedding his tie at the banister, then his suit coat, which he draped over a Louis Fourteenth chair in the hall. It would drive Mai crazy, and ordinarily it would have driven him nuts as well, but tonight he didn't care.

He took the day's mail with him, intending to work until dinner, but as soon as he closed the study door behind him, he heard the whisking sound of denim on suede.

Hannah was curled up in his favorite oatmeal-colored chair, one now-bare foot propped on his hassock.

"Daddy?"

"What?" He'd pretend not to know what she wanted; maybe she hadn't heard very much.

"I want to know what Mother meant."

"About what, hot stuff?"

"Don't be thick. About 'peddling blue jeans.'"

Welles sprawled on the love seat across from her. He couldn't quite meet Hannah's eyes. "I had a call yesterday, baby. From the States."

"From Quinn Tyler?"

"Yes." He decided to just get it over with. He'd thought she had a right to know anyway, no matter that he'd covered up with Quinn.

"Daddy, that's terrific!" Hannah said when he finished explaining about Priceless. "Awesome!" When Welles said nothing, her features fell. "I know what Mother said, but can't you make her say yes instead? Please?"

"No, Hannah. I'm sorry."

"Why not? I heard you. You wanted to tell me last night, didn't you?"

"Your mother and I decided—"

"*You* wanted to. Why are you always so careful to please her? She's not right, Daddy." Hannah flew off the chair and over to Welles's bookshelves. Unerringly, she pulled out a scrapbook stuffed full of pictures: all Hannah, in the last two years, the most impressive lay-out from the French *Elle*. "They said I was good, you know they did. They said I have a 'quality.' So did Quinn."

"You sure do, baby." But Welles shook his head. "You have finals to consider," he said.

"But when school's out? All the American kids fly home for summer holiday. I could go too—and work the rest of the summer. I could even go to school there in the fall if I had to."

"You're too young, Hannah."

"This is what I want to do, Daddy. I have to do it while I'm young."

"So Quinn tells me."

"Then why can't we say yes?"

"It wasn't a formal offer, just a teaser. There'd be contract negotiations and probably a test shoot."

"Then, okay," Hannah said, seeing her chance. "If I make it, great. If I don't, no big deal."

Welles couldn't help smiling. "You sound more American every day. Your mother would have a fit if she could hear you."

"All my friends are from New York and Los Angeles and Chicago and Palm Beach. They have rich parents who are all divorced, so they ship the kids over here to keep them out of trouble."

"You happen to attend one of the finest schools in Geneva. Don't knock it," Welles said.

"And it's expensive, right? If I was working, I could pay my own tuition."

"Hannah, we don't need the money."

Her look was winsome. "Please, Daddy? You can convince Mother, I know you can. And Quinn's awfully nice. She sent me those magazines I wanted—didn't even expect the postage—"

"She did?" He'd never seen them.

"She'd be fun to work with. Have you ever seen her ads for Sterling Tea, with the couple who fall in love?"

"Yes, I've seen them. They're good."

"So it wouldn't be 'peddling jeans' like some sleaze-ball at a carnival, would it?"

"No," Welles admitted. He'd blasted Quinn about her business, but his heart hadn't been in it. Her work was damn good, classy. Like the lady herself.

"Then, *please?*"

The hardest thing in the world for him was to say no to her. But he and his wife had long ago decided to keep a united front with their precious only child—not to be overwhelmed—and Mai did have some good reasons, mainly the continued contact with Quinn Tyler.

"Hannah, we're of one mind on the issue. Let it go."

Crossing the room to him, she changed moods as swiftly as location. The growing pout turned into another grin, her eyes brightened, and she slipped into his arms. "I can change your mind," she said. "I can wear you down."

"The curse of indulgent fathers."

"How much will it take?"

"Forget it this time, hot stuff."

She dropped a kiss on his nose, then on both cheeks. Their old game, which they'd played since Hannah was a baby; which they'd played the last time when Quinn came to dinner.

Welles pointed to his chin. "Plant one here."

"Where else?"

He grinned. "Right ear."

"And?"

"Uh, forehead." By now, he was laughing and so was she.

Hannah leaned back in his arms and Welles realized all over again what a blessing she was, this child who still loved so freely—as he never had, except with her. "Why do you call me hot stuff?"

"Because you are."

"You mean . . . sexy?"

Welles was shocked. "Good Lord."

Hannah looked wounded. "You don't think I'm sexy?"

"I think you're terrific. But your poor father isn't prepared to fend off callow youths at the door. Save it for a few years, can't you? I'm too young to think about giving you away."

"I'll never leave you, Daddy."

Which showed him just how young she really was. Welles decided Mai was right entirely. And he hadn't considered Hannah's leaving for New York, to work. Leaving home.

"Someday you'll change your mind," he said.

"If I can, then you can. About Quinn."

Welles groaned. Only too easily, he thought. "Hannah."

"You don't have to change it tonight," she said. "But you will think about it?"

"I'll think about it."

He'd given her the old parental dodge. For once, Welles was grateful it held the same old meaning: no. Especially where Quinn Tyler was concerned.

9

Quinn had a grease spot on her skirt—the least of her problems. That morning she'd bought a French cruller, her favorite, on the way to work, but as soon as she settled at her desk and took the first bite, Frank Murray called. He was in her office now and Quinn folded her hands in her lap, hiding the stain.

"I'm trying," she said again. "It's not easy, finding the perfect spokeswoman for Priceless. You ought to know. You thought Ilse Jansen was just right, but—"

"Don't say it."

"—now she's costing your company twice what she signed for to break the contract."

Frank, who'd been pacing Quinn's office, halted at the windows to look broodingly at St. Patrick's spire. On a rainy August morning, it was shrouded in mist worthy of a melodrama.

"Don't be dramatic," he said, raking a hand through carefully styled dark hair.

"I'm not. From all I hear through the grapevine, Ilse is." Quinn added, "I'm also sure the numbers I hear are a lowball estimate. I'm just stating facts, Frank."

He turned to study her with nearly black eyes, obviously looking for sarcasm—or some sign that she was interested in more than their discussion about Priceless? In turn, Quinn studied him. An attractive man, she thought. Tall, spare, a real clotheshorse in his gray suit and silk paisley tie, he seemed about her own and Welles Blackburn's age and he'd made half-hearted passes once or twice. Under her continued scrutiny, he straightened his tie and shot his starched white cuffs. Quinn thought of Welles's similar neatness. In Frank Murray, the same trait irritated her. He didn't turn her on either.

"Facts?" He echoed Quinn. "Well, let me give you some. Our CEO's making my life a living hell. Priceless is a family business, three generations' worth, and he's taking a personal interest in this campaign. The guy calls me ten times a day—which is why I've been calling you every hour on the hour, why I'm in this office now. I need a solution to this thing."

"I've given my presentation. Your CEO—and the rest of management and marketing—agree. Now it's simply a matter of finding the right girl."

The task, Quinn thought, would have seemed simpler if it hadn't been for one thing. Three days after Welles's refusal about Hannah, Quinn had received a package from Geneva. Inside, she'd found enough photos of Hannah in various poses, all appealing, to make her curse both the solid family unit that wanted to keep the girl at home and her own reluctance to pursue the matter any further.

The photos had come from Hannah herself, so Welles must have told her about Priceless. They'd been sent not to her office but to her apartment, the address presumably taken from Quinn's package of American fashion magazines to Hannah, but she had no idea where Hannah's pictures were at the moment. Typical of her, but just as well.

Frank walked back to Quinn's desk. With a gesture at the array of photographs and contact sheets spread across its surface, he said, "Strange, how beautiful women all start to look alike."

"That's my point." She riffled through the stack. She'd long ago broken down the pictures into groups. Then into one group: sleek, dark-haired young women who could pass for any number of nationalities. The more exotic-looking, the better. None of them seemed right to her.

No, she corrected. One of them was right. It was simply fortunate she couldn't find that particular set of photos.

"There's never been an oriental spokeswoman for a major product," she said, tapping a glossy 5 by 7 photograph. "Except for this one, the others are too . . . American. And thus too narrow for the global campaign image we've all agreed upon."

"The Japanese girl's okay, but she doesn't say sex."

With the last word, Quinn said a prayer of thanks as Valerie clomped into the office, wearing green lizard cowboy boots and a turquoise tent dress.

"Christ," Frank murmured.

Valerie shook her wild, frosted mane of hair, which set her silver earrings jangling. From Quinn's view they appeared to be horse-shaped, with elaborate liquid silver tails, their eyes set in turquoise.

"Good morning, Frank. You're looking scrumptious today."

He didn't answer.

"Andrew would have said I was giving him indigestion," Valerie told Quinn. "Frank's the strong, silent type. And I love a challenge."

"What did you want, Val?" Quinn guessed from the

stiff set of Frank's shoulders that he was about to
explode.

"Nothing urgent. Just had a question on that mouth-
wash commercial I'm doing, but it can wait."

"By all means, don't let me stop you." Frank grimaced. "What could be more important than solving
America's problem with bad breath in the morning?"

"Val," Quinn began and Valerie shrugged an apology.

"Pardon my presence. I'm outa here," she said.

When they were alone again, Frank turned to stare at
Quinn.

"Frank, I don't know what else to tell you." She made
a futile gesture at the photographs strewn across her
desk. "What can I say?" She slapped the file shut. "It's
not here. It's not anywhere."

"Splendid."

"Frank, I'm no magician."

"That's not what I was told. Priceless hired you as the
wunderkind of innovative advertising, famed for the
launch of new products, the woman with the Big Idea."

Quinn sighed. "Perhaps the well ran dry."

God knew, she had problems enough to dry up her
creativity.

Frank paced the room again. His shoulders were
tight and the back of his neck looked red. Violet Red,
Quinn thought, as if he were in one of her coloring
books. When he paused at her drafting board, his dark
hair gleamed in the pearly light through the windows,
the way Welles Blackburn's had looked in Geneva. She
was still having those dreams.

"Hell," Frank muttered, "I don't want to take this
launch to Ogilvy or Dellafemina, but it's coming to
that." Over his shoulder he gave her a weak smile.
"Things would be simpler."

"What things?"

"You," he said, "and me. We'd be free to explore . . . other fascinating possibilities."

"Such as?"

He grinned. "You and me."

"I'm a married woman," Quinn said, a ploy she rarely used in self-protection. She stood up.

"So?"

"So forget it." She was rounding her desk, intent on throwing him out of her office, when he flipped open the Beauty and the Beast coloring book she'd left on the drafting board.

"What's this?"

"Oh, Lord."

Quinn prepared herself for embarrassment, but several glossy contact sheets had slipped from between the pages, and her pulse skipped.

He gave a low whistle. "Wow."

"No way, Frank."

"Easy for you to say. I'm a susceptible male." He turned, Hannah Blackburn's pictures in hand. "Why are you holding out on me, Tyler? She's fantastic."

"She's also fourteen years old."

"And?" Some of the most successful models weren't much older, as Frank knew.

"She's the daughter of . . . a friend."

He squinted at the photographs. "This is the look you said you wanted. Yes or no?"

"Yes," she said weakly.

"Innocent but sexy, exotic . . . what is she? Korean?"

"Amerasian," Quinn said. "Her mother is Vietnamese, her father's American."

Frank whistled again. "Wartime hanky-panky?"

"Hardly. She wasn't born that long ago." Her hand shaking, Quinn took the pictures. From Frank's reaction, she could appreciate Welles's refusal to see his daughter in magazines all over the world. "Her parents met there, though. Now they live in Switzerland."

"You said they were friends of yours."

"Casual friends."

"You don't look casual," Frank said. "You look nervous."

Quinn turned her back. She strode to her desk, dropping the pictures on it. So that's where they had been. Her heart was thumping. "My friendships, casual or otherwise, are none of your concern. I've told you, she has the look I want but she's not available. I've already asked and the answer was an unqualified no. Her parents are dead set against such public"—she reluctantly used Welles's word—"exposure."

Frank's eyebrows lifted. "That doesn't sound like Quinn Tyler to me." Over her shoulder, he examined Hannah's pictures again while Quinn fought the urge to step away. He pressed closer, his chest to her back. "Beautiful girl. Have I seen her before?"

"No." When he appeared to be waiting, Quinn said, "She modeled in Europe the last year or two, once for *Elle.* I understand they wanted her back again, but her mother refused. The girl's an A student and her education is paramount just now."

"Is that so?" Frank said, as if he didn't believe a word. He fanned pictures across the desk until he found the clip from *Elle,* showing Hannah in a white maillot swimsuit, her long black hair flying gently in a breeze, her tanned thigh sprinkled with glittering white sand, her eyes laughing. In spite of herself, Quinn caught her breath.

"What's the real holdup?" Frank asked.

Quinn shook her head. She was still smarting over her last contact with Hannah's father. That one overseas phone call hadn't proved harmless at all. The mere sound of his voice made her remember everything she was trying to suppress, and she'd become so rattled she'd neglected to ask him the one question she really wanted answered about Jay. It was a good thing Welles had said no about Hannah. The image that seemed so perfect for Priceless would mean talking to him, even seeing him again.

Frank waved the photograph. "There's not a guy with blood still moving through his veins who won't take notice of this, of Priceless jeans with her in them. Not a woman in the world who won't want to look like that, who won't imagine her own wide fanny to be as skinny and tempting as this one if she just buys Priceless jeans." He pushed the glossy paper in her face. "You want to work in this town again, you want the *chances* this account can get you, then you take this to little Miss Saigon, by God, and come back with a yes this time!"

"By Monday, Frank?" Quinn had an almost over-whelming urge to slap him.

"You got a mouth on you, you know that?"

"So I've been told."

"Then use it." When he waved the picture again, Quinn batted it away. It fluttered to the carpet, where Hannah's smiling face, pert and mysterious at once, smiled up at her.

"You fly back to Switzerland," Frank said, "and ask those people—ask her—how she'd like to make a million bucks?"

"Money's not the issue. It won't work."

"Make it work." He grabbed his briefcase and stormed toward the door. "Tell you what." He paused with a hand on the knob, his gaze flicking over her from head to feet. "I'll go with you."

"That's not ne—"

"You always run a classy campaign, Tyler. Remember, there's not a soul in this world who can't be bought."

As soon as the door closed, Quinn sent the pictures flying. "Bastard."

The door immediately opened again and Valerie stepped in, looking back over her shoulder toward the elevators, in Frank's direction.

"He has a point," she said.

"You were eavesdropping?"

"Waiting," Valerie corrected. "Shooting the breeze with your faithful secretary until you were finished." Quinn's glare didn't faze her. "Priceless wants to shoot as soon as possible. Don't be so hard on him. I think he's kind of—"

"Challenging?" Quinn raised her brows.

Valerie grinned. "He has possibilities."

"You'd be better off trying to make friends with Andrew." Quinn bent to pick up the photographs. The trouble with grand gestures was you had to clean up after them. "Frank Murray has only one use for any woman, and that's on her back."

"Hmmm. I'll have to consult his horoscope."

Already angry, Quinn warmed to her subject. "Frank wasn't born, he was cloned. I've met a hundred just like him—good looking, well-dressed, in love with nobody but himself—and so have you. Val, if you really want to land one, there are better fish in the sea." She slipped the pictures back into her file. "Frank Murray is a bonafide shark."

No better than loan sharks, Welles thought, as he looked around the conference table at his colleagues. The consensus of the meeting seemed to be that a deserving Third World country, which had struggled valiantly and without bloodshed to solve its problems, was about to be foreclosed upon.

His fault? Earlier, Welles had argued in favor of trying for a partial interest payment, with a further generous extension on the loan itself, but nobody was buying.
Considering his own pending promotion, he'd decided,
at the same time hating himself for the decision, not to
continue trying to change the minds of the six other
bankers around the elliptical rosewood table.

Quinn, he suspected, would have shoved the table
over to make her point.

He slouched deeper in his chair. Thornton, who
favored full repayment of the loan, shot him a self-satisfied
look. Sharks, he thought. In his own home, Welles was
considered one of them.

Hannah hadn't spoken to him since he'd promised to
rethink his position on her modeling opportunity with
Priceless and then told her no. Now, a week later,
Mai—who might have snapped Hannah out of her
pout—was still in Florence and his evenings at home
had all the stimulation of a tomb.

When Hannah came in, she either went straight to
her room or, as Welles suspected, ran upstairs when
she heard his car. She ate alone. Went to bed early—or
at least turned out her lights. The few times he'd
tapped at her door, hoping they could talk, she tearfully
told him to go away. Each morning she was gone before
he woke up.

Welles had developed a permanent knot in his
stomach.

He balled a piece of notepaper in one hand.

His job, his wife, his daughter . . . Quinn. There were
days, this being one of them, when he actually envied—

"Blackburn?"

Welles glanced up. Six faces regarded him expectantly.
He'd missed something.

"May we have your concurrence?" Thornton asked.

Welles threw down the crumpled paper ball. "Why not?"

"Then it's unanimous. You'll inform the Finance Minister of our decision?"

"First thing." He'd okayed the loan; he'd have to wield the ax. Nothing could have pleased Thornton more, or Welles less.

When the president's gavel ended the meeting and the room cleared, Welles stayed in his chair, his arms folded. If he moved, he was afraid he might smash Thornton. If he went back to his office, he'd have to make that call. And if he went home. . . . There were days when he would gladly have traded places with Jay Barron to keep from going crazy.

Welles straightened, shuffling papers on the table into a neat pile. At last his hands stilled and he stared at them. Jay, he thought, and the years peeled away. Sweet Christ, Jay. . . .

Welles Blackburn and Jay Barron couldn't have been more unlikely friends; in fact, in the moral world Welles still envisioned, they would never have flown together, front to back in an F-4 Phantom jet.

Jay, he remembered only too well, had been the glamour boy, tall and lean and loose, looking just what he was: a favored son of American aristocracy. If his attorney father had pulled a few political strings, Jay would have avoided Vietnam entirely, would have stayed safe in law school—and probably married Quinn.

But Jay had a reckless streak a mile wide. For the first twenty-three years of his life, Welles knew, while Jay had been a star Little League pitcher, an honor student, then one of San Francisco's coveted escorts of debutantes, he secretly craved action, adventure. After quitting law school, he became the perfect naval officer, an image even his conservative parents could admire. Jay told them he intended to come home a hero.

Welles, on the other hand, had no such illusions. Until he met Jay Barron, he didn't believe in heroes. All he'd wanted from the Navy, ironically, was peace and three square meals a day.

His earliest memories were of his mother, stumbling through their two-room apartment in Shreveport in the dark, telling Welles how tired she was from waitressing when he knew, even at the age of five, that she was drunk again.

Welles always forgave her. Rubbing sleep from his eyes, hitching up his too-big undershorts—a hand-me-down from someone else's kid—he'd tug at her hand and lead her off to bed. "Come on, Mama. I'll tuck you in."

As she fell onto the double mattress, the smells of sweat and man would rise into the air. Welles would pull off her cheap high-heeled pumps, carefully loosen her skirt and blouse. By then, she was already asleep, passed out.

Welles slept on the living room sofa, which always smelled of beer, his mother's usual breakfast. She tried to take care of him but it just wasn't in her, not responsibility and not love.

He didn't blame her for that either. He didn't know who his father was; but then, neither did she. So how could she love him? He'd been an accident, nothing more, the by-product of a night in bed with some man or other, one of the "uncles" who drifted in and out of her life and his.

Some of them were okay. Some weren't.

By the age of eight, when Jay Barron would have been collecting stamps and visiting his father's law office on Saturdays to learn about his future, Welles had been taking care of his mother more than she took care of him.

He bought food for them with the tips he found in her wallet. When there was no money, he scavenged from the trash cans behind local restaurants or occasionally slipped a package of meat into his jacket at the supermarket. He scorched hamburgers; dusted the apartment; sponged the spots from his clothes and hers; dragged his baggy underwear and her stale sheets to the laundromat. If she couldn't love him, at least he would love her, care for her.

In the end, it hadn't worked.

When he turned sixteen, the year Jay Barron finished college, Welles learned to drive. They didn't have a car, but he needed a license. The week he got it, having borrowed a friend's jalopy for the test, he gave it to a neighborhood wizard who, for a price, altered his birth date.

Welles easily passed for twenty. He was big for his age, strong and broad-shouldered. He'd worked with weights to build muscle, to protect his mother from her newest boyfriend. When he signed up, using the license and his also-"fixed" birth certificate, the navy recruiter never batted an eye. They needed cannon fodder, he supposed.

Two years later he was in Vietnam, assigned to fly with Jay Barron. Still, they wouldn't have become friends.

At the controls of his aircraft, Jay could be brilliant— or like a kid playing hooky. Their first week Jay had done a fly-by past the carrier deck, a dangerous stunt that incurred the wrath of their superiors but which Jay had undone with his next textbook-perfect mission. "You and me and this old Louisville Slugger," he crowed, sending the powerful jet into a climb, freezing Welles's blood. "Man, we are invincible."

Welles wasn't so sure. But he had his own bravado, and he and Jay looked enough alike to earn the nickname The Terrible Two, which they stenciled on the F-4's fuselage. People kept pairing them off duty until it stuck, and Welles, in Jay, felt that he had found his hero. No matter how different they actually were, they had looked enough alike to fool Quinn Tyler twenty years later. . . .

Welles gathered his papers from the conference table. The Terrible Two. He could remember Hannah at that age, small and light-framed but so gutsy, defiant, and strong-willed. It was a stage, all right, which in his opinion Jay Barron hadn't outgrown.

Sometimes Welles thought he'd become a banker because of his own need for safety in figures; at other times he thought it had more to do with a need to live his life as Jay Barron might have done—if Welles had let him.

Shoving away from the table, he left the room. He had just enough time to call the South Cileanese finance minister before going home. What else could he do?

He was living his life in the most honorable way he knew. Taking care of Hannah. Taking care of Mai, who sometimes needed him even more than his mother had. Yet the first time Welles had seen Quinn Tyler's picture, twenty years ago, he'd felt the swift kick of desire. A picture, for Christ's sake!

Now, at last, he'd met her—and couldn't seem to get her out of his system no matter how he tried. Forget, dammit! He could forget anything if he tried hard enough; he'd been forgetting since he was five years old.

The next afternoon, just when he'd begun to believe his own advice, he heard from Quinn again.

The sound of her voice went through him like a song, and he knew just how wrong he was. Since Paris, when he'd seen the back of her coppery head, she'd been in his gut. So, he reminded himself, had the havoc she could wreak on his life. So had Jay.

Subic Bay Naval Base
The Philippines

Tossing fitfully, the man struggled with the damp sheets, with his own panic. The dream still had him in its grip, razor-sharp talons piercing him with relentless pain. Yet he fought to stay within the nightmare. Consciousness hurt more.

"Commander?"

The silken voice hovered near his ear. He batted at the intrusion of reality, rolled deeper in the tangled sheets. The jet was screaming, the jungle rushing past, then the jarring crash halted its momentum, a giant tree limb shattered the cockpit windshield—and he felt nothing.

How long? How many minutes, hours, days had he been trapped in his safety harness, drifting in and out of consciousness, always hurting, hurting worse than he did when he was awake?

"Wake up, Commander."

"Go 'way."

Don't leave me, he'd shouted. Get me out of here before they find us. Don't leave me!

Silence. The eerie silence had been worse than the agony in his chest, his legs. Worse than the blood that flowed, then trickled, then seeped down his flight suit into his boots. Worse than the blood, or the flies that fed upon it.

When would the patrols find him? Kill him?

Finish the job, he'd thought a thousand times in the silence.

But he wasn't alone now. He couldn't stay in the dream. Nothingness slowly gave way to an insistent hand on his bare shoulder, gently shaking him. "Wake up now. It's all right."

"Hell."

Opening his good eye, he gazed up at her in the darkness. He hadn't been asleep long, he guessed; it couldn't be past the middle of the night. He never got used to it: the impenetrable darkness.

"Shh," *the nurse whispered. He could see the whiteness of her uniform and cap, the whiteness of her smile.* "It's all right. Would you like me to get you something?"

"Another needle? No," *he said, but groaned. With consciousness had come pain again, the pain she was so good at easing.*

"I can make you more comfortable."

"I've been comfortable before." *Dependent, he thought. His reliance on someone else had nearly killed him then, driven him mad.* "I'll pass."

She sat on the edge of his bed. "They don't give medals for bravery before surgery. And you need some rest before morning. You needn't suffer."

"I'm not suffering."

"Perhaps not," *she agreed,* "except here." *She smoothed damp hair from his forehead, her touch light and cool.* "Physical pain can be managed more easily than that of the mind."

"I'm not crazy." *He pushed her hand away.* "I had a goddamn nightmare."

"You have them every night."

"So do most of the men I've ever served with"—*he waved his good hand toward the doorway, the hall* beyond—"so do most of the screamers in the ward. You think I can't hear them?"

"They hear you too." She touched his shoulder again, and his skin warmed. "Let me help you."

"You want to help me?" His groin was suddenly aching. He flipped the sheet back. "Climb in here and push your skirt up."

He'd shocked her, as he meant to. With one eye, he appraised her, imagining her blush in the dark. She was pretty enough, small and dark, her black hair confined beneath the peaked nurse's cap. He wondered how long it was, how it would feel slipping through his hands. But she was young and he hurt and maybe he was crazy too.

"You must be getting better," she said. Then she stood beside the bed.

He didn't believe in apology. The people who owed him had never delivered, had left him trapped and helpless, abandoned him without a backward look. So much for the fine manners his mother had instilled a lifetime ago. Now, more often, he thought of murder.

When the nurse walked toward the door, his voice stopped her.

"What's your name?"

"Helen."

He laughed. "What kind of name is that for—"

"A Filipino? You won't make me angry, Commander, so don't keep trying. I know a lot more about you than you do about me, about what happened to you in the highlands weeks ago, and what happened in Vietnam."

His pulse lurched.

"Then, you crash-landed a jet in dense jungle and were badly hurt. You were left for dead by someone you trusted. More recently, not far from here, you walked into an ambush."

"There was no ambush. No someone. I work alone!"

She touched his arm. "Let me get you a—"

"Fuck your needles! Fuck your goddamn pills! You think I can't live with pain? Pain's my only friend, except for the gun they took from me; it's what tells me I'm still alive."

He sank back against the pillows. Nothing had happened, nothing except Vietnam, and he knew how to deal with that. As soon as he had his strength. . . .

"Commander?" Her tone was hushed. "Who was Cochran?"

Even the name made him strong with rage. With the need to survive.

"Cochran?" he repeated as if he'd never heard it before.

"Yes," she said. "It's the name you say when you're back there, in the dream. The one from Vietnam, I mean. Maybe you're not ready to think about the other, but if you talked about him first—"

"There's nothing to tell." He closed his eyes. "Except he's a bastard and I intend to kill him when I get out of here. As soon as I find him. Now leave me alone."

10

Quinn had never expected to see Welles Blackburn again. As she entered the Geneva restaurant, her heart fluttered in her throat, and she wondered at her own nerves. Priceless had insisted on this trip, she reminded herself, and Quinn too still believed that Hannah Blackburn would be a perfect spokes-woman for her client, yet she couldn't help wondering what effect tonight—or any future dealings with Welles—would have on his young daughter. For an instant, she wanted to turn and run, certain that she had no right to invade the Blackburns' lives again. To disrupt her own.

Leaving Andrew in New York the night before, she'd found him in his den, bent over his worktable, his bad hand clutching one of the thick colored pencils Valerie had given him.

He dropped it as soon as he saw her.

"Don't think I'm working," he said.

"Then what are you doing?"

"And don't smile. I'm proving a point." He stepped

aside, letting her see the formless scribbles on the drawing pad, disconnected streaks of blue and red.

"I see a beginning," Quinn said and, aiming a kiss at
his cheek, swept from the room with the excuse that she
was late. She didn't want him to see the tears in her eyes.

"I'll need more than a beginning, like some kid with
piano lessons"—Andrew followed her—"now that you
and your marketing executive have decided to mix business with pleasure."

"Frank Murray?" Quinn was shocked.

"I've seen him. Tall, dark, good-looking," he said.
"Smooth."

"This is a business trip. Nothing more."

"Ah," he murmured. "Those expense-account lunches,
dinners, a nightcap together, just to discuss the evening's
meeting of course. Adjoining rooms in the same hotel. A
few extra hours for sightseeing—or location scouting."

Quinn bristled, all the more because of guilt. "We're
both professionals," she said, hating the fact that she
was defending herself. "Some people would abuse such
a trip, but I'm not one of them." With Welles, she'd had
Jay for an excuse.

"Proximity's a wondrous thing."

Quinn would have taken pity on him, but she dreaded the trip with Frank. As if to prove Andrew right, ever
since the Blackburns had reluctantly agreed to hear
them out in person, he'd invented excuses to touch her.
"If it were my choice," she told Andrew, "I'd be going
alone and coming back the same day. But it's not my
choice. Neither is Frank Murray."

The guilt she could deal with, Quinn had decided.
She'd lived with it long enough. But she hadn't wanted to
feel relief when the L-1011 jet rolled down the runway at
Kennedy and rose into the dark skies over Jamaica Bay.

Quinn insisted on their flying First Class. She used

the excuse of needing the extra room to spread out, to work, but the truth was she didn't want to sit any nearer to Frank than necessary.

By the time they'd landed and reached their hotel at noon, Quinn's nerves were jangling. Eight hours later, they still were.

It had taken her most of the hour while she dressed and made up for tonight's dinner with the Blackburns to realize that she was again staying at the Beau-Rivage, which, although she liked the hotel, irritated Quinn, who didn't consider herself a creature of habit.

Change could be tumultuous, but it was what she knew. Until now, she'd always derived a certain pleasure from it. Until Paris, she corrected. She supposed that if she'd gone there again instead of coming to Geneva, she would have stayed at the George V.

That realization displeased her even more.

She wouldn't need chance tonight, or coincidence, or her own mistaken eyesight. She'd called Welles to make the dinner date herself. Surprisingly, he accepted, with only a bemused explanation about teenage daughters twisting their fathers around their little fingers. Yet Quinn sensed that the change of heart had come against strong opposition from Mai Blackburn.

Standing in the restaurant foyer, Quinn felt her palms grow damp. Not normally vain, she turned away from Frank Murray to double-check her image in a nearby mirror. She'd dressed carefully in a gray-green silk suit, loosely structured and fluid, an ivory silk tank top for evening, a long gold chain, and hoop earrings. Simple, understated, businesslike. That's all tonight was, she thought, a business meeting with her career—and Hannah's future—on the line. Still, she hoped she looked feminine too.

"They're late," Frank murmured at her elbow. "What time did you say?"

"Eight."

He checked his watch again. "It's already eight-fifteen."

"People in Europe eat later, Frank. Relax."

"Relaxing's not in my nature, babe."

"Don't call me babe."

He smiled, reaching out to her. Frowning, Quinn took a step back. Then she felt another hand, warm and obviously male, touch her elbow. Turning, she saw Welles Blackburn.

Her gaze met his, then slipped down his lean frame over the beautifully tailored dark suit he wore with a deep-red foulard tie. A festive touch? Valerie would consider that a good omen. Quinn looked up, hoping he couldn't see the nerves she felt. She had been prepared for Welles's physical presence, but to her dismay other feelings tried to surface.

She tamped them down. "Welles. How nice to see you again."

"Quinn," he said with a nod but didn't smile. He was giving Frank Murray a measuring look, avoiding her.

She didn't reach out a hand and neither did he. Quinn turned to include the woman beside him, introducing Frank Murray. "Mrs. Blackburn, how good of you to join us."

With a cool nod, Mai Blackburn brushed past them in a soft rustle of white linen, her sleekly coiled hair a sheen of jet black under the restaurant lights. "I believe our table is ready."

"This isn't going to work, you know," Welles murmured just before Mai stopped, smoothly positioning herself next to Quinn, leaving the two men to follow into the dining room.

Quinn had declined the Blackburns' invitation to dinner at their home. Remembering Mai's hostility the last time, she wanted more neutral territory and countered with her own request that they meet in one of Geneva's finer French restaurants.

But the Blackburns had come alone. Her heart sank.

"Hannah is an impressionable girl, easily lured by the promise of bright lights and attention," Mai explained. "We thought it best not to include her this evening."

Typically brash, Frank Murray responded. "Mrs. Blackburn, there's not a girl her age in Geneva or anywhere else who wouldn't relish the opportunity to—"

"Frank," Quinn warned.

They had agreed that Quinn would do the initial talking. As a representative of Priceless, Frank had a natural tendency to market his own firm, exactly what Quinn wished to avoid for the moment. He sat next to her at the table, facing Mai Blackburn, with Welles across from Quinn.

"My husband and I," Mai continued, "will hear what you have to say, then see whether it alters our decision."

Quinn smiled. "I hope we can change your mind."

Over drinks before dinner, she tried to keep the conversation flowing around harmless topics. Mai, who seemed to be constantly assessing Quinn, blocked all her attempts at ice-breaking, and not once did Welles smile. He kept his gaze, that penetrating blue, trained either on the cocktail fork he was nudging around by his service plate or on Frank Murray. Quinn could see he didn't care for Frank, which came as no surprise, but why was he treating her as if she wasn't there?

Quinn was suddenly glad she'd neglected to ask him about Jay, about the coordinates when his plane crashed. For that, she'd need his goodwill and some privacy, neither of which it appeared she was likely to get. She'd be lucky to get an answer she liked for one question: about Hannah. Which was why she'd come here, Quinn reminded herself.

She waited until they'd been served their entrees

before she took the plunge and talked about Priceless. "Your daughter sent me some contact proofs of herself from the *Elle* assignment, some other shots too. She's extremely photogenic. Her pictures make her appear older, more mature."

Mai glanced at Welles. "Hannah sent them herself?"

Clearly, she'd taken Mai by surprise. She didn't want to betray the girl, but she needed Mai Blackburn off balance and she'd counted on Hannah's enthusiasm to turn the tide. But obviously, Hannah had sent the pictures on the sly. "She had my address after my last visit."

"The fashion magazines," Mai murmured, disapproval clear in her tone. "She pored over them for days. I was sorry you'd put ideas in her mind."

It was Frank's turn now, and Quinn signaled him with a glance. On the plane, they had rehearsed what he would say. He gave enough figures about Priceless to impress Welles as a businessman, if not his wife. Frank had also brought a letter from his CEO to sweeten the pot.

"The company would pay private school tuition in New York?" Mai frowned. "Why would that be necessary?"

"According to Quinn's plan for the campaign, they'll be shooting ads almost continuously from late August or early September through December. A media blitz. Print ads and TV. And if the campaign hits—" He looked at Quinn. "Why don't you show the Blackburns exactly what you have in mind?"

Quinn reached for her briefcase, pulling out a sheaf of papers, thinking that she and Frank should take their act on the road. "This is a rendering of the presentation I've made to Priceless Sportswear." Pushing her own plate of veal française aside, she quickly laid out the drawings, anchoring them with the salt and pepper shakers. "You'll note there's a minimum of color, a maximum of black and white." She tried a smile. "I've decided in retrospect that your beautiful home was my inspiration."

"Black and white," Mai said, "like life itself."

Quinn's fingers tightened on the drawings. "I prefer a few grays here and there—or, in this instance, a splash of crimson. This would be the first ad, and after that we'd choose a different accent color for each commercial. But the basic impression will remain black and white: stark, mysterious, sophisticated, innocent; take your pick. I feel this deceptively simple campaign should appeal to a wide variety of women buyers."

"And to men?" Mai's look was shrewd.

"Men often pay the bills," Quinn said. "Less so these days, but there are plenty of indulgent fathers whose daughters buy blue jeans."

"Fathers like Welles," Mai said.

Frank sent him a man-to-man look. "I'm not married, but I enjoy giving presents to the ladies. And they sure like getting them."

Welles leaned forward. For a moment Quinn thought he would take Frank by the throat, but he only pulled the drawings closer. "These are impressive." He shoved the papers toward Mai.

"The image isn't what I expected," she admitted after a moment, "but it's not enough to change my mind. I will tell you a story, Ms. Tyler, Mr. Murray." Ignoring Welles's dark look, she said, "When I was a child, living in Saigon before the war—or at least before the American presence in it—a small circus came to town. My parents, who had already suffered their share of tragedies, refused to allow me to attend."

Welles settled an arm on her shoulders but she pulled away.

"Please let me finish." Her dark eyes shone brightly when they met Quinn's puzzled look. "A school friend of mine went to the circus that afternoon, as did many of my classmates. During the performance a Siberian tiger attacked its trainer in the ring, tearing the man to bits before it could be shot—in front of all those onlookers, who had expected only a pleasant afternoon watching elephants dance and beautiful girls walk the tightwire."

"What's the point, Mrs. Blackburn?" Frank asked, frowning.

"My daughter will not be going to any circus, Mr. Murray." Mai rose from the table. "I came tonight because I am tired of her sulking about Priceless, but we have a pleasant life here in Geneva, which is where she belongs. I wish you luck in finding a spokeswoman for your blue jeans."

Welles reached out for her. "Mai, wait. Dammit." For the first time, he glanced at Quinn and her heart turned over. "This had no other end," he said. "I agreed to this for Hannah's sake but—"

Mai cut him off, her eyes black as night. "Thank you for dinner, Ms. Tyler. Mr. Murray. I'm sorry your trip was wasted."

"Hey!" Frank was on his feet.

"Never mind," Quinn said.

She watched Mai walk regally from the room toward the exit, with Welles following, his shoulders stiffly set, as they had been the first time she saw him standing at the window of his office. Her impression then had been one of loneliness, of frustration. It hadn't changed.

Quinn *had* changed, though, and now she identified the real reason for her nerves. She'd never blamed herself for reacting to Welles Blackburn physically. Quinn enjoyed as much as anyone else—married or single—the assessments of strangers that she sometimes shared with Valerie. Yet her sense of unease tonight didn't come from simple chemistry.

That she could live with, even ignore.

No, she'd been nervous about seeing Welles again partly because of something equally basic, but far deeper, which she'd just seen in his eyes too. How much had his kiss at Cointrin or the words "No goodbyes" had to do with Jay Barron?

Welles drove home with his teeth clenched tight, his foot heavy on the gas. He hated ordeals, and tonight certainly qualified. At the house Mai left him to close both car doors, which he slammed. Welles strode after her, his temper held in check only by curiosity. He never knew what Mai would do next.

Inside, she swept through the foyer and up the stairs.

He stayed two steps behind her until she banged into Hannah's room, switching on lights, flipping the covers back.

"Get up," she said, "and explain yourself."

Hannah sat up, blinking.

"Mai, for God's sake." Welles brushed a hand over the wall switch and the overhead light went out. Now only the bedside lamp illuminated the room, sending long shadows across the walls and ceiling. Lit from below, Mai's face seemed all angles, harsh white and black as she bent over their daughter.

"Of all the impetuous, ill-considered actions in your life, this must be the worst." She hauled Hannah from bed by one arm. "What on earth were you thinking of, sending photographs to that woman in New York?"

Welles took a step. "Her name is Quinn Tyler."

Hannah's face looked pasty. "I didn't mean—"

Mai whirled. "Or was all this your doing, Welles? The two of you, plotting while I was away?"

"Don't be absurd." Welles saw that Hannah's eyes were wide with fear. "What does it matter? She sent them and Quinn saw them; so did the people at Priceless. Let her go back to bed and we'll discuss this, as you insisted on doing tonight at dinner, with only the adults involved."

Mai's cheeks flushed. "You are truly incredible. I don't care to discuss a thing." Her grip tightened on Hannah's arm. "I've had enough of your permissiveness. I leave this house for little more than a week, and in my absence everything falls apart. My daughter takes it upon herself to defy my wishes. What did she do, Welles? Corner you as soon as the taxi pulled away for the airport that night? Plant some kisses on your chin and convince you there was no harm in sending a few pictures to New York?"

"Let her go," he said. "We talked about Quinn's call, yes. I told Hannah we agreed that she shouldn't do the ad."

Mai twisted her grip, making Hannah whimper.

"That's enough." Welles moved, prying Mai's fingers loose. "What in hell's wrong with you?"

"What do you think? You managed to cajole me into dinner this evening, letting me believe we'd simply hear those people out and confirm our decision; then they'd leave and that would be the end of it. But don't think I was fooled."

He led Hannah back to bed, tucking the covers around her. He kissed her forehead, trying not to notice the tears that brimmed in her eyes. "Sleep, baby."

"I shouldn't have sent the pictures, Daddy. I'm sorry."

"Shh," he murmured. "I wish you'd asked me beforehand, but there's no real harm done. Your mother and I will resolve this."

When he faced her, Mai's dark eyes were bright with fury. "I know exactly why you arranged that dinner. I was humiliated. If I wasn't a lady, I would have emptied my plate in her lap, silk suit and all. Because—"

"Downstairs," he said, turning her around.

Mai slipped free. "If Hannah considers herself to be

a grown-up, capable of making decisions without her parents, perhaps she should know about this woman whom she so admires—"

"Mai—"

"A woman with a husband in New York, traveling with that odious man, a woman who cannot keep from looking at my husband—"

"Jesus Christ!" The words had sent a perverse flash of desire through him. He'd walked into that restaurant, determined not to let Quinn get to him again, and after one look at her legs he was gone. Her suit, her hair, her smile, all were perfect; but she'd had a narrow run in one silk stocking.

"Deny it, Welles. Oh, don't think I couldn't see what you were doing. I've seen it before. That careful avoidance of eye contact with her didn't fool me for a second. Neither did your contrived absence from the office the last time she was here, and—"

"You're behaving like a lunatic!"

Her voice dropped. "Am I?"

Glancing away, he met Hannah's wide-eyed stare. "Yes," he said, "you are." He couldn't reason with her; she'd never gone this far before. She'd never been right before. Feeling sick, he started toward the door. "I can't talk with you when you're like this."

Mai dogged his heels. "Yes, that's it. Place the blame on me. How convenient. Because you're an honest man, Welles, aren't you?"

"Think what you like," he said, knowing she meant the opposite. "You always do."

And, as always, her hard demeanor slipped, collapsing with a sudden sag of her small shoulders, the weakened tone of her voice.

She murmured the words in Vietnamese, then in English. "We need to talk."

"Not tonight, we don't."

"Welles? Where are you going?"

"Out," he said and left the room, the house, with the image of Hannah's white face, and of Mai's, in his mind. And worst of all, the face of Quinn Tyler.

Quinn was brushing her teeth the next morning when someone rapped at her door. Frank Murray, she thought, wanting her to join him downstairs in the terrace restaurant for breakfast. After last night with the Blackburns, all she wanted was to get on the first plane to New York and figure out how to salvage Tyler & Devlin Advertising. It could be a cold day in hell before she snagged another client as big as Priceless or a model as potentially exciting as Hannah.

The knock sounded again and Quinn sighed.

"Just a minute."

After rinsing her mouth, she opened the door—to a still-unsmiling Welles Blackburn, his eyes a deep cobalt blue. Before she could speak, he stepped inside the room. Without a word, he slammed the door behind him and pushed Quinn up against it, then without warning brought his stern mouth down on hers, stealing her breath. All she could manage was a stifled cross between a moan and a whimper, as instant need streaked through her and her limbs turned to putty.

His lips slanted across hers, changed angles again, lifted a scant inch for a gulp of air, then plunged into another, deeper kiss. And she'd thought he meant business the last time. Quinn didn't even think of fighting him. She sagged against the door, feeling the metal frame of the room's emergency exit map against the back of her neck, the graze of his fingers over her breast, the press of his thighs into hers. The entire length of his body, hard and hot, held her captive; her arms dangled at her sides, her mouth open under his.

Immediately, the kiss softened. "Better than Cointrin," he whispered, took a few light, testing bites of her lower lip, then her upper one, and let her go. At first, Quinn wasn't sure she could stand. She certainly couldn't speak. Taking deep, calming breaths, she inhaled the scents of gasoline and damp grass, of flowers, blowing in from outside. Quinn always slept with her windows open, and now she could hear Geneva's morning traffic building and the hotel gardeners talking as they watered the roses.

Welles pressed his forehead to hers. "I spent half the night driving around, thinking. About you, about Mai and Hannah. I even drove back into town in the middle of the night, parked at the front entrance of the Beau-Rivage, and called myself an idiot for wanting to take the elevator upstairs to this room."

She heard more than passion in his tone. "Welles, what happened?"

He pulled back, framing her face in his hands. "I had a helluva fight with Mai. She was furious that Hannah sent you those photos."

"I thought as much," Quinn said. "I shouldn't have mentioned them." She ran a hand through her uncombed hair. "I didn't mean to put Hannah at risk in any way."

Welles made a sound.

"I didn't, did I?" She didn't know Mai Blackburn well. She only knew that she'd distrusted the woman the first moment she laid eyes on her. "Welles?"

Briefly, he explained the scene in Hannah's bedroom. Quinn was shocked. "Lord, I'm sorry."

"She wasn't hurt, just scared, though that's bad enough. Mai . . . sometimes she loses it. She never hits Hannah or anything, I wouldn't allow that, but—"

"What did you do?"

"Took her down a peg or two," he said wearily. "You have any coffee? I went home for the second time last night after three A.M. and left before anyone was up this morning. I'm sorry about dinner last night, and I know I don't deserve either your sympathy or breakfast—"

"I'll call room service."

While they waited, Welles used her bathroom and came out, his face freshly washed, his hair damp, the night's beard stubble still on his cheeks. He looked tired but rakish and, Quinn couldn't help seeing, terribly vulnerable. "I'm sorry, Quinn, about barging in on you like some caveman."

"Why did you?" she asked, her pulses still thumping.

He cracked a smile. "That's it, give me a little sass. It sounds good to me right now." He waved a hand. "I don't know why. I was driving around this morning again, remembering how you looked in the restaurant foyer in that suit with your green eyes wide as saucers, scared to death—"

"I was not."

"Yes, you were. So was I. After I saw that run in your stocking," he said, "I knew damn well I couldn't keep from staring at you all night, couldn't keep Mai from seeing it."

Quinn's pulse jumped. "So the fight wasn't only about Hannah."

"Bingo."

"Oh, Welles."

"I came to apologize," he said, just as Quinn realized she wasn't objecting to the notion of familiarity between them, of intimacy. Maybe those kisses against the door had knocked down more than one barrier. "I'm sorry. For everything. And I'm sorry as hell that my wife—"

"Picked up your vibrations?"

"Ours, I think. Just as I picked up yours. I'd never have pushed my way in here this morning if I hadn't felt them coming from you. I did, didn't I?"

Quinn didn't have to answer. Another knock sounded at her door and a voice called out, "Room service."

Over English scones and coffee, she pondered her answer to Welles's question.

"You're not going to answer, are you?" he finally said, refilling his cup, then carefully adding cream.

Quinn shook her head. "I don't think I'd better." Let him think that she could turn her back on a physical relationship, especially one that jeopardized both their marriages, as long as he didn't guess that her feelings ran deeper. She'd only realized their depth last night and needed time to make sense of them.

Their eyes met, but Quinn looked away first.

She had the privacy she wanted and his goodwill now. In a few hours, she'd be flying home again—this time for good. With only a brief twinge of conscience that Doug Lloyd was right, that she should let Welles have his peace, she took a breath.

"I have a question for you," she said. "The one I didn't ask before." She picked up her scone, and raspberry jam squirted onto her lap. "It's about Jay."

"Quinn, Jesus." He stood abruptly, jostling his coffee. He paid no attention to her sticky lap. "We've been through all that. I told you—"

"Jay's dead," she said. "Yes, I know what you think."

"What I know."

"You don't know for certain that he's dead. You saw the plane but not a—corpse."

"Shit." Welles rubbed the back of his neck. He went to the open windows and stared out at the traffic.

Giving up on the raspberry blot on her eggshell linen

slacks, Quinn rose and walked toward him. "If you survived," she said quietly, "maybe Jay did too."

"Maybe he didn't. Probably he didn't."

"I'm an optimistic person," Quinn said.

"In this case, I'm not. Sure, I came through, but I
was . . . lucky."

She angled in front of him, dipped to meet his downcast eyes. "Jay was the luckiest man I ever knew."

"Surviving's also a matter of being—oh, hell—in the
right place at the right time. Or the righter place," he
said, "if there was such a thing over there."

Guilt tugged at her, but she ignored it. Doug Lloyd
asked uncomfortable questions too. So did Andrew.

"Then it's possible—"

"There were . . . lots of planes in the air that day.
Ours, theirs. Lots of antiaircraft fire." He paused. "I
don't know what really happened. My plane took some
hits, probably sprung a fuel leak, went down." He hesitated again. "So did Jay's, just . . . not in the same place."

"Exactly."

He glanced up and Quinn gave him an encouraging
smile. "You must remember something: landmarks,
coordinates. Even if his plane landed a mile or so from
yours, the numbers wouldn't be that dissimilar, would
they? What were the latitude and longitude?"

His eyes darkened. "All I remember was the plane losing altitude. When it slammed into the ground I blacked
out on impact. I lost days of my life, unconscious."

"Yes, I know," she said. It really was painful for him
still, so painful that he'd used Mai as a buffer when talking about the experience before. But she sensed he
knew more than he was telling her. She laid a hand on
his arm and felt the muscles tense.

"What the hell difference does it make, whether I
think Jay's dead or you think he's alive?"

"A big difference. If he's alive, I want to find him."

"Why?"

Quinn shrugged. This was always the tough part. Andrew asked her, so did Doug. Even Valerie. "I want to know. It's called closure. I need—"

"You can't still love him." He caught her shoulders, his hands bruising her skin through the pomegranate-colored cotton sweater she wore. "You know what your problem is?"

She didn't answer.

"It's easier to keep pining away for Jay Barron, for a dead man, than to admit your marriage is in trouble—or that you feel something for me."

Quinn pulled away, shaking. "The only thing I feel for you is pity. You invent correct little stories about your war experience, stories to hide behind. Do you think for one minute that I believed everything you told me about Jay being dead?"

His face was pale.

"I told you the truth."

"No," she said. "Your wife told me."

Silence.

"Is that why you stay with her, Welles? For protection from something? Some memory of the past you can't face?"

"Go to hell. I don't owe you any explanations."

"Then I don't owe you any. But I'll give you one," Quinn said. "Yes, my marriage is troubled and I don't know how to fix it." She thought of the scene with Andrew before she'd left home. "Do you know why? Because I'm the one who broke it. Maybe you're right: I was still pining for Jay and I married Andrew in part because we could laugh and cry at the memories, who knows? People marry for all sorts of reasons."

"Try love," Welles said.

"Is that why you married Mai?"

After a moment, Welles shook his head. "I probably married her for some of those same reasons. Because of what we'd been through together. She can be hard and difficult, even cruel sometimes, but she crumples so fast— and then she's just a little girl again, lost, without her family, looking from Saigon to Hanoi for her only brother."

"She found him," Quinn said.

"Oh, yeah. But he was a real bastard. Mai was only five when he headed north to join the cause. There'd been a bitter fight with his parents and, as you'll recall, he took Mai's inheritance—the Tears of Jade. When Mai found him, she was fourteen and her father had just died, a broken old man. She was the youngest; the rest of the family had all died in the war. Her mother was killed during a street riot when Mai was ten, an innocent bystander who got in the way of a Molotov cocktail."

"How terrible." Quinn shuddered.

"He wouldn't return the necklace and earrings. And he didn't want Mai around, unless it was to offer her to his friends in the North Vietnamese military."

"God," she said. "So of course she ran and found refuge with the villagers who took you in. That's a sad story." It almost made her feel sympathy for Mai Blackburn. "I feel responsible for Andrew too," she said, adding, "It's my fault that he can't work, or even walk that well."

Welles waited for her to go on and Quinn haltingly told him what had happened at Christmastime six years ago.

"It was an accident," Welles said, just as Doug always did. He took her hands, warming them in his. "You weren't at fault. Even if you were, that was a long time ago. Hasn't he tried to come back? To function again?"

"He tries."

"How hard?"

"As hard as he's able to."

"I lay in a thatch-roofed hut full of fever for three, four days and woke up with my leg three times its normal size. For two months I couldn't take a breath without knives going through me from my broken ribs. But I decided one thing early on, Quinn. I would survive—I'd keep my leg and I'd walk again. I'd put my life back together."

"Maybe you're a stronger man than he is."

He pulled her closer. "So what do we have here?" he asked. "Two people locked into marriages that don't work, that they can't seem to dissolve without a lot of guilt. I tried, you know, recently. The night I saw you in Paris—from the back—I was with Mai's uncle. He's lived there since the early sixties. Very proper, tough as nails, family oriented to a fault. When I told him I wanted to divorce Mai, he talked me out of it."

"How?"

"I let him," Welles said. "So where are we now?"

"Nowhere."

"You're wrong. I'm here," he said, "and not just to apologize."

Quinn, leaning back in the circle of his arms, looked up into his eyes. By degrees, she saw them lighten. "What?" she said.

"First, say it." She tried to pull away but he held her. "Say you liked the kiss at Cointrin, the kisses at the door—"

As if he'd given a cue, someone knocked again and Quinn jumped. "Who is it?"

"Frank."

"I've already eaten. You go ahead without me."

"Have another cup of coffee," he called through the door. "We need to talk."

She looked helplessly at Welles. "All right. Give me a few minutes."

"Come on, Tyler, open up." His tone was seductive. "I'll wait for you. Help you dress."

"Meet me downstairs," she said, noting Welles's darkening expression. She heard Frank grumbling away toward the elevators.

"Say it," Welles murmured, lowering his head. He kissed her, once at each corner of her mouth, then again until Quinn's lips parted. "Say, 'Welles, I want you too.'"

When she would have shaken her head, he held it still and took her mouth again, his tongue slipping inside, tasting, savoring. He groaned and Quinn murmured, "Yes. I do, but—"

"That's all I want to hear. For now." He set her away from him. "You'd better get moving. By the way, did I tell you that I hate Frank Murray's guts? It was all I could do last night not to punch him out. I'll try to control myself and wait here."

"For what?" Quinn asked.

He smiled. "We have things to talk about. Hannah, for one."

"Hannah?"

"When I went home at three this morning, Mai was still up. She can be obsessive about our relationship, but she'd do almost anything to preserve it. I don't like knowing that I take advantage of that sometimes, but I do."

"You mean—?"

His smile grew. "She'll make her own rules, insist on clauses in the contract that will drive you crazy, but yes. She'll let Hannah do at least one commercial for Priceless."

Quinn's heart was in her throat. "Welles, that's wonderful. Why didn't you tell me before? Of course we'll have to insist on more than one—"

"Not now," he said and kissed her. "Later. We'll work something out."

He didn't mean only the contract, Quinn knew.

11

Welles drove a hard bargain. Yet by midweek he'd had more than he wanted of Frank Murray, of the bevy of corporate lawyers Priceless had sent to Geneva, and far less than he needed of Quinn.

In a small conference room at the Banque Internationale, across the table from her, he found his attention wandering. He imagined her legs, now hidden from view by the rosewood table, wondered whether, today, she also had a fine-line run snaking from one slender ankle toward her silky thigh. He wanted, badly, to get her alone to find out.

She smiled at him across the table, and his groin tightened.

"Very nice," Welles murmured, shifting. Frank Murray was staring at him, waiting for some answer.

Quinn came to his rescue.

"I can't see that Hannah's education needs to be compromised in the least. I've already made some calls, and all the top private day schools in New York are more than willing to interview her. Just say the word, and I'll set up the appointments."

Dinner that night, necking with her the next morning in her hotel room. . . . He looked into her eyes and straightened in his chair.

"I'm afraid that doesn't solve the problem," he said and thought, No kidding. "My wife travels a great deal on business of her own. She's fund-raising liaison for the World Refugee Foundation. She couldn't possibly live with Hannah in the States, and of course I have a job here to think about."

Frank Murray looked to the Priceless attorneys.

"An apartment might be provided, a woman hired as guardian," one of the lawyers suggested.

Welles mentioned some legal terms having to do with responsibility, culpability, insurance liability.

The lawyers rose in one motion. They'd check with Corporate, the Priceless CEO, who wanted personally to be involved in all decisions. Tomorrow morning the meeting would resume precisely at nine o'clock.

Frank Murray stood too, gesturing Quinn to precede him to the door. She hesitated briefly and Welles saw his chance. Still uncomfortable, he got to his feet, cursing. Maybe he should content himself with just looking. At the same time he reached over to touch her arm as she gathered pen and note pad and stuffed them in her briefcase.

"Wait."

"Quinn, come on," Frank Murray said at the door.

"I'll be right there." Her gaze held the same ambivalence Welles felt.

"Help me out here," he murmured.

She started to shake her head, then thought better of it.

"Frank, I'll see you in the lobby. I have some things for Mr. Blackburn's daughter, and he—"

"Sure you do," he said.

"Maybe you could get us a cab."

After a moment, the door to the conference room swung closed and they were alone. Quinn snapped her briefcase shut, the sound of the lock like a gunshot in the empty room. From far below, the muffled rush of traffic and the blare of horns reached them.

"That wasn't very smart, Welles. Now Frank will be sure there's something between us."

"There is."

Her head down, she turned away and walked to the windows. "What a lovely view," she said. "How do you ever get any work done? The water's sparkling on the lake and you can see the Jet d'Eau from here. I could watch it for hours." She paused. "From my office I can see St. Patrick's Cathedral. Sometimes, when the light is just right—"

"What are you trying to do?" Welles stepped behind her, his fingers itching to take hold of her shoulders, to draw her back against him. "Remind me that we each have separate lives, obligations? That you belong in New York with Andrew, and I belong here, with Mai and Hannah? I already know that." He gave in to the urge and touched her. He could feel her spine tense, then forcibly relax.

"It's the truth, Welles."

"Right."

And oh, he prided himself on truth, didn't he? Yet she'd sensed before that he hadn't given her all of it. She believed Jay was still alive, and the only way he could think of to change her mind was to tell her the rest. If he did, he might as well drive her to the airport, put her on a plane, and this time say goodbye.

"I may not love Andrew in the best way," she said, "but I am married to him."

"I'm married to Mai, but since the night she went after Hannah, I wonder what's left. The morning I came to you, she disappeared—on business, she said—and I haven't heard from her since. As soon as this contract business gets straightened out, as soon as the yearly staff reviews are over here at the bank. . . ."

"Then what?" Quinn asked when he didn't go on.

Welles sighed. "Hell, I don't know. In her own way she's as sick as Andrew, as disabled, whatever. Christ," he said, "that makes me sound as if I think I'm some kind of saint to stay with her."

"Relationships are rarely simple." She shrugged, the slight movement making awareness shiver down his spine. The silk of her hair brushed his fingers where they rested on her shoulders, and he inhaled sharply, tightening his grip. "Marriage most of all, I suppose," she said. "Yours, mine. What are we doing?"

"Shhh." Softly, he massaged the tension away, using the excuse to keep on touching her. Sixteen floors below, a steady flow of taxicabs streamed past the building. Frank Murray would be hailing one by now, perhaps waiting impatiently with the rear door open, his eyes narrowed on the bank exit, looking for Quinn. "The other night at dinner, that run in your stocking drove me crazy."

"Welles," she began and would have turned, but he held her in place, her back to him, his hand sweeping aside the hair at her nape.

"Just like the first day in my office, when your slip was showing." He bent his head, pressing his mouth to her fragrant skin. She smelled like roses. He trailed kisses across her neck, into the hollow of one shoulder. And, triumphant, felt her shudder. "You know what I wanted to do? I wanted to reach out under the table, to slip my hand under your skirt, up the inside of your thigh. . . ."

When she whimpered, he knew he had her.

"Quinn." She turned, and he murmured, "Oh, yes."

But instead of sliding into his arms, she pushed lightly on his chest and stepped back. Welles blinked.

Striding to the conference table, she hefted her briefcase.

"I can't handle this," she said, not looking at him. "I don't know what this means, but I can't."

"I don't know either." He reached her in soundless steps on the thick off-white carpet, reached for her again. Quinn evaded him.

"Frank's waiting."

"Quinn, all I know is, I want you. With your peeka-boo lace, your pantyhose run, with raspberry jam in your lap—"

"Have a good night. I'll see you in the morning, Welles."

He had to admire her. She left him feeling almost grateful that she'd saved him from himself. She left him aching.

Quinn didn't sleep until late that night. Then she dreamed erotic dreams of Welles and, finally, of Doug Lloyd and happiness. The next morning she stood under a hot shower for twenty minutes, willing her muscles to relax.

After toweling dry and trying to rub some color into her face, she dressed in the brightest outfit she'd packed—a white linen suit paired with a teal-blue camisole, a blue paisley-print bow at the nape of her neck holding back her hair—and permitted herself an extra scone with jam for breakfast. Grape jam. None of her usual pick-me-ups seemed to be working. She didn't know how she'd get through the day.

"What's with you?" Frank Murray asked in the cab on the way to the Banque Internationale.

Quinn toyed with her purse strap. "A bad dream."

"Should have phoned me," he said, trailing his index finger up her arm. "I'd have come over, rocked you to sleep."

"My worst nightmare." She drew away and Frank dropped his hand.

"You can be a real bitch, you know that, Tyler?"

"I didn't mean you," she lied.

"Yeah. You did."

"Not exactly."

Frank stayed silent the rest of the way. Entering the conference room behind him, Quinn hung back. The lawyers sat deep in a huddle at the coffee urn, but Welles was already at the table, nudging papers around.

Looking at his strong hands, Quinn could have groaned. They were long-fingered and lightly tanned. She could still feel them at her neck, brushing her hair aside. Then his mouth—

"Good morning." He'd caught her looking at him and glanced up. "Did you have a nice evening?"

"Not especially. I think I'll have another cup of coffee." She moved toward the silver pot. "I can't seem to wake up this morning. Would you like some?"

He gestured at the white porcelain cup at his elbow before his eyes met hers again. "I can wait."

Quinn sat down. She wanted these meetings over with so she could fly home, away from Welles's intent blue gaze. It made her weak in the knees, like a schoolgirl. She hated herself for responding, and Frank Murray's eyes followed her every move.

Frank wasn't the most discreet man she'd ever known, and he didn't like being rebuffed. When Welles refilled her coffee cup an hour later, when his hand lingered on her back after he set her cup down before taking his seat, Frank quirked an eyebrow. At lunch, he didn't miss the fact that Welles maneuvered the other men into position, leaving himself next to Quinn at the table.

Negotiations had stalemated again just before noon, and Welles suggested they adjourn to fresh surroundings. The northern Italian restaurant was sun-washed, filled with hanging plants, the food superb. Quinn picked at her salad, only half hearing the conversation around her. The lawyers worked even when they ate, their words sounding cold and clinical to Quinn.

"I wish Priceless could guarantee Hannah's safety in New York," one said to Welles, "but it just isn't possible. We'd do everything we could—provide a rental in a security-intense building, rides to and from any local ad shoots, interviews, back and forth to school. . . ."

Quinn grimaced but, having no immediate influence on the proceedings, she stopped listening to focus on her own dilemma. She'd never had to worry about her personal reputation before—an archaic term—not that Frank was likely to call Andrew with his suspicions about her and Welles. But she didn't want to be a laughingstock in the advertising world, to jeopardize all her hard work and Tyler & Devlin.

In the noisy, crowded restaurant she and Welles were jammed into a leather banquette with one of the attorneys, the other two and Frank across from them, and she could feel Welles's shoulder against hers, the heat of his thigh alongside her own. Hell, she'd made the contact with the Blackburns. Other than producing the commercial Priceless wanted, she had done her part. But when she thought of Priceless, she thought of Hannah too. Go home, she ordered herself, before she gets hurt, before you do something foolish.

"Sorry." Reaching for the antipasto dish, Welles leaned into her. His eyes were warm, as if he sensed her discomfort and was enjoying himself. The lawyers' conversation, Frank's mumbled replies, buzzed in her ear like bumblebees.

"Is there something else you can't reach? I'd be happy to get it for you."

Offering her the antipasto, Welles grinned.

Lord, she'd been giving him openings all morning for

double entendres, and—probably because of the day before—he was taking them. Quinn dropped a piece of prosciutto.

Welles picked it up, holding the small piece of ham in front of her, until Quinn obediently opened her mouth, then rolled her eyes at its succulent delicacy.

"Good?"

She swallowed, feeling as if he'd plied her with an aphrodisiac, not the warmth of his fingers. "Yes."

His tone was husky, for her ears alone. "They have the best in Geneva in this place. If you need help ordering. . . ."

Quinn remembered the blood pudding in Carouge. She sipped at her wine. "I try to learn from my mistakes."

The lawyers were arguing a point among themselves and Frank Murray for once seemed to be listening, rather than watching Quinn.

Welles draped an arm over the back of the seat. "What makes you certain something's a mistake?"

"My instincts," she murmured.

He leaned closer. "I could prove you wrong."

On the verge of answering, she relaxed as their waiter appeared to take the order. Twenty minutes later Quinn was halfway through a bowl of *zuppa de pesce* she didn't want when she suddenly stiffened. Something warm and vibrant had touched her knee and instinctively she glared at Frank, who sat across from her.

"What?" he said just as Quinn realized the hand belonged to Welles.

"I—uh, just remembered that you had some bright idea last night in the cab going to the hotel. I haven't heard you mention it today."

"The limo and driver," he said in disgust. They'd been finalizing details on the subject for most of the morning.

"Oh," Quinn said. "Right."

"You better get some sleep tonight, Tyler." He looked at Welles. "Drink some warm milk before bed, so you don't have those nightmares again."

Quinn looked down. She couldn't eat another bite. She also couldn't squirm away from that warm hand on her knee without attracting more attention. Welles knew it. In the next moment, he slipped past the hem of her skirt and up underneath it, along her inner thigh. Her pulse leaping, Quinn shot him a look. Welles looked back with bland innocence.

"Would you please—" Conversation stopped and everyone looked at her. "Uh, pass me the sugar?"

"Sweet," Welles whispered.

Frank Murray choked on a hot pepper from the antipasto. The lawyers thumped him on the back, and the one on Quinn's side of the table went to fetch a glass of water.

"Stop," she said, just loud enough for Welles to hear.

"Stop what?"

Quinn glared at him. "Fondling me."

His hand slid higher, making her gasp.

"Don't kid yourself, Quinn."

"You may make a habit of lunchtime flirtations, but I—"

He leaned toward her. "I don't make a habit of this, but you're driving me nuts. I want—"

Quinn coughed. Frank had recovered and everyone was looking at her again.

"Want what?" Frank asked.

Quinn took a deep breath and said, "Mr. Blackburn was just agreeing to a condition I've proposed."

The three lawyers looked expectant.

"Excellent," one said.

"Nothing like good food to get the brain moving," said another.

The third added, "I feel a breakthrough coming."

"Let's hear it," Frank said hoarsely, still coping with the aftereffects of the hot pepper.

Quinn desperately searched her mind for some answer. "Well, I—uh—"

Welles's hand stopped. "I'm afraid I pushed Ms. Tyler a bit too far," he said, giving her time.

"Not at all." Quinn smiled at the others. She'd learned long ago to fake it when things got tough. "Mr. Blackburn's concern for his daughter's welfare is obvious and—uh, it occurs to me that—"

"Quinn, never mind."

Looking guilty, he moved his arm from behind her on the banquette, withdrew his other hand slowly from her skirt, and rested it in his lap. Horrified, knowing his penchant for honesty, Quinn felt sure he was about to confess.

She couldn't let him embarrass himself and her. She wanted the negotiations to end successfully, didn't she? But she also wanted to avoid getting hurt—and hurting Hannah.

Yet the girl was all but signed, sealed, and delivered to Priceless in a flood of clauses and legalese. As the idea came to her, she glanced at the three lawyers. Did they even realize that they were discussing more than a corporation and its profits? They were talking about a fourteen-year-old, who was about to be taken away from her home, her family, her friends, even the school where she was an A student. No matter how exciting the Priceless opportunity might be, Hannah would have adjustments to make—adjustments that, in their own way, could prove as wrenching as Quinn's at the same age.

She shared Welles's concern for his child. Maybe that should be the only thing they shared. It was time, she decided, to use the spare room for something more practical than her own dreams.

"No," she said, "I'm perfectly aware of the problems, but I see no reason to withdraw my offer."

"Offer?" Welles repeated.

"I'd be delighted to have Hannah stay with me in New York."

She leaned weakly back in her seat as Welles let out a breath. His hands were folded now on the tabletop and he was staring at them.

"That's not necessary," he murmured.

But the lawyers were already talking more clauses and guardianship, sprinkled with Latin terms. And Frank Murray was smiling.

"I'd be happy to have her," Quinn said. "And so will Andrew."

"I thought you were coming home." Lying on the sofa, Andrew shifted his weight onto his good hip. "Alone."

Quinn spoke softly into the receiver, her tone placating. "I was, then the Blackburns—at least Welles—accepted the idea of having their daughter stay with us, so there are a few more ends to tie up."

"I don't know anything about kids."

"Neither do I," Quinn murmured, obviously stung by the reminder that they were childless, "but we can learn."

"Don't we have enough problems here without some intruder hearing every word?"

"She's a delightful girl, excited about coming to New York. You might summon some enthusiasm, Andrew, and think about welcoming her."

"She's your project, not mine." He could hardly keep from adding, Like Frank Murray. Andrew propped his foot on the living room's slate blue hassock. He knew he wasn't making it easy for Quinn but he didn't care. She hadn't apologized for their quarrel before she left, and now she not only wasn't flying home on schedule—again—she was moving a stranger into the apartment. "Where would she sleep?" he asked.

"In the spare room."

"The nursery?" He closed his eyes. "Does that mean you've given up badgering me about a family?"

Pained silence.

Then Quinn said, "If you don't want her there, I can find her an apartment. But her parents' agreement hinges on my serving as guardian. She's only fourteen."

Why couldn't Quinn see he was suffering? He'd been suffering for six years and couldn't see any light at the end of his tunnel. "Do what you want."

"Fine," she said. "I know the timing stinks, but that's not up to me. I'll be home as soon as I can and we'll talk, all right?"

"Whatever."

"A few more days. I know you must be lonely."

Andrew sat straighter, swinging his stiff leg off the hassock. "Actually, I'm not. I have my work to keep me warm."

She paused. "Are you drawing again? I knew you could."

"I'm headed for the top of the kindergarten class."

The pause was longer this time. "If they're handing out awards for self-pity," Quinn murmured, "then I'm sure you are."

"It beats wondering where my wife is every night, and with whom. You give Frank my best, will you?" He struggled to his feet, the cordless phone tucked under his chin. "Be sure to tell him how you like your back rubbed, and that your left breast is the sensitive one—"

"Andrew, for God's sake."

"And that I'd really prefer he practice safe sex."

"Frank Murray is on a plane headed for New York

right now. His part of the negotiation process is finished. The three Priceless lawyers are all workaholics who get turned on only by fancy clauses beginning with 'Whereas.' I'm having dinner alone tonight and sleeping by myself." Her voice rose slightly on every word until Andrew was holding the phone away from his ear. "Thank you for your unshakable trust in me. I'll be home when I can."

She always hung up without saying goodbye, but this time, even with the phone held ten inches away, he heard the slam of the receiver.

Andrew jammed the phone into its cradle. He stalked the living room—as well as he could stalk, dragging one leg like some caricature of a Civil War battle victim. Clumping into his den, he switched on the light. She'd probably stay an extra week in Geneva to spite him.

Let her, he thought. She'd be that much later getting her messages and the latest letter from PRISM, the MIA group. Not that there was anything new. He'd opened the letter himself.

Christ, what was happening to them? When he and Quinn were first married, he'd thought they had a chance, though he knew she didn't love him. As Jay always told him, he had no edge; he was just good old Andrew Devlin, everybody's friend in a pinch. Pull Jay out of a bar, or out of a ditch when he'd been drinking. Patch up his quarrels with Quinn, as if he were John Alden. Hold her, after Jay came up missing in Vietnam, and dry her tears. And, always, he'd hoped.

But she would never love him. And he really couldn't blame her.

He'd married her, hadn't he, under false pretenses? Hell, sometimes he wished Jay Barron would walk in the door, wearing that broad shit-eating grin, expecting the world to go his way. Especially Quinn. Maybe now she'd be able to see him for what he was: a rich, spoiled flyboy who loved Quinn mainly because she adored him. But then again, maybe she wouldn't.

Andrew searched through the papers on his drawing table, finding the PRISM letter. He tore it across and watched the pieces flutter into the trash basket. Then he eased himself onto his artist's stool and pulled Valerie Mason's pack of brightly colored pencils toward him. He might not have an edge, but he was no liar.

Two hours later he was bent over the drawing pad, sweating and periodically brushing back a strand of damp hair that kept dropping over one eye when Valerie rang the bell.

"What do you want now?" he asked.

He heard the jangle of bracelets, the metallic music of earrings in motion as she pushed past him into the apartment before he could slam the door.

Peering around him in the dark foyer, she looked toward the den. Light streamed from the open door and she smiled. "Quinn asked me to check on you. She said you were working again, but I didn't believe her."

"I'm not working. I'm playing."

"All the better. Let's see what you're up to."

Andrew tried to step in her way. He was slow, and she'd marched halfway down the hall before he reached her. She carried a tote bag, stuffed full as always—the thing must weigh fifty pounds—in teal-blue canvas to match her pants. Her gauzy summer blouse in blinding orange did nothing to conceal her extra pounds. "Those things in your ears are as big as wind chimes," he muttered, "and just as irritating."

She circled with a smile.

"Don't try to insult me. I'm in an excellent mood tonight."

He followed her into his den because there seemed no way to stop her. She stood an inch taller than he, and probably outweighed him. She was certainly more aggressive, so much more that she tired him. Then she spoke and he felt wired.

"You *are* working." She leaned over the drawing pad. "I'm glad Quinn was right. She believed you."

"She always does."

"What's this?" Valerie asked, pointing.

"If you can't tell, I'm not working very well, am I?"

Over her shoulder she gave him a look. "I'm blind without my reading glasses. I've worn them since I was ten. I have a lazy right eye." She tipped her head to show him. "Mostly when I'm tired; that's when you can really see it."

"You must be exhausted. It's drifting toward your nose."

She grinned. "We had some day at Tyler and Devlin, stuff hitting the fan right and left. One of my ads got lost, and a model broke her leg at a shoot. . . ."

She had trailed off and was staring at him. "What?" he said.

"When you smile, your whole face lights up." He watched the lazy eye move a little. "I don't think I've ever seen you smile before."

"Don't get too excited." He dropped his gaze, found himself staring at her mouth. Tangerine lip gloss.

"If I did, there'd be no controlling me." She turned back to the drawing board. "Now explain to me what you've done. I left my glasses at work."

She'd remembered food, though. No surprise. Fish and chips, which he despised but ate anyway—it seemed easier than listening to her bully him—and a gooey chocolate cake from the French bakery on the corner. Quinn bought flaky croissants there when she was home on weekends. Andrew didn't care for pastry either but he cleaned his plate, and at midnight, when Valerie still hadn't left, he ate a second piece.

"You shouldn't be discouraged," she told him, scooping frosting from the cake plate onto her index finger. "The seascape isn't bad."

"Without your glasses," he said.

"Or the city view from your window either. The perspective's nice, kind of scrunched up but long and leggy, the skyscrapers kicking at the air."

He shook his head at the nutty description. "Where in hell did you come from?"

"Brooklyn."

"I should have known."

"A street of rowhouses. Lots of noise, so I learned early to shout and be heard. Three brothers, a sister. Our parents fought all the time so they didn't get in our way much." Her gaze dropped and he sensed she wasn't telling the truth. "Your typical lower-middle-class upbringing. Pa with his lunch pail, Ma with her—"

"Her what?"

"Laundry. She hung it out back on these sagging, dirty lines every morning at six o'clock, and soot fell on the clothes all day."

"What were you going to say, Val?"

She looked up, startled. "Wow, two firsts in one night. I've seen you smile and I've heard you say my name—the familiar form, yet." She paused. "I wasn't about to say anything else. I had an idyllic childhood. Playing in the street, running from the gangs, scraping my way through school."

"No," he said.

"No what?"

"You're like Quinn, one of those super-achievers who always get A's. You're too well organized not to have done your homework."

"Me, organized?"

He flicked a glance at her orange and blue outfit.

"Oh, you look like a bag lady with flair—somebody really ought to introduce you to a color wheel someday and teach you about contrasts—but inside, your mind's a computer."

"How perceptive."

She didn't like that, he could see. Andrew discovered he liked having the upper hand for a change. Her eyes narrowed, and slowly she lifted her index finger with the dab of chocolate frosting to that slash of tangerine-glossed mouth he'd noticed earlier. "Don't," he said. "That's a disgusting habit."

Reaching across the table for her hand, he watched her eyes widen, watched the lazy one track again to his right. It made her face arresting. She had regular features otherwise, level brows and a straight nose that seemed a bit too short for her face, a chin and jaw that just missed being stubborn. And that mouth. Surprising himself, Andrew lifted her hand to his own lips, drawing her finger into his mouth, sucking long after the chocolate frosting was only a lingering sweetness on his tongue.

"That's a disgusting habit, Andrew."

"But it feels good." To his surprise, his blood was thumping, hard.

"Does it?" she asked, her eyes on his. Then she rose from the table, bending for her tote bag. "I think I'd better go."

Andrew saw her to the door. She could easily have made it first but she slowed her steps, staying just ahead of him, her head bent, her shoulders rounded.

When Andrew touched them, she jumped.

"You know what would feel even better?" he said.

"I'm afraid I do." She turned, her gaze defiant. "And I suppose my reputation as a man-crazy bitch has preceded me, but I won't let you punish Quinn by using me. Good night, Andrew."

He caught her arm. "I meant, having you come for dinner tomorrow night. Quinn will still be away, but we can be trusted, can't we?" He gave her another quick smile. She was right; he didn't smile often, and his face felt as if it might crack. "Our housekeeper makes a mean lasagna. I don't think I can stand any more take-out food, but I would like . . . some company."

"You're kidding."

He shook his head. "Tomorrow's Friday," he said. "What else do you have to do on a Friday night?"

"I might have a date. It's not impossible."

His smile broadened. "Do you?"

"No."

"Then say yes, and I'll show you how much my drawing has improved in twenty-four hours."

"My God," Valerie whispered. "That's three shocks in one night. I don't think my heart can stand another." She was trembling under his hands at her shoulders.

"Come early, and we'll see what we can do about your color blindness."

"How did you—?"

"Six-thirty," Andrew said, pushing her gently outside.

Nothing would come of it, he told himself. As Quinn had said, he was feeling lonely and so was Valerie. It took one to know one. And then there was that lazy eye, that soft, warm mouth. He closed the door as she got into the elevator. Once, he would have felt he was cheating on Quinn. But now things were different.

12

Welles was the first to arrive the next morning in the small conference room at the Banque Internationale. He arranged his papers, laid his favorite pen on top, straightened his tie, and poured himself a cup of coffee. All the while, keeping one eye on the open doorway for Quinn, he silently rehearsed his apology. Perhaps they would have a few minutes alone. . . .

But the lawyers, arriving en masse as usual, beat her by a good quarter hour. Quinn came late, hustling into the sun-flooded room, briefcase in hand, her coppery hair flying. "Sorry. Were we to start at nine? I overslept." She slipped into a chair at the table, nodding in turn to the three Priceless lawyers and avoiding Welles, who soon saw that things were worse than he thought.

Quinn didn't spill coffee in her lap, but she dropped her pen half a dozen times in ten minutes. He might have smiled at that latest small glitch in Quinn's elegant image, which touched him. Like the run in her stockings, it made him want to hold her; but when she stood, just before noon, nothing else marred her perfection. The ivory blouse, the charcoal-gray pin-striped suit, the long slim length of her legs all looked flawless. Yet she had a scattered look that made him frown. As she poured coffee—her first of the day—he saw her hand tremble.

The morning's subject again had been Hannah's education. Mai would have a tantrum before she signed the papers, Welles suspected, but he'd given his okay, provided Hannah lived with Quinn and her husband, to a six-month contract with Priceless.

"You'll take care of those admissions appointments we discussed, Ms. Tyler?" one of the lawyers asked. "I believe Mr. Blackburn gave you his New York choices."

"Yes, I have the list of schools." She rummaged through her briefcase. "Taking the time difference with New York into account, I'll make the calls this afternoon." A small frown appeared, and she drew her lower lip through her teeth. Papers flew onto the tabletop, Quinn's frown growing deeper. "I had the numbers yesterday. I know they're . . . somewhere." Another scramble through the scraps of paper in front of her, and Welles heard her mutter a curse. "I think I've left them at my hotel."

The lawyer's tone was patronizing. "We won't need you this afternoon. Why don't you make the calls from there?"

Welles swore silently. Earlier he had suggested she use his office. He'd been planning to talk to her there. He tried to catch her eye now but she was gathering up papers, tossing her pen into the briefcase, snapping it shut.

"Gentlemen." Priceless's senior attorney rose with her. "Let's have lunch and wind up these negotiations." He looked past Quinn, obviously irritated by her disorganization. "Welles?"

"Thanks, but I have some paperwork to catch up on at my desk. I'll order out today. See you around two o'clock."

The lawyers left, but Quinn was already out the door. Swearing, Welles reached the hall only to find her gone. His heart sank. He'd have to follow her to her hotel. Then he spotted a flash of bright copper turning the corner and his spirits lifted. She hadn't headed for the elevators but for the cloakroom off the reception area. She was pulling her trench coat from the rack when he entered the small room.

"Quinn?" Her body stiffened, and his heart felt as if it were climbing into his throat. "Yesterday I behaved badly, coming on to you like a Neanderthal again, like some street-tough punk who just wanted to score—the kid I used to be. Don't stay mad at me."

"I'm not." She started to put on the coat, but Welles held it for her. "I'm not awake," she said. "I didn't have time for breakfast, barely enough time to shower. I raced over here in a panic. I hate being late, as if everyone wouldn't still be here, but I often am. I wonder if I'll need this coat. It was cool this morning—"

"It wasn't that cool." In fact, Geneva was enjoying an unsual warm spell. He smoothed her collar down. "Why won't you look at me?"

She shook her head. "It's not you," she said.

"All right, but it's something. Somebody. Who?"

The tiny shrug tore at his heart and he decided to gamble. Welles pulled her back against him, lightly, letting her know that if she wanted to be free instead, she only had to resist. Instead, her muscles went slack under his hands at her shoulders and she let her back settle against his front. Welles suppressed a smile of relief. The position was rapidly becoming his favorite. Taking another chance, he swept the silky hair from her nape and dropped his head low to kiss her.

"Oh, damn," she whispered.

"Is it Andrew?"

She nodded, her neck moving just enough for her fragrant skin to tickle his lips. "We had another quarrel." Her tone was hoarse. "I don't know how to deal with his self-pity any longer. Nothing I say or do seems to make a difference. I feel . . . hopeless. I'm so tired, Welles, of being punished for ruining him."

"You didn't ruin him. He's ruining himself."

The coat's fabric rustled as she turned, her gaze at last meeting his. At the open look in her eyes, Welles felt his heart slide back into place again.

"You do understand," she said.

"It's how I feel about Mai," he reminded her.

"Has she come home yet?"

"No."

"What will she think about Hannah staying with me?"

Welles shook his head. "I never know what she'll think. Or do. But I think it's right for Hannah, and I have to go with that." He looked into Quinn's eyes. "Yes, I understand frustration. Yours with Andrew, mine with Mai"—his thumbs caressed her cheekbones—"with you."

"Welles, don't."

"I want you to know I've never cheated on her," he said.

Quinn smiled. "That doesn't surprise me. You're an honorable man, touchingly old-fashioned. I saw it the first day we met in your office."

"Not always honorable," he said, and then, "Quinn, we're done here. The lawyers will fly back to New York to draw up the final contracts, I'll probably fight Mai so that

Hannah can attend school in Manhattan and stay with you, and you'll go back to Andrew and his spineless self-pity."

"You make us sound trapped."

He smoothed her cheeks, then the hair at her temples. They wouldn't be alone much longer; someone would need a jacket from the rack, a hat. "That's not meant as an excuse, and if I could change things between us, I would, but you know as well as I do what this is all about. Where we're headed."

"Not where you think we are," she said.

When she moved, he drew her close again, his voice urgent. It occurred to him that he'd never taken so many chances with a woman. He'd never wanted to before. "Listen, I told you I have a ski house near Zermatt. Mai never goes there. Hannah and I use it on weekends—there's skiing year round at Théodule Pass—but Hannah's spending the next few days with Mai's uncle outside Paris. She has a school friend there. I want time with you, alone."

"I've never been unfaithful to Andrew either, and I don't think this is the time to change. It wouldn't solve anything."

Unable to help himself, Welles pressed against her. "It would solve one thing."

"I doubt it." Picking up her briefcase, she started for the door. Welles let her step over the threshold before he spoke.

"You don't like to ski?" he asked, which stopped her cold. "I thought you grew up in Colorado. I'll bet you were on skis before you could run."

"You louse."

He grinned. "You love to ski, don't you?"

"Yes, but I'm still not going." She paused. "There's no future in this, Welles. We both know that."

No safety either, he thought. If she got him alone, she'd

start in again about Jay, and he'd either have to tell her the
truth—in which case she'd certainly hate him—or he'd
have to lie. And prove he wasn't an honorable man.

"I thought you were a risk taker," he said.

"I thought you weren't."

"See? We have a lot to learn about each other."
When she stayed silent he said, "You know what I think?
I think you'd take any outrageous risk that came to mind
in your career—and, by God, make it work—but your
personal life's a different matter."

Quinn whirled in the doorway. "Yes. It is. So don't try
to manipulate me as you do Mai. What I do or don't do
in my personal life is none of your business."

He held up a hand. "Okay, fine." He paused for a
heartbeat. "If you change your mind, just call the
concierge at your hotel. There'll be a car at your dispos-
al for twenty-four hours."

He didn't wait for her to leave; he pushed past her,
heading for his office. He didn't look back. She was
right about him, but so was he, about her, and the realization depressed him. He didn't think for one minute
that she'd pick up the glove he'd thrown down.

When Quinn reached her hotel room, she was still
shaking. She had to force herself to function, something
she'd become even better at over the past week in
Geneva. She found the scraps of paper with the phone
numbers she needed under that morning's newspaper
on the desk; she ordered a late lunch and talked with
New York while she ate; she ended the afternoon with a
headache and half a dozen firm appointments at six of
the most prestigious private schools in Manhattan.

Which meant another few days, she realized, of
possible contact in the States with Welles.

Quinn phoned Swissair but couldn't change her flight. She was stuck in Geneva until morning. She decided to eat dinner in her room, then went to bed early with the chain on her door and her phone off the hook.

The next morning there were no messages waiting, no commanding knock at her door. Quinn felt vaguely disappointed. Her breakfast croissant tasted stale, which she knew it wasn't, and her coffee seemed bitter. She'd made the right choice, she kept telling herself; hadn't women through the ages always had to be the voice of reason? Men let their hormones do the thinking.

Holding a black lace camisole in one hand, a clutch of pantyhose in the other over her opened suitcase, she stopped. She'd thought he was a cautious man; she'd been wrong. Welles Blackburn, his cuffs so neatly rolled that first day, with his evasions about Vietnam; Welles, his hand snaking up her thigh under the table. He wasn't always the rigid man she'd thought; but then, she wasn't as gutsy as he remembered, through Jay.

She tossed the lingerie into the case. She had an hour and a half before her plane. She wouldn't miss it this time; wouldn't spend a sweet, early summer afternoon with Welles in Carouge; wouldn't taste his kiss at Cointrin. That hadn't been so cautious either, she realized.

But someone had to be.

Just before bed the night before, she'd called Andrew again. Quinn didn't like flying home across the Atlantic with bad feelings between them; what if the plane crashed and Andrew spent the rest of his life remembering that they'd parted in anger? Doug Lloyd always insisted on peace before bed—even that last time, after she'd run away from Bella Sharp's foster home. But last night, her attempts at peacemaking with Andrew hadn't worked. He'd even sounded . . . different.

Quinn fought down a surge of guilt. How could she have hurt him again? She'd turned her back on Welles, hadn't she?

She shut the suitcase. After a last check of her make-up, she'd call the bell captain. Quinn glanced at the bedside alarm and frowned. If anything, she'd be early this time. She'd have that much more time to worry about Andrew and tell herself she'd made the right decision about Welles.

Why mess up her life any further? On the way home she could think of what to say to Andrew, how to reach him. Was it possible?

Start thinking about your own happiness. Doug Lloyd's advice stopped her halfway to the dressing room mirror. *I can hear the need in your voice, even when you talk about a stranger.*

In the bathroom, she applied lip gloss. Fighting the urge to do something she would surely regret, she avoided her eyes in the mirror. Her makeup in one fist, Quinn tossed it into her purse and closed it.

A stranger like Welles Blackburn. Dark hair, those blue eyes, his strong hands. *I thought you were a risk taker.* Damn him. Damn Doug too. She reached for the telephone.

"I believe a car has been reserved for me. Could you send it around, please, to the front entrance?"

"Oui, madame. Quinze minutes." Fifteen minutes.

She hung up, shaking again. Praying that Doug Lloyd was right. That Welles was too.

Quinn's first surprise met her at the front entrance of the Beau-Rivage. A car, he'd told her, and she already felt the first stirrings of guilt. She had envisioned a dark limousine with tinted glass and a stern, certainly judgmental chauffeur, but as she left the hotel lobby, a black Chevy Blazer pulled out of line at the entrance and stopped in front of her.

"*Le voici, madame,*" the doorman said.

While he stowed her bags in the rear, Quinn leaned down to look at the driver, another surprise. At the wheel sat Welles himself. "Get in and let's go," he said.

He was wearing snug blue jeans with a green polo shirt and a scuffed pair of American cowboy boots. Quinn had never seen him so casually attired.

Tipping the doorman, he put the Chevy in gear as she slid onto the passenger seat. "Fasten your seat belt."

The words made Quinn remember the old Bette Davis line about preparing for a bumpy night. Suddenly, for the first time in years, she felt truly free, exhilarated—and scared out of her senses. "I don't think I know you at all," she said with a smile. "You've got a crazy streak. Like Jay."

Welles focused on the road, his mirrored sunglasses hiding all but a slight frown. "Once we're out of the city, the scenery becomes increasingly breathtaking." He glanced at her. "But if you don't mind, let's leave Jay Barron in Geneva."

Irritated, Welles stayed silent most of the way. He was having second thoughts, of course, and didn't want to take them out on Quinn. Maybe he was middle-age crazy after all. He'd just get her out of his system in the next few days, then let her go. He'd be safe then, from wanting a woman he couldn't have much longer than that; safe from Jay Barron and the truth that would make her hate him.

By the time the Blazer rounded the last hairpin curve and swung into, then straight up, Welles's unpaved driveway, the afternoon light was already shifting. Zermatt lay in a hollow, but he'd built outside the town on steeper ground, and the magnificent Alps that ringed the village were even closer here, casting long deep shadows over the earth, framing the ski house like a stage set. With a sigh, he switched off the ignition, glad to have reached his refuge again.

"Good Lord, how beautiful," Quinn breathed, stretching. She grinned. "The house too."

All glass and angles except for the huge curve of window wall in back that overlooked the drop-off to the valley below, the bleached redwood house, in harmony with its environment, soothed his spirit. He watched Quinn scramble from the car, sucking in deep breaths of cool air so clean, as always, that it hurt his lungs. So did looking at her in another, more pleasurable way.

"I love Colorado, but it's nothing like this," she said, circling with her arms spread to take in the view.

He studied her for another moment. She looked in tune with this place herself. Then Welles stepped out and began pulling suitcases from the back of the Blazer. "You're used to younger mountains. They have some growing to do."

"Have you ever seen the Rockies?"

"No. But this is where your Olympic hopefuls come to ski."

"How provincial," Quinn murmured. "We'll have to broaden your horizons."

He had two cases stacked under one arm. With the other, he pulled her near to kiss her cheek. "I hope so."

Inside the front entry, she looked around and gasped. The house shot upward like the nearby mountains, like the steep slope on which it stood. The great room soared two stories high with a balcony running around it on three sides. The large kitchen was state-of-the-art with its own breath-stealing view of mountains and an alpine meadow dotted with wildflowers.

"Is there edelweiss?" she asked, peering out the window above the sink.

"It's a weed."

"Ha. I'll bet you've never seen *The Sound of Music* either."

"That was Austria."

"They're the same mountains, aren't they?"

Welles grinned, leaning against the ceramic tile counter. "I'm gonna remember that. Wait until you've skied Zermatt."

"You must be laboring under a misconception. I'm no beginner."

"I hope not," he whispered, leaning closer for another kiss, this time on her mouth.

They packed food and supplies into the cherrywood kitchen cabinets, left a bottle of white zinfandel to chill, changed clothes, and headed for the lifts. It was either that, Welles told himself, or drag her upstairs to bed, and he wasn't sure Quinn was willing.

After three races down the mountain, she was breathing frost and obviously frozen to the bone. Welles had won all three.

"Unfair," she complained, breathless in the mountain air, trudging behind him toward the Blazer. "You know these trails like your own face in the mirror. How could I possibly have beaten you?"

"Be glad I'm carrying your skis for you tonight. Tomorrow I show no mercy."

"I didn't have a chance."

"Different mountains. Thinner air." He turned and grinned. "Poor Quinn, you're gasping. What's the altitude where you ski?"

"About eight thousand feet."

He pointed in the direction of the triangular mountain. "The Matterhorn—Le Cervin to the Swiss—is fourteen thousand plus."

Quinn had a blister on one heel and tended it at the house while Welles fixed dinner. "I feel like a sissy," she called from the great room by the fire. "First you beat me by a mile, now you're preparing the victory feast."

"Does wonders for my male ego."

"It doesn't need feeding," she said, "after that hat trick on the slopes. And I didn't know you could cook."

"Necessity being the mother of invention, as they say. Even if she didn't hate this place, Mai is a lousy cook. I don't think she's been here twice. She's always afraid Hannah will break a leg or an arm or worse. Hasn't seen her ski since she was seven years old."

"Is Hannah good?"

He laughed, coming into the room with two glasses and the uncorked bottle of wine. "She would have been down that mountain half a dozen times to our three. At her school she's captain of the ski team."

Quinn clicked her glass against his. "To Hannah," she said.

"And to Priceless jeans." Welles poked at the fire in the fieldstone hearth. When he turned, he caught Quinn staring at him, and his pulse jerked at the soft look in her eyes. Could something that felt so right between them be a mistake?

"I think I'm glad I'm here," she said.

He cleared his throat. "What did you tell Andrew?"

Quinn looked into her glass. "I told him we had a few more clauses to iron out because of Hannah's staying with us."

"Will he call your hotel?"

She shook her head. "I don't think so. We aren't on good terms, but I'll call him later before he goes to bed.

That's always his worst time—when he's alone and the pain gets bad."

Welles studied her. "I didn't have to lie to anybody. Hannah's away and so was Mai, still, when I left." He paused. "I hate to ask this, but if the telephone rings here . . . ?"

"I won't answer."

"Right," Welles said and disappeared back into the kitchen.

He went, feeling as if he'd deliberately distanced himself from her. He didn't like stealing time anymore than she did.

When Quinn took her wine into the kitchen, he was standing at the double stainless sink, the window reflecting black night now outside, concealing the riot of wildflowers on the hill. At her approach he turned on the water, rinsing a colander of vegetables.

"Welles?"

"Don't say it."

"I think I need to go back."

His shoulders tensed. "Just help me set the table, okay? This'll be ready soon. We can talk after dinner if you want."

He'd cooked homemade spaghetti sauce, thick and rich, with chewy bread, but the salad was completely American. "Where did you find Wisconsin cheddar?" she asked when they sat down to eat.

"It costs an arm, but Hannah and I are addicted. We order it from the States."

"Hmmm," Quinn murmured. "The man drives a Chevy Blazer, wears Texas boots, and likes his cheese flown in from the Midwest. How uncivilized."

"Enjoying good food's not the same thing as running for your life in Central Park."

"I think you're homesick."

"Wrong," he said. "I don't own a thing from Shreveport."

After dinner, Quinn groaned when Welles brought her a plate by the fire. "I can't lift a fork. My muscles are screaming and I'm already stuffed. Pecan pie with whipped cream? Cruel."

"Hannah and I keep them in the freezer."

"Did your mother make pecan pies when you were a boy?"

Welles smiled faintly. She wouldn't let up about his being homesick for the States. "No, I was always a better cook than she was. I was great," he said, "with boiled hot dogs and turkey pot pies."

"Ugh." Quinn took the plate. "Didn't your father mind?"

"I don't know. He wasn't there."

Welles sat cross-legged on the carpet beside her. The rug, a Navajo design, had made Quinn smirk when she first saw it. In fact, he'd done the whole house in Southwestern decor, something Welles hadn't consciously thought of in years. "I don't know who my old man was," he murmured.

Quinn looked shocked but she recovered quickly, reminding Welles that she was a posthumous child herself. "But at least I have my father's picture."

"My mother didn't know either, if that's what you're wondering." He dug at his pie, pushing nuts around. "Hell, she probably never asked for his last name."

"She was a . . . ?"

He set the plate aside. "She never took money for it that I know of. If she had, I guess we'd have lived better." He passed a hand over his face. "Christ, that's a lousy thing to say."

"After my father was killed, my mother had a hard time. She was just starting to be happy again, I think, when she died."

Quinn talked about Doug Lloyd and how the court had taken her away from him. Then she told him about the foster homes, about Bella Sharp's and how she'd run away rather than be molested, maybe raped. Welles couldn't believe how matter-of-fact she was.

"The Sharps were good people, and I think, more than not wanting to be hurt myself, I didn't want them to find out what that boy had done. So I ran."

"Where to?" Welles leaned on an elbow, pouring them both another glass of wine.

"Back to Doug Lloyd."

"And he let you stay?"

"He would have, but of course nothing had changed. I was three months older, that's all. He was still single and 'unsuited' to be a father on his own." Quinn told him about the night she'd shown up on Doug's doorstep, cold and wet from rain and very scared. "He shoved me into a hot shower, fed me, then tucked me in bed—and all the while I kept praying he wouldn't tell them where I was."

"He's the first person they would have called," Welles said.

"Yes, he was. I wasn't thinking clearly. The next morning I woke up, feeling the world had gone right again—the sun was streaming through my old bedroom window, I could smell Doug's bacon frying downstairs and hear oatmeal bubbling on the stove—and when I opened my eyes, I was staring right at the welfare woman who'd taken me away before." Quinn grimaced and took another sip of wine. "She wasn't bad, really. But I should have seen it in Doug's eyes the night before, that sad way he had of looking at me even when he smiled. The way he kissed my forehead when we said good night." She looked at Welles. "Maybe he knew I'd feel betrayed. Which, like a typical teenager, I did. It was years before I saw him again, and I'm sure he still thinks I blame him."

"Do you?"

"Maybe a little," Quinn admitted. "God knows, I haven't been to Colorado since Andrew and I moved to New York." She paused, then changed the subject. "Where's your mother now, Welles? Still in Shreveport?"

"She's dead. Cirrhosis of the liver. About ten years ago, I understand."

"She was an alcoholic?"

"Yeah." He looked into his empty glass. He was still half afraid he'd follow in her footsteps.

"You didn't go home when she died?"

"No."

"Why did you leave in the first place?"

"When I was about fifteen," he said, "she brought a guy home one night and he was still there the next morning—the next month. He moved in with us. We hated each other on sight. I was pretty tough then, getting in trouble at school and generally making things rough for myself—hell, the guy had a point. But after the first few times he beat the crap out of me, I'd had enough. Enough of her too, I guess." He looked at Quinn. "I'd sure as hell been more her mother than she was mine, pouring her into bed at night, hiding her booze. I was damn glad to get out of there."

"So you signed on with the Navy."

"Lied about my age, yes."

"And ended up in Geneva." She'd bypassed his time with Jay, as if sensing he wouldn't want her to bring him up tonight.

"Not a pretty story," he said. He reached out, tracing a light line down her arm with one finger, then up again.

"That's why you like it here, where it's clean and neat."

"I guess so."

"Even though you miss the States."

"I didn't say I did." His gaze met hers. "We all like to be safe, I guess." His fingers grazed her skin again, then smoothed the faint frown from her forehead.

"Welles, I don't know if I can do this. What happens when I have to face Hannah? When I'm living with your daughter under the same roof?"

"She doesn't have to know."

"But I'll know," Quinn said, "and so will you."

He glanced into the fire and felt his own resolve waver briefly. "Do you want to go back to Geneva tonight? I'll take you if you need to go." Then his eyes sought hers again, begging for another answer.

As his hand lifted to her cheek, Quinn turned her face into his palm and kissed it with trembling lips. "No," she whispered, "but I'm still not sure about us."

Through the darkened wall of windows, just a black reflection of the night, he could see nothing. They were alone in the darkness, in the house, with each other. He could feel his pulse throbbing low in his gut. He had enough certainty for both of them. He'd never been more sure of anything in his life.

"Welles, I don't know who I am when I'm with you."

"Yes, you do." He moved closer, his hand at the nape of her neck, and drew her to him. Quinn stared at his mouth until his head lowered, stared into his eyes until he let them drift shut and his mouth dropped the last inch to cover hers. "When you're with me," he said, "you know exactly who you are."

She moaned, slipping her arms around him.

"And so do I," he whispered.

13

After long moments, Quinn ended the kiss.

"I don't know what you want from me," she whispered.

"Everything."

The feel of his arms around her, tightening, the force of his next kiss seemed to draw the battle lines between them, as if he wanted all she had to give, and would have it, or destroy her in trying. Without conscious thought, Quinn found her arms twining around his neck, felt herself lifting into his kiss, even as Welles gently but firmly—accepting no resistance—eased her down onto the Navajo rug in front of the fire. "This is a corny seduction caper, Blackburn," she tried and felt him smile against her lips.

"No sass," he murmured.

He silenced her with another kiss, hot and open, that stole her breath away. Her breasts, though still clothed in the soft white cotton turtleneck she'd worn over navy stretch pants to ski, rubbed against his black pullover, and her nipples began to tingle. Quinn searched for his tongue with hers, beginning a tender duel that left them both gasping, wanting more. And then, still more.

"Welles."

"It's all right."

He slipped the shirt free from her waistband, skimming a hand up inside to capture a breast. With practiced ease he flicked the front catch of her bra, then shoved her shirt high, the cooler air warring with the heat of the fire, the heat of his mouth on her naked skin.

And as fast and hot as the desire that made her legs weak, made her spread them at the first nudge of his knee between hers, panic streaked through her. Quinn had had only two lovers in her life. Jay Barron had taken her virginity. He'd taught her, teased her, coaxed her first responses from her— and made Quinn feel, for the first time, like a woman.

She moaned now as Welles dropped both hands to her hips, pushing gently at the navy stretch pants, easing them down her legs. She was breathing hard, watching him with fixed concentration, wanting, wondering. What would he be like?

When she'd first married Andrew, the loving had been sweet and simple—until the accident.

Now Welles sat back on his heels and gazed at her, his eyes dark in the shadowy firelight, his handsome face devoid of anything but hunger.

"You're scaring me," she said, then reached for him anyway, knowing Welles Blackburn was neither patient nor passive. He would pull Quinn's passion from her, then draw out more until, she feared, he had her very soul.

Quinn, with her hands at his waist, stopped moving. She turned her mouth under his until she was free again, and to her surprise Welles stopped too, looking down at her, half naked and vulnerable to his gaze. His eyes met hers.

"I'm afraid, Welles."

"So am I." He waited.

She stared into his eyes, saw the caution there, the hope. He seemed all the more dangerous for that. The careful way in which he lived his life: shirt cuffs neatly rolled. His devotion to Mai, his love for Hannah. He wasn't here as Frank Murray would have been, to tumble her in front of the fire for a night, then walk away—even if he didn't know that yet himself.

And what of her? If she let her feelings deepen . . . ? Better to stop now while she still could, while he had some control. But with the thought, she eased both hands under his shirt and pushed upward, baring his flat belly, his torso, his chest. "I do want you. . . ."

"But what, Quinn?" His tone was hoarse, thick.

"I think you'll take too much."

"No more than I can give."

Arms behind his neck, he pulled the shirt over his head in that peculiarly masculine and fascinating motion men used, revealing skin and muscle in one swift assault on her senses. Quinn took a shaky breath. His shoulders gleamed in the soft light of the fire, dusky gold and looking sleek and hard, so she had to touch them.

"I'm not good at this," she said, realizing it was true as she said the words. "I've lost every man I ever cared about. My father and Doug Lloyd. Jay. And now, maybe, Andrew. I don't think I can—"

"They don't matter." Welles worked off his ski pants without ever taking his eyes from hers, his gaze fierce, warlike. "Mai and . . . nobody else matters. Not tonight, Quinn. If you can't put them out of your mind, your heart—"

She laid a hand across his mouth. "Can you?"

He kissed her fingertips, whispering, "Yes."

"Then you're stronger than I am."

He shook his head. "No, weaker. More selfish."

She thought of Doug Lloyd. "I'm told selfish can be good." Quinn's gaze traveled slowly down his body, taut and glowing in the firelight, to the hard strength of his erection. "There's nothing weak about you," she said with a half smile. "Not your will and not—you make me selfish too." She touched him. "You have a beautiful body."

When she looked up again, her cheeks warmer than the fire made them, he was smiling too. But his eyes were hotter and she could almost feel him wanting to lean toward her, to have her take him in. The look frightened Quinn, who sobered.

"There's nothing but this," she said, "for either of us."

"I don't care."

"I don't either, right now," Quinn said. "But I think—"

"Don't think. Just want this as much as I do." He reached out, gently removing the last of her clothes, then his. When he finished and they were naked to each other for the first time, he let his gaze warm Quinn until she held out her arms.

Hesitating, Welles looked at the Navajo rug beneath her, at the rough hearth, at the darkened room. "No cheap seduction scene by the fire," he murmured. "Let me take you upstairs."

She couldn't help echoing, "Take me—?"

But his eyes stayed somber, intense. "The bedroom has skylights. On a clear night like this, I want to make love to you under the alpine sky, under a blanket of stars."

He took Quinn's hand, leading her with only the red-gold glow of the fire to guide them, through the dark room past the curved wall of windows, a mirror of blackness, and started up the open stairway. He stopped along the way to kiss her, or Quinn stopped him, and soon they were both breathless. Halfway up, Welles pulled her around for another melting kiss, urging Quinn down onto the stairs. Broad and thickly carpeted in pale beige, they felt as soft as fur against her bare skin.

"I can't make it any farther." His mouth still on hers, Welles ran his hands lightly over Quinn's body, her breasts. He lingered there, grazing her nipples, peaked hard from cold and excitement. "Oh, Jesus." He stretched out over her, their bodies fitting perfectly, his arms braced at either side of her head. Quinn stared, fascinated, at the definition of his biceps. His arms were trembling and so was she, all over.

"Welles—"

"You're the only woman who's ever made me shake," he whispered, then lowered his mouth to hers again, and for long moments there was no sound except the crackling of the fire and their soft groans, not from discomfort. The carpet was plush and the incline only pushed them closer to each other.

Quinn felt the last of her strength, her resistance, begin to ebb. Mouths, hands, a tangle of legs. . . . She moaned into his mouth, receiving in answer the light nip of his teeth on her lower lip, the hot brush of his mouth over hers, warm and wet. His fingers sought her, found her damp and open, ready. Then she felt the hard press of his penis against her softer warmth and cried out.

"Oh, Welles!"

"Give up," he whispered and, on a long sigh, entered her.

Quinn felt her body go lax, stretch, and lengthen to accommodate him. He began a slow, steady pumping in rhythm with the deep kisses that had her arching up like a sacrificial offering. Her heart clamored, her lungs seemed to quiver. Quinn wrapped her arms, her legs around him and knew she was lost.

"Don't. Or I can't—"

"Now," she urged him. "Please, now."

In that instant Quinn knew what her deeper feelings for him meant. She loved Welles Blackburn, and this seemed the greatest terror of all, the greatest joy.

With the next frantic lift of her hips, Welles grunted. Then she felt him push deeper and let go, felt herself fly into fragments as he flooded her with warmth, with a groan of surrender that matched her own.

◦ ◦ ◦

Later, Quinn was lifted in a tight embrace and carried the rest of the way upstairs. Much later, she awoke, warm and cozy, between the feather bed's comfort and the goosedown quilt on Welles's bed, her nose tickled by the silky dark hair on his bare chest. She woke up to bright sunlight, blushing.

After their first lovemaking, they'd fallen into a doze on the stairs, exhausted, but Welles had roused her with kisses, with his hands, and the battle with him taking care to protect her this time, had begun anew. Once again during the night, at last in his bed under the stars, he'd turned to her, and each time the loving seemed more fierce, more elemental, more richly fulfilling—and, to Quinn, more terrifying.

They might be lovers, but still there was no future for them except separately, with Mai and Andrew.

When she opened her eyes, she found Welles already watching her with that light in his eyes she'd come to know so well in the night. In spite of her fear, it made her smile.

"When I was younger," she began softly, "and started to notice men looking—"

Welles dropped a kiss on her bare shoulder. "Is this my reward for performing with valor in the field? As soon as I open my eyes, you're reciting your other conquests."

She traced a finger over his smiling mouth. "No, it's just that men always look intense, almost angry when they . . . assess a woman. I could never figure out what I'd done to a perfect stranger." She smiled. "Like you, this morning."

"After last night I'm not a stranger."

"As soon as I opened my eyes, I got that hostile stare."

"It's a predatory look."

"Mmmm."

"A man on the prowl for a mate."

"Mmmm," Quinn said again, trying not to flinch.

She wasn't his mate and perhaps needed the reminder.

"No complaints?"

"It's hard to find fault with perfection."

He laughed, a rich male sound of satisfaction, at the same time lowering a hand under the covers to lightly swat her bottom. "So, you want breakfast? Or you want to try for a perfect ten again?"

Quinn pressed her forehead to his shoulder, and he waited a minute before easing her back to look into her eyes. She blushed again. "I'm a morning person. I can do without coffee."

She watched his eyes darken in a way that was also familiar now, also perfection. He threw the covers back, baring her to his gaze, and gave a low, appreciative whistle.

"You look even better in sunlight than you did by the fire. Talk about perfect." He lowered his head to nuzzle her breasts. "The weather's good too, but I don't think we'll get much skiing done today."

Quinn tugged at his head, drawing him up into the first kiss of the day. She cared, had known for certain since that night in the restaurant—perhaps Mai had seen it too?—and the caring had led them, as he'd promised, to bed. Where else could it lead? she wondered. She loved him, but she couldn't say what was in her heart; she hoped her feelings showed in her eyes.

Welles teased her lower lip with his teeth. "Glad you . . . came?" he asked, then grinned. "I mean, Zermatt too."

"Yes. Don't be crude."

"You inspire me."

Within moments, Quinn decided that she could suppress thoughts of tomorrow for a while. His touch sleeked over her skin, her hair, her mouth, her breasts; he kissed and licked and suckled and teased until she felt as if her body, like the glowing embers in the hearth downstairs, had flared to life again.

As he moved into her at last, Welles smiled down into her eyes. "I'm glad . . . I came too."

They ate breakfast at three in the afternoon, following bouts of teasing talk and lovemaking in bed, with the second-story windows open to the alpine breeze and the scent of wildflowers from the meadow. Quinn discovered she was starving and asked for another helping of pancakes with strawberries.

"It's lovely to let someone else—a man—nurture me," she told Welles, who ignored the oblique reference to Andrew.

"I think I have a bulletin for the folks at Tyler and Devlin."

Quinn smiled. "Don't you dare. I'm supposed to be masterminding the Priceless campaign, and if I make a wrong move this time, I'm finished."

"Practice makes perfect," he said, feeding her another plump strawberry from the bowl between them at the white tile-topped kitchen table. "Remember what we did together, upstairs, before you finally made coffee."

Quinn flushed but bit her lip. She'd never be able to forget. Last night she'd thought there was no future for them and earlier she'd tried to be content with now, but in the light of day, like most women, she needed the reassurance he couldn't give. Yet she'd never felt so sated in her life, so . . . loved. She only wondered when it was going to end.

In late afternoon, Quinn took a spill on the slopes, sprawling off the trail, against a tree trunk, in a flurry of arms and legs.

Welles dropped down next to her. "Are you all right?"

Groaning in frustration, Quinn sent her poles flying

and one ski. On the other, the binding had snapped. The ski itself had cracked against a tree, splintering on impact. Worrying about tomorrow, she hadn't been paying enough attention.

"I'm fine." She even laughed as Welles ran his hands over her, searching for breaks.

He looked into her eyes but Quinn knew he was really checking her pupils. "You could have been killed."

"I'm okay. Don't worry about me more than you would Hannah."

"Hannah's practically a pro." He forced a smile. "You look pretty rusty, but then you've only run down those puny Colorado peaks until now."

She started to punch him on the arm, but his expression changed so rapidly from anxiety to need that she drew him down with both arms around his neck.

"I'm okay," she said again.

Welles's mouth met hers and the kiss, which started out soft and cool from the lowering temperatures around them, turned hard and hot. "That's for you," he whispered. In seconds, Quinn was clinging, oblivious to the fact that Welles lay cradled between her legs not six feet off the trail.

A skier raced past, hooting back at them.

"Jealous," Welles murmured.

With the next kiss he got serious, and Quinn's body heated another few degrees. Her borrowed parka felt stifling and she unzipped it, then tore the ski band from her hair. Welles cupped her head, sifting the strands through his fingers, spreading her hair out on the snow, then kissing her again, his body moving against hers.

"We shouldn't," Quinn said.

"This one's for me." And he lowered his head again.

So late in the afternoon, the crowds had dwindled, but a loud whistle shrilled back to them on the wind as another skier shot by. Quinn froze.

To cover her embarrassment, she pushed Welles away and lay back, as if exhausted, slowly sweeping her arms and legs back and forth over the snow. Welles grinned, his eyes still intense with unspent arousal.

Before he could move, Quinn struggled to her feet, brushing snow from her parka. This wasn't the place for intimacy, and she felt the need to remove herself from him emotionally as well.

"Lord, I haven't made snow angels since college in Boulder, when Jay—"

"Quinn, don't," Welles cautioned.

"—and Andrew and I used to lie together on a hill in the freezing cold, during a snowstorm, flapping our arms and legs like windmills. One night—"

"Quinn."

"Jay was always the best," she went on, unable to stop herself. "He had longer arms and legs, but he said enthusiasm won every time—"

"Fuck Jay!" Welles jumped to his feet, his eyes stormy. "Or is that what we're really talking about here? He always talked big, so tell me the truth." He grabbed Quinn's arm. "Forget the snow angels. How was he in bed?"

That quickly, the sunlight seemed to dim, as if someone had flipped a switch, and long shadows moved across the trail.

Quinn looked at his unhappy expression. "You're a wonderful lover," she said, carefully freeing her arm.

"Come on, Quinn, did he make you moan the way I did last night?"

Her cheeks flamed. "I didn't know we were holding a competition."

When she turned aside, he turned her again. "No, you started this, dammit. You pulled back, just like last night, trying to leave. Just like this morning, about other men sizing you up."

"I'm not comparing you to anyone."

"It sure sounded that way." With a last angry look, he started down the hill. "It'll be dark soon. We're not that far from the bottom. You can carry your own skis. Let's go home."

Numb with cold and shock, Quinn trudged after him to the Blazer. She didn't know whether Welles meant home to Geneva or to the cliffside house in Zermatt. At that moment, filled with the memories he wanted to avoid, the memories she needed to cherish, she didn't care.

Welles slammed the Blazer's gearshift into park. He got out and released the skis from the roof rack, shouldering them and heading across the lawn to the darkened house. He hadn't meant to blow like that, but he knew something now. He wouldn't get Quinn out of his system with one night. He hadn't even made it upstairs then, and minutes ago he'd lost control on a ski slope, for Christ's sake—until she dumped ice down his neck by mentioning Jay.

He recognized the tactic. He'd used it himself, by bringing up Mai the night before. In the back entryway, a long room studded with shelves and hooks for equipment, he stashed the skis—dropping the one with broken bindings on the floor. Still angry, mostly with himself, he kicked it aside.

Quinn spoke to his back. "Why is it that every time Jay gets mentioned, you slam a door on me? What's so terrible about a memory?"

He rounded on her. "Hell, maybe I'm jealous!"

However true, it was an easy out.

"I was pea green the first goddamn time I kissed you, and I'm sure as hell jealous now." He looked away. "Let me be ashamed of myself in peace, will you?"

"No. I won't." She made him look at her. "Talk to

me, Welles. Or you can just get back in that American car of yours and drive me straight to Geneva."

He waited a few seconds. "Is that what you want?"

"No," she said. "Didn't this morning tell you anything, or last night?"

"All night." He stomped into the kitchen.

Quinn followed. "I live with someone who's cranky. Believe me, you won't win the prize."

He turned on her. "Why the hell live with him then?"

Quinn in New York, he thought, with that self-serving jerk. Him in Geneva with Mai. What had last night accomplished anyway? It had only made things worse. It had given them the power to hurt each other. At the sink, he grabbed a pot and filled it with water.

Quinn snatched it away. "I'll fix dinner," she said. "You sit. And start talking."

His heart thumped. "Forget it. I'm going to take a shower."

He'd taken three steps when Quinn caught his elbow. "You know, I've noticed something about you. When you get scared, you clam up. You get cautious, Welles. What are you so afraid of?"

"When *you* get scared, you get sassy," he said and, removing his arm from her grasp, he headed for the stairs.

He'd made a mistake, a whole series of them. This house was his and Hannah's. He had no right to bring another woman here, no right to make demands on Quinn and then send her away. She wasn't his.

But she wasn't Andrew's either.

While Quinn made dinner, he stood under the hot shower, cursing as the water sluiced over his shoulders, trickled off his buttocks. When he squeezed his eyes shut, the water sounded like rain and he groaned. Tropical rain.

It had been raining that night too, he remembered,

when he'd dragged Jay out of a bar in the Philippines, where they'd been sent for a week's rest and recreation.

"Are you crazy, Barron? Picking up one of those bar girls when she's with someone else? Starting a fight? Besides, she's probably loaded with disease," he had said. "Let's get out of here."

But on the way back to their quarters, Jay lectured him. "Some freakin' nerve, messing with my good times. We been flyin' together for months, you never screw up. I'd like, just once, to see you miss the coordinates. Hell, I'd like to see you drink more'n two beers in one night." He slurred his words more with every step. "Like to see you get laid for a change."

"You and me both," he had muttered under his breath.

"You are one spooky character, my friend." Jay staggered on the uneven sidewalk. "For a tough guy from Lou'siana, you sure as hell don't know how to relax. Good with the weapons, good with your fists, but what d'you do for fun? Besides ogle my pictures of Quinn, I mean."

"I don't ogle them." His fantasies were his own.

"I mean, hell, Quinn's my lady, but she's prob'ly at some movie or frat party right now with my old buddy, Andrew Devlin. You can't trust 'em. Even if Quinn's good in the sack—"

"Shut up, Jay."

"Hell, I taught her everything she knows. I'm tellin' you, all I have to do stateside is snap my fingers"—he tried but failed miserably—"and she's on her back."

"Shut the hell up!"

The shower water pelted Welles now, reminding him of the hard Southeast Asian rain that night. He shut off the faucets and stepped out into the warm, humid bathroom to towel-dry. He'd been crazy for her then, based on nothing but a few snapshots, a few stories; Quinn had been crazy for Jay Barron.

She still was.

Welles came downstairs to find dinner waiting—and Quinn, her face expectant. A little hurt. He slipped an arm around her waist and nuzzled the soft place beneath her ear. "I'm sorry."

She clung to him for a moment. "We shouldn't be here," she said, "doing this. We were bound to feel guilty afterward."

At the table Welles couldn't have said what she served. Whatever, it tasted like sawdust to him, and Quinn picked at her food in silence. Finally, he pushed away from the table, leaving his meal half eaten. "Quinn, I want to talk to you."

He couldn't read her expression. "Let me finish up here first." Keeping her face averted, she cleared the table, then went into the great room to sit in front of the fire. She hadn't looked at him once. "I can't seem to get warm," she said. "I guess I shouldn't have made those snow angels."

"I shouldn't have lost my temper." He sat beside her, taking her hand. It was cold. What did she think he was going to say? That last night had been a mistake?

"I want to tell you about the war," he said.

"You don't have to." Her glance slid quickly away. "Doug Lloyd's right. The war was too painful for a lot of men even to think about now, and I should let you have your peace."

Welles shook his head. "No, I saw a lot of shit over there, I did things that you won't . . . approve of, that you won't like me for, but—oh, God." His heart hammered as he raised her fingers to his lips. He felt sick with fear. "I need to tell you, Quinn."

"All right," she whispered, pressing her palm to his mouth again. Welles kissed it but said nothing for a moment.

"I don't know where to start," he said, still holding her hand, then thought of Mai. It had always been safer, easier to talk about her. He'd ease into the rest, he decided.

"You already know about Mai's brother and the Tears of Jade."

"The necklace and earrings," Quinn recalled, "that belonged to her. He'd stolen them."

"When Mai ran from him she took the jade with her, and he turned the countryside inside out looking for her. Mai hid with the same people, as you know, who took me in. I was there in the village—nothing more than a camp, really, with a few huts—when Nguyen homed in on her. And found me too."

"An American airman would have been valuable."

Welles nodded. "Mai bargained for her life—and for mine. Nguyen needed money. Badly. He'd held onto his mother's stuff as long as he could, but the war was winding down. He was a colonel then, running out of supplies, ammunition. Mai promised him the Tears of Jade in exchange for her own freedom and safe passage for me. If not, she said, he might as well kill us both. He'd never find the necklace or the earrings without her."

"She'd hidden them?"

Welles nodded. "She didn't even tell me where. Nguyen agreed, after a lot of jawing back and forth. He disappeared for about three days—the time he needed, he said, to get us phony passports and papers—but when he came back, he double-crossed her."

"How?" Quinn asked.

He paused. "He brought another man with him. He thought the two of them could easily overpower me—I was still pretty feverish from the leg—and Mai, of course."

"What happened, Welles?"

He hesitated again. When he spoke, his tone was hoarse.

"They jumped us, and I killed him—Mai's brother." He tried not to see Quinn's shock. "With his own knife—and my bare hands."

Quinn stared at him. Then, finally, she said, "It was wartime. You had to kill him, or he'd have taken you—and given Mai to his friends."

"To his superior. Some general or other. She'd shamed him by running off. He had to save face somehow." Welles paused. "That's not all," he said, "I . . . killed the other man too."

He glanced at Quinn's trusting green eyes, her look of acceptance, and lost his nerve. He couldn't take the risk.

"Nguyen's sidekick."

"In self-defense," Quinn murmured.

"Then Mai and I ran like hell."

"She had to leave the jade behind?"

He shook his head. "No." The memory still made him sick. "She told me to get out of the hut, that she'd search her brother's body for the pouch the jade was in. She brought it with her. I thought that once we got out of the north, Mai could find an aunt or cousin—whatever—and I could go back to my unit. When we stopped late that night to rest, I asked if I could see the necklace and earrings. I said at least they were worth all her troubles, that now she'd be able to take care of herself."

When he didn't go on, Quinn said, "What happened?"

"She tipped the pouch into my palm. And a bunch of riverbed pebbles fell out."

"Just stones?"

"Just stones. Worthless." He gazed into the fire, remembering his fear, the taint of blood on his hands, the eerie nighttime cries of animals and birds he didn't recognize. Or were they signals from men looking for him? "I said, 'Now, instead, you have nothing and no one.' And Mai, so small and dark and helpless, looked up into my face, her eyes black as ink, and she said, 'I have someone. I have you.'"

"That's why you feel responsible for her."

"She saved my life."

"And you saved hers," Quinn pointed out.

"Maybe. Or maybe I was just so gut-scared I would have killed my own mother"—he winced—"not that I hadn't thought of that before. I acted on reflex, Quinn. Nothing braver or more noble than that."

Quinn touched his hand. "You still feel guilty about it."

He shrugged, his pulse pumping, his stomach churning. "Sick is more like it." Christ, he couldn't tell her the rest. Quinn believed him; she didn't blame him. "Whenever I think about that night, about all the nights after . . . my plane went down, I feel sick. Maybe Jay Barron was lucky after all."

He let the sentence hang there, but Quinn misinterpreted him.

"When I get back to New York, I'll see whether the MIA people I've contacted at PRISM have anything new for me."

"You've already been in touch?"

"Again," she said. "You can help with the question I asked before. I'll get some maps, and maybe you can pinpoint the coordinates where Jay's plane went down."

"I'm not helping with that wild goose chase. I know what happened, and I don't want to live through it all over again."

He was sweating.

"Why are you being so unreasonable?" Quinn asked. "You wanted to talk about it—"

"Jay Barron is dead, goddammit!"

"Not to me," she said. "Not without proof."

Oh, Jesus, he couldn't tell her. "You've been carrying him on your back for twenty years. You married a man you don't love just to keep the memory going—"

Quinn jumped to her feet. "That's not true!"

"—because you can't face losing somebody. You can't face the fact that people like your father die and Doug Lloyd can't replace him. You came here with me for the same damn reason. Hell, you came after me in the first place just because I look like Jay Barron."

"You say that as if he were something terrible—"

"He was a great guy, but he had another side. He took chances, Quinn: with his own life, with other people's, with his plane—"

"He was a good pilot! A decorated hero."

"Believe whatever you want, but you're not using me the way you use Andrew Devlin."

Quinn looked horrified. "I haven't used you."

"No? What about last night?" Welles tried to calm his pulse. He said coolly, "We tried every position I know. You used me, all right. You set me up, but I'm not helping you dig up old graves in search of some illusion."

She hadn't used him, he thought. He had used her. And he still wasn't safe.

"What are you hiding from me?" she asked.

"Nothing!"

She was halfway to the stairs when he caught her.

"Where the hell are you going?"

"Back to Geneva. If you don't want to drive me, I'll walk."

14

 Stuck in Friday afternoon traffic on the Long Island Expressway, Quinn cursed inwardly. The past month had been tough enough, with Frank Murray calling every five minutes to say "Can't you speed things up?"—which was Quinn's own feeling at the moment. Then, today, she'd lost Hannah's flight information among the Priceless ad drawings on her desk. By the time she found the arrival time, she was late and quaking with nerves. Once, she thought, she had looked forward to this meeting.

"Can't you go any faster?" Quinn asked the cabdriver.

"Not unless we fly," he said, and she subsided against the seat, swearing again.

Trying to relax, instead she remembered another tense drive from Zermatt to Geneva four weeks ago. In the midst of Quinn's hasty packing after her quarrel with Welles, Hannah had called the ski house. Her friend was ill, she said, and Hannah had come home a day early. Frowning, Welles squelched her intention to join him in Zermatt; he'd see her at home, he told Hannah. To Quinn, he didn't say a word.

At the hotel Welles had double-parked, yanking her suitcase from the Blazer with the motor still running.

Quinn pulled the case from his grasp. "I can carry it."

She'd taken no more than two steps before he spun her around. "Quinn, I don't know what to say."

"Don't say anything. I'm sure we both feel guilty enough—which is why you were spoiling for a fight and got one. Let's leave it at that."

"Like hell."

With a dark look, he jerked Quinn to his chest and kissed her, as much in fury, she thought, as in regret. The kiss was hard and she pushed back. When he let her go, she grabbed her suitcase and stalked into the hotel lobby.

Quinn felt her shoulder wrench as Welles snatched the suitcase. "Don't be an idiot," he said. Then his eyes suddenly widened, and when Quinn followed his gaze across the lobby, she felt shock run through her too.

Hannah Blackburn had just stepped away from the registration desk. Seeing her father in that same instant, she stopped dead.

Quinn's first reaction was relief that Hannah hadn't seen Welles kissing her. As Hannah's gaze ran over Welles in jeans and boots, over Quinn in stretch pants, Quinn saw the mix of emotions cross the girl's face: recognition, delight, then confusion, and the same shock Quinn was feeling.

Hannah looked from her father to Quinn. "I called the Beau-Rivage after I spoke to Daddy and they said you were still staying here. I came to talk about New York."

Giving her father one wounded, accusing look, in the same manner Mai had used at the restaurant, she swept past him and Quinn. Soon enough she'd see the Blazer, which Welles only used for Zermatt.

"See what we've done," Quinn had murmured.

Drumming her fingers on the seat now, she silently urged the taxi to hurry. She already had two strikes against her with Hannah.

Two weeks ago Hannah and Mai had come to New
York without Welles for the school interviews. Quinn
invited them to dinner. Even if Priceless hadn't been picking up the tab, she wanted to take them somewhere
memorable like Lutèce or Windows on the World. A
glamorous introduction, she thought, to Manhattan and
Hannah's exciting new life there. Instead, Mai insisted on
an early meal at a restaurant near Quinn's office. By eight
o'clock, mother and daughter were at Kennedy Airport for
their return flight to Geneva and a disappointed Quinn
had finally realized she was trying to overcompensate.

She glanced at her watch. If Andrew had come with
her, she might feel better, but Andrew had been in one of
his sulky moods that morning so she hadn't even asked.

"Which terminal, miss?" The cabbie finally swung
onto the access road at Kennedy.

"Swissair."

Her heart began to pound. She'd pushed the driver
all the way; now she prayed for a few more minutes to
prepare herself. The taxi lurched to a halt at the terminal,
and Quinn shoved bills into the driver's hand. "Wait for
me." Inside, after a swift check of the monitors for Hannah's gate, she was running along the concourse, cursing her own disorganization.

She spied Hannah, a canvas pack over her shoulders,
coming toward her. She'd already cleared Customs.

Pasting on a smile, Quinn relieved her of the bag and
gave the girl a quick hug, feeling her slender body tense.
"Welcome to the Big Apple. We're going to have a wonderful time."

"I came to work, Ms. Tyler. That's the only reason I came."

Dammit, she thought. "Then let's get your bags into
our taxi and get you home and in bed. Monday we start
bright and early."

On the way, the only safe topic seemed to be Priceless jeans, and for the first time in weeks Quinn felt only too happy to talk about the ad campaign.

"We'll be shooting right here in New York first. The Plaza Hotel ballroom instead of Versailles"—she smiled—"then the Waldorf-Astoria lobby, and maybe the garden room at the Four Seasons. I think we'll get a pretty exotic look, but my plan is to warm things up as we go."

"You must be good at that," Hannah murmured, gazing out the side window at what Quinn had always considered the ugliest cemetery in America. It ran on for miles through Queens, and Quinn always turned her head away.

"I'm good at my job, yes."

Her tone must have put an end to it, because Hannah said nothing more, even when they reached Manhattan. In the mirrored elevator of Quinn's apartment building she clenched her hands in front of her, gaze fixed on the flashing numbers above her head. But her cheeks were pink and Quinn fought a smile. She'd win her over yet.

"Here we are." At her door, Quinn rang the bell, then fished for her key. She'd give Andrew some warning.

She had the key in the lock when he opened the door, leaning heavily on his blackthorn stick, his eyes vaguely unfocused.

"Did we wake you?"

"I wasn't sleeping."

Quinn urged Hannah into the apartment. She set the canvas pack and a suitcase by the foyer closet, waiting for Hannah to add the two she carried. "This is our star boarder." Then she fumbled the introductions. Andrew's eyes looked wary, Hannah's suspicious.

"You don't like me," she said.

"I don't even know you."

"Andrew doesn't like anybody when he first meets them," Quinn said, and he turned away, thumping down the hall. Looking after him, she sighed. "Come on, Hannah.

I'll show you where everything is. Would you like something to eat before bed?"

"I'm not hungry. I'm not tired either."

In Geneva it would be the middle of the night, Quinn thought; but then she smiled. In spite of herself, Hannah must be too excited to sleep. She followed Quinn through the apartment, saying in a begrudging tone that it seemed larger than she expected.

When they reached the hallway to the bedrooms, Quinn opened the door to Andrew's den, where she found him again—to her surprise, with Valerie Mason. They stood, hunched over Andrew's drawing table, shoulders touching, and when Quinn cleared her throat, they both jumped.

"Val, I didn't know you were here," she said.

Valerie grinned. "Just dropped by to see what kind of trouble I could get Andrew into."

Feeling uneasy, Quinn made more introductions. "Hannah, you'll see a lot of this lady. She's slaved for me since I started the agency."

"Is she good at her work too?"

Quinn followed Hannah's gaze to the two pairs of hands close together on a sketch of Manhattan. "Yes," she said, her stomach tightening as Andrew and Valerie exchanged looks that Quinn could only label fond.

Then she took a second look. Valerie wore simple gold studs in her ears, a taupe linen pants suit, and an off-white shirt.

"You look wonderful, Val."

"Gee, thanks." Valerie looked down at the sketch pad.

What was going on here?

She hadn't seen Andrew smile in weeks, and he'd never said a civil word to Valerie, much less looked in her eyes as if they shared some wonderful secret. The new clothes, Quinn decided.

Her own guilt over Zermatt had simply clouded her judgment.

"Go on with your sketching," she said and kissed his cheek. "I'm proud of you, Andrew."

He didn't answer. Quinn, feeling as if she'd patronized him, led Hannah to the spare bedroom. When she opened the door, she experienced a pang of longing. She'd considered painting the room herself but decided against it; the room would be Hannah's, at least for the duration of the initial Priceless ad campaign, and she should make it her own. At the moment, however, it was still the nursery Quinn might never fill.

At a loss, she turned. "I hope you like it. This is the smallest bedroom but it has the best light. You can do whatever you want with it. If you'd like to choose other furniture"—she'd culled a few pieces from the apartment, bought a simple bed—"we can go shopping."

"My mother gave me money. I can shop by myself."

Quinn forced a smile. "Bear with me. We'll need to set a few house rules, but those can wait until tomorrow. For now, I'll leave you to unpack your bags."

In the hall, she leaned weakly against the door. Had Hannah told Mai about the scene at the Beau-Rivage? Maybe this wouldn't work out and she'd have to ask Priceless about another apartment, another guardian.

Her legs were shaking, and she put a hand to her empty stomach. *I don't know anything about kids,* Andrew had said, but neither did she. Quinn didn't have brothers or sisters, and she'd never stayed long enough in any foster home to make a surrogate sibling bond that lasted; the only child she'd ever carried had died in the first hours after Andrew's accident, without ever being born.

What had she done in taking Welles's only child to care for now? Quinn might know nothing about children; but this one knew entirely too much about her.

∘ ∘ ∘

Without Hannah the house seemed much too silent, Welles thought a week later, his footsteps along the marble hallway echoing as if in a mausoleum. He had missed his daughter emotionally during her silent treatment of him before leaving for New York, but he hadn't prepared himself for her physical absence.

He'd stayed late at the office again tonight, which he'd done every night since Mai put Hannah on the plane.

"I don't want you to see me off," she'd told him, just as she'd told him to stay home while she interviewed at private schools on the first trip.

He'd tried to change Hannah's opinion of him before she left, inviting her for a last weekend at the ski house. Despite some resistance, she had gone, a good sign, Welles had thought. Then she gave him the cold shoulder for two days, staying on the slopes all day without him. Welles spent the weekend knowing he'd made another mistake, hoping she couldn't smell roses in the air at the house, wouldn't find a stray stocking under his bed.

All Hannah said as they loaded the Blazer to drive home was, "I don't like the ski house anymore. Maybe I'm growing up."

Standing in the foyer with Mai looking on that last day, Hannah's bags stacked by the door, Welles tried once more to win her over. "Come on, plant one here," he said, pointing at his cheek.

Hannah only stepped back. "I'm too old for silly games."

She didn't kiss him goodbye, and in that moment Welles hated himself all over again, hated this house— which, he supposed, made a convenient scapegoat.

His steps haunting him, he went into his study, shrugged off his suit coat, stripped off his tie, and opened his shirt collar. The nightly ritual didn't make him breathe easier. He felt suffocated, lonely.

Not for the first time, he wondered what kind of treatment Hannah was giving Quinn.

He'd talked to Quinn only twice since Zermatt, both brief conversations in which he warned her of Hannah's hostility. She never let him say more than that.

Had she forgotten that one enchanted night on the ski house stairs and in his bed under the stars?

Welles poured himself two fingers of whiskey from the bottle he'd recently bought. The house seemed quiet as death itself. He imagined he heard the silence broken by Hannah's girlish laughter, the clatter of her footsteps on the stairs.

He shut off the study lights and left the room. If he stayed there, he would have another drink—despise himself for dealing with his problems as his mother would have—and brood.

In the dark, carrying the dregs of scotch in his glass, he climbed the steps. He stood in Hannah's doorway, missing her, praying that she'd forgive him. Stepping into her room, he glanced at the clock beside her canopied bed. It was ten in Geneva, only four in New York. Needing to know if she had, he reached for the telephone.

Quinn's secretary, Daisy, made him wait, and when Quinn came on the line she sounded breathless. "Hello?"

"Hi," he said.

"Welles?"

"Yeah." He kicked off his shoes and settled back against Hannah's headboard, letting the sultry sound of Quinn's voice run through him again.

"I'm in a meeting. You shouldn't have called."

"I thought it better to phone you at work than at home." He paused. Clearly, she didn't want things to get personal. "How's it going?"

"We've been doing test shots. Hannah's wonderful, all legs and those mesmerizing eyes, and her skin . . . it's sheer radiance. You should see—"

"I mean, does she give you a hard time?"

There was a silence. "Well, now that you mention it. . . ."

"How hard?"

"Like a rock."

"I've been there," he said.

"Can you blame her?" Quinn asked. "I can't. She's fourteen years old, and the man she adores broke her heart. She won't talk about you. She calls you 'my father,' but only when she has to."

Welles sat up. "Do you have to rub salt in the wound?"

"Maybe so. If it makes you see things as they are. You can't expect to call me, here or at home, and get a tender reception. What do you want me to say? That everything is all right, that Hannah thinks I'm the perfect role model and her best buddy in New York? That she's forgotten all about . . . us? I just thank God she didn't see you kiss me."

"What do you want *me* to say?" He tossed back some scotch.

"Nothing. Frank Murray and I are in the midst of a disagreement about location sites."

"Give him my love," Welles said tautly.

"I shouldn't have left the meeting."

"Why don't you say the rest?"

"What?" Quinn murmured. She had her caution too at times, her self-defenses.

"That you're sorry about me."

"We're grown-ups, Welles. We made a mistake."

He emptied the glass. "Following you into the Beau-Rivage was a dumb move, Quinn, but Zermatt?" He hesitated. It seemed they were trading places: Quinn becoming cooler, more reserved; he, taking chances he had no business taking. "Quinn—"

"Don't," she whispered. "I'm doing the best I can with your daughter. Don't ask me for more than that. We both have troubled marriages to tend."

He wondered whether she was crying and felt like an ass. "I need to talk to Hannah," he said.

"Then call her at the apartment. Week nights. Before seven o'clock. That's when I usually get home."

"Quinn!"

As she hung up, Welles slammed his glass down on the table. Goddammit to hell. If Quinn Tyler wanted something, she had the tenacity of a pit bull; when she didn't, she could be just as persistent in reverse.

With a sigh, he ran a hand over Hannah's white crocheted coverlet, then got off the bed and went across the hall.

"Is something wrong?" Mai, already in bed, pushed hair from her face, a slight frown marring her smooth features.

"No, nothing. I thought you were asleep."

He began undressing in the dark, hoping she wouldn't press things.

"I heard your voice. Who was on the telephone?"

"New York," he said.

"Hannah?"

"Yeah."

Maybe Quinn was right about him, that he'd been spoiling for the fight in Zermatt. He wanted to blame Mai somehow, for Hannah and for Quinn, but he could only blame himself for stealing a few hours of . . . what? Good sex? It was more than that, he knew, which only made him feel worse.

"How is she?" Mai asked, and his pulse skipped.

"Who?"

"Our daughter. Welles, what is wrong with you?" Watching him shuck his pants, she came up on her knees. "You've come home late every night since Hannah left—and I know things weren't right between you when she did."

"We had a small quarrel. Nothing major," he said, relieved. He'd been wondering what, if anything, Hannah had told her mother. "You know how it is. Teenage girls and their fathers. I suppose I'm feeling left out all of a sudden after years of being a priority in her life."

"I wouldn't know," Mai said, meeting his eyes. "My own father seemed to die with my mother when I was much younger than Hannah." She paused. "I never really had him in my life, it seems. And with you, your first priority has always been Hannah, not me."

"Don't start, Mai. I'm exhausted."

"No wonder. You come home at ten o'clock every night for a week, miss dinner, drink scotch in your study until midnight—"

He pulled off his shirt. "I've had a lot of extra work. The peer review's coming up and—worse luck—I have to rate Thornton."

"Are you worried he'll get the promotion instead?"

"It's a good possibility."

"I doubt that," she murmured. "My uncle—"

"Doesn't need to intervene on my behalf, dammit. I've told him so. He thinks he can keep me in line with the promise of an executive vice-presidency, responsible for all of Eastern Europe—" He broke off. "I don't want to talk about work. I'll never get any sleep if I do."

"We were talking about Hannah."

Welles shook his head. "She's still a kid, as you're always quick to point out. She gets moods. She'll get over it, and so will I." Or so he hoped.

"Then I'll let you work it out between you."

Welles slipped between the sheets, remembering the night she'd hauled Hannah out of bed. "I'd appreciate that."

Mai moved close to rest her head on his shoulder. She smelled of gardenias, heavy and cloying, and he closed his eyes. "We have tickets for the Music Festival tomorrow night. Please don't be late," she murmured.

Welles turned on his side but she followed him, pressing herself against his spine.

"I'm lonely too," Mai whispered. She touched his shoulder, ran a hand down his arm. "Could I have at least a kiss good night?"

Turning his head, Welles kissed her with his lips closed.

Mai's face appeared over his shoulder, her dark hair falling around them like a heavy drapery, the gardenias stronger. She took his mouth again and slowly turned him, her hand under the covers, searching for him.

He was half hard in spite of himself when everything in him turned cold again. "Mai, I can't." He pushed her hand away.

"We have our problems, Welles, but we've never brought them to bed."

"I know. I'm sorry."

"Please tell me what's wrong." He could hear the tears in her voice. "If it's something I've done. . . ."

Since the night in Hannah's room, since her own flight from home—she'd never said where—since Hannah's leaving, she'd been too eager to please. Welles turned over, drawing her near. "You've done nothing. It's work," he said. "Hannah. Me." He forced a laugh. "Hell, maybe I'm getting the male equivalent of empty nest syndrome."

"It's an adjustment. But now I have you all to myself."

Her words sent a chill down his spine. Mai's agreement about Priceless, even her approval of Quinn's *in loco parentis* guardianship, had come much more easily than he expected. Why hadn't he seen before?

"We'll have more time together now," she said.

In the darkness, he frowned. With Hannah at Quinn's away from her father, and Quinn serving as substitute parent—not pursuing a relationship with Welles—Mai had them both under control. The pathetic ploy tightened his embrace. Hadn't Quinn said they both had marriages to mend? Pushing the memory of Zermatt and roses from his mind, he willed himself to sleep.

Quinn couldn't sleep. Distressed and guilty, replaying the sound of Welles's voice in her mind, she tossed and rolled until dawn lightened the sky over Manhattan. Quinn had hoped for blue skies but the sun never came up, and by the time she and Hannah left the apartment for the limo ride uptown to the Plaza Hotel, a depressing drizzle was falling.

"So much for the park today," she murmured as the big car shot around a stalled bus. "We'll take the ballroom shots instead and save the Boat Pond in the park for tomorrow. I hope."

At eight o'clock the hotel lobby was fairly quiet and they swept through it, then up the broad stairs to the mezzanine level. In the ballroom, technicians were already at work, stringing lights and testing camera angles.

Hotel workers milled about, interested—despite the everyday occurrence of such events—in the ad shoot, and at a white-draped table along one wall a woman served coffee and doughnuts to the crew. Quinn grabbed a French cruller, offering one to Hannah.

She shook her head. "No, thank you. I never eat junk."

"Mmmm," Quinn agreed and went in search of Tony Fisher, her director.

"I hope we haven't a teenage prima donna in the making," he said, casting a look at Hannah, who was now surrounded by makeup people and Valerie Mason, holding up one prop, then another.

"Not if I have anything to do with it."

Tony grinned. "I remember Versailles."

"And Ilse Jansen."

"Bite your tongue."

"I've practically bitten it through," Quinn said. "I'm past rational planning or the appreciation of camera lenses and the newest filters. I'm ready for witchcraft, chickens' feet, and little dolls I can stick pins in."

Tony kissed her cheek. "Leave everything to me. We'll get this on the first take."

Eight hours later, Quinn could have made him eat his words.

Priceless jeans, she thought. The ad shoot from hell.

All day, while Hannah posed under hot white lights and the prismed brilliance of chandeliers, Welles's daughter tracked her with unwavering dark eyes until she began to feel like a woman on parole.

"What's with her?" Valerie finally asked.

"You noticed."

"Who could help it? Even the electrician changing bulbs over there asked me why Hannah Blackburn keeps looking at you as if you were Lucretia Borgia and Mata Hari rolled into one."

Quinn brushed hair from her eyes, pulling it up into a ponytail. She secured it with a rubber band, wincing. Her hair's thickness could not be tamed in such damp weather; Hannah's, thank fortune, remained like heavy silk. "She's not taken in by my charm."

"Did you murder her grandmother or something?"

"No." Quinn hesitated. "I slept with her father."

Valerie rounded on her, eyes like saucers. "You're kidding."

"I wish I were." Almost, she thought. "The worst part

is, I can't even blame her for glaring daggers at me. In her place, I'd do the same." It was the way Quinn had felt about the county welfare agent who took her from Doug Lloyd and the only emotional security she'd known.

"When?"

"During the contract business in Geneva." She told Valerie about Zermatt and the stars above Welles Blackburn's bedroom skylights. "Do you think I'm terrible?"

"I said he was a hunk. Though I don't think I expected you to take my advice. What happened to the search for Jay Barron?"

"Thanks for reminding me." She'd come home to find no messages, no letters, nothing but the same dead end. "Val, what am I going to do? In every way Welles was a bad judgment call. If it wasn't for wanting to know about Jay, we'd never have met. . . ." She trailed off, remembering the fond look between Andrew and Valerie a week ago.

"And?"

Quinn frowned. "I think he's miserable too—God knows, I am. Hannah found out and blames both of us. No," she corrected. "She blames me. She's not speaking to her father, but she still loves him."

"Do you?"

Her frown deepened, her heart went wild. "For heaven's sake, it just . . . happened. I was upset with Andrew; Welles was feeling trapped with his wife."

"Who wouldn't, from what I've heard." But Valerie's tone sounded thin.

"Marriage is a two-way street," Quinn said.

She went back to the shoot, and to Hannah's glares, for the rest of the day. At six o'clock Frank Murray strode across the ballroom to Quinn's side.

"Beautiful," he murmured, sliding an arm around her waist. "A beautiful job from a beautiful lady. Time to knock off, Tyler, and join me for a drink downstairs in the Peacock Lounge. Whataya say?"

"I say no, I'm sorry, but us working girls have to get home." She looked toward Hannah, who still wore Priceless jeans and a white silk shirt, Valerie's dark red feather in her black hair. Hannah was watching.

"Don't give me that, Quinn. You know you want to."

Before Quinn could duck away, he lowered his head and nuzzled her throat. "Stop it, Frank."

"If I didn't know better—that you're devoted to Mr. Andrew Devlin-Tyler waiting at home—I'd think you had something on the side."

"Think what you like." Quinn's heart raced.

"Somebody with the initials W.B."

She stepped out of reach. "You stupid moronic—"

"Watch it, Tyler. The young lady's coming this way. Looking as if she knows it too."

"You're scum, Frank. You clean up good"—she glanced at his hand-tailored navy suit, his Brooks Brothers tie—"but you're still scum. You always were."

As Hannah reached them, her eyes bright with the censure Quinn had come to know only too well, Quinn led her toward the ballroom doors. "We'd better get home," she said. "Lotte promised pot roast tonight, and Andrew likes to eat early whenever possible."

Outside, rain poured from leaden skies. The chauffeur met them at the hotel entrance with an umbrella, and Quinn collapsed onto the back seat of the waiting limousine with Hannah. Being with a model on the rise had its advantages; if Hannah weren't staying with her, Quinn would be trying to hail a cab in the torrential Manhattan downpour at rush hour. Instead, she let the plush luxury of the upholstery cradle her exhausted body and closed her eyes.

On the screen of her eyelids, she saw Valerie and

Andrew looking at each other. Maybe she shouldn't have confided in Valerie, who'd been her closest friend for four years. Then Frank Murray intruded with his sly smile and all-too-accurate innuendos. Had Frank seen how she felt? She didn't trust him at all. Finally, she could see Welles himself, damn him. She'd fallen for him like a struck set at the end of a successful shoot. She'd made a grave error and didn't know how to rectify it.

Opening her eyes, Quinn found Hannah studying her. She hadn't said anything in the ballroom, but she said it now, her dark eyes on Quinn, a small smile on her still-painted lips.

"You are exactly what my mother said you were."

The words went through Quinn like a needle in wool, like her own guilt. Oh, yes, she deserved it. But she also knew how to fix things after all, if not with Hannah, then for herself.

She'd dig for more information about Jay. If he was dead, she'd tell Andrew, who might have turned to Valerie for comfort, nothing more, and put the past behind her; if Jay was still alive . . . well, then at least she'd know. She could put an end to things—to Welles Blackburn—and put her life right again for the first time in nearly twenty years.

Subic Bay Naval Base
The Philippines

He'd been telling her for a month to leave him alone, yet every time he had the nightmare she was there. Sweating, cold, and shaking, he would jerk awake in the predawn stillness, and against every inclination of his mind his eye would seek her out. Finding her now, he slumped back onto the hot, damp sheets, flinging an arm over his face.

"Rest now, Commander."

"Why do you do this?" he asked wearily. *"Is this part of private duty? I doubt it."*

A cool cloth swept over his forehead, his bare arm. *"You'll be released soon. Your injuries are healing well. You must shed your anger now, as if it were more burned flesh, so that the healthy parts can grow."*

He took his arm down and looked at her. Her blue-black hair still shone; her eyes held a faint smile. Reprimand, he thought. She was good at that. In her quiet way she could dig at his spirit and almost make him like it.

"If I'm so damn healthy, why are you sitting up with me half the night every night?"

The smile reached her mouth. *"You keep the others in the ward from sleeping."*

He'd been screaming then. Again.

"So you try to keep the top-brass medics from transferring me to the psych bin. Is that it?"

"At one time, perhaps." The cloth touched him again, bathing his sweaty cheeks. *"Now there is no need. You are ready to talk—about Cochran."*

Still trembling, he shoved her hand away. *"Why don't you go home, wherever that is, and stop picking me apart? I've got no pretty stories to tell."*

"I don't care for pretty stories."

He almost smiled. *"I should have realized."* She'd given him a stack of Stephen King novels the week before, the first time in years that he'd read anything but coded messages, orders, intelligence information. *"Those books turned my blood cold."*

"A masterful storyteller."

Cochran, he thought. He had a thousand stories about that bastard—all except the last one.

"No happy endings," he told her.

"In this place I don't expect them." She sat on the edge

of his bed. "You are a very troubled man, commander. Such problems become a dam against the heart's feelings, constricting a man until he can't breathe for so much hate."

"I have reason to hate him."

"Because . . . ?"

"Damn you, I trusted him! I had no reason not to. I was his superior. He was younger, greener than me, new to Vietnam when we were assigned to fly together. No threat." He burrowed into his pillow and closed his eyes. "Or so I thought."

"And then?" Her small hand stroked his arm.

"We flew together," he said bitterly, "and all the jolly camaraderie, the nights together in local bars, the run-ins with the MPs, the fucking confidences from the midnight bunk across from mine: all of that got blown away in a burst of antiaircraft fire."

"Your plane went down," she said.

"Sheared right through the trees, plowed into the ground like a goddamn pickax." He took a shaky breath. "Why talk about it now? It was years ago. I've had plenty of time to think about it, to remember."

"You were hurt in the crash."

He snorted at her prompting. "Pinned into my seat like a moth on a mounting board. My harness jammed. The smell of jet fuel was everywhere." He passed a hand over his eyes, felt the strange comfort of her hand against his thigh. He was shaking, but he wasn't alone now with the memories, with his rage. "I begged the bastard to get me out." Struggling up in bed, he stared into the darkness. "'Cochran, for Christ's sake, this Slugger's gonna burn. Get me outa here!'"

"Softly," she said. "Go on."

He shook his head.

"He left you there," she said. How much had he babbled in his nightmares?

"He left me to die, and when I get out of this place I'll—"

"He may be dead himself."

"I doubt it." After his own rescue by the North Vietnamese, after his injuries healed enough to escape, to travel, after he got the morphine monkey off his back, he'd made inquiries. *"He made his way to Europe, I know that much."* That's what his fellow agents, French-based, had found out. *"If he made it back, deserted the war and his own men, I think he was too strong to die. He came from trash. A streetwise kid who knew how to survive. I had to learn. No,"* he said, conviction giving him strength, *"he was a lying bastard then; he's still lying. Somewhere. Waiting for me to pay him back."*

"Bitterness is a poison, Commander. It might kill you first."

"What the hell do you know?"

"Only what I have heard at night from your own lips."

Through the thin cotton blanket, her hand grazed his thigh again and he caught her fingers. His skin was tingling. *"What else have you heard?"*

"Enough to know that, of all your hurts, Vietnam is the safest to remember."

"Tell me, damn you." He squeezed her hand, hard.

"Vietnam, this Cochran, is not your only poison. You have suffered recently, even more deeply—"

He twisted her wrist. *"You conniving bitch!"* Cochran wasn't classified information; but those terrible hours in the nearby highlands were, and like the good operative he was, without heart or soul, he had repressed all memory, all information, as if erased from a computer. She'd almost brought it back again. A test? A trap? His tone was silken, deadly. *"Nice try, sweetheart, but don't dig any deeper. There's nothing there."*

When she tugged, he released her hand, then moved swiftly, silently, in the darkness to haul her close, to flip her over and beneath him in an instant. If she'd been an *assailant, she would be dead by now. He could imagine the weight of the blade in his hand, now tangled in her black hair, could feel it slip between her ribs and into her heart. He froze.*

"Commander."

He heard fright in her voice, but passion made as good a substitute for anger as the knife. She wanted to know him. And she would. "Shut up," he whispered.

"Rape is an act of violence."

"So is love."

Raising her head, she looked sadly into his eyes. "You are more troubled than I dreamed."

He had meant to frighten her and then let her go, so she wouldn't come back again, but in the same instant her mouth parted with the words, he covered it with his. Hard and angry, at the first touch of her hand on his cheek, the kiss turned soft and heated, making his head spin. In seconds he was hard, harder than he'd been in twenty years.

"Helen. . . ."

"It's all right," she said. "Why do you think I've stayed with you so many nights and listened to you crying?"

"Oh, God." He buried his face in the warm hollow of her throat, pressed his mouth against her skin. She was young, delicately dark, and lovely—a fact he'd been hiding from himself—and when his hand slid beneath her uniform skirt, shoving it high, he groaned with wanting.

Twining her arms around his neck, she groaned too.

"Commander."

"I'm not navy," he whispered as she opened his pants. "I haven't been for a long time. I'm not a commander."

She waited and he said his name, the real name he'd nearly expunged from memory for the last twenty years, and for a while, in her arms, he moved out of the shadows into the light.

"My name is Jay Barron."

15

At 8 A.M. Quinn snapped off her desk lamp and slumped back in her office chair, longing for that brief, simpler time in her life when she had loved Jay Barron and didn't worry about anything else. Instead, the night before, after another day of rain, another go-round with Frank Murray, she'd quarreled with Hannah. Then with Andrew. And ended up working half the night. Or, rather, coloring.

"We're still impressed with the girl," Frank had said the day before. "But there's something missing from the first ad. Nobody here knows what that is. We don't have to. It's your job to supply the magic."

Quinn had to admit he was right. The proof now tossed on her desk lacked some essential quality. Too bad that the night hadn't given her any answers; yet if she hadn't worked, she would have suffered one of her recurrent dreams of Welles that, since Zermatt, had become even more erotic. Nothing missing from those, she thought; nothing left to her imagination now.

Setting aside her coloring book, she straightened in

the chair. Morning sun streamed between the thin slats of her miniblinds, striping the office floor, gold on brown, like a tiger's pelt. At least today the sun was up. They could try shooting at the Boat Pond, then the fountain in front of the hotel. With luck and Valerie's help and Tony's eye, they just might make magic.

Quinn hoped so.

Between living with a hostile Hannah and a surly Andrew whose drawings never met his expectations, and with both of them taking things out on her, her personal life seemed to be a shambles. Always before, she had fallen back on her work.

Quinn forced her attention to the Priceless ad proof: a wash of light, the glint of mirrors out of focus as a background, the glow of white candles in white ceramic holders. On a white marble couch, simple and Roman in style, Hannah Blackburn reclined on her side, wearing Priceless jeans, a white silk shirt, Valerie's dark red feather in her hair. A splash of matching crimson over the shirt's breast pocket gave the photograph an air of mystery, a sense of something about to happen. Or perhaps, the picture hinted, it had just happened and that was why Hannah smiled so secretively, so softly.

Quinn frowned. Maybe Hannah's slender hand cupping her head, fingers buried in its black silk, was wrong. Maybe the feather itself said too much, or not enough.

She poured a cup of coffee from the silver carafe on the sideboard, but she'd already downed most of the pot and her stomach felt sour.

Maybe Hannah herself was wrong; or, more likely, the bad chemistry between the girl and Quinn simply showed on film.

"I'm not a baby," Hannah had said last night. "I don't need a stupid curfew. When I'm ready to come home, I will. You're not my mother."

"I'm your guardian while you're here," Quinn argued. "I'm responsible for you. This is New York, Hannah. If your parents knew—"

"My father, you mean." She gave Quinn a level look.

"Your mother too. If we can't come to some agreement here, I'll have to call them."

"Suit yourself." Yesterday's rain had canceled the ad shoot. Having spent the hours after school wandering the city, having missed dinner, Hannah shouldered her backpack and went to her room. "I'm sure you'd love that," she said, just loud enough for Quinn to hear.

To Quinn's amazement, Andrew had sided with Hannah.

As far as Quinn knew, they rarely spoke to each other, yet the two seemed to share a wavelength—or a mission, she supposed. Punishing her with silence or sarcasm seemed to be a favorite household pastime.

"You can't expect to monitor her comings and goings as if she were a five-year-old," Andrew said. "She's a bright kid. A working kid at that, with a pretty hefty income—so I hear." His tone made it clear that he'd learned from someone else.

"Valerie told you?"

"Yes, while we were working on the charcoal sketch of the view from my den the other night. My God, that girl, precocious as she may be, earns more than I ever did"—he paused—"even when I was whole."

"She's still a child. And while she lives in this house, she will do as I say." Quinn could have groaned at her own words. Yet although she empathized and couldn't blame Hannah for her dislike, she had a responsibility to Welles's daughter. She couldn't let her run wild.

"What's with her father?" Andrew asked, making Quinn's pulse jump. "Every time the guy calls, Hannah tells me to tell him she's not at home. If I'm out of the room, she lets the phone ring or the answering machine pick up. If you ask me, he sounds pretty desperate."

Quinn looked away. "He and Hannah had a falling-out about . . . her coming to New York. He's quite protective."

"Of you too?" Andrew asked. She could feel his gaze on her.

"I don't know what you mean."

"The other night when he called, Hannah was out so he asked to speak to you. When I told him you were still at the office, he said he wouldn't disturb you. He asked me how you were."

The phrase hung in the air. Quinn forced herself to meet Andrew's eyes. "We share a common interest," she said, "in Hannah—and in Jay's whereabouts. He still believes Jay is dead, but he knows how frustrated I've become with my search." She frowned. "I can't imagine why I haven't heard anything from PRISM since I got back from Geneva."

His tone turned harsh. "I think Blackburn's right."

"He's entitled to his opinion. So are you. I happen to disagree." She shook her head. "I really can't understand it, though. In the past those people have been so responsive, even apologetic that they can't seem to help more."

"Quinn, they must get a hundred calls a day. Everybody wants a neat answer. Your question's not top priority, I'm sure."

Another dead end, she thought now, and made a note on her desk calendar to call her New York contact if she didn't hear within the week. A phone call, a letter, the maps she'd requested: there should have been something by now.

Quinn set aside her cold coffee and went down the still-empty hall to Valerie's office, hoping she had come in early. Right now she had an ad to reshoot, if they decided to scrap the red feather—as they had Ilse

Jansen. At least Hannah Blackburn was a go. For once, she thought with a rueful smile, she and Frank Murray and Priceless Sportswear agreed on something. Now if she could just get the right picture. . . .

"Dammit."

Valerie rummaged through a suitcase of props again, the lakeside breeze in Central Park blowing scarves and rippling the fingers of a pair of pale pink satin opera gloves.

"Nothing?" Quinn asked with a sinking feeling. She cast another hopeful look along the path. Hannah was late.

"We tried the gold . . . the white sequin-embroidered blouse, didn't we?"

"Yes."

"I thought so." She dug deeper, coming up with a long gold rope braided with lapis silk. "How about this?"

"Interesting."

Valerie unfurled the chain. "If we used it single length, it'd fall to Hannah's waist, make a good foil against the white shirt, and the blue would pick up the denim of the jeans. What do you think?"

Quinn frowned. "Let's ask Tony."

"He never replies, except to peer through his viewfinder, hunker down, or shift to one side for the right angle and say, 'Ask Quinn.'"

She had to laugh. "I thought that was a game only kids played, pitting their parents against each other." Though she had little firsthand experience, Quinn had seen more than one natural child in a foster home manipulate in just that fashion. For that matter, in a more privileged setting, Hannah Blackburn had done it too.

Valerie looked away. "Parents can play. Mine were especially good. Pros, in fact."

Quinn glanced at her friend. Valerie rarely spoke of

her family, and Quinn had learned long ago not to pry.
All she really knew was that Val had come from a large
family in Brooklyn.

"Come on, Quinn," she said. "Forget Tony. You're
the creative director, so direct and create."

"Let's try the lapis and gold," Quinn said, though she
still wasn't sure. She was in danger of losing confidence
in her own vision of the Priceless campaign: a background of white, the snug blue jeans, Hannah's exotic
beauty—and splashes of color, different for each ad.

"Uh-oh, here we go." Valerie's undertone brought
Quinn's head up. "The princess arrives."

Hannah strode toward them, the sun shining brightly
on her jet-black hair, her walk slim-hipped, loose, and
leggy, making all heads along the nearby path turn. "Hi,
sorry I'm late. The limo got tied up on Fifth, and before
that Andrew fell in the bathroom and I had to help him
back to bed."

Quinn's heart was instantly racing. "Is he hurt?"

"He's tougher than he looks," Hannah said. "He
bumped his bad leg, but other than swearing his head
off and looking like thunder, I think he's all right. He
said you'd call him to make sure."

Valerie seemed intent on their conversation as Quinn
murmured, "Did he really?"

Hannah said, "He knows you think he's helpless. So
he acts like a baby."

Quinn gaped at her.

"Well, you do," Valerie said, "and he does."

Hannah flicked her long hair back in a coltish gesture. "My father's really tough when he gets hurt. He
doesn't say a word. Once"—she glanced at Quinn—"at
our house in Zermatt, he sliced his shin open on my new
ski. Know what he did?"

"Sewed himself up with fishing line?" Valerie guessed.

Hannah laughed. "No, he just turned white, splashed alcohol on his leg, then said that with skis like those I was really gonna fly down the mountain."

Quinn wondered whether her cheeks looked pale, wondered how much more punishment Welles's daughter meant to inflict. Trying to sound uninterested, she said, "Male machismo."

"He's not like that." Seemingly unaware that she was doing so, Hannah defended her father. "But he was hurt in Vietnam, got smashed up in a plane crash, and I guess nothing hurts as bad now as it did then, lying there with the bone sticking out all night."

Now Valerie turned pale. "God."

"That was when he was young, though," Hannah added, making Quinn smile faintly for the first time that day.

"Everything's relative. Come on, let's get to work," she said. "We want the best light and this is it. Look at that blue sky this morning."

"My God."

"Val, if you're going to faint, please sit down. The story wasn't that bad." Then she took a quick breath, seeing at the same instant what Valerie had seen. "Good Lord."

With a hand on Hannah's arm, Quinn swung her gently around.

At the slight movement, the sun flashed around Hannah's head, prisms of light striking the air, sending arrows of color everywhere. Quinn could only stare. At Hannah's earlobes dangled exquisite diamonds and pearls above perfect droplets of lustrous jade. The earrings made the lapis and gold chain look like dime-store junk.

"Where did you get these?" Quinn asked.

"I've never seen anything like them," Val said.

The design was certainly unique but Hannah simply shrugged. "They came in the mail."

"In the mail?"

"With a note from someone. It wasn't signed," she added. "It just said, *From a fan.*"

"Ah, stardom." Valerie brushed Hannah's hair back to take another look at the stones, which Quinn could see were set in fine gold. "The first ad hasn't even come out, my pretty."

"Maybe whoever it was saw my pictures from *Elle* last season."

Unconvinced, Quinn fingered the jade. In the sun, warmed by Hannah's skin, it felt smooth as water running over marble, but it raised the hairs on Quinn's neck.

She'd never seen the earrings before, yet they stirred something in her: She had the uneasy feeling that she knew exactly what they were, even though Hannah didn't seem to recognize them.

Hannah tossed her head, throwing off Quinn's touch. "You can't make me send them back. There wasn't a return address. Besides, they're only costume jewelry."

"I don't think so," Quinn murmured.

"What else could they be?"

"The answer to our prayers," Valerie said, leaning closer for a better look at the earrings. "Priceless will love this."

Hannah grinned slowly. "You mean, use them for the shoot? Oh, wow!"

"The color is—"

"Perfect," Quinn agreed, "but we're not using them." At Hannah's instantly mutinous look, she said, "We're talking antique settings here, twenty-four-carat gold, and, if I'm not mistaken, some pretty impressive, beautifully matched natural pearls, not to mention the jade itself. I'd bet my job at Tyler and Devlin that the earrings are real and worth a lot of money. We can't just—"

Hannah's lower lip jutted out. "You wanted the right

prop for the ad. This is it. Valerie says so too. So will Tony."

"They may be right, but we can't use them until we trace where they came from—and from whom—and, if necessary, get permission."

"We use them," Hannah said, "or I take the day off." Quinn opened her mouth but didn't get to speak. "I won't work! Do you hear me? And if I don't work, nobody does. I'm not taking the earrings off! They're mine now, and—"

Quinn had her fair share of empathy for Hannah. She'd betrayed the girl with Welles and, because she understood both Hannah's pain and the adjustments she was undergoing in New York, she'd given her as much space as possible. When it came to work, Quinn had to be less flexible.

"You'll work if I say you will."

"You can't make me!"

Hannah started walking toward Tony, who was waving madly in her direction.

"Let's go!" he shouted. "You're late, and I've got sparkle on the water."

"Besides, you're probably wrong and the gold will turn green tomorrow," she called back over her shoulder. "So no sweat."

"Fine," Quinn said through gritted teeth. She was already striding toward her director. "We'll work."

Val followed her. "Why do I feel I missed something?"

Quinn stepped between Hannah and Tony. "We're going to try two versions of this ad today. The lapis and gold chain first"—she looked evenly at Hannah—"then the jade earrings. Go find your mark, Miss Blackburn, and let's shoot some film." As soon as Hannah left them, she drew Tony aside. "I'll need close-ups of the earrings. Fine detail. As soon as you have prints, I want them."

When Tony returned to his cameras, Valerie grinned. "Priceless. But I've got a feeling, and your horoscope today said—"

"Don't tell me." But feeling closer again to Valerie, Quinn forced a smile. She had a feeling too—about the jade. When the prints were ready, she'd find out whether her hunch was right.

When the doorbell rang that evening, Andrew considered ignoring it. Quinn was working late and Hannah also had a key, so he bent over the drawing board again, slashing another line of magenta across his pad, his heart pounding. He could guess who was leaning on the bell, and—dammit, his hand and eye never seemed to coordinate. The line had veered off again.

Throwing down his brush, he shuffled into the hallway. Maybe he'd send her home this time. He didn't need her constant prodding or his own disturbing reaction to her.

Opening the door, he smelled wine and seafood.

"Filet of sole Florentine," Valerie said.

He leaned against the doorframe. "Did Quinn send you?"

"No," she admitted, "but I knew she'd be working late. The shoot went great today and—"

"Lotte made veal tonight."

She stepped inside, brushing against him, sending his heart into a spin he still wasn't used to. "Did you eat it like a good boy?"

"No."

She grinned. "You waited for me."

Desire streaked through him, as much of a surprise as it had been the first time, when he'd sucked chocolate frosting from her finger while Quinn was in Geneva. Andrew shut the door, closing them into the narrow foyer under a soft spray of light from the beveled glass fixture overhead.

"Yes," he murmured, "I think I did."

Her mouth opened, but before she could say anything, Andrew leaned near to kiss her. Soft, warm, loose. He felt the sensations like a roller-coaster ride from his head to his loins. Finished with the first kiss, he went back for more.

When he finally lifted his head, he was breathing as if he'd run a marathon on his bad leg. Valerie's eyes looked glazed and liquid, and he noted that the right one—the lazy one—was drifting.

Again she opened her mouth to speak, but he closed it with an index finger across her kiss-warmed lips. "Let's eat first," he said, "then I'll show you what I've been working on. And then. . . ."

He trailed off. He wouldn't let it happen again, he promised himself. . . .

Several hours later Quinn still wasn't home, neither was Hannah, and he and Valerie were closed in his den, Andrew cursing himself for locking the door as if he had in mind something more than sketching. The air conditioner hummed but he was sweating.

Valerie waved an airy hand sporting thin silver rings over his sketch pad. "You've been painting scenery for weeks. Why not people? Faces? Animals? Life?"

"I'm not ready for forms."

"Bullshit."

Andrew gave her a look. "Your language needs work, though you've improved tremendously otherwise since I made you aware of what goes with what." He'd learned she wasn't truly color blind. In her work Valerie combined colors masterfully, or played one against another like a skillful politician; but in her own dress, she put together outlandish costumes and colors. The paradox made him smile—until he remembered her crazy upbringing. Maybe she'd needed to show the world she existed; to flip the voters the bird. But he didn't welcome such insights. His gaze swept from the ice-blue gauze shirt that defined her full breasts to the trim length of matching slacks to the simple dark flats she wore. "You even seem to have lost a few pounds."

"You should know."

His eyes met hers again. She was actually smiling, making him remember how her bare skin felt, as sleek as Quinn's. "That was a mistake," he said.

"Which time?" Valerie waited but he didn't answer. "The first time, when you all but dragged me off to the spare room while Quinn was still in Geneva, or the night after that, or three days ago?"

He turned his attention to the drawing pad and his nighttime view of Manhattan. "All of them," he said, then scowled at the sketch. "You push your way into my life, into this apartment while my wife is gone, into my work"—he jabbed a finger at the still-wet watercolors—"and tell me how wonderful I am with *this,* how wonderful in bed—"

"You are."

"You're a desperate woman, Valerie. I'm only half a man and not even half an artist, and I goddamn never will be anything but parts."

She reached for the drawing but he had it first. "You're a coward, Andrew. It's easier for you to give up than to keep trying."

"I *have* tried!" He held up the picture. "You're right about one thing. This is no damn better than the first sketch I did weeks ago when you pushed those stupid pencils at me." His blood pounded in his ears. "I don't see things the same way with one good eye. I can't draw with my left hand."

"Then train it."

"Give it up, Val."

She gave him a jaundiced look. "If I'd given up just once in my life, I'd still be sweating it out in Brooklyn, taking care of three brothers and a sister, because my mother spent all her days at the track losing the little money my father brought home. Sometimes I wonder about you, Andrew. You must have grown up in luxury, never having to do a thing for yourself."

He flushed. "I was hardly Jay Barron," he said, "but my parents were reasonably comfortable. My father was a dentist, my mother a nurse."

He'd piqued her interest in something other than his drawing. "What were they like?"

Andrew shrugged. "He could be heavy-handed. She always smoothed things over. I was their only child."

"So they let you get away with murder."

"Your interpretation," he said.

"I'll bet your mother still picks up your socks when you visit them."

"I didn't lack for anything," he said.

"You never had to struggle." Her look told him he was an appealing but spoiled child, like Hannah Blackburn. "I struggled plenty," Valerie said, "and I'm not a quitter, Andrew. If you want to take the easy out—"

He grasped the sketch in both hands, struggling to hold it with his bad one. "Giving up isn't easy, don't you understand? But it's better than knocking my head against a wall every day when I know what I do here will never be of publishable quality."

"Really?" Valerie smiled. "Quinn thinks I'm a little nutty for believing in horoscopes. Does she have any idea that you can see into the future?"

"Thanks to her, I don't have a future." The paper trembled in his hands, and he couldn't bear to look at it any longer. With quick jerks of his fingers he tore it into pieces, letting them sail through the air—over the drawing board, onto the carpet, across the tips of Valerie's shoes.

"Feel better?" she asked in the heavy silence.

"No." He felt ashamed of his outburst, as if he'd confirmed her opinion of him, then figured in the next breath that he might as well go all the way, leave no doubts in her mind. "But in the next few minutes I might," he said, and before she could react he took her shoulders, her mouth, and pushed her against the slanted drawing board, pressing her body flat with his. He'd made mistakes before, with Quinn too, so he couldn't see the harm in one more.

Valerie's moan only drew him closer, like the soft swell of her breast beneath his palm. Lush and giving, she was a woman to sink into, and in seconds more he did, the incline angle of the drawing board allowing him to push deep. He'd been hard for hours.

Valerie whispered in his ear. "If three times is a charm, then—"

"Four's eternal damnation."

"Not the way we fit together." Turning her head, she sought his mouth again. "Paradise," she told him and sent him soaring.

Welles rarely admitted, even to himself, that he hated flying. In the waiting area by his gate at Cointrin, he kept glancing at the departure monitor, wishing his flight would be canceled. Already sweating in his custom shirt and new navy suit, he tugged again at his tie.

"Stop fidgeting," Mai said, laying a hand over his. "You'll be in Paris by noon."

"You didn't have to see me off." He traveled on business all the time. Suddenly, with the exception of one brief trip of her own, Mai was sticking to him like Velcro now that Hannah was in New York.

"I have a meeting at the Foundation this morning anyway. I was happy to come with you." Her smile was soft. "You're usually gone when I get up. It was nice having breakfast together again."

"I enjoyed it too," he said, almost meaning it. Hannah had left a big hole in his life; despite his resolve, so had Quinn.

"Why don't we spend the weekend together when you get back?" Mai asked, moving closer. "It's been weeks since we made love. I miss you. Just as you miss Hannah."

"That's entirely different."

"Of course," she said, "but still . . . or is it Hannah who really makes you feel lonely?"

Welles felt his pulse flutter.

"Hannah wouldn't let you see her off here. She wouldn't say why not. I keep wondering what might have happened to tear the bond between you."

He glanced at the monitor again. The flight was still listed as being on time. "She's a teenager. I told you."

"And perceptive."

"Mai, for Christ's sake—"

"We have not made love since Hannah left the house to stay with your Miss Tyler-Devlin. The first night she came to dinner with us, Hannah bubbled over with excitement." She paused. "Yet when I put her on the plane to New York, she had tears in her eyes and she was not speaking to the father she adores."

The gate attendant announced boarding for his flight and Welles stood, his hand white-knuckled on his briefcase. "We'll talk about this when I get back. I'll give your regards to Uncle Tran."

Mai rose with him, her fingers clutching at his sleeve.

"Don't be angry. I can't help wondering what happened while I was gone, after our quarrel about Hannah and Qu—"

"Nothing happened. They're calling my row. I have to go."

Her fingers only tightened. "I've loved you since the first moment I saw you, lying unconscious on a straw mat in a jungle hut, your leg broken—"

"That was almost twenty years ago. Stop reminding me of it." As he started walking, his leg began to ache. Thanks to Mai, he could hear the whine of jet engines long ago, the pop of antiaircraft fire, the shriek as the plane went down into the tangle of earth and trees. He could feel the pain again.

"I saved you, Welles. I loved you then and I still love you. I want to know now, not two weeks from now, whether you and that woman—"

"You're being ridiculous."

People were staring, and his natural caution made him ease her away from the crowd into a nearby ell where they might have some privacy. He held himself rigid, feeling the knot of the tie at his Adam's apple, the warmth in his armpits. Oh, Quinn, he thought. "I don't know how to reassure you—"

"Tell me there is nothing between you and Quinn Tyler-Devlin."

He heard the final boarding call but only shook his head. How could he say that? After Quinn's rejection, how could he not?

Mai's eyes filled. She ran her hands over his lapels, up and down, the tears falling. He'd never dreamed he could hurt her so deeply. "I've known about her for a long while, Welles. You needn't pretend."

"Known about her?" How could she? Until July, Quinn had been nothing more to him than a photograph, a fantasy, a few anecdotes told by a drunken Jay Barron. Until the George V.

"All those years ago when you were delirious with fever," Mai said, "I heard you call her name. I didn't know then who Quinn was. But I know now—and so, I think, does Hannah."

He was going to miss his flight. And in that moment he suddenly wanted to be on the plane. Whether it made the trip to Paris or crashed.

Welles cupped her face in his hands and bent low to kiss her mouth. "We'll talk when I get back," he said, and could have cried himself.

She tasted of café au lait and smelled of gardenias, when he still wanted white wine and roses.

He would speak to Tran again, Welles promised himself. He didn't want to hurt Mai, but there must be some sane solution. In the two weeks he'd be gone, first to Paris and then on for discussions with the South Cileanese government, he'd figure a way out.

Two weeks later, when Welles walked into his office at the Banque Internationale, he saw there would be no escape. Tran had even warned him. On his desk lay the Priceless photographs from Quinn that had come while he was gone.

Pictures of his beautiful Hannah. Wearing the Tears of Jade.

16

Quinn set the jade close-ups to one side and frowned at the longer shot that would make any client turn cartwheels. It didn't get better than this: Hannah Blackburn's global beauty with those jade-and-pearl-and-diamond earrings that said Priceless. Quinn had been in the business for fifteen years, had had her share of successes and a few failures, and, like Frank Murray, she knew a Big Idea when she saw one. Too bad she might never be able to use it.

She was wondering why, in the two weeks since sending Welles the pictures, she hadn't heard from him, when her intercom buzzed. Had she been wrong about the jade?

"What is it, Daisy?"

She heard a slight commotion in the background, then her secretary's protest came clearly through the door as it swung open and Mai Blackburn breezed into the office on a drift of scent, redolent of gardenias.

"Ms. Tyler-Devlin." Mai crossed the room, her black hair sleekly coiled into a knot at the nape of her neck, wearing a white linen double-breasted jacket with a short skirt that showed her slim legs to advantage.

Unable to stop herself, Quinn looked beyond Mai and her heart pounded. With Daisy poking her head in behind him, Welles stood in the doorway, his dark hair ruffled from the stiff breeze that had been blowing off the East River when Quinn arrived at work, his blue eyes shadowed behind his tortoiseshell glasses. He looked as harried as her secretary, and her heart, despite all her harsh words by telephone, went out to him.

"I tried to tell them—" Daisy began.

"Thank you. It's all right." Rising from her chair, Quinn dismissed her secretary but stayed behind her desk.

It was Welles who stepped forward, thrusting the glossy close-ups she'd sent him, that she'd been looking at herself only moments before, into her hands. Quinn felt a flash of dread. She still had to admire the sparkle of diamonds, the luster of pearls, the smooth, milky green—

"The Tears of Jade," Welles murmured. "Where did you find them?"

"I didn't. We'd been casting about, looking for the right prop for the product, something to showcase Hannah. . . ."

"And they just happened to turn up?"

At the sarcasm in his tone, Quinn stiffened her spine. "Hannah came to work one morning wearing them."

"Right," Welles murmured. "And of course you recognized them."

"I'd never seen them before. All I knew was their basic composition and that the jade was teardrop-shaped. That's all. And that much I heard from you. Why do you think I sent you these pictures?" Quinn asked. "I wanted to know exactly what they were, who owned them, and if we needed permission before we used them."

"You've already used them."

She shook her head. "Your daughter threw a temper tantrum worthy of a two-year-old, and it seemed the

only way to get any peace was to photograph her wearing the earrings. So I asked Tony—my director—to take
some close-ups and I sent them to you on a hunch."

"What about the ad itself?"

"The proofs have just been approved." When she saw
his features tighten, Quinn hurried on. "In her first ad,
Hannah will be wearing a lapis and gold chain with gold
hoops in her ears. I must say," she murmured, "it's
taken you long enough to respond—and with such
urgency—to the package I sent."

"I was out of town."

"Really."

Mai's smooth brow furrowed slightly. "The earrings
and its matching necklace have been missing for twenty
years. Now, all at once, they are a photographer's prop,
as you say, for a commercial."

Quinn came around her desk. "It's not as if we
picked them up in a local pawn shop or swiped them off
the jewelry counter at Bloomingdale's."

Welles met her gaze for the first time, sending an
unwanted electric charge through her. "For God's sake,
the earrings aren't exactly priceless—to make a bad pun—
but they are valuable. Having been handed down in my
wife's family for centuries, perhaps they're of more emotional than monetary value, but they're still worth thou-
sands with the necklace. Where did Hannah get them?"

"She said a fan sent them to her."

"A fan? Oh, come on!"

"Hannah showed me the mailer. It came from London via a package service and we traced it back to their
drop-off office, where no one remembers the person
who sent the package and paid for it." Quinn took a
breath. "The name and address they have seem to be
false. That didn't bother me," she added, "until just now.
Fan mail is often anonymous. But because I didn't hear

from you right away, I'd almost decided I was wrong about the jewelry. Hannah didn't seem to recognize it."

"We've never told her about the jade." Welles thrust a hand through his hair. "I entrusted my child to your care. Against my wife's better judgment, I trusted you not to let Hannah come to any harm."

"I haven't. I—"

"Then I go to Paris and the Middle East on business for two weeks, only to get back to my office and find this"—he tapped a finger against the ad close-up in Quinn's hand, narrowly missing contact with her—"*this*, waiting for me. What the hell kind of game are you playing?"

"I'm not playing games. What are you so frightened of? Hannah is perfectly safe and well."

Quinn noted that Welles was pale under his tan; Mai had stepped back so that Quinn and Welles seemed to be facing off for a fight. Zermatt had never seemed farther away.

"How safe do you think she is with some kook out there, sending her messages through the mail? What's next, Quinn?"

"I don't know! What message? What are you implying?"

Mai stepped between them.

"Perhaps the earrings are fake," she said, touching Welles's arm, "a near thing that needn't concern us. An astonishing facsimile and nothing more."

"Who would want to copy a family keepsake?" Welles asked.

"Just so. In which case perhaps Ms. Tyler-Devlin is correct and we have overreacted. Perhaps there is a simple explanation." She looked at Quinn. "My husband has been suffering some strain lately in his work." Her hand moved slowly along his arm as if to comfort. "He is always inclined to protect Hannah, even when she doesn't need protecting."

Welles jerked his arm away. "You thought the jade was real enough when I first showed you the pictures. You thought so on the plane from Geneva. Why change your mind now?"

"I am merely weighing alternatives, which I must urge you to do also."

"Christ," Welles said, "that inscrutable mind of yours." He walked to the window and inspected Quinn's view of St. Patrick's Cathedral. He spun around, nailing her with his piercing blue gaze. "We'll need to have the jade appraised." He leveled a finger at Quinn. "If it is authentic, then we'll call our respective lawyers, because Priceless Sportswear's need to make a buck doesn't concern me in the least. My daughter's safety does."

Quinn didn't trust herself to speak. If the jade was real and Welles felt Hannah was in some danger because of it, she'd done the right thing. Yet to Quinn, Welles sounded paranoid. Even Mai seemed to think so. This was her last chance, Quinn thought, to prove herself with the Priceless ad campaign. Damned if she'd declare bankruptcy to indulge Welles.

"That package had nothing to do with Priceless. Hannah's first ad—without the jade—hasn't been released yet."

"Nor will it be."

Then Quinn turned and wasn't sure she could trust her own eyesight. Welles had missed the look but she hadn't. Mai Blackburn was smiling, her black eyes filled with triumph.

In the cab going uptown, Welles seethed, and not only because he disliked riding in New York taxis as much as he hated flying. Sharing the rear seat with Mai, he kept his face turned to the window and said nothing as he tried to avoid reacting to Quinn's presence. She sat in front beside the driver; he wondered why. To give him and Mai some privacy? Or to stay away from him herself?

Hell, after he'd blasted her in her office, he couldn't blame her. Welles realized that half his anger was fear for Hannah; the rest, anger at Mai. Why had she turned ambivalent just when he needed her?

He stared at the back of Quinn's head. Welles had only seen the Tears of Jade on one occasion himself, and he hadn't been at his best. Feverish, his leg throbbing with infection, he couldn't fully appreciate the gleaming pearls, the winking diamonds, or the smooth, celadon-hued jade. Within the hour the jewelry had been gone, turned by some sleight-of-hand of Mai's treacherous brother into a handful of river pebbles. So who now owned the Tears of Jade—and had sent the earrings to Hannah, a gift from "a fan?"

His heart beat faster. In Paris he'd thought Tran was up to his old tricks, nothing more, when he said, "You are foolish to stir up the leaves in the bottom of the teacup again."

"So you keep telling me. But Mai and I have little future, Tran. Her love is too possessive; it isn't love at all. She's never had reason to mistrust me."

"And now?"

Welles kept his gaze steady. "She still has no reason. I met a woman but it hasn't worked out. That's not the point. I've decided it isn't fair to stay with Mai when I . . . don't love her."

"Love becomes more habit than desire."

Welles shrugged.

"You are not old enough to believe that, I see." Tran closed his eyes briefly. "A divorce would shatter my beloved niece, and as for your own advancement—"

"You can take the bank and shove it. Give my job or the promotion to Thornton."

"And what of Hannah?"

His blood chilled.

Tran smiled faintly. "A lovely child, though you have permitted her to become too western in Mai's view also. No," he murmured. "I am afraid it is not in your best interest—or in Hannah's—to seek a divorce."

Welles had stood, throwing his napkin down on the table of the small Left Bank restaurant. He'd refused to meet Tran at the George V. "That's blackmail."

"Perhaps."

"Christ, Tran."

"You must reconsider your decision, J. Welles Blackburn." Deliberately he used the whole name—the invention that had given Welles a life, ensured his privacy. "I do not wish to alarm you, but inquiries have been made."

Welles sank down in his chair again. "From whom? Where?"

"It is not possible to say. I can tell you only that I believe Hannah is most vulnerable. And, through her public exposure with the American blue jeans people, a connection might be made to you."

"Jesus." After all those years, he thought. He'd almost stopped expecting the past to boil up again, except with Quinn.

"Go home," Tran had said, "and guard your back."

Now, as the cab hurtled up Fifth Avenue, Welles stared at the back of Quinn's coppery head and wanted to groan. He'd come home from Paris to find the pictures of Hannah—for all the world to see, he'd thought—wearing the Tears of Jade.

A warning? he wondered. From whom?

And why?

If only he'd asked his secretary to open the package from Quinn in his absence. But Quinn had marked it personal and he'd reasoned that she'd rethought their relationship, that it had something to do with them, not Hannah. If Hannah's well-being was involved, he'd been certain, Quinn would have come after him.

Nearing her apartment, he shifted on the hard taxi-cab seat. Tran was right, blast him. On some level he had never trusted Welles, but he loved Mai with all his heart and Hannah too. If the jade proved real, Welles had to take his family home, to ground if need be. Still, his palm itched and he wanted to lean forward, to stroke that copper-colored hair, bright as fire in the sun.

But was Quinn Tyler the best thing that had ever happened to him—or his punishment for Jay Barron's murder? Since the moment they'd met, the past had been welling up in him like blood from a wound. It just might kill him.

"I'll die if I can't stay here!" Hannah whirled away from Quinn's outstretched hand. Standing closest to her, Quinn meant to restrain the girl, but Hannah, jade earrings swinging, ran from the living room into the hall. "I came to New York to be the Priceless spokesperson and I will be, even if I have to disown my parents!"

"Hannah." Welles's tone was one of command.

"The earrings are mine and nobody else's, and if Priceless wants me to wear them, I will."

"Hannah!"

Quinn took a step. "Welles, don't. She's upset."

"She is badly spoiled," Mai said and followed her daughter into the hall. "I'll speak to her. She's had a shock."

"Not as much as I have," Welles muttered. When they were alone, he turned to Quinn. "Christ, she won't even talk to me."

"Do you blame her?"

"Yes," he said. "I held Hannah in one hand when she

was born, held her even before Mai did. I've loved her all her life and she knows it. I've tried a dozen times to explain about Zermatt, but she won't listen."

"You can't expect her to understand, Welles."

"Why not?"

Quinn found the remark typically masculine. She said unhappily, "Because I'm old enough to be her mother, and I don't understand Zermatt myself."

He lowered his voice. "If we were really alone right now, I'd make you understand. In fact—"

In the narrow hallway, his eyes dark with need and obvious frustration, he reached for her.

Quinn held out a hand to stop him. "Andrew isn't twenty feet down that hall in his den, pretending to be working but probably hearing everything that goes on. And have you forgotten? You were firmly convinced not an hour ago that I was some sort of jewel thief or con artist!"

"For Christ's sake, don't exaggerate."

"Don't make threats to me, especially about sex." She wasn't sure she wouldn't throw herself into his arms.

"I didn't mean sex." Welles hung his head. "Quinn, hell, I'm sorry. This is your home, your marriage, and the three of us and our problems are intruding."

"Hannah's welfare is important to me too," she said, realizing that despite the antagonism between them, she cared deeply for Welles's daughter, saw in Hannah the confused young woman she had been herself—and possibly, though older, still was.

"We'll be out of your way as soon as Mai calms Hannah down," he said, just as the two appeared, Hannah striding toward them with tear streaks on her face, Mai reaching out to grasp her daughter's elbow.

"Let me go, Mother. I need to show him too." Hannah held out the mailer in which she'd received the jade earrings. "See? I'm not lying."

"No one said you were." She showed Welles the note too and he said, "*From a fan.* That doesn't tell us much."

Mai smiled. "Of course it doesn't. This is not the issue. The appraiser will be able to tell us whether the earrings are real—or simply paste—which is what does matter."

"You're awfully calm about this all of a sudden," Welles said. "Do you think they're paste and someone's idea of a joke?"

Her eyelashes fluttered. "No. I think they're real."

"Then it's nothing to smile about."

Mai's lips made a flat line, but her eyes held amusement. This time, Welles could see it too.

The appraiser couldn't see them until the next afternoon, and then at his office on 46th Street in the heart of the diamond district. Afterward, Quinn refused to let Welles drive her home.

"It's not that far," she said, troubled by the outcome of the appraisal, by the grim look on his face, "and I doubt if we have anything to say to each other."

But Welles insisted, which under other circumstances might have made her smile. He could be as persistent as Doug Lloyd accused her of being, and Quinn was forced to see that the trait could be as irritating as Mai Blackburn's contradictory behavior.

"We need to talk," he said, steering Quinn toward his rental car, "and I'm headed for your place anyway to see Hannah. Whether she wants to talk to me or not."

He dropped Mai first at their hotel, and to Quinn's greater surprise Mai didn't protest. Quinn supposed that, after the past twenty-four hours, nothing about Mai Blackburn should surprise her. She settled into the Lincoln Town Car's plush passenger seat and tried not to let her nerves overwhelm her.

"I wish you'd reconsider," she said, as Welles pulled into the midafternoon traffic heading up Fifth Avenue outside the Sherry-Netherland Hotel, where the Blackburns were staying. She wondered whether Mai was already upstairs in their suite, looking down on the car and her husband with another woman. "Even if the jade is real, as the man said, and part of Mai's inheritance, you have no evidence that anyone wants to hurt Hannah."

"Then why send her the Tears of Jade? Can you answer me that?" He glanced over at her, his eyes unreadable behind mirrored sunglasses. "It was a message for me, Quinn."

"What kind of message? What are you hiding?"

"You've asked me that before," he said.

Quinn looked down at the padded leather armrest between them. She didn't want to watch the heavy traffic. Since the accident with Andrew, she hadn't driven, and she never relaxed in a car with anyone else. Yet on the drive to Zermatt and now, she had to admit that Welles was a skillful driver.

A hesitant glance at his hands on the wheel made sensation spiral low in her stomach, as she remembered those hands on her body in Zermatt.

She studied his profile, the strength in it, and the surprisingly sensual shape of his mouth; she remembered his kiss.

". . . not proud of that," Welles was saying as he threaded the powerful car between a bus and a cab with all the skill of a tailor finding the eye of a needle, "but I told you, I've done things I'd rather not think about."

"Killed two men, you mean." Quinn looked down at the taut pull of his trouser material against his thighs. He wore a pin-striped suit with the kind of sexy, understated elegance that a clotheshorse like Frank Murray could only envy. "If they're both dead," she went on, shifting in her seat, "who could want to harm you—or Hannah—now?"

"I don't know. That's what scares me."

"Enough to take Hannah back to Geneva? I didn't think you were a coward, Welles."

His hands tightened on the wheel. "Sure, I'm a coward. I'm afraid of convincing Hannah that she has to come home."

"And Priceless?" Quinn asked. "How will you convince them?"

"I won't. My attorney will."

"You have nothing to support cancellation of that contract, and you know it."

"Do you ever think about anything but your job—except Jay Barron, that is?"

"Yes, I think about something else." Quinn turned sideways to face him, frustrated that she couldn't see his eyes. "I think about Hannah, but I seriously doubt your daughter is in any real danger. And let's forget me. What about Mai? She doesn't seem terribly unhappy about the course of events since she saw that picture of Hannah wearing the Tears of Jade. She came into my office yesterday like a prizefighter entering the ring for a sure win, and she went out smiling. Victorious. She pitted us against each other."

"That's why I left her at the hotel while I take you home"—he gave her a dark look—"and talk to Hannah."

"Hannah's staying in my apartment," Quinn said. "Be fair, Welles. Be honest. You know I wouldn't let anyone or anything harm her."

"This isn't a judgment of your capabilities."

"What is it, then?" She paused, her throat constricting. "A way to end things after Zermatt?"

His jaw tightened. "I thought you already had."

Quinn didn't answer. She lapsed into silence, her

hands clenched. He had taken her heart, and if he got his way about Hannah he'd quite probably take Quinn's career as well, and yet she absorbed his presence as if he were the only breath of air that might keep her alive.

She cared more for him, for his child—a child she might easily love, given the chance—than she did about Priceless. The knowledge came as a surprise. He was right. It had been a long while since Quinn had cared about anything more than her work. She hadn't let herself.

Welles sighed. "Sorry. I'm on a short fuse today." He swung the car around the corner and past Quinn's apartment building. "I *am* a coward, and not only where Hannah's concerned. And a liar. And, in my time, a murderer. What kind of honor is there in any of that? You were sensible to send me packing while you had the chance, smart enough not to want me in your life."

The admission stunned her. Quinn pointed at the parking garage entrance and Welles spun the wheel. A whoosh of air, the sound of screeching tires on another level, and they were inside, past the guard booth, into a sharp right turn and up the ramp, then down a long aisle dotted with parked cars on either side. Again, she gestured at her space.

Quinn didn't own a car, but she and Andrew reserved the space anyway, and Quinn had a loose arrangement with a wealthy neighbor who used it whenever he was in town, staying at his pied-à-terre to dabble in antiques. He was now spending a month in Maine at his vacation home.

Welles braked the Lincoln, cutting the engine.

At the end of the row on the second level, Quinn's space occupied a dark, cool corner. At four o'clock no one was around; the rush home hadn't yet started. She became suddenly aware that she and Welles were really alone together for the first time since Zermatt; aware that, as much as she'd been fighting for the Priceless account and Hannah's future, she'd also been fighting herself about him.

Welles was the strongest man she'd ever known, except for Doug Lloyd. He was even stronger than she remembered Jay. It touched her that, at the most unlikely moments, his self-confidence deserted him.

"I do want you," Quinn murmured, looking at her lap.

"Christ." Welles was staring at his hands.

"I don't want to but I do."

Before she finished speaking, he slammed the arm-rest up, moved toward the center of the seat, and hauled Quinn across his body. When his mouth came down on hers, hard, she didn't even think of protest. In the same instant their mouths met, she flowed into his arms, arching closer to the hard contact with his chest, the quick throb of his heartbeat against hers.

Quinn gave a low moan and stopped thinking about Priceless, about anything. Her mind emptied, and her soul filled with Welles and only Welles. She opened her heart to him, and then her mouth.

His tongue met hers as his hand slipped into the opening of the surplice-wrapped bodice on Quinn's dress. "God, I love these things," he said on a groan, and she half smiled against his lips, wondering whether he meant the dress or the soft overflow from the lace bra he pushed lower, then lower still, until he held her bare breast in his hand. "Quinn—"

"I can't stop thinking about you."

"I can't get you out of my mind, my gut." His thumb grazed her nipple, raising it into a tight, hard button. As sensation raced through her, Welles tore off his sun-glasses and tossed them on the dashboard. He glanced around. "This is as private as we're going to get," he said and then, "What can we do?"

"This." She'd hate herself later, but in the next instant Quinn turned, throwing a leg over him, straddling him. Her dress rode up, revealing black garters and stockinged thighs, and Welles made a tortured sound.

He lowered a hand to her thigh, the garter, toying with it. "Leave 'em on." He kept his hand there, teasing, stroking, while Quinn cradled his head to her breast. Blindly, Welles pushed the dress opening wide and took her in his mouth, kissing, suckling. His moist, shaken breath whispered over her skin and Quinn arched higher, bowing her back, shielding him with her body.

"I can't forget Zermatt," he whispered brokenly. "It only makes things worse, makes me want you more. I keep remembering what it was like: your mouth"—he lifted his head to kiss her—"your hands"—he turned enough to kiss her fingers at his shoulder—"your breasts"—and he went back to them, a hand cupping the left, his lips upon the right one.

"I kept having these dreams." Quinn's breath came rapidly. "It was like everything all over again."

His mouth feathered over her, his tongue soothing where he nipped. "I keep thinking what it was like to see you"—his kiss puckered her nipple into a harder point—"naked . . . to feel you come apart in my hands . . . what it was like to get inside you. . . ."

His hand skimmed lower, making her moan at the first light touch between her legs.

"Let me, Quinn."

"Now," she urged him.

Groaning, he pushed her skirts higher around her hips, his fingers hot and digging deep into her bared flesh as she dropped a hand between them to work his zipper down. "Hurry," he said.

Then, with Quinn over him, her thighs bracketing his

lean hips, she took him in. One long sleek stroke and they were joined. Welles made a sound, half grunt, half sigh, dropping his head back against the seat. Quinn followed, pressing more tightly to him, sheathing him deeper, as her mouth sought his.

Lifting to her, Welles began a slow, deep rhythm that soon intensified, then quickened until they were both gasping. "This is gonna be fast," he said, and with the words Quinn felt him tense, felt his mouth harden in a final kiss before he came in a rush that sent Quinn spiraling into her own climax.

For long moments after, she held him close, Welles's mouth open but unmoving on the hollow of her throat while his breathing slowed. "I didn't use anything," he said.

"There wasn't time." She smiled faintly against his dark, silky hair and hugged him tighter, hoping—against all intelligent thought and conscience—that he'd just given her his child. "It should be all right, though."

"I'm not carrying anything . . . diseases, I mean."

"Neither am I." But the words seemed to bring reality into the car again and Quinn drew back, trying not to notice the steamed-up windows. At least no one could have seen them. She pulled her clothes together, dragged a hand through her hair and then through his.

"We'd better go upstairs," he said, tracing a light line with both hands over her forehead, over each cheek, his fingers meeting at her lips. He bent to kiss her, as soft as a breeze, then got out of the car.

In the elevator neither of them spoke. Quinn focused on the floor numbers flashing one by one, though she could feel Welles's eyes on her all the way to number seventeen. When the car stopped, he punched the HOLD button with one hand so the doors didn't open; with the other he snagged Quinn's wrist and pulled her near.

"I haven't begun to get enough of you," he whispered

and kissed her again, hard, then let her go with a knowing smile that said he knew just how deeply he had
affected her.

Quinn was still shaking so badly when they walked
down the hall to her apartment that Welles had to take
her key.

What had changed? she wondered. Nothing. She still
loved him, and Welles still meant to nullify the Priceless
contract that could keep Quinn in the business she'd
given her life to, a job she not only enjoyed but needed.
Even though she cared too about Hannah, they might as
well be enemies, she thought, instead of guilty lovers.

As the door opened, she looked into Andrew's eyes.
He stood in the foyer, his quizzical expression slowly
turning into a bleak frown. He was looking not at Quinn
but at Welles and, as if some mark were upon them both,
as if their scent filled the air, he seemed to know—as
Mai Blackburn must—that he had been betrayed.

"Is Hannah here?" she asked, stepping away from
Welles and riffling through her mail on the foyer table.

"She's out with Valerie. Shopping."

"Avoiding me," Welles murmured.

"Perhaps she knows something that Quinn hasn't
seen yet," Andrew said, then disappeared into his study.

Quinn headed for the kitchen to fix drinks. She had
just dropped a bottle of soda on the floor and was mop-
ping it up with a sponge when Welles came through the
swinging door.

"Be careful," he said, "you'll cut yourself. Let me
help."

"I can do it."

Her face hidden by her hair, Quinn swept up broken
glass, managing not to nick herself. Every time she
glanced at Welles, she had to look away. His eyes were
dark, still hot.

Finally, he hunkered down in front of her. "Don't shut me out again," he said, but Quinn rose before he could touch her.

"Stop looking at me like that."

"Like what?"

Color washed over her cheeks. "As if you want to do, all over again, what we did in the car."

"I do want to."

So did she. "Andrew sees us looking," she said. "He saw right away when we came in. Things aren't good between us, but I don't want to hurt him, Welles."

"You made that decision," he said, "the day we met."

Late that evening, Quinn threw down her pen and shoved the household bills back into her desk. She couldn't concentrate. She kept remembering the afternoon's lovemaking with Welles and feeling guilty; she kept waiting for Andrew to walk into her office, demanding some explanation.

Next door she could just hear his voice, on the phone with Valerie. She'd called Quinn to say that Hannah wanted to spend the night with her, then had asked to speak to Andrew. Quinn heard him laugh, soft and warm, the way he'd laughed with her when they first knew each other.

She was still frowning long after he disconnected the call and the apartment fell silent again. Then the phone rang a second time, and Quinn jumped as she snatched up the receiver. Welles, wondering if Hannah had finally come home? No, it wasn't. Still, the deep, familiar voice went through her like an old remembered love song, a pang of memory.

"Hello, Quinn."

"Who is this?" she asked, but the caller wouldn't

say. He asked a question of his own and then hung up.

"Whatever happened to Jay Barron?"

The outskirts of Olongapo
The Philippines

Jammed into the Phantom's safety harness, he screamed his head off. "Cochran, come back and get me! Come back, you bastard. Don't leave me here!"

All around he smelled jet fuel, spilling from the tanks, soaking into the jungle leaves, just waiting for a spark. He was a dead man. "Cochran!"

The face appeared above him. Dark, enigmatic, as hard as the city streets, the slum that had spawned him.

The knife raised high, Cochran grinned. One stroke and the competition would be gone, eliminated as if by a Mafia hit squad or, more likely here, a gook patrol.

"You have no tolerance for anyone outside the Social Register," Cochran had said once, chiding him for prejudice. "How do you explain Quinn to your folks, Barron?"

"I don't," he said.

"How do you explain her to yourself, then?"

"She's a good lay."

He'd read parts of her letters aloud, just to make Cochran squirm. Jay knew he had a thing for her. Crazy as hell, falling in love with someone he'd never meet. Cochran frowned and said, "She loves you."

"Yeah," Jay said. "She sure does."

"She thinks you're going to marry her."

He laughed. "She's wrong—but it keeps her nice and sweet."

The knife arced over him and Jay screamed again. He wanted to beg but it was too late. He wanted to say he'd lied, that he felt more for Quinn Tyler than that, though he didn't know how much, but he'd underestimated the kid from Shreveport. The knife flashed—and while he was still praying for a swift death, he was free.

The harness sprang apart, straps falling to either side, and his body was lifted from the jet's pilot seat. He stared into Cochran's smiling face, but in front of him the blue eyes turned dark, the dark hair became sandy-brown, and blood burbled from a gaping wound in his chest.

Not Cochran now. It was years later and he was in another jungle, wearing camouflage clothing, waiting for a drug shipment to fly in. When the plane landed, he and Sandy would open fire and another two-bit heroin dealer would die before he could blink.

The plane touched down, a perfect landing. The cargo door opened—and automatic weapons fire sprayed the stand of trees where he and Sandy lay hidden.

Blood all over his hands, his shirt. Blood all over the partner he'd shared the past ten years with.

"Sandy! Sandy, damn you, don't leave me!"

His heart slamming, he jerked awake in a cold puddle of sweat. Goddammit. He was at Helen's place, not the hospital, and he'd had the dream again, only this time it had been different all around. In the total darkness just before dawn he lay still, listening to his pulse thunder.

He never dreamed, never talked, about Sandy.

Eyes closed, he took a shaken breath. He hadn't moved, not a muscle, but a hand, small and smooth, reached out for his.

"Jay?" she whispered.

As if he were spring-loaded, he sat up, then stood fast enough to fool her that he had no pain. His aching leg felt stiff as he crossed to the window and stared out at the last of the night. Thank God. It would soon be morning. "I had a kinky dream, that's all. Go back to sleep."

He could hear Helen sit up, yawn. "About Cochran?"

"Yeah."

"And what else?"

"Jesus, you pick at a man. Give it a rest, will you?"

"When you do," she said.

He shook his head.

"Does that mean you think I am a nuisance, or that you can't rest from the dream?"

"Both."

She glided to him like a spirit, her body pressed to his back, her small hands meeting at his belly, her palms pressing against his naked skin.

He shivered. "I dreamt that Cochran was about to kill me."

"I thought it was to be the other way around."

"So did I," he murmured, dragging a hand through his hair. He'd discovered a thinning area at the crown the previous morning, just before he saw the photograph in the magazine. As a reminder of how much time had passed and that he was growing older, the bald spot shocked him. So had the picture and the connection it had given him at last.

The girl in the advertisement for Priceless jeans was a perfect blend of both her parents. She had the Vietnamese black hair and dark eyes, but their shape was more West than East and her smile was all Cochran. Could it be?

Jay leaned an arm against the window frame.

Lord, he'd never even imagined that Cochran would not only get away but marry the girl named Mai who had so adored him. Now it seemed they had a child together, a child who was about to become famous, if the appeal he saw on the magazine page was anything to go by. And still, he might have missed it or thought he was mistaken— except that she was wearing the I'll-be-go-to-hell Tears of Jade for which Nguyen, Mai's brother, had given his twisted life.

"Cochran killed my erstwhile partner," he murmured, *half forgetting that Helen was still listening, "and left me for dead. Twice."*

"In the plane and in the hut," she said.

"Yeah." Then his vision dimmed as he remembered the face that had turned from Cochran's into Sandy's. He felt sweat seep from his pores and began to shake. *"Sonofabitch,"* he said.

Helen's arms tightened around him. *"It will be all right."*

"When?" He spun away from her. *"When, Helen? After I kill that bastard for leaving me behind?"* He closed his eyes, seeing the plane on the screen of his lids. He swallowed, feeling sick. The harness had stuck, and with Sandy—*"I didn't mean to,"* he said softly. *"Jesus, I never meant to."*

"What, Jay?"

He shook his head but couldn't seem to clear it. The picture, like the magazine photograph of Cochran's daughter, stayed in his mind. The gunfire in the highlands flashing. The airstrip belonging to the drug lord the agency had wanted to bust—in any way possible. Dead or alive. Sandy, being shot. Sandy, falling. Bleeding.

"I only had one chance," he said. *"He was dying, maybe dead by the time I ran."* He rubbed a hand across his eyes and felt wetness. *"There wasn't any way for both of us to survive. I didn't have any fucking choice."*

"No," she whispered.

"I couldn't have saved him." He heard himself sobbing. *"He was already dead."*

"Yes." Helen moved against him, rocking, soothing.

"I had to leave him behind," he told her.

"You had to. That's better, Jay. That's better now."

She led him back to bed, as if he were a child again in Pacific Heights. His mother, smelling of verbena sachet, her lace negligee sleeve brushing his cheek when she tucked him in at night after a bad dream. "My little hero," she always whispered.

He had wanted to be a hero for her, for his father, for his brother, Charles. He wanted to escape the strictures of the life they wove around him like a snare.

"I left," he said, his tone hoarse. "Just like Cochran."

"Shh." Helen crawled in beside him and held him like a baby in her arms.

His eyelids felt heavy. He had never been more ready for sleep in his life. "I wonder if Cochran had any choices."

"No happy ones," Helen said.

"I wonder if he has nightmares too."

"Then you still think he is alive?"

"I'm sure of it." Jay had spent the day before making calls, his excitement growing with each new connection after he'd seen the magazine ad. Small world, he thought, as he drifted into sleep with the tears still rolling down his face. Full, as Quinn always said, of surprises.

They were both alive, he and Cochran. Both intimate with oriental women, Helen and Mai. Both still somehow a part of Quinn Tyler's life as well. Her voice on the phone had even sounded the same: soft, slightly husky, greatly bewildered. And hopeful.

Maybe it could end, he thought. He would find Cochran and Quinn. And then . . . ?

He held Helen tightly, her cheek nestled in his shoulder. And then maybe, at last, he could go home.

17

Welles entered the coffee shop on the lobby level of Quinn's New York office building without taking off his mirrored sunglasses. He needed the anonymity they provided, the screen of privacy, protection.

He hadn't seen her since the afternoon in the parking garage, and the first sight of her now, two days later, set his blood simmering. She knew he'd spent the intervening time trying to get Hannah out of the Priceless contract, and her expression looked carefully blank. Was she about to trash his ego?

Welles stopped at the rear booth, from which Quinn had a perfect view of the restaurant entrance.

"You wanted to see me," he said.

"Sit down."

Welles slid into the booth alongside her.

"I meant on the other side," she said.

"I like it here."

She looked around then at her own reflection in his glasses. "Where's Mai?"

"At the hotel. Sleeping." He'd be damned if he'd ask

about Andrew. "We were up early, on the phone to Geneva. Afterward, she went back to bed."

He gestured and the waitress brought him a cup of coffee, refilling Quinn's. Quinn waited until they were alone again to speak. "And what does your lawyer say this morning?"

"The same as yesterday." He pulled off the glasses, giving her a glimpse of penetrating, naked blue eyes that couldn't quite focus. "It seems you were right. We have no case."

"Priceless people—Frank Murray included—can write airtight contracts. You shouldn't have wasted your time."

"It reminds me of the Banque Internationale. I'm feeling right at home."

Quinn sloshed hot coffee down the front of her blouse, giving Welles the opportunity to touch her. He dabbed at the stain with his napkin, moistened in her water glass.

"Keep your hands down," he said.

"How can you see what you're doing?"

"I can't. I just close my eyes and grope—from memory. I'm thinking again," he added, his hand warm against the valley of her breasts, his gaze on her mouth, "of saying good morning in the right way, of really getting to you."

Quinn pushed at his chest. "Half my staff will be down here any minute on a coffee break. So will Valerie, who's become close as bunnies in a hutch with Andrew lately. And I have a meeting at ten o'clock." It was nine forty-five.

Welles retreated, draping an arm over the back of the booth. "So what did you want to see me about? If good old Frank has a counter offer, I'm not interested."

"You know there's no offer." Quinn slapped a rolled-up magazine open on the table and sighed. "Lord, I might as well just say it. We have a new problem, and it's a honey."

Welles felt his stomach clutch. "What?"

His gaze dropped to the fashion magazine in front of

him as Quinn tapped a finger and he felt his breath catch. From the full-color page a lithe, jeans-clad Hannah smiled slyly at him, teardrops of jade gleaming in her ears.

"Jesus H. Christ." He stared. "I thought you said—"

"The ad wouldn't come out. I'm sorry."

Welles looked at her. "Are you, Quinn?"

"Believe it or not, yes. Very. And I'm as surprised as you are." Her gaze drifted from his. "My phone started dancing off the desktop at seven this morning. When I came into the office, I had messages waiting, most from overseas." He watched her swallow. "The good news is, only one magazine seems to have printed the wrong ad."

"How the hell did this happen?"

"Frank Murray." Her voice was a breath of sound. "At least that's what I think happened. Frank was in my office when I got the proofs of the ad we shot using the lapis and gold chain and the extra pictures I'd had Tony take of Hannah wearing the jade. That, and the close-ups I sent to you."

"And?"

She glanced up again. "He loved the earrings on her. Raved about them. He said the oriental jewelry with the Amerasian model made exactly the right statement—mysterious, exotic, it was the magic he'd asked for—and the CEO at Priceless would probably fly through his office ceiling with joy when he saw it."

"And then?" Welles prompted.

"He asked me why I hadn't thought of it before. Weeks ago," she said. "Then he kissed me on both cheeks and sailed out of my office."

"With the jade pictures."

"He must have picked up copies," Quinn murmured, "along with the lapis ad. The one we planned to use."

"Goddammit." He looked down at the ad again. "What are you going to do about this? What's Murray going to do?" Then he smiled grimly. "He may just have handed me the gun I need to get Hannah out of that contract and damn quick."

"Welles, I know what you think about me and my work, but I swear I'd never intentionally put Hannah in jeopardy—even possible jeopardy—or expose her at all if it went against your wishes. This was an accident, even on Frank's part, I'm sure. I swear, I didn't know. . . ." She trailed off.

"Some accident." Welles touched her fingers, which were wrapped around her coffee cup. "Your knuckles are white, your hands are cold. What else, Quinn?"

Staring at his hand on hers, she shook her head.

"Tell me."

"I don't know if I can," she whispered, turning her hand to hold his, sending a flash of heat through him. "It's not about Hannah and the ad." She met his gaze and took a deep breath. "I had a telephone call the night before last. I decided you should know about that too."

"What kind of call? Obscene?"

Quinn shook her head. Her eyes were wide, clear green, and the words seemed difficult to say. When she finished, she was looking just past him, over his shoulder, at the opposite wall. Just as well, he thought. He could feel his color fade, feel his skin turn clammy. In that moment he stopped thinking about Hannah's ad. In all his imaginings, even of Quinn's rejection, he'd never expected this.

"You don't seriously think it could have been Jay Barron?"

"It sounded like him."

He looked away from the hope in her eyes. "Quinn, you haven't heard his voice in almost twenty years."

"Voices are distinctive," she insisted. "How many times do you answer the phone without having to ask who's calling? Even if you haven't heard from the person in a long while?"

He didn't answer. He didn't touch her. "I thought we'd put an end to that in Zermatt."

"He called me. I didn't call him."

"Where was he—this person—calling from?"

She hesitated. "I don't know. I've told you exactly what he said: 'Whatever happened to Jay Barron?' He said it and hung up, Welles. That's all I know except that he knew my name and where to find me."

"Did Andrew hear the call?"

"Why?"

"Did he?" Welles pressed.

"A witness? Do you think I'm making this up?" Quinn tried to move from the booth, but Welles trapped her in the very corner that had given her refuge moments before. "I shouldn't have told you," she said, frowning. "I should have known you wouldn't believe me."

Welles leaned close, his voice taut, his heart pounding. "Jesus, can you blame me? How the hell many times do I have to say it? He's dead, Quinn. Our plane went down and Jay didn't make it! He was dust and bones and the goddamn fillings in his teeth a helluva long time ago. That's all." He spaced the words. "He's never coming back. He sure as hell isn't making any telephone calls from God knows where."

"Then why are you sweating?"

Welles wiped his upper lip. "Because I don't know how to make you face facts."

"No good," she said. "Don't tell me again that I married a man I don't love to keep Jay's memory alive. Or that I miss the father I never knew. Or that I've used you and pushed you away because there's no room in my mixed-up life for—"

"All right, dammit." He'd expected a brush-off. Instead, she'd given him the shock of his life. He felt very close to going for broke. "He died in that crash," he said in a hoarse tone. Then, slowly, his eyes lifted to meet hers. "I left him for dead."

He knew, deep in his gut, that she didn't want to surrender even the least bit of her belief in Jay Barron, but her fingers fluttered near his cheekbone before she pushed her hand down into her lap. "What really happened, Welles?"

He could only shake his head.

"It's possible he's alive," she said. "Admit at least that it's possible."

How could he tell her that it wasn't, that he'd sent a knife deep into Jay Barron's flesh, between his ribs? He stared at his hands, as if the blood were still on them. He could barely get the words out. "Quinn, I don't—"

"Yes, you do know."

Welles could hear his own breathing. "Even if he did survive somehow, where could he have gone?"

"And where is he now?"

"You tell me."

Her tone was dry but shaky, an attempt at the sass she used to shield herself. "I didn't have time to trace the call. He could have been in San Francisco—or right here in New York."

The awful thought zipped through his brain. "What about London?"

Quinn stayed with him. "You mean, the Tears of Jade?"

"*If* he's alive, he knows where I am." Who I am, he thought. "Somehow, he knows that Hannah is my daughter. He could have sent her the earrings." He still didn't want to believe it.

"But how would he have found me?"

"Through Doug Lloyd, maybe. Or through Hannah— that damn ad?"

"Wait a minute. That's it!" Quinn tapped an unsteady finger against the open magazine on the table. "While I was waiting for you, I kept pondering the vagaries of distribution, because I knew how upset you'd be when I told you the ad was out. When I reached the office this morning, I was horrified to learn about Hannah's ad, then puzzled because the messages waiting—the same messages that tipped me off to its release—had mostly come in from abroad. When Daisy tossed this magazine, the U.S. edition, on my desk, I did some research." In front of his eyes, she became the consummate professional woman again. "If a certain magazine hits the stands in Manhattan and, say, Geneva on the same day, allowing for the time difference, it usually follows that it will be available around the world within the same twenty-four hours. Yet with Hannah's ad, in addition to its being released in the first place, something went wrong." She paused. "Or very right."

"Meaning?"

"I had that telephone call two nights ago. The first copies of *High Fashion*"—she touched the ad page again—"appeared here in New York this morning. But for some reason nobody understands, they went on sale in parts of Southeast Asia two days ago."

"Holy Christ."

"Jay might have seen the ad and the earrings and with another phone call or two been able to connect me to Hannah."

"If it's Jay, he'd hate me, Quinn. Now he can get to me through her." It was beginning to make perfect, horrible sense. "Where is Hannah right now?"

"At school, of course."

Welles dug in his pocket, pulling out several bills. "I've got to go."

"But he didn't say anything about—"

"Jay didn't always say everything he meant, and he didn't mean every damn thing he told you, Quinn. Let me tell you what I really know about Jay Barron. He comes first, last, and always. If you think for one minute that he wouldn't have bartered your soul if he had to to save himself, you're as naive as you were then, at nineteen."

"You're wrong about him." Quinn pushed out of the booth after him, her eyes blazing. "You're dead wrong. I'll find him myself, and when I do you'll see how wrong you are."

Welles gripped her shoulders. "Can't you understand?" Jay had fought him to the death once, or so he'd thought. "He'd kill me if he could. And consider he was doing the world a favor."

"I'll find him," she repeated and left Welles standing in the crowded coffee shop, staring after her, her last words slicing through him like another slash of his own knife. "You couldn't have done anything terrible enough to make him hate you."

"Maybe he did, darlin'."

Doug Lloyd's tone was comforting, but his words weren't. Quinn tipped back in her desk chair at home that night and frowned when Doug went on.

"And maybe this isn't the first time we've heard from Jay."

She sat up again.

"Some years back," Doug said, "when you and Andrew were first married, I had some strange calls: a man who wanted your new phone but wouldn't give his name. So I wouldn't give him your number. The voice sounded familiar but different somehow . . . more grainy, coarse."

Like the voice she'd heard. "Why didn't you tell me this before?"

"I had no proof. I didn't think your happiness would be well served by opening up old wounds. The calls stopped coming, so I assumed that was the end of it."

"I can't believe you never told me."

"Blackburn may be right, Quinn. People change. Life changes them," he said, "not always for the better. Have you thought about that?"

"I have to find out for myself."

She could hear the faint smile in his tone. "Well, that doesn't make my head spin around. I'd be surprised if you gave up. From what I've heard, Blackburn would too."

They spoke for a few more minutes, about the Priceless ad, agreeing that the damage had been done and all Quinn could do now was to contain it.

"Frank assures me that *High Fashion* was the only leak for the wrong ad."

The conversation turned to Andrew's dissatisfaction with his work, and Quinn's mind wandered. Maybe tonight the phone would ring again and she'd know.

". . . think about that too," Doug was saying.

"I'm sorry. I didn't hear."

His tone was patient. "I just invited you to the ranch for Thanksgiving. I'll put fresh sheets on your bed if you promise to roast the turkey—and fix me some home-made cranberries with oranges in 'em."

"Doug, I don't know. . . ."

"Been a long time since you were home yourself." His voice lowered. "If Andrew doesn't want to come along, bring Blackburn. Among us, we might just get to the bottom of things, darlin'. Everything," he said and hung up.

Quinn stared a moment at the receiver, then dropped it in its cradle. Calling Doug had only raised more questions without answers, and his neglect in telling her about what had possibly been earlier calls from Jay rankled. She felt torn between anger at him and at Welles and the growing, exhilarating conviction that Jay was really alive.

Just as she'd always thought.

Quinn began scrambling through the papers on her

desk. If she hurried, she might reach PRISM, the private MIA/POW group of dedicated volunteers that had never answered her recent inquiries, before the office closed.

Five minutes later she slumped back in her chair.

"I wish I could help," her contact had said, "but other than the letter I sent you—"

"Letter?"

She heard a groan. "No, don't tell me the U.S. mail sent it to Jacksonville for a vacation. It won't be the first labyrinthine rerouting I've heard about. Let me send you a copy." She paused. "It didn't say much, though. I wish I had something concrete."

When Quinn related the telephone call from Jay, she heard silence for a moment.

"You realize you're fulfilling the fantasies of every frustrated family from Manhattan to San Diego? Let me ask around some more. I'm not quite sure what we're dealing with here, but there's a new group I can try."

"I'll appreciate anything you can turn up."

It seemed to Quinn that she had better information, better contacts—if only Welles would open up. She felt sure he knew more. Funny that letter hadn't reached her, though. Quinn riffled through more papers, coming up with Charles Barron's San Francisco phone number. She dialed with shaking fingers.

"Ah, Quinn," Charles said, the austere silence of his paneled law office seeming louder than voices in the background. "What can I do for you?"

This time, she heard in his irritated tone.

She'd barely launched into her story of the mysterious telephone call when Charles cut her off. "You have your nerve. The last time you called, I thought I made myself clear. My brother is dead."

"And if he isn't, Charles? If he was there with you now, at home again—would you even admit it?"

She heard him make a strangled sound. "My God. When Jay knew you, none of us approved. You fancied yourself in love with a man far above you. You were an orphaned girl looking for a society meal ticket, nothing more. Do you think my parents didn't see through that? Even Jay saw it," he said, "so you seemed harmless enough. If he were alive now, do you think he'd give you a second's thought, much less a phone call? You've become a vile, sick woman. Don't bother me again." He slammed the phone in her ear.

Quinn sat trembling, willing the phone to ring again and Jay's bright voice to say, "Hi, beautiful, don't let Charles get you. I'll be right over and we'll—"

What? For a moment, Quinn stared at her desktop, unable to remember what she and Jay had enjoyed other than finding a dark, quiet corner somewhere in which to kiss and fondle. So long ago.

Her memories weren't happy ones now. The phone call from Charles to say that Jay was missing. The bad dreams about the crash. *Our plane went down and Jay didn't make it.*

Quinn's breath caught. In the coffee shop Welles had said *our plane*—not two planes but one. A slip of the tongue? Or the truth he'd been trying to hide?

She remembered Mai Blackburn's story, sounding so carefully rehearsed that first night in Geneva. Remembered Welles's caution. But under pressure, with his defenses lowered, the story might crack.

Flinging her file drawer open, Quinn rummaged through it. Damn. *Surely you remember landmarks, the coordinates?* she'd asked. But there was no picture in the drawer of Jay and his flying partner. Andrew could have burned it too.

Maybe Doug was right and Welles had done something terrible after all, something that made him fear Jay Barron's being alive.

The possibilities spun through her mind like a gyroscope out of control. Maybe Jay had a perfect right to want him dead.

"Andrew?"

She slammed the drawer shut. If he'd burned a picture that could answer her question, he had to have looked at it first. What was it he'd said about Hannah and Welles? *Perhaps she knows something that Quinn hasn't seen yet.*

Quinn ran into the hall. "Andrew!"

"I don't think I can get up," Andrew said.

Valerie smiled thinly as Andrew slipped from her onto his side. "You seemed to be up all right a few minutes ago."

"Go ahead. Make a dirty joke of it." He struggled to his feet. He was already leaving her again; he could feel distance settle like the weight of his Oxford cloth shirt on his shoulders as he shrugged it on. "What else is this? I'm still a married man."

"You're a grouch," Valerie said, but she hadn't been herself tonight either. Turning, she found her sweater on the den carpet, having insisted on making love after another fruitless discussion of his latest sketches. "But I have faith. Tomorrow morning you'll be at your drafting table bright and early—before noon at least—with a new vision."

"Not likely."

He zipped his pants, watching as she smoothed her bright red sweater over full breasts. Her nipples were still hard as a ballpoint pen tip and he looked away, despising himself for the fresh tug of desire low in his belly.

"You disappoint me, Andrew."

"I disappoint myself." He eased into his loafers. "For God's sake, I heard Quinn slamming around in her office. She could walk in at any—"

"I locked the den door." But Valerie's tone lacked its usual bravado, and he realized their lovemaking had been not only furtive but desperate. "Just in case we felt naughty tonight."

"Naughty?" He shook his head. She rarely took anything seriously, especially him, unless they were flat on the floor, buried in each other. "We really lost it this time." He hobbled toward the door. He should never have let her come over, not when Quinn was home. He felt depraved.

"Do you still love her?"

The bleak tone stopped him. "Quinn and I have been together for a long time," he said.

"So have Patience and Prudence."

Unlocking the door, he frowned. "Who?"

"The stone lions that guard the New York Public Library. That doesn't mean they love each other."

"Look," he said, propping his walking stick against the wall, "Quinn and I aren't close these days. I admit that. She's been preoccupied with the Priceless thing, we've had our celebrity boarder of course, and I've been—"

"Preoccupied with me?"

"With trying to make something of my work again. Val, this thing between us has no place to go. You knew that coming in. I should never have let things get started."

"Then you do love her."

"Well, sure. But not as if we were just seeing each other or newly married. . . ." He trailed off, with a miserable glance at the wastebasket and the shards of paper he'd thrown away. Like him and Quinn. "I'm not about to leave her for you, if that's what you're waiting to hear."

Valerie came toward him. "My horoscope this morning informed me that I 'have personal problems to attend to before love can find a way.'"

"Shit." Andrew stepped back, wincing as pain shot through his bad leg. She'd been making odd allusions to trouble all evening, but he'd assumed she meant his drawing. Now he saw her lazy eye was drifting. "What personal problems?"

"You."

"Valerie, I'm not the man for you. I can hardly take care of myself these days. You wanted to get laid, so we did it. But you know damn well I'm not the guy who's going to marry you by Christmas."

"Quinn always says that life is full of surprises."

"She's my wife, dammit."

"Oh. While we were rolling around on the rug—this time—I forgot." Close to him now, Valerie blinked. "Proper Andrew. The only child, the good little boy, the A-plus student, the talented artist." She paused. "The hapless invalid."

"I'm not—"

"You keep leaning on Quinn much longer, you'll fall down."

Andrew's shoulders sagged. He'd had the same thought himself, most recently in his own foyer when she'd walked in with Hannah's father, both of them looking guilty—and sated. He recognized the look.

"God, Val. I think Quinn's fucking Blackburn."

Her gray eyes widened. "I suppose it's possible."

"Come on, you work with her," he said, not really wanting the answer. Needing it. "You went to Europe together that time when she met him. You're good friends, and women talk."

"I'm not so sure we're good friends now." Valerie caught his hand. "But yes, she told me herself. It's true."

First Jay Barron, now Blackburn. . . . Feeling sick, he snatched his hand free. "How long have you known? Is that why you decided to declare open season on her husband? Took advantage of Quinn's affair and brought me food and drawing pencils and hung your tits in my face until I had to—"

"Stop it," she said, blinking again. "I love you."

"There's nothing to love, Val."

Before he could push her away, Valerie's arms came up around his neck. She pressed close to him, her lips at the hollow of his throat, which was still bare because he hadn't bothered to button his shirt, her hands sifting through his hair. From out in the hall, he could hear Quinn calling his name.

"What about the moments we've shared in this room? The hours at your drawing board, making your pictures beautiful again?"

"They're not beautiful. I could never publish them."

She ignored that, as she usually did. "What about the days, the nights, talking? The way you've made me see color and texture and taught me how to dress to please you? The way I've made you laugh sometimes?"

"Val, don't." But his mouth made its own way to the tender spot beneath her ear, and he groaned softly.

"And what we've created here together. What about that?"

He tensed. "Created?"

"Andrew?" Quinn called again, in a panicky tone.

He was drawing back when Quinn pushed open the door, nearly knocking him over. Valerie whirled, frosted hair flying, her gray eyes wild. Quinn looked from her to Andrew, then back again.

"Am I . . . interrupting something?"

He groped for his blackthorn stick, his heart in his throat. Valerie's voice sounded thick but defiant.

"I was just telling Andrew that I'm pregnant."

18

Quinn stood frozen in the doorway.

It took a moment before her thoughts became coherent again. Lost in misery over Welles's probable deception, she'd jumped to the conclusion that Valerie's child was also Andrew's.

There'd been other men, she knew: a Japanese businessman, the friend who had married the client's model while on location. She didn't know how many others, or when, but Valerie had been on the prowl.

"Pregnant?" Quinn asked at last.

Andrew grasped Valerie's inner arm, swinging her around. "What is this?"

"We made a baby, Andrew. You and me." She looked away, at Quinn. Valerie's face had turned pale, her eyes misty. "He can't deny it. We've been lovers since your second trip to Geneva."

Quinn made a small strangled sound. Disbelief threaded her voice, though she'd certainly seen the signs. "You? And Andrew?"

"He seems to find me attractive enough."

"Convenient," he said.

"How could you?" she asked. "How could you both? We're friends, Val."

"Maybe you shouldn't have trusted me quite so much."

Andrew steered Valerie toward the front entry, leaving Quinn to compose herself. She blocked her ears with both hands, but she could hear every word of their exchange: Andrew's accusations of carelessness; Valerie's promise to have the baby, with or without his help. By the time the front door slammed and he shuffled back into the den, Quinn's face was devoid of expression, but she gripped her upper arms with cold fingers in self-protection.

"All these years," she said half to herself, "wanting a baby, a family together, waiting for you to get well again and want one too."

"I didn't plan this, Quinn."

"But it is your child?"

"Yes. I suppose so."

The word was torn from her. "Why? How could you do this to me?"

"What do you want, some glib answer? Do you want me to say I was lonely and alone too much? That she forced herself on me? That I wanted to find out what it was like for a change to know that a woman desired me—"

"Oh, Andrew."

"This is your fault," he said.

"I won't accept that."

"From the night of the accident—"

"You can't live the rest of your life blaming me, Andrew." Quinn's flesh began to warm. "I made a mistake, one I've paid for dearly. We pulled up roots in Colorado so I could make things up to you, so I could support us. I left a good job for the risk of opening the agency here and proving myself in a bigger arena." She swept an arm around the den. "You live well enough for a man who hasn't worked a day in the past six years."

"Are you calling me a parasite?"

"No, I'm calling you weak." Quinn gestured at the drafting board with its expensive adjustable lamp. "You've had every opportunity, every advantage. I've worked myself sick providing for you. I don't resent that, but I do resent your not making the most of your opportunities." She paused. "I'm happy that you've been trying to draw again. But don't you think I see what's happening?"

He said nothing.

"You're giving up, just as you did with therapy, as you did with all the doctors—the specialists—I brought in to help you."

"You're a regular saint, Quinn."

"No," she said, "no, I'm not."

"How true." He stumped toward her, leaning heavily on the blackthorn stick, stopping with his face inches from hers. "You think I'm blind as well as crippled? You think I haven't guessed what's going on under my own nose? Forget Valerie."

"I can't." The night had been filled with betrayals.

"Well, I'm not about to forget Blackburn either."

She'd been expecting it, but Quinn took a breath anyway. "I suppose you're right. In this, at least, I am at fault. I didn't mean to let it happen," she said, "to have things go as far as they . . . did."

"Don't try to tell me the grand passion is over. I saw you with him, right here in my own home, two nights ago."

Quinn nodded, unable to speak past the lump in her throat.

"You're sleeping with him, aren't you?"

"Was," she murmured.

"Until his wife objected?"

"Until he lied to me. I'm sorry."

"And here I thought it was Frank Murray." He ran a hand through his hair, eyes raised at the ceiling. "What in hell happened to us, Quinn?"

"Too much," she said sadly.

"We had a decent marriage, two good jobs, a great house—"

"A baby on the way."

She couldn't look at him. Quinn studied the dark carpet, which she'd never liked. Deep brown shot with green and gold, the heavy tweed had been Andrew's choice for his den, colors he would never have chosen before the accident.

"We lost it," he said. "Whatever we had, we lost it long ago." He waited until she looked up to say, "Maybe further back than six years. Hell, maybe the day we married—and moved Jay Barron into the house with us."

"You loved him too," Quinn said.

"Past tense. You still do."

She hesitated, unsure that she should tell him now about Jay's call. When she did, Andrew looked astonished.

"Jay, alive? When are you going to rid yourself of this crazy obsession? Quinn, you're losing your grip."

"I'm telling you, Jay called. I talked to him, Andrew. Do you really think, because you destroyed that scarf, a letter, and maybe some photographs, that ends it?"

"You're deluding yourself! And I didn't burn any pictures." He shuffled toward the door. "But there's a point. You know what Jay Barron's always been to you, Quinn?" She couldn't answer and he said, "Not a flesh-and-blood man—like me or even Blackburn, damn him—but a romantic daydream. A happy ending that never quite resolved itself. That's a hellish obstacle for any man to overcome, even Jay himself. Frankly, I hope you never find him or vice versa. Because if by some remote chance he is still alive, even he won't live up to your expectation."

Trembling, Quinn hugged herself tighter. "The only thing I've ever wanted was to know what happened to him."

"And then what?"

"And then?" She shrugged, her shoulders stiff.

"That poor bastard." Andrew turned away. "Blackburn, I mean. I shouldn't envy him."

"You don't have to," she said. "Just get out."

His tone sounded of self-pity again. "I suppose you mean you want me to pack my things. Leave."

"Yes."

"I don't know where—"

"You'll find a place. Valerie's."

"I don't want Valerie."

"Try a hotel, then. A nice, efficient hotel where they'll cater to your every whim, where the maid who breaks her back dusting your furniture and changing your sheets won't care if she comes in and finds you in bed with someone."

"Quinn—"

If he begged her to let him stay, she'd scream. All she wanted at the moment was to be left alone, to make sense of all the lies, but she couldn't help asking. "What will you do about Valerie?"

His head down, he studied the floor as if for answers. "I don't know, but we all make mistakes, it seems. I sure as hell won't get down on my knees and ask her to marry me. If I were you, I wouldn't expect Blackburn to leave his wife either."

As soon as he'd left Quinn that morning, Welles had begun searching for his daughter. He didn't expect to spend most of the day hunting for Hannah, and by the time he rapped on the door of the suite at the Sherry-

Netherland, he was hot, tired, furious—and scared. His wife didn't help matters.

Opening the door, she gave him the cool, inscrutable look that was her specialty. "You're late," she said.

"I need a drink."

Welles strode to the full bar across the suite's living room and poured two fingers of whiskey. He could feel Mai's disapproval, as if she were head of the local temperance union.

"Don't say it," he warned, letting the scotch trail fire from his throat to his stomach. He didn't need another lecture on the dangers of following in his mother's footsteps. He tugged off his tie, draping it over a chair.

"Where's Hannah?" she asked.

Welles snorted. "That's anybody's guess."

On Quinn's advice, he'd tried the school first. Small and exclusive, it boasted a student population of fewer than three hundred from kindergarten to twelfth grade, and the headmistress knew each child.

"Quinn said she'd ridden in the limo with Hannah to school, but Hannah wasn't there."

Mai, who'd been standing ten feet or so behind him, began to move, a sure sign of tension. He shouldn't have mentioned Quinn's name, he supposed, but he was beyond caring.

"I saw Quinn this morning. For coffee in a public restaurant. She had something to tell me." After telling Mai about the Priceless ad, he paused. "Mai, it's been a helluva day. She also thinks she's heard from Jay Barron."

Mai showed no response at all. She picked up his tie, folding it neatly. "We were talking of Hannah."

"The headmistress said she was absent." He tossed back the rest of his drink. "Then she noted that Hannah's best friend was also missing. 'It seems we're dealing with a classic case of hooky,' she told me. 'Strange, our children always wonder that we see how transparent they are, when they leave such a broad trail to follow.'"

"The school is responsible for her, Welles. So is your friend Quinn."

She's more than that, he thought; she's the woman I love. He'd never admitted it to himself in so many words. Welles shrugged out of his jacket, dropping it on the bed where Mai's suitcases lay, open and half filled. Lingerie, blouses, suits, and dresses—all crisply stacked and folded with tissue layers between.

"Yes," he said, "but Hannah's fourteen and New York is a big city. She's also angry with me, and not too happy with you. She doesn't get on with Quinn very well, and God knows Quinn's husband can't have much influence. The toughest thing he does in a day is lean on that walking stick of his."

"The man is ill," Mai murmured. "Why must you defend her? I shouldn't have altered my decision. You sent Hannah here, and that woman has let her do as she pleases."

Welles recalled the headmistress's words: *It's a difficult age*. "Control is often a matter of luck."

"You've spoiled her rotten."

Splashing more scotch into his glass, he said, "Maybe I have. And maybe, just now, I regret it. But regrets—or blaming Quinn Tyler—won't find Hannah. And if Jay does first—"

"If the headmistress knows her students so well, she must know where Hannah and her friend might be."

She'd given him a phone number and address. Hannah's friend lived in an Upper East Side brownstone. Her father was a Broadway producer, her mother a cabaret singer of some renown. Both parents had left for California two days ago.

"I tried the house," he said. "No one answered. Another classic case. An empty house, a bunch of teenagers, a liquor supply, God knows what else."

"Do something, Welles."

"What? I staked out the house for most of the after-noon. The girls didn't come home." He rubbed the back of his neck. "Maybe the party moved elsewhere. All I know is, there were beer bottles in the trash and half a dozen pizza boxes."

Mai made a sound. "This is deplorable. Our plane leaves in three hours." She turned, swiping his suit coat off the bed, straightening it as she walked toward the closet, hanging it squarely on the rod. "We'll take Han-nah back to Geneva, enroll her again in the day school where she belongs, one we can trust, in which we'll know her friends and their connections"—Still the Saigon aris-tocrat, she almost sniffed at the notion of Broadway pro-ducers and nightclub singers—"and we will take up our normal lives where they left off. No more frantic trips to New York, no more public exposure for an impression-able child." No more Quinn, he thought. "Uncle Tran will get us out of the Priceless contract."

"Didn't you hear me before? I said, Jay Barron is alive."

"I heard you."

"Then don't be so damn single-minded. We can take another plane. Someone called Quinn the other night just when I was beginning to think I'd jumped overboard with my suspicions. She's certain the voice was his."

"She has always believed he was still alive. Because that is what she needs to believe."

Shoving his glass along the bar top, he said, "That's what I thought too. Now I'm not so sure. I've had this feeling. . . ." He looked at Mai. "If she's right and it is true, Hannah is in more danger than we thought." He slammed a fist on the bar. "Where the hell can she be?"

It seemed to Welles that the more agitated he grew, the calmer Mai became. With graceful motions, she emptied his glass in the sink behind the bar, washed it, and rinsed it. "You must call Ms. Tyler-Devlin and inquire further about Hannah's new friends."

While Mai finished packing, Welles spoke to Quinn, feeling his wife's eyes on him the entire time. In the brief conversation he could hear Quinn's concern, but her voice sounded flat. He hung up with half a dozen names and numbers and Quinn's promise to let him know the minute Hannah came home.

The numbers proved futile.

"Then we must call the police," Mai said, smoothing a last pair of slacks into the suitcase and closing it. The locks snapped shut.

"They won't file a missing persons report until she's been gone at least twenty-four hours."

She went to the bureau, where her papers made a neat pile squarely in its center. She picked up her Swiss passport.

Welles snatched it from her hand. "What the hell is wrong with you? Our daughter is missing. I spent the whole goddamn day looking for her while you fussed with a bunch of clothes." He gestured at the bed. "Aren't you worried?"

"You are worried enough for both of us."

He waved the passport. "I want her out of here! I want her safe. I want all of us safe and—" He stared at the passport, which had fallen open, showing the recent Customs stamp from their arrival at Kennedy Airport. Welles barely noticed it. He was looking at the previous page.

"Calm yourself, darling." Mai tried to take the passport from him, to close it on the other Customs mark, but Welles held on.

"When were you in London?"

"A few weeks ago." She looked away. "You can see for yourself. The date is there."

He felt dizzy. "It's the same date as on that mailer, the one that contained the jade earrings sent to Hannah by 'a fan.'" Hannah had made a point of showing it to him, but there was no fan. And probably no Jay Barron threat either.

"Coincidence," Mai murmured.

"You're the last person to rely on coincidence." He glanced about the painfully tidy room. Not an article out of place. Not even his. Shock made his blood run cold, his skin clammy. Welles shook his head. "You sent them, didn't you? My God, you've had them all this time. For twenty years, you've had them. The necklace too?" he demanded. "Where is it, Mai? Hidden somewhere until you need to scare me half to death again? To pull me back where I 'belong'?"

"I did it for us, Welles."

"Bullshit." He slung the passport across the room. "You did it to make me think Jay knew where I was, and Hannah too. How did you manage it? After I'd left him for dead on the floor of that hut in Laos?" They'd run through jungle, up hills and down into ravines, falling, scrambling, his leg on fire, the fever turning his brain to mush. He sank down on the bed, his tone thin with disbelief, his voice seeming to come from far away. "How did you make the switch? The pouch of jade for a bunch of river stones?"

She twisted her hands together. "You were sick. I had already switched them to cheat my brother of his theft, to regain the legacy that was rightfully mine."

"You switched them in the hut? And took the phony pouch after your brother was dead?"

"After you killed him, yes." She'd gone back to make sure, she'd told him. She'd gone back to get the jade.

"And later you showed me the pebbles and I felt sorry for you," he said. It had been the pattern of their lives together. "I felt so damn obligated . . . responsible."

He remembered the long journey to Paris, the proximity of two people on the run; the first time she'd convinced him to make love and the pregnancy that resulted. She'd lost the baby right after they married—or so she'd claimed. "That first pregnancy was false, wasn't it? There was no baby."

Mai didn't answer.

"All lies," he said, holding her dark gaze, "and by the time I started to wonder—"

"You were sick again. In hospital."

Except for that, it had been the same as with his mother. He was always responsible, always taking care. Feeling trapped.

"Your mind needed rest," Mai whispered. "Tran and I protected you."

"From what?"

"From life"—she hesitated—"and from Jay Barron."

"Then you did a lousy job. I had nightmares of him every single time I closed my eyes. I guess I wanted to believe this morning that Jay is still alive, I guess part of me needed that as much as Quinn does. Even if he came after me. He won't," Welles said. "He can't." He rose and paced the room, feeling Mai's gaze upon him with every step. "He's dead."

"Welles—"

The full reality hit him then. "By God, we're married to a pair of liars, Quinn and I. Who else could have made that late-night call, who else would have known what to say that would touch her most except her own husband? Hell, Andrew Devlin was Jay's best friend before the war. He knew as much about him as I did. Maybe he got tired of living in Jay's shadow and decided to give her what she wants. To shake her up enough to turn to him again for comfort. Just as you tried to bind me to you with the jade."

There was no danger to Hannah at all, no danger to him. His own wife had sent the Tears of Jade for the same reason, to frighten him into going home. Her possessiveness had driven their entire marriage. Welles could barely contain the sick feeling in his belly, the disgust in his heart.

"Welles."

"It's over, Mai. I'm filing for divorce. Get on that plane to Geneva and out of my sight."

"I'll sue you," she said, her voice trembling, "for custody of Hannah. You'll never see her again."

"I'll see her before you will," he said. "I'll find her." Sudden rage at her threat sent him to the telephone. "On second thought, I'll get the bellhop, then I'll drive you to the airport myself. I'll put you on that plane and watch it take off. What you do when you get to Switzerland is your decision, but remember this: I'll fight you every damn step of the way. You and Tran."

Turning, he watched her crumple, as she always did when he fought back. Her voice thick with tears, she said, "You can't send me away. I won't let you. You're wrong about Andrew Devlin. You want to be safe, Welles, but you're not. You want to push the past back, but you can't. It's here. It's real."

"What the hell are you talking about?"

"Jay Barron," she said. "He *is* alive."

Welles paused with one hand on the telephone.

"How do you know that?"

She sent the jade, he told himself. Andrew made the call.

"Jay was looking for you long ago. In Paris. It was when we were living with Tran and you were drifting in and out of unexplained fevers, despite the fact that your physical wounds were healed. Someone—not Jay himself—called the house and then Tran's office at the bank in Paris."

"You didn't tell me."

"Reality, Tran said, would be too much for you at the time."

"Post-traumatic stress syndrome," Welles said. For almost a year, she and Tran had made all his decisions while he sat it out in a Swiss sanitarium.

Welles dropped the receiver and went to her. She was standing in the center of the room, her head down, her dark hair coming free of its knot at her nape. The warm strands drifted over his hands as he shook her. "What, damn you?"

"The next time we had a call Tran told the man—a government agent, he thought—that you were dead." Welles inhaled sharply and she went on, her tone desperate. "He said you had fallen into a deep depression over your war experience and committed suicide."

Welles spoke in a whisper. "Jesus Christ."

"We even held a funeral. You never knew it, but in a small cemetery on the outskirts of the city there is a marker."

"With my real name on it."

"Yes," she whispered.

"You expect me to believe all this?"

Dark and wild, her eyes met his. "Jay had a score to settle, the man said. Instead, your death would tell Jay what a complete coward you were. That's why afterward, Tran suggested that we relocate to Geneva, where he was trustee for the Banque Internationale. He suggested you take another name, not only because you had deserted the military."

He could have received amnesty, but Welles had taken the name to cleanse himself, because he'd killed one of his own men and had no place else to go and wanted no reminders of the life he'd squandered. He would begin again, he'd thought. With Mai.

"He got me new papers, a job, and managed to convince me that it was all my own idea." He laughed bitterly. "I played right into his hands. And yours."

"We did it for you, Welles."

"You did it for yourself."

He felt the slickness of silk under his damp fingers and let her go, disgusted by the feel of her. The sight of her. He smelled gardenias and his stomach rolled. The scent seemed southern, cloying and heavy; it had always reminded him, he realized, of his Shreveport beginnings.

When he reached once more for the telephone, Mai's hand covered his. "I love you, Welles."

"On your own terms," he said. "I may have needed that once, but I don't now." He punched in the bell captain's number and waited.

"I am telling the truth," she cried. "You are not safe, so neither is Hannah. Jay Barron is very much alive. Tran knows it too. Call him if you don't believe me."

"I'll take my chances this time."

When the front desk answered, Welles spoke rapidly, softly. A strange peace had settled over him. Hanging up, he doubted that either he or Hannah was in any danger, doubted that Jay really was alive or a threat. But if he was, the confrontation seemed long overdue.

"Please believe me. He will kill you, Welles! Hannah—"

"Get your passport and let's go."

Mai tugged at his arm. "If I can't have you, neither will Quinn Tyler-Devlin."

He opened the door, waiting for her in the hall.

"You'll come back to me," she said. Her voice lowered, becoming the sultry promise he knew too well. For twenty years, it had had the strength of handcuffs. "I'll fix everything. And then you'll come back."

19

Two days later Quinn looked up from some sketches on her desk to find Valerie standing in her office doorway, eyes smudged with fatigue, her lids puffy. Quinn tried to harden her heart at the signs of obvious and recent crying, but she couldn't. Besides, she was trying to overcome her own latest personal shock.

"Come in," she said. "Sit down before you fall down."

"I wanted to talk to you."

"Sure." Quinn swiveled in her chair. "As long as we both understand that certain topics are off limits."

"Andrew came to my place the night you kicked him out."

"That's one of the topics," Quinn murmured, shoving aside the drawings for the next Priceless ad. "I've been pondering possible locations while we still have Hannah."

"Welles didn't take her home?"

"Not so far." As Daisy brought in the mail, Quinn looked up, tensing. Earlier, she'd had a telephone call from PRISM and was still trying to forget the message. "He and Mai are getting a divorce." She took the stack

– 319 –

of mail with a thin smile that dismissed Daisy. "It must be catching."

Valerie looked at her hands but said nothing. Apparently she'd decided not to risk their tentative communication with any more loaded subjects.

Quinn said, "Welles has spent most of his time in the last two days either tracking down his daughter or trying to convince her that he's still her father."

"She blames him for the breakup?"

"Right now she seems to blame him for everything." She gestured at her cluttered desk. "Because I can't seem to help, I've been spending a lot of time here, keeping out of the way."

"Things will get better," Valerie murmured. "At least that's what I tell myself every morning. Then I open the newspaper and read my horoscope. *Pay close attention to relationships,* it says, or something similar. *Now is not the time to rock the financial boat.*"

Quinn toyed with her latest sketch for Priceless. "Maybe things would get better if you'd stop believing in fortune-tellers."

"Meaning?"

"Life's not the same as fantasy. Andrew's not a knight on a white charger."

Valerie made a small, miserable sound, and Quinn glanced sharply at her to make certain she wasn't crying again.

"Sorry, my tongue's a bit sharp these days."

"I'm having this baby myself," Valerie informed her. "Andrew acknowledges that it's his, but he wants nothing to do with it."

"No surprise."

"Quinn, I know how many years you've wanted a family of your own. Now the two people you trusted most—"

"That was my mistake," she said. "I refuse to wallow in self-pity, and I'd advise you to do the same." She let her chair turn, facing the windows, as if she were an ostrich; if she couldn't see the source of her pain, it wouldn't hurt. "Andrew led us both on."

"What about Welles? At least you're free now to work at something better with him."

"Welles lied to me," Quinn admitted, "which is nothing more than I should expect from a man cheating on his wife. So we both have tarnished dreams, don't we?" She turned back. "I suggest we chalk things up to experience and go on."

"That's not you, Quinn."

"It is now." The PRISM message flashed through her mind, bringing a fresh wave of pain, of betrayal.

Valerie shifted in her chair across from Quinn, the desk between them like a wall blocking their friendship. Quinn noted Valerie's pale features, her dull hair.

"Are you feeling lousy? Physically, I mean?"

"Queasy. Bloated. Dragged out." She forced a weak smile. "Nothing that a few more weeks and a gold band wouldn't fix. Guess I didn't pick my quarry very wisely. I want you to know it wasn't intentional."

"Come on, Val. You waved a horoscope under my nose when we flew to Geneva and told me you'd be married by Christmas."

Rising, Valerie walked behind her chair, gripping the back with both hands like a shield. "Maybe you're right that I shouldn't trust predictions. I've thought Andrew was a damned appealing guy for years, I admit that. But I'd never have gone after him, Quinn. It . . . just happened."

They were her own words. "Yes."

"It happened with you and Welles Blackburn too."

"So it did."

Looking at her hands, Valerie blinked. "I don't know

what else to say, except I'm sorry, and that doesn't seem to cover it." Her voice thickened. "I came in here to apologize—and to tender my resignation."

Quinn hadn't expected that or the surprising twist of anguish she felt. "Do you have another job offer?"

Valerie shook her head.

"Then don't be hasty. The economy stinks, but if Priceless can keep Hannah Blackburn, as it appears they might, Tyler and Devlin will be solidly in the black. You're a good stylist, Val. A good copywriter too. And a damned good right arm when I need an extra one." She avoided any mention of their friendship. "You have a baby on the way to think about."

Valerie's lip trembled. "You want me to stay?"

Quinn's hesitation was slight, her tone faintly husky. "I want you to stay."

"Well." Valerie took two steps backward toward the door, which stood ajar.

From the anteroom Quinn could hear the soft tap of Daisy's computer keys. Work goes on, she thought, though she wasn't as sure about her personal life. The emptiness had never mattered so much before.

Valerie took another step, then stopped. "We've never talked much about our lives," she said, "before advertising. I know you had no father, and a mother who died young, but I grew up in a big family, doing the work my parents should have done. I've been taking care of other people all my life, Quinn. Telling myself it didn't matter, that I enjoyed it. Making a big joke of everything, talking tough, wearing kooky clothes. Andrew made me see myself as a serious person, but you know what?"

Quinn looked at her expectantly.

"I was taking care of him too," Valerie said softly. "Now I have a child to consider. I guess it's time I stopped believing in horoscopes and happy-ever-after and started taking care of myself." In the doorway she paused. "Thanks, Quinn. I appreciate the job."

"We women have to stick together," was all she said.

When Valerie's footsteps died away in the hall, Quinn put her head down on her folded arms, letting her hair sweep the desktop, the ad sketch she couldn't focus on.

She'd been telling herself for two days to buck up, to tough things out. Now she wished she had been able to confide in Valerie instead of hiding behind her professional facade, taking refuge in the seemingly magnanimous offer to let Valerie keep her job. In truth, she needed Valerie and going it alone scared her.

God knew, she should be able to understand. Yes, Welles Blackburn had "just happened" too, but what a mess the day in Carouge and the night in Zermatt had made. She wondered whether she could even put them—him— behind her, as Valerie seemed about to do with Andrew.

She wondered about Jay.

Welles had told her of Mai's deceptions, about the Tears of Jade and his own theory that Andrew had made the telephone call. He'd agreed that Hannah could stay with Quinn while he and his wife worked out the terms of their divorce. But Welles wanted one thing and she needed another. Two nights ago he'd decided Jay was dead—always had been—while Quinn remained certain he was alive.

Was she deluding herself? Again? Andrew would say.

Even thinking his name still hurt. She would never forget standing, arms folded over her breasts, in the entryway while he dragged his luggage to the elevator. A dramatic gesture, throwing him out? Or, as he claimed, had she been doing it over the years with every mention of Jay? With every small rejection of her own marriage? Quinn squeezed her eyes shut. Had she driven him to Valerie? Used Welles Blackburn as an excuse for her own distance?

Raising her head, Quinn tried to force the thoughts away.

She hadn't been a bad wife . . . had she?

He hadn't given her that much as a husband.

Quinn cast a glance out her office window, then squared her shoulders. She had no more time for guilt or, after the call from PRISM, for more lies.

"We've been in touch with a new group in Hanoi," her contact had said. "These people are investigating old crash sites from the war."

Quinn held her breath.

"They sift bones and debris, try to make identifications. There were a number of downed fliers in the area you're interested in, but on the day in question there was only one Navy F-Four Phantom."

"Not two?" she asked. "You're sure?"

"Just one. I'm sorry, but that's all I could find out. When they get to it, if there's any evidence—"

"There won't be."

Shaking, Quinn had hung up. Now, certain she'd had all the bad shocks she was likely to get for one day, she reached for her mail.

The top mailer bore a Geneva return address label, which she recognized. Frowning, she ripped it open and a small photograph tumbled out.

Quinn's pulse pounded. Welles was still in New York, and so was Hannah. There was no note, but Quinn didn't need one. The only other person she knew in Geneva was Mai Blackburn.

She picked up the photo and read the caption on the back.

"Oh, God."

Then, knowing what she'd see, she turned it over. Jay

Barron stood with one arm on the fuselage of a Navy F-4 Phantom jet, against a gray background—the carrier deck, she assumed.

Somewhere in the South China Sea, November, 1972, the caption read.

His other arm was around a pair of broad shoulders clothed in the same military garb. Jay grinned at her from the creased picture. So did a younger, huskier Welles Blackburn.

Maybe he did do something that terrible, Doug had said.

And with the thought, she reached for the phone. Valerie was right. Quinn too should start taking better care of herself, and of all the lies she'd heard in the past two days, Doug Lloyd's seemed the least harmful; he'd only been trying to protect her, and he was still the only family she had ever known. The only home.

Having to roast a turkey seemed a small price to pay for spending Thanksgiving with someone she loved, someone she could trust. She fingered the Priceless ad sketches. With business also in mind, she'd head for Colorado and kill two birds with one stone.

Her gaze returned to the tattered photograph, on which Jay had written, *Me with Mike Cochran.*

Welles had even lied to her about his name.

Early on a Wednesday morning four weeks later, Welles walked briskly down the corridor from the elevator on Quinn's floor and jabbed a finger at her apartment bell. The ringing on the other side of the door vibrated through him like a tuning fork, and he wiped both hands on his thighs as he waited for someone to answer.

He'd waited long enough. A month ago, certain that Jay Barron posed no threat, he'd left Hannah in New

York with Quinn. He'd grounded her though, for playing hooky—the first time Welles could remember having disciplined his daughter. Then he'd gone back to Geneva to settle things with Mai. The experience had drained him; through it all there'd been Hannah's balky silence, Quinn's avoidance. He wasn't leaving the building without breaking down the barriers both women had put up.

Quinn answered his second ring, one hand sweeping hair from her face, the other covering a yawn. He sensed she'd been hesitating behind the door, inspecting him through the security viewfinder, because she didn't seem surprised. "Hannah's still sleeping," she said coolly. "I'll have her call you later."

"That won't be necessary. I'll stay right here."

Ignoring Quinn's shocked expression, he pushed past her through the foyer and into the slate-blue living room. Neither the soft color nor the pale November sunlight soothed him. "Do you have any coffee?"

"I just got up." With a vague gesture at her gray sweatpants and the shirt that cradled her unbound breasts, she started toward the kitchen, then stopped. "Try the deli on the corner. They have great cheese Danish too."

Welles gave her a look. Stepping around her, he went into the kitchen, grateful that Andrew was gone. He felt territorial himself. With quick motions he located a canister in a cupboard, put water and coffee in the machine, and flipped a switch to start it. Behind him, Quinn hovered in the doorway.

"I don't know what you're trying to prove," she began.

"I'm not proving anything. I'm making coffee. After that I'm going to talk to my daughter, and then to you."

"I have nothing to say. Frankly, I doubt if Hannah does either." Quinn walked closer. "You have more nerve than I gave you credit for."

"And you have less."

"I don't care what you think of me," she said, eyes flashing. "But that *child* is troubled."

Welles felt his temper slip. "I told you once, that child is my life. And for the past three months she's barely spoken to me. She won't listen, and she won't let me touch her. Now the same, for some reason, goes for you. I've had enough."

"Oh, fine," Quinn murmured. "Why don't you just storm into her room and bully her out of her own feelings?"

"I didn't mean—"

"She's had her heart broken—partly my fault but mostly yours—and I'm just as tired as you are of feeling guilty about it, but you can't make things right just because you want them that way."

"I don't see why not," Welles said under his breath. "It seems to work just fine for you with Jay Barron."

He turned his back on the enticing aroma of coffee brewing and of Quinn, who smelled faintly, even in the early morning, of roses, and headed for Hannah's room.

She wasn't sleeping. He could see the tight set of her shoulders, her back, as he eased the door open and crossed the room. "Hey, hot stuff, it's me."

"Go away."

Welles sank down on the bed. "I went away," he said, "for several weeks. It's you and me now, babe. Talk to me."

Hannah's voice came muffled from the covers pulled over her head. "Mother found out about you and Quinn and made you leave. I'm glad," she said thickly.

If she said he was a bad father too, Welles thought he'd shatter. He wanted to hold her, to talk and hear the love coming back, but he held himself rigid. "Hannah, your mother and I had problems long before—"

"I don't want to hear it!"

Welles stood, pacing the room. In two months she

had made it her own: rock posters on the newly painted rose-colored walls, a bulletin board studded with pastel letters from friends in Geneva, copies of the first Priceless ad with the lapis and gold chain and the one from *High Fashion* with the Tears of Jade, and scattered around the room Hannah's most treasured stuffed animals, peering at him in reproach.

Quinn had told him this wouldn't work.

"Look, I know you're angry with me. I know you're hurt." He heard a sniff. "Well, I'm hurt and angry too," he said. "I want the chance to explain, and when I do I need you to listen. So here's what we'll do." Having paced to the door, he turned. Hannah was leaning up on one elbow now, staring at him, her eyes red and her mouth trembling. "Tomorrow is Thanksgiving. The American Thanksgiving. It'll be our first time here, and I think we ought to spend the holiday together, eat roast turkey. And I have something for you—from home."

She didn't accept the bribe. "Quinn is taking me to Colorado."

Welles couldn't mask his surprise. "What for?"

"To see the ranch where she grew up. To ride. To meet her father."

"She doesn't have—" Welles cut himself off. "You mean Doug Lloyd?"

"I think that's his name." Hannah sat up. "We might go skiing too," she said.

He heard no pleasure in her tone, but Hannah loved to ski. "You'd rather spend the weekend with Quinn than with me? It was my impression you don't get along."

Turning her back, she flopped down on the mattress. Welles said nothing because he knew he'd only feel as if he were talking to the stuffed baby fur seal on her headboard, not his daughter. "The restaurants are open on Thursday," she said, "but you'd better make a reservation." She pulled the covers over her head again.

Welles struggled with his urge to yank the sheets down and blister Hannah's bottom, but he'd never spanked her and now wasn't the time to start. When Hannah's emotions turned raw, she hid them behind Mai's inscrutable mask. Perhaps she was more her mother's daughter than his after all.

Leaning against the doorframe, he watched her long enough to make Hannah uncomfortable with the silence; then he slipped from the room with a suppressed sigh and went in search of Quinn.

"Strike one," he said behind her in the kitchen.

Hot coffee splashed over the counter but Welles didn't move to mop it up. Pouring himself a cup, he followed Quinn to her bedroom, where she tried to shut the door in his face, only to find his coffee mug raised between them. "You want to ruin the carpet, go ahead," he said. "Slam this door and see if I help you clean up this time."

"You really are a bastard."

"Yeah, I can be." He bird-dogged her every step of the way to the bed. What the hell had happened? he wondered, and felt his temper slip one more notch. "You don't do a bad imitation of a bitch either."

When she backed up, Welles took another step.

"Why so sour, Quinn? You got what you wanted. Even Mai didn't fare as well." Mai's opposition to the Priceless contract had proved futile; she couldn't demonstrate that any threat to Hannah existed, and she'd given the jade to their daughter herself. Priceless didn't need permission to use it. "The lapis ad was good for business, and from all I hear, now the new ad's been released, so is the one of Hannah wearing the jade earrings."

"You think that's all I care about? We're selling blue jeans, yes. By the carload, I understand."

There was little pride in her tone. A suitcase lay open across the unmade bed, tumbled with clothing. Quinn plucked an ecru nightgown trimmed in black lace from his fingers as soon as he picked it up and the sheer fabric, her touch, sent a rush of yearning through him.

"Hannah's going with you to Boulder?" he said. "She'll make the weekend hell."

"No more than it already promises to be." She dropped the froth of ecru and black lace onto the pile in the open suitcase. "Besides, it's a working vacation. Doug's willing to let us use the ranch for the next Priceless ad. With the mountains as a backdrop—"

Welles spun her around. "You really think I'm going to stand here and watch you drag my daughter away for the weekend?"

"Did she want to spend it with you?"

"No," he admitted.

"I didn't think so."

"Quinn, I'm sick of this. I've asked too many times what's bugging you. I've spent weeks fighting Mai for custody and every other damn thing. I've moved out of my own house. Hannah won't talk to me. At the bank—"

"I don't want to talk to you either."

"Why? Because Jay hasn't called you again?"

Looking at him as if she'd stepped into something unpleasant on the sidewalk, she went to her bureau, opening the top drawer. Welles watched her pull out two airline ticket folders and a photograph. Quinn stuffed the tickets into the outer pocket of a leather handbag. Then she walked toward him, Welles's eyes never leaving her, his heart beginning to thump louder as she pressed the picture into his hand.

Welles looked at it and flinched. He saw Jay Barron's grin, the F-4 Phantom they'd flown together, his own smile.

"Mai isn't the only one who lied, Welles. Or should I say Mike?"

His stomach bottomed out. The past had found him after all, was blowing his life wide open as he'd known it would the day he met her. He opened his mouth but nothing came out.

"And I thought you were an honorable man," she said, "a man of integrity, a man I could trust, when all the time—"

"Where did you get this picture?"

"It doesn't matter."

His blood ran cold. She'd said she would fix everything.

"Did Mai send it?"

Silence.

"Did she? Tell me, dammit." He took a step, and Quinn stepped back. "Of course she did. Can't you see she's trying to turn you against me? She's done it before. She thinks she can get me to come home, that everything will be just as she wants it again."

"I don't care what she wants. I don't care what you want."

"I'll show you what I want." His hand shot out, grasping Quinn's wrist and pulling her to him. Before she could react, he bent his head and brought his mouth down hard on hers.

With a muffled sound, Quinn tore her mouth away, wrenching free as her hand lashed out, slapping him full force across the face, jerking his head to one side.

"You're a liar! Nothing but a liar. 'I've lied twice in my life,' you said, to get into the Navy and out of Laos, but that's only the tip of the iceberg, isn't it?" Her green eyes were flashing. "'I don't make a habit of it,' you told me. But what about your job and your family, your fancy home in Geneva and the ski house in Zermatt full of furniture and food from America? The Chevy Blazer you drive? What about that plane crash twenty years ago? And Jay?

Every evasion about him, every half-truth was another
lie."

"Quinn."

"Damn you. Your whole life is a lie!" She was practically
sobbing now. Welles reached for her. Quinn spun away.

"Well, let's not put too fine a point on things," he
said. "You stay in that glass house of yours long enough,
somebody's going to lob a rock through the window.
You reek of self-righteousness, you know that?" He was
desperate now. "Go ahead, judge me—but don't forget
yourself." He waved a hand. "Don't forget all the years
with Andrew, playing it safe as his nursemaid, telling
yourself how much happier you would have been with
Jay. Telling yourself you deserved to be unhappy
because of that damn car accident. Don't forget the self-
pity on your part because your husband wouldn't give
you the kids you want—"

"Nice try," she said, "but I'm not buying. Andrew
always did that, turned the problem back on me. Your
manipulations won't work. Whatever I am, whatever I've
done or haven't done, doesn't change a thing about you."

"You've been hiding too, Quinn, afraid to—"

"Get out of here!" She dragged a hand across her lips,
scrubbing away his kiss. "If you don't want your image tarnished further for Hannah, get out now, or I'll scream."

Welles clapped a hand over her mouth, hating himself. But he'd come here to make someone listen, and by
God she would. She was right, but she'd listen. For
almost twenty years he'd been running from his past,
denying who he was, even to himself. Mai had lied to
him, and now he knew exactly how that felt. He couldn't
blame either Quinn or Hannah for despising him, but
the lies stopped here.

"I'll tell you everything," he whispered urgently, then
let her go.

"I won't believe you."

"I'll make you believe." His throat felt tight; his voice was husky. His cheek stung like blazes. "I'm up against the wall here. Please, Quinn."

She dropped her head, avoiding his gaze. "What good would it do?" In the same instant her eyes came back to his. "I don't even know who you really are."

The vulnerability he saw made him bold. Welles brought his hands up to her cheeks. "You know," he said. "I'll tell you everything, but you already know."

"Zermatt's not enough, Welles."

"It doesn't have to be."

She shut her eyes briefly. "I won't be patronized. I want—"

"The truth," he promised. His thumbs stroked her cheekbones and he looked deeply into her eyes, fighting a smile. If he gave in to it, she'd slap him again. But though she didn't know it, she trusted him more than she knew; she had called him Welles and she hadn't pulled away. "We'll straighten things out, the three of us. You, me, Hannah. Together."

She hesitated.

"Take the risk, Quinn," he said. "Personally, this time."

Lightly, he kissed her cheek. Then he went to her handbag, pulled out the airline ticket folders, and sat on her bed. "I'm coming with you to Colorado."

"You won't get a seat the day before Thanksgiving."

"They'll accommodate us in First Class," he said.

Her cool tone sounded ironic. "For a man who—I've always thought—preferred the status quo, you're making a lot of changes."

"Watch me," he said, reaching for the phone.

20

Picking at her Thanksgiving dinner, Quinn knew she was being watched. The feeling was driving her mad. They'd been in Colorado for twenty-four hours and Welles had barely taken his eyes off her. She kept waiting for him to say something, to tell her about his past, as he'd promised; she kept waiting for the last of her faith in him to die.

Why was it so much easier to keep believing in Jay? In the last month there'd been no more phone calls, even though Hannah's Tears of Jade ads were waving like signal flags at every newsstand, and he knew where to find Quinn too. Or was she really still hiding, as Welles had said?

Quinn glowered at her plate. She hadn't taken three days off in the past six years, and personal risk didn't seem to be her bag. Pushing cold whipped potatoes around, she tried to think of work, but even the memory of Frank Murray's praise before she'd left New York didn't relieve her nerves.

"You did it, Tyler," he'd said. "Profits at Priceless are going through the roof. The lapis ad got attention, but the jade's selling better than rubbers at an orgy. By year end, Hannah Blackburn will be a household word. Women all over America will be naming their babies after her."

"That's nice," she murmured, feeling nothing more than her usual vague distaste for Frank.

"Looks like we'll be doing business for a long time." His leer hadn't fazed her. "Too bad I can't talk you into some extracurricular activity."

"You can't."

But she would rather have spent the weekend fending off Frank or fighting over the next ad than fidgeting at Doug Lloyd's table.

Why, when she had so much at stake, did Welles look good enough to eat, damn him? In his western boots and jeans, a dress shirt with the sleeves rolled back his only concession—like Doug—to the holiday, he even fit the scenery.

Quinn pushed her chair back and, hefting the turkey platter, hustled into the kitchen. Once safely through the door, she banged the platter down on the center island and leaned against the counter, shoving a dish of dripping cranberries aside. She'd had all she could take of this "family Thanksgiving." The term was Doug's, but the feeling was her own.

It wasn't as if the group was a happy one. Hannah had been surly from the moment Welles informed her of their change in holiday plans; on the plane she'd sat across the aisle from him and Quinn, every glance in their direction a dart of disapproval, though it was Hannah who insisted on sitting alone. A trap, Quinn supposed.

She gazed around the homey red-and-white kitchen of the sprawling ranch house. Earlier she'd hoped Hannah would help with dinner, but minutes later Hannah had dropped a paring knife for the third time into a bowlful of carrots. "I don't know how to do this," she said, hands on hips, and Doug poked his salt-and-pepper head into the kitchen again.

"Come on, little darlin'." With big, capable fingers he fished the knife from the bowl, handing it to Quinn. "I promised you a tour of the barns. It's getting time for the horses to wander down off the hill for Thanksgiving supper. Might be a good time to meet a few of 'em. Pick out one you like."

Little darlin', Quinn thought.

Hannah needed attention from someone like Doug just now, but Quinn didn't like his attitude toward *her*. His only comment about her pending divorce had been, "No more'n I've expected ever since the wedding. Maybe you'll start lookin' forward now, instead of back." And on the one occasion they'd been alone, he flatly refused to listen to another word about Jay Barron. "So what if he is alive?" he said. "Past history's as dry as wash on a line in the noonday sun."

"Since you leave your laundry out until you happen to remember it, I suppose you'd think so," Quinn had answered.

Now she looked away from the restaurant-style range heaped high with dirty pans and picked at a nail. Then she stared at the row of spices above Doug's pock-marked porcelain sink—the sink her mother had kept spotless—and mentally arranged them in alphabetical order. She'd had enough of being watched, as if she, not Welles, were the one on trial. She couldn't go back to the dining room.

"I thought we were getting pumpkin pie," Welles said, coming into the kitchen. "With whipped cream."

"In the fridge."

When he bent over to peer inside, her heartbeat skittered. He had the best butt she'd ever seen, which only irritated her. How could she still be attracted to a man she couldn't trust?

Quinn pushed away from the counter, wiping her hands on her jeans. She hadn't dressed for dinner deliberately. Welles's gaze went to her softly worn blue shirt anyway, homing in on her breasts. She folded her arms.

"Well?" he said, holding up the deep-dish pie plate and a glass bowl in which Quinn had whipped cream until it nearly turned to butter.

"Go ahead. Slice the pie"—she waved toward the opposite counter and a stack of waiting plates—"then serve it." She started for the door.

Welles blocked her.

"You want to talk now?" he asked, his eyes that penetrating blue, enhanced by the dark frames of his glasses, and a flash of sick fear raced through her. Did she really want to know the truth?

"No." The firmness of her reply surprised Quinn.

"Then why ruin Thanksgiving? You're making things uncomfortable for Doug, and he's a damn nice guy."

"Yes. I've noticed you're fast friends already."

"He gives a man some room. A chance to explain himself."

"He still believes in the tooth fairy," she said.

"You'll believe in something too when I'm done with you."

"In what?" she said, glad that both his hands were full.

"Me."

With an incredulous sound, Quinn stepped around him. Then she couldn't resist. Stopping, she dipped a finger into the bowl of cream he held and carefully set a dollop on the end of Welles's perfectly straight nose. "Careful, Pinocchio. You know what happens when you lie."

Welles let her reach the door, let her hand lift to

push against the panel, before his laugh warmed her from head to toe. Quinn glanced around to find the pie plate and bowl on the counter and Welles licking his finger. "Sweet," he said; then, as Quinn went through the door, "but you've got cranberry jelly on your cute little ass."

"Did you always live here?"

Hannah's lukewarm tone made Quinn stop smoothing the yellow blanket on the bed. The big square room in the back corner of the house, across from Doug's, had been Quinn's as a girl, but to her surprise he had steered Hannah toward it the night before. Then he'd guided Quinn and Welles to the two rooms on opposite sides of the hall at the top of the stairs. Quinn was still wondering at his arrangements.

"Only for a few years," she finally said, telling Hannah about her parents. "My mother was Doug's housekeeper until she died. Then I went to a foster home."

Hannah frowned. "Did you like it there?"

"I had several. Some I liked, some I didn't." She leaned over to plump the pillows. This was the most conversation she'd had with Hannah since meeting her at Kennedy, so soon after Zermatt. "I suppose, with one exception, my teenage years turned out as well as anyone else's."

"Then what did you do?"

Quinn sat beside her, letting the soft light on the bedside stand soothe her, enjoying the quiet talk. She hadn't realized how much she craved Hannah's acceptance—on any level. She told Hannah a few stories about college, and meeting Andrew, but didn't mention Jay.

"Did you love him?"

"Andrew?" Quinn glanced up. "Yes, of course I did.

Before he hurt his leg, he was charming and funny, and he smiled more than he does now."

"Is that why you fell for my father? Because Andrew stopped loving you and you were lonely?"

Out of the mouths of babes, Quinn thought, and tried not to wince. "Maybe I was lonely, but I didn't look for a man—any man—to replace my husband."

"All my friends think my father's sexy."

"Yes," Quinn said. "He is."

Hannah hesitated, the frown plowing a furrow between her dark brows. "I'll bet he's a good kisser too."

Quinn got off the bed. Her pulse pumped harder, and she could feel her face heat. "Why are you asking me this?"

"I want to know, that's all." Hannah's voice was deceptively lazy, her glance sly. "Is he a good kisser?"

"Hannah."

"And good in bed?"

Quinn whirled. She'd been set up again, and she had tolerated enough bad behavior, no matter how understandable it might be. "You have no right to speak to me like that, little girl!" She started toward the bed. "You're fourteen years old and precocious, I admit, but whatever your father and I have done together is none of your business. Do you understand me?"

"But I—"

"Your parents may put up with impertinent questions about subjects that don't concern you. They may tolerate rudeness, or late hours without permission, or prying into their most private lives—but I will not. If your father is willing to answer you, fine. Let him tell you every little detail of his problems with your moth—"

"Is that why he left her? Why she kicked him out?"

The suddenly small voice took the wind out of Quinn's sails.

"Is it my fault they're getting a divorce?" Hannah

asked. "If I was good, would he have stayed at home with me?"

As her voice broke, Quinn gathered her close, meeting no resistance. Hannah's arms wrapped tightly around her neck and held on as if Quinn offered the only refuge.

Hannah buried her face against Quinn's front. "I shouldn't have said that. I was trying to make you mad. I make my mother mad all the time, even when I don't want to."

"Don't cry," Quinn said helplessly, patting her shoulder, smoothing the black silk hair from her face.

"I'm not a bad girl."

"No, of course you aren't." Quinn hugged her tighter. "It's hard to grow up, isn't it? You left home to come to New York to work and live with me—when I know you don't like me much—and there's been nobody to talk with."

"My father made me sad, Quinn."

"Yes, I know. And so did I."

Hannah gazed up at her. "I liked you when you came to our house for dinner that night and when you sent me the magazines. I even liked you when I didn't want to, after I saw you with my father at the hotel."

"Shh, it's all right. You don't have to like me, Hannah. Right now I don't like myself."

There was a brief silence.

Then Hannah said, "Did you feel hurt sometimes when you lived with other people? And didn't have any mother and father?"

"Yes, sometimes I hurt very much."

"What did you do then?"

"I called Doug and we talked. And then I felt better."

"He's your substitute father?"

Quinn smiled faintly. "Yes, he is. He gives good advice."

"I'd rather talk to my real father, since I have one."
Hannah shuddered with the last tears and snuggled

closer to Quinn, her coltish legs tangled in the blankets. "Is he mad at me, Quinn? For being a brat?"

"I don't think so, but maybe you should ask him yourself."

There was no answer, and after a few moments Quinn felt the slow breathing rhythm against her side as Hannah drifted into sleep, exhausted. She should have taken a stand before, but she'd been afraid. And the timing had been wrong. Tonight Hannah needed a woman's understanding. Quinn rested against the headboard, closing her eyes briefly, glad she'd been there for the child. When she opened them, she saw Welles in the doorway, his glasses in one hand, the other wiping his eyes.

"You heard?" she whispered.

"Enough."

"She'll be all right. She knows you love her."

"I need to tell her," he said, but Quinn waved him off.

"Later." She curved against Hannah, inhaling the sweetness of skin and soap and the faint, milky scent of whipped cream. Six years ago she'd lost a child: perhaps a little girl who would have grown like Hannah into a lovely young woman with joys and sorrows and confusions of her own. Quinn had mourned her baby. But until now she hadn't fully realized what she'd lost.

The next morning Quinn woke with gritty eyes and a crick in her neck; she'd fallen asleep very late the night before with her head at an angle on Doug's too-plump feather pillow.

The house was empty, or at least no one was around.

A note in the kitchen told her that Doug and Hannah had gone riding, which left Quinn alone in the house with a still-sleeping Welles.

She took a cup of coffee out into the yard and, as she always did in Colorado, sniffed the sharp clarity of a Rocky Mountain morning. Overhead the sky was a big blue bowl and the air was crisp, yet not cool enough. No clouds heralded a blizzard or the chance to ski, except on artificial snow. Even the weather this weekend wouldn't cooperate, Quinn thought.

She strolled toward the corral next to the weathered gray-shingle barn. One of Doug's geldings nosed her, looking for carrots, and Quinn laughed. "You always were a pig." She turned slightly, letting the horse nuzzle her backside, then pulled out a sugar cube. "With a sweet tooth to boot. Enjoy."

Except for the gelding, the corral was empty. Doug's hands were probably riding fence before winter set in. Leaning against the rail, she gazed into the distance at the Foothill Range, rising from the flatter surroundings like huge gray fingers pointing at the sky. On the slopes she saw patches of white, which soothed Quinn slightly as she forced herself to think of work. Valerie would arrive on Monday to help choose the specific shooting site and props for Hannah's next ad.

At a sharp whistle, Quinn turned around. Welles was walking across the barnyard, one of Doug's sheepdogs nipping at his heels. Quinn faced the corral again and talked to the gelding, offering him more of his favorite sugar.

"Guess I'm the last one up," Welles said, coming up beside her. He folded his arms across the top rail next to Quinn. "The coffee's pretty thick and black as tar."

"The price you pay," she murmured. "You didn't talk to Hannah?"

He shook his head. "Not yet. I don't want to talk about Hannah now." He looked at her, his eyes soft and hazy without glasses. "How long can we step around each other, Quinn?"

She tossed her coffee grounds over the fence into the corral, watched the horse toss his head at them and jog away.

"I promised you the truth," Welles said.

Quinn turned and started walking toward the house. "The truth isn't always easy to take."

His hand caught the crook of her elbow before she'd taken two steps. "We're alone. There won't be a better time."

Looking beyond his shoulder, Quinn went boneless with relief. "I'm afraid there'll have to be," she said, and in the same instant Hannah cantered into the yard from the nearby scrub woods on a paint pony, Doug right behind on his current favorite, a black stallion.

"Hey, you two." Doug's ruddy cheeks looked even more red after his ride. He reined the black to a halt in a small cloud of dust.

"How was your ride, Hannah?" Quinn asked, moving away from the fence.

"Fantastic. This is the first time I've used a western saddle. Right?" Her dark eyes sought Welles, who stood just behind Quinn.

"Right," he said, his voice taut.

"Maybe we could use my pony in an ad. Okay, Quinn?"

"We'll see. It's not a bad idea." The horse was black and white, and against a stark background of mountains and corral, the picture just might fit the Priceless image.

"You could have come with us, but Doug said you needed your beauty sleep."

"Thanks."

Doug grinned at her. "Thought it might help your disposition." He turned in the saddle. "Why don't you take the horses into the barn and unsaddle 'em, little darlin'? I'll come help you groom soon as I talk to your daddy and Quinn."

He dismounted, and Hannah took his reins as if

she'd been born on the ranch. As she led the horses off, Doug looked from Quinn to Welles.

"Am I in the middle of somethin' here, or what?"

"No," Quinn said.

"Yes," Welles murmured.

Doug scratched his chin, which was stubbled with gray whiskers he hadn't bothered to shave. "Wanted to ask you—if it's all right with you, I thought Hannah and me would drive over to Grand Junction tomorrow. I've had my eye on a perky little mare I might breed to my black. Thought we'd spend the night at a friend's place there."

Quinn's startled gaze met his. "Doug, I need Hannah to—"

"Fine with me." Welles settled his hands on Quinn's shoulders before she could move. "We have things to talk about."

"I figured." Doug gazed thoughtfully at Quinn, who could feel her face heat. Then he looked back at Welles. "Think I can trust you two in the house alone?"

"No," Welles answered.

Doug grinned. "You're all right, Welles. I like a man knows his own mind." He took a few steps toward the barn. "Lack of communication can kill a relationship faster'n a loose woman after someone else's man." He looked back at Quinn, his grin widening. "You listen for a change, you hear?"

The mantel clock ticked loudly in the silence, broken only by the creak of the rocking chair by the fire. Welles shifted on the sofa across from Quinn. Doug and Hannah had left before noon, and at eight o'clock Welles and Quinn were still circling each other.

He had made a dozen starts and stops. When he told

Quinn everything, another slap was the least he could expect.

"Jay's dead," he said now, his voice husky and his eyes avoiding hers. "I don't know where else to begin except with that. It's the truth, Quinn. I know you don't want to believe that, but—"

"I can't believe it."

Welles ran a hand through his hair. "All right. I can't change your mind about that phone call, but maybe I can change it about the rest." He sat up straighter, his hands locked between his spread knees. "Remember when I told you I'd killed two men the night Mai and I ran from Laos?"

"Yes."

Her face looked pale. His heart thumped in time with the clock. "One of them was Jay."

Quinn jumped up. "You're lying. Do you ever tell anything but lies?"

"Shreveport, my mother's drinking, the fact I had no father I could name: that's all true. I'm not proud of it, but it's fact."

"And Jay?"

"Most of it," he said. "When I got into the Navy— yeah, by lying—I did pretty well in training so they sent me on. When I got to 'Nam, I was assigned to fly with Jay. He was confident and cocky, I was . . . just cocky. Maybe that's why we hit it off. Only he saw right away that my arrogance covered up a teenage kid, straight off the streets and scared out of his shoes." Welles shrugged. "He took me under his wing, as they say. Taught me everything about that Phantom and turned me into a pretty damn good aviator. Jay was crazy himself sometimes, taking chances, pulling stunts in the air, but he knew his stuff. After a while, so did I."

"And then?"

"We flew north as part of the President's stepped-up bombing campaign that Christmas. And we didn't come back."

"And when the plane crashed? Not two," she said, "but one?"

Welles went to the fireplace, adding more logs to the fire and poking at it until sparks showered onto the grate. "Jay got caught in his safety harness. I couldn't get him out. I'd been hurt myself—smashed my leg up pretty bad, as you know—and I kept blacking out. There wasn't much pain then, I was in shock and feeling numb. All I remember was smelling jet fuel, leaking all around us." He turned, his gaze bleak as it met Quinn's. "'Get me out of here, Cochran!' he yelled."

"But you left him," Quinn accused.

"No." Welles shook his head, trying to clear it of the memories he could no longer avoid. "No, I—I had this cheap knockoff of a Swiss army knife, but when I tried sawing the nylon straps in two, the blade snapped. I could smell the jet fuel, stronger now, could hear Jay yelling. Cussing me. Begging me." He pressed two fingers to the bridge of his nose. "I didn't have any choice, Quinn. I had to leave the plane and try to find help."

"So you told yourself."

"Yeah, maybe. Maybe I did. I crawled away from that wreck just as I'd left Shreveport—any damn way I could."

"And for the same reason."

"To save my own ass?" He smiled bitterly. "Right again. Maybe you ought to tell the story."

Her look was cool. "Doug's accused me of not listening; Andrew, of persisting in my own obsession. Go on," she said. "I won't say a word."

"I don't know how long it took me to get away. I limped and fell and crawled and passed out, then limped again. The next thing I knew I was on a straw mat in a hut and Mai was bending over me."

"And because of that, you think Jay is dead?"

"No," he said.

She couldn't help adding, "That's what you told me."

"I didn't tell you everything. By the time I could send somebody to look for him, he was gone and the plane was just a shell. The plane didn't explode, but they torched the cockpit, I guess."

"Who?"

"Vietcong. They took Jay and held him. When I saw him again two months later—" He broke off. "Quinn, he'd had some pretty bad wounds himself. While he was laid up with the VC, someone decided he'd be a better patient if they took the edge off his pain with some horse."

"Heroin?"

Welles nodded, his throat tight. "He got in with Mai's brother, who was a real bad actor. When Nguyen tracked her to the village where I was staying, he brought Jay with him."

Quinn put a hand to her heart.

"Jay called me a traitor," Welles went on, "a killer, a lot of other names I probably deserved. But he was out of his head from the drugs, so I didn't pay much attention."

Quinn leaned forward, listening raptly.

"As you know, Nguyen tried to bargain with Mai for the jade." Welles shook his head again. He was back in the hut, which smelled of sweat and rotten fish, of fear. His words came haltingly. "When the switch was made, Nguyen saw his chance and jumped us. So did Jay. He did everything Nguyen told him like a robot. He must have had a lot of shit on board that night, or else he could have taken one look in my eyes and known that I was going to try to help him."

"Jay fought you?" Quinn asked.

Welles rested his forehead against the mantel. "Nguyen came after me first. I used my survival training to put him away. Surprised the hell out of myself, because I never thought I could snap a man's neck with my bare hands."

"Dear God."

"One second he was flying at me; the next he was on the dirt floor of the hut, stone dead." Welles raised his head. "Jay came at me then, in a rage. Nguyen had messed up his head, I suppose; it was like he was in some cult or something and had to act, had to get me for getting Nguyen. He yelled some stuff, I don't remember what—about being left behind, I guess—then he pulled a knife on me."

"I can't believe Jay would—"

"He wasn't the Jay Barron you fell in love with, Quinn. He probably hadn't been for a long time, if he ever was. All the masks got ripped away over there. The pretenses. In those moments he was far from being the golden boy of Pacific Heights, the Navy hero. He was a strung-out junkie with a bunch of half-healed wounds, most of them infected, and out of his mind. I was the kid from Shreveport again, fighting my way to school every day and up against the wall with another gang member shoving a blade at me." He gazed past Quinn into the middle distance, as if seeing the fight again. "The kid won," he said. "I'd been getting ready for that fight all my life."

"You really killed him?" Quinn said.

"He fell at my feet. His own knife in his gut. Blood everywhere. . . ."

She buried her face in her hands. He hated himself.

"You wanted the truth, Quinn."

Lifting her head, her eyes wide, she stared at Welles and he stared back.

"Do you believe me now?" he said.

"Yes." The word was a whisper. "You couldn't have made that up if you tried."

The clock ticked louder. The fire crackled as a log fell, splintering through the grate. Embers shattered like Fourth of July sparklers, pinpoints of fire showering onto the tile hearth.

"So now you know," he said.

"Now I know." Her voice sounded as taut as his, and he watched her bite her lip.

"I didn't want to tell you, Quinn. I didn't want to hurt you. I thought if I told you—when I told you—you wouldn't believe me." He held her gaze with his. "I think it's even worse that you do." And with a last look, he left the room to climb the stairs.

Quinn sat in the deathly silence for long moments, feeling numb at first, then feeling the pain of knowing at long last, before, surprised at herself, she went after him. His bedroom door was already shut, and no light shone under it. Quinn knocked lightly but there was no answer.

She pushed open the door into darkness and more silence.

"Welles?"

Nothing. Her pulse thumped as she felt her way across the room, bumping into a chair near the door, then the edge of the nightstand by the single bed.

He was sitting on the edge of the mattress, holding his glasses, his gaze fixed on his hands.

"Welles?" she whispered, rubbing her shin.

"My name's Cochran." His voice broke. Quinn sat beside him. "Jesus, when I saw that picture, saw myself again. Christ, I was just a kid. I never wanted anything more in my life than to get out of that crummy apartment and away from my mother, to be somebody else. But you're right, I've never been anybody except Mike

Cochran, looking over his shoulder, waiting for the phone to ring, for the knock on the door." He shivered. "Jay could be a crazy bastard, but he was my best friend—my only friend—and I took his life."

"He would have taken yours."

He glanced up, obviously surprised at her acceptance; then he looked at his hands again. "I killed him, Quinn. And part of me wasn't even sorry. Part of me wanted what he had . . . the family, the money, the chances." He looked at her from the corner of his eye. "I fell for a bunch of anecdotes about this sweet, gutsy girl with a fragile heart under all the sass, and maybe I was glad when he died. Maybe I thought I'd have you."

"Don't," Quinn murmured.

"I've had all the years he didn't." The glasses snapped in his fingers. "In Geneva," he said, "living my careful life with Mai and Hannah, my job at the bank."

She pried the glasses from him and set them on the table. "It's been a good life. Not perfect but good."

"Has it? I wanted to be like him, so much that when I chose my own name, it even had his initials. JWB . . . WJB."

"Those initials led me to you," Quinn murmured.

His gaze jerked up, meeting hers, and she saw the light in them even in the darkness. "Quinn?"

"Hold me."

Welles reached for her, groaning as they came together, leaving no space between, like two matchsticks in a full box. Quinn pressed her cheek into the hollow of his shoulder, pressed her mouth to the soft cotton of his shirt, and Welles wrapped her in his arms.

"I was so afraid to tell you," he whispered. "The only thing that kept me going was that you used my present name, not my real one."

"Welles is your real name now." Quinn tried to smile

against his shirt, but her lips quivered. "You've had it longer than the other one."

She heard him take a shaky breath. In the dark he bent his head and lifted her chin, his eyes closing, his mouth groping for hers. "Quinn. God, don't turn me out."

Her mouth opened under his and her tongue went seeking. Spirals of dark sensation made her heart speed, her limbs feel weak. She felt the muscles in Welles's arms tremble as he drew her closer, their bodies touching from shoulder to hip, then eased her back onto the narrow bed.

The subtle scents of clean skin and woodsmoke seemed intensified by the friction of his clothes against hers, and suddenly Quinn had no patience with confinement. She twisted, fumbling with his buttons and zippers, pushing cotton and denim aside.

Their fingers brushed as Welles drew her jeans down her hips, her legs, and over her bare feet. His hand skimmed up, past her narrow waist, to the half-open front of her shirt, pulling the last buttons free, pulling it over her shoulders and then off completely. All the while, his mouth stayed on hers and she could hear her own breathing. She had her arms around his waist, yanking at his shirt. She lay trapped beneath him, Welles with one leg over her, the hard ridge of his erection at the juncture of her thighs.

She had never wanted him more.

He'd told her a tale of deception and death, a tale in which Jay Barron no longer played the more innocent role. Quinn fought tears at the thought of a younger, terrified Welles and moved closer still, moaning into his mouth as he changed the angle of their kiss.

"Welles."

"Wait." He rolled off the bed, groping his way to the

chest across from it. Quinn heard a drawer scrape open, then close, but when he came back to her he didn't bring only the protection she expected. In the darkness she saw a flash of light, then another, like stars tumbling from the sky. He leaned over her, pouring diamonds and milky pearls and soft green jade across her breasts. "I wanted to show you these."

Quinn lifted her head to stare down at herself. In the room lit only by a pale yellow slice of moon, she watched the gems wink and glitter. "My God. The necklace. The Tears of Jade."

Their eyes met, his somber, before Welles bent, arranging gold and green and cream and utter clarity over her until all Quinn wore was a delicate collar gleaming in the moonlight. She held her breath.

"But where—?"

"From Mai," he whispered. "Shh."

His mouth, warm and open, lightly grazed her skin from shoulder to shoulder. Then his lips planted kisses there, as if he were seating gems, carefully, one by one, in another golden setting.

"But this is Hannah's," Quinn whispered.

Welles lifted his head and stared into her eyes, letting a finger follow a single setting in the necklace's arch from prismed diamond to perfect pearl to jade droplet and onto Quinn's bare skin. She felt both cold and warm, the cool diamonds, the heated gold.

"We shouldn't—" Quinn raised a hand but Welles captured her fingers before she could pull the jade away.

"For twenty years it's been a lie, causing pain . . . except for Hannah, except for you." He lowered his head to trail kisses over her naked skin, to drag the jade lightly from her shoulders to her breasts to the narrow indentation of her waist. "Wear it, just this once, so it won't make me think of darkness and sorrow when I see it again."

"Oh," Quinn cried, her body curving upward, offering her breast. His mouth closed over it and, like the sweep of his tongue on her nipple, she felt the jade slide, warm and fluid, on her bare stomach, in Welles's hand.

His breathing was ragged. "I make you hot, don't I?"

"Yes."

"Hotter than with Andrew?" he said, his mouth on the tender spot beneath her ear. The jade tingled her navel and Quinn groaned.

"Yes!"

In the same instant, with a soft grunt that seemed almost a prayer of thanksgiving, he entered her. She circled his hips with her legs, holding tight, and followed his rhythm, slow at first, easy, and then faster, harder.

"Hotter than with Jay?" he demanded.

"*Yes!*"

And with the next thrust of his hips, Welles sent caution scattering like pins across a marble floor, like the rest of reason. Only one thing mattered now, to either of them.

As the jade fell from his hand and flowed over her hip as if its gold setting were molten, and dropped with a soft plop onto the carpet, Quinn shivered.

"Let it go, baby." He arched deeper. "Let him go."

"Oh, Welles. . . ."

"Trust me." The climax burst in her like a thunderstorm over the mountains, and as Quinn shuddered in his arms, he shuddered too, breathing the words into her mouth. "I love you."

21

Andrew had long ago stopped believing in love. Or in much of anything, for that matter. So he couldn't answer his own question as he shuffled down the jetway on Monday into Denver's Stapleton Airport: What the hell was he doing here?

The question stayed in his mind as he rented a car, then drove to Boulder. He was still asking it when he turned off the highway onto the dirt access road that led to Doug Lloyd's ranch.

Andrew was a city boy. The dust rose in cotton puffs around the car, choking him. Yet he knew this road like his own hand, like the scars that mapped his leg. He knew every bump and hollow, no matter how many times Doug had scraped or filled them over the years, knew the exact instant when the rental car would bounce on its springs into the barnyard and the two-story sprawl of a house, weathered shingle with a red roof and a wraparound porch, would come into view.

Still, when it did, his heart seemed to stop. Andrew nudged a button, and the car window rolled down. He heard the bawling of cattle from the nearby pasture, the greeting call and answering whinny of two horses in the corral. A sheepdog yapped from the front porch of the house, and a rooster crowed in the distance. Far off, in the direction of the bunkhouse, several doors slammed.

Then he realized that one of them had come from much closer. The screen door of the ranch house was still quivering on its hinges and Doug Lloyd himself stood, spraddle-legged, on the top step.

"Afternoon, Andrew." In a red wool shirt and jeans, his ubiquitous cowboy boots worn at the heels, Doug stamped toward him. "What brings you west after all this time?"

Andrew couldn't say. He repeated his own question to himself. Considering Quinn, Doug wouldn't have much use for him now and Andrew couldn't blame him.

"I missed Thanksgiving," he said, climbing slowly from the car and dragging the blackthorn stick off the seat. His leg had seized up during the trip from the airport, the first time he'd driven since the accident. "I thought maybe you'd have some leftover turkey and cranberries for a sandwich."

Doug sized him up. It took one lonely man to recognize another, Andrew supposed, as he had with Valerie.

Doug squinted at the clear sky, then the snow-covered peaks in the distance. "Quinn's over on the far side of the barn in the pasture. Has some idea that these mountains and one of my horses make the right background for Welles Blackburn's daughter and those jeans she's selling."

He hadn't mentioned Blackburn by mistake. Andrew inhaled the aromas of fresh-cut grass and animal sweat that always pervaded the ranch, a thousand memories of the years past and his marriage. "I'm not looking for Quinn," he said.

He started walking, but Doug blocked his way. "You hurt my girl again, I won't care about that walking stick of yours. First thing I'll do is kick it out from under you."

"Quinn should have done that years ago," Andrew said, and headed for the pasture gate.

Inside the fence, he stopped to prop the blackthorn stick against the rails. Perhaps a hundred feet from him, Quinn and Valerie stood in a huddle. In the sun Quinn's hair was a bright bonfire, her form slim and sleek, but it was Valerie he focused on, Valerie he began walking toward without the aid of his crutch.

His leg throbbing, he was almost there when she must have sensed his presence and turned, her mouth set in a straight line. "What are you doing here?" She asked his own question when he was still ten feet from her.

"I came to see you."

Her eyes flickered and Quinn looked over her shoulder, gaze widening too.

"You're a little late," Valerie said.

"Better late than never."

He took the last few painful steps and stood, staring at her in the bright sun, hearing the lowing of cattle all around them. He didn't realize they were alone until he glanced up, away from the smokiness of her eyes; Quinn was strolling back toward the gate.

"I feel like a fool," he said. He turned back and found Valerie watching him. "I know you're angry and you have a right to be. I said a lot of things I didn't mean—"

"You meant them."

He lifted his brows. "Yes, I guess I did. At the time. There's nothing like sitting alone in an empty one-bedroom apartment to put a man's feelings—his priorities—into perspective."

"Don't you dare make some half-assed apology and

then thump your way out of my life again—" She broke off, looking at his leg. "You're not using your stick."

Andrew smiled faintly. He felt shaky, but he was still on his feet. "Doug and I agreed a few minutes ago that I don't need it anymore."

"Really." Her right eye was drifting.

"My leg's not good just yet," he went on, "and your eye"—he lifted a hand to touch her—"isn't working so well right now. Maybe we're okay for each other."

Valerie swatted his hand away. "I'm okay for myself, Andrew. That's all I can handle."

Taking another step, he brushed his fingers over her stomach and his own belly tightened. Had she done something crazy while he was making up his mind? "What about the baby?"

Her eyes closed briefly. "The baby's fine too."

Andrew let his breath out. "That's good. I'm glad."

"The baby doesn't care if I wear funky earrings or purple harem pants with a red cossack shirt. When I feel like it," she said, looking down at her jeans and plain white shirt with the tails out. "He loves me just as I am."

"What makes you sure it's a boy?" he said, and then, "I love you too."

Her gaze flew to his. She took a deep breath, her cheeks pink, her lips parted. "If you're lying, so help me, Devlin, I'll stampede these cows and let them trample you into the ground."

"No more than I deserve." His hand, which he realized still rested on the faint, soft roundness of Valerie's stomach, drifted higher. Over her still discernible waist, over the swell of her breast. "You're bigger. You feel okay?"

"I feel fine—now."

Andrew took her shoulders, pulling her tight against

him. His lips moved in her hair, the slight breeze blowing strands across his cheek. "I missed you," he said. "I sat in that furnished apartment on Thanksgiving night, eating a TV dinner, and I cried. I realized that I've been unfair to Quinn for a long time—even realized that our marriage was as much a mistake on my part as on hers, that I was hedging my bets just as she has been, obsessing about Jay Barron. Then I realized what I really needed."

Waiting, Valerie leaned back in his arms.

"Therapy." He tightened his hold, because she looked vaguely disappointed. "I called some people. Doctors Quinn found for me when we moved to New York, specialists who wanted to help me then—but I refused to let them." His mouth quirked. "I start treatments next week and they're really going to make me sweat. I might be looking at more surgery, but the prognosis is pretty good."

"Quinn always said so."

"She was right about a lot of things. So were you." He hesitated. "But I went through my drawings, and about them I was right. They're not good enough. I thank you for your encouragement, for your support—"

"You sound like an acceptance speech at the Emmy awards."

But he had to say it all. "And I'm sorry for the abuse I heaped on you in my own frustration. I won't publish again, at least not for a while. So I went out and got myself a job—or the promise of one."

"A job?"

"You've never known me when I was gainfully employed," he said, beginning to smile. "It seems that the art department at NYU needs an instructor with my background, just a few classes to start with, but once we work out the details I can pick up in January with the new semester."

"Andrew, that's wonderful!"

"I don't know much about kids," he said, glancing at her stomach again, "but I've been around Hannah for a few months and didn't do so bad. In grad school I was a teaching assistant. Maybe those college kids won't think I'm too much of a jerk now."

"You're showing definite signs of improvement."

Andrew lowered his head, nuzzling her throat. He locked his arms at the small of her back to bring her closer, to stabilize himself. "What do you think about me as a father?"

"You're already a father. Biologically speaking."

His lips stilled against her skin. "Ah, Val. It's been a long time since I thought about the future. About life being good again." He raised his head to look at her. "So what do you think?"

"You might make a darn good daddy once the baby gets here."

Andrew's slow smile turned into a grin.

"Gives me something to shoot for," he said. "By the time he's ready, maybe I'll be able to show him something about baseball and football."

Valerie groaned. "Why not drawing lessons?"

"That too," he said.

"Don't tell me I'm going to be a sports widow, a mother, and a bride all at once." Then her cheeks colored. "You *are* going to marry me, aren't you?"

Andrew's grin broadened. "What did your horoscope say this morning?"

"'Be prepared for a new beginning and a surprise visit from an old friend.'" Valerie was smiling too.

"Did you make that up?"

"No."

"I'll marry you anyway," Andrew told her, then touched his mouth to hers. The question had stopped ringing in his mind. He'd known the answer all along.

Moments later, walking Valerie back to the house, he hoped Quinn would find hers with Welles Blackburn.

Welles kicked his horse into an easy canter and headed back to the barn. He didn't consider himself much of a rider, but Doug Lloyd had assured him the gelding had good manners and could be trusted to bring him home again. Just behind Welles, Hannah loped along on another of Doug's placid quarter horses, as silent as she'd been for the past hour.

Not even the breathless scenery, a long stretch of green grass that seemed to end abruptly at the face of a mountain, or the vast blue sky had brought a response. If the crisp thin air, still sharp in midafternoon, cleaned New York's pollution from her lungs too, she didn't say. She hadn't spoken a word to him during the enforced ride, and the back of Welles's neck prickled.

Maybe he shouldn't have insisted on this time alone. They certainly weren't working things out, but he'd run out of excuses to wait. She'd been with Doug in Grand Junction at his friend's ranch, buying a mare, until late Sunday. This was his first chance with Hannah—or so he'd told himself—since he'd seen her with Quinn on Thanksgiving night, and he'd blown it. Royally.

Welles shifted in his saddle. Of course he'd already blown it that morning with a half-dozen steps down Doug Lloyd's hall.

He'd spent the night with Quinn again, slipping into her room after Doug and Hannah finally went to bed, and had all but forgotten they weren't alone in the house. At first light Quinn kicked him out. Heading for the bathroom with his unappeased morning erection zipped into his pants, he ran into Hannah.

Her gaze jerked from his bare chest to his jeans, then

to Quinn's bedroom door. Her face flushed, she turned and ran while Welles cursed himself.

Later, as they'd saddled their horses at his insistence, Hannah had flirted with one of Doug's young hands. Soon she'd be dating. Welles tightened his grip on the reins. If he didn't regain control, his influence on her would be gone; Hannah would be lost to him forever.

"Look," he said, pulling his horse up short, "we're not going back to the damn house until we have this out."

"Have what out?"

"You'll make me say it, won't you?" Just like Mai. She wouldn't look at him, but her horse stood quietly and Welles kneed his gelding closer, facing her. "All right. I slept with Quinn last night. I slept with her in Zermatt and while you and Doug were gone."

When Hannah tried to ride past him, Welles caught her reins.

"Listen to me, dammit. I've had enough of your judgments against me and Quinn. I'm not just your father. I'm a human being. A man. I love Quinn, and I think she loves me." She hadn't said as much, though, a small detail that had been sticking in his mind. "Hannah, I know it's tough but try to understand. When your mother and I get divorced, and Quinn's is final too, I want to marry her."

"Divorce his, divorce hers." Hannah's voice quivered. "You make the perfect modern couple. I suppose you'll have kids together."

"I hope so."

"Then I'll be like everybody else in my school, with half sisters and brothers all over the place. Parents here, parents there."

"Would that be so bad?"

She shrugged, and at her obvious misery Welles nudged his horse closer. Hannah's gaze met his, then flickered away.

"Don't you love Mother at all?"

He couldn't answer directly. "Your mother and I went through a lot together," he said. "No matter how we've ended up, that bond will always be between us—but no, I don't love her the way I love Quinn." He paused, searching for the right words. His voice had gone hoarse. "Hannah, sometimes people fall out of love with each other just as they fall in love at the beginning. But that's a man-woman, not a parent, thing."

Her voice was barely audible. "Mother wants custody, doesn't she? Will she get it?"

Welles looked at the sky as if for answers. "I don't know, Hannah. I hope not. We'll work it out."

She raised her head, eyes brimming. "But who will I live with?"

The words had been torn from her, and they slammed him in the gut. God, he'd been worried about Quinn when all along Hannah had been wondering where she belonged. At her age, in Shreveport, he'd wondered the same thing himself. "I don't know," he said, not wanting to push. His heart beat erratically. "You're old enough now that sooner or later some judge may ask your preference. I'm not asking which of us you'll choose—"

"I choose you!"

With the words, Hannah tumbled from her horse into his arms. He had no choice but to let her horse go free, watching it head—as Doug had told him it always would—for the barn. His own horse danced, so Welles held his daughter with one arm while he brought the gelding under control with the other. They stood for long moments, the horse shifting restlessly beneath them at the extra weight, Welles's embrace tight and sheltering.

He stroked her back, his tone thick. "Hey, hot stuff. I love you."

Hannah only buried her face deeper in his shoulder.

"You know that, don't you? Nothing will ever change that." Another shrug, another blow to his gut. "Oh, baby," Welles murmured in amazement. "You don't know that."

"As much as you love Quinn?" She lifted her head.

"Every bit as much. Just different, that's all."

"Man and woman," Hannah whispered. "But I'm your girl?"

Welles shut his eyes. "There you go."

"Daddy?" She waited for him to look at her. "I like Quinn too." She corrected herself. "Not all the way, but I'm working on it. Are you really going to marry her?"

"I'm gonna give it my best shot, gorgeous."

Hannah giggled and the horse snorted.

"Come here," Welles said, gathering her close again. His thighs were half asleep and his back ached but he didn't care. "Let's get something else straight. Your mother's right and so was Quinn. I've spoiled you. There'll be some rules from here on, and you'll stick to them. Understand me?"

"Mm-hmm."

"Then plant one here," Welles murmured, pointing. With a laugh, Hannah kissed his chin. "Here," he said, getting another smacking kiss on his cheekbone. "And here."

Hannah kissed him soundly on his nose. "I love you too, Daddy. Even when I was mad at you, I still loved you."

"There you go," he said again. For a while longer, he had his Hannah back. Welles let the reins slacken, taking her face in his hands. "I want you to know one more thing. Your mother loves you too, baby. I know sometimes she doesn't show it, but she does. When I left Geneva, she gave me a gift for you—a very special gift."

Hannah's eyes brightened. "The jade necklace?"

"It's yours." He couldn't tell her that Mai had flung it

at him with the words, "Take it! You've taken everything
else I love." Quinn had helped him free himself. For too
long he and Mai had kept any knowledge of the jade
from Hannah, but now whatever she didn't know but
wanted to learn, he'd tell her. He cradled Hannah close
for a moment. "She hopes it will give you the happiness
it would have given her, if her mother had been able to
give it to her when she was your age."

"Is it at the house?"

"Yes."

"Let's go see."

"Turn around." She swung her leg over the saddle,
facing forward in front of him, and Welles nudged the
gelding into a slow trot. Quinn, Hannah. He'd faced his
past and his daughter, and the future looked just fine.

So why was the back of his neck prickling, as it had
on the day Jay Barron took that old Louisville Slugger
skidding down through the jungle and almost killed
them both?

His neck was still tingling when Welles rode back into
the barnyard and dismounted, helping Hannah down.

Frowning, he said, "Why don't you go back to the
house while I rub the horses down?"

"Can't they wait, Daddy? The Tears of Jade—"

"Have been in my room for days. They can wait a
while longer, but these horses can't." Leading his own, he
walked over to the corral fence where Hannah's gelding
stood, feet splayed, neck down, munching tufts of coarse
grass. He was still saddled, and no one else seemed to be
around. Then Welles noted a car, Andrew's, he supposed,
parked near the front porch at the house. "Doug has
company. Maybe you could help him out and put a pot of
coffee on for me at the same time."

"Okay, Daddy." Hannah, like any teenager, seemed only too happy to be relieved of her chores. She liked horses, she'd told him, "but not the way they smell on your hands after you brush them."

In the barn doorway, holding two sets of reins, Welles paused to look after her. The back of his neck prickled again, but he pushed away any dark thoughts. Force of habit, he thought; he'd spent twenty years looking over his shoulder for trouble.

He went into the barn out of the sunlight, blinking at the darkness, and hooked both horses to their crossties in the aisle. He unsaddled them. Then, his eyes growing accustomed to the lower light, he found Doug's grooming box in the tack room and began brushing the horses down as Doug had taught him earlier.

The work was mindless, soothing, and he let his thoughts drift. The divorces, the custody suit for Hannah, his own job problems . . . all would end in time. His promotion at the bank belonged to Thornton now of course, thanks to the divorce and Tran, but he'd been thinking about a change anyway. He had the contacts, the knowledge to do well in a venture capital firm. He'd get work in New York, and he and Quinn would buy a house in Connecticut or a co-op in the city, if Hannah wanted to stay in school there. Maybe tonight he'd take Doug and Hannah and Quinn—hell, Andrew and Valerie too; Quinn had told him about them as he saddled the horses—into town for a celebratory dinner.

Nice and civilized, why not? The thought calmed him.

One of the horses snorted, swinging its head around to peer at the open door. "Easy, boy." At first Welles could see nothing but a mote-filled shower of sunlight. Then the other gelding whinnied and stamped a foot, his shoe ringing on stone, and Welles stared more closely at the doorway.

He felt his heart skip once, then thud heavily again. Tall and broad-shouldered, with a build similar to his own, a figure stood there. As his pupils adjusted to the light, Welles couldn't help but recognize him. Silent, the man walked into the barn, his steps measured and soundless, his expression shadowed.

Although Welles tried to tell himself he was wrong, he knew better. He knew the cocky walk that was a near swagger. And in that instant he knew he'd been wrong; on one count at least, he was no murderer.

Resting his hand on the horse's warm side, Welles leaned against the animal's greater strength, feeling his own muscles turn to water. He wasn't sure how long he could stand up.

"Jay," he finally managed.

"Stinks in here," Jay Barron said. The closer he got, the more familiar he became. Welles looked for changes. His lighter brown hair still seemed the color of coffee, but he wore it longer now. "That you or these horses?" he asked, with the same arrogant grin that had haunted Welles's nightmares.

"Both," he whispered.

"Never thought you'd end up mucking stalls for Doug Lloyd and smelling of . . . is that sweat or fear?"

"Both," Welles repeated.

He looked into Jay's brown eyes and swallowed. They were the same, yet not the same. Still with a hint of the wise guy, they appeared older, harder. He had that thousand-yard stare Welles had seen so often in Vietnam, as if he rarely focused close up—as if he couldn't afford to if he wanted to stay alive.

Welles dropped his gaze, unconsciously searching for the barrel of a gun or the glint of a knife in Jay's hand.

When he'd believed Quinn that Jay was alive, after the telephone call, he'd welcomed a confrontation, the chance to put his past to rest. Instead, he'd decided Jay was dead and he'd given Quinn the truth as he knew it. Now he had Quinn and Hannah and a future. He didn't want to die.

"Cochran, for Christ's sake. You look like your heart's about to give out." Jay peered into his eyes. "The way you must have looked in that damn cockpit when we crashed. Bloody hell," he murmured. "Am I that much of a surprise?"

"A man doesn't look his own mortality in the face every day," Welles said. But seeing no weapons, he took a chance and turned his back. His fingers clutched the grooming brush with white knuckles, but he forced his hand to make long, sweeping strokes over the horse's hide. He didn't know where to begin with the questions. "How'd you find me?"

"After looking for you nearly half my life? I saw that Priceless ad and the jade earrings—and the girl wearing them. She looks just like her mother did twenty years ago." He stood on the other side of the horse, facing Welles. "She's got your ears and your smile. Hit me right between the eyes like a gook bullet."

"Jesus, Jay."

"Relax. I'm not going to kill you." The tough tone softened. "I wouldn't mind if you wet your pants or something, though. Show you missed me a little, wondered what happened to me."

Welles couldn't speak. He felt as if his past and Jay's hands were around his throat again, squeezing.

Jay shook his head. "You left me on that hut floor for dead. Your mistake, pal. The knife missed anything vital, and your village buddies fixed me up. I can't recommend their brand of medicine, but I survived."

Welles nearly choked on the words. "And Mai's brother?"

"Deader than a raccoon on a road, I'm happy to say. But

I'm afraid you'll have to meet your maker on that one."

His whole body was trembling. Twenty years, he thought.

While Welles made shaky strokes over the gelding's hide, Jay told him about kicking his heroin habit and then escaping from Laos, about working for a top-secret branch of Intelligence ever since. "I wasn't allowed to contact anybody," he finished. "Not even my own family or Quinn. I did call Doug Lloyd once or twice to ask how she was." He grinned. "Doug—upstanding lawman that he was—wouldn't give me her number. I ought to thank him. It wasn't the wisest thing I've done. I'd have blown my own cover and made her miserable."

Welles tightened his grip on the brush. "She was miserable enough," he said, "wondering where you were. She's believed all these years that you were still alive."

"You thought different, of course."

"She put her life on hold for you, Jay." The notion didn't seem to concern him. "If I have any say, that's over now." He paused. "I love her. I never thought I'd love anyone in my life as much as I love Quinn."

"Doug told me she was married."

"To Andrew Devlin," Welles admitted.

Jay tilted his head to study Welles. "So tell me, Cochran. How'd you end up here with my woman? Put a knife through Devlin?"

Welles stroked the horse's hide. "They're getting divorced."

"How'd you meet her in the first place?"

"She met me," he said. Briefly, he talked about Geneva. "She thought, from the back, that I was you."

Jay threw his head back and laughed. "Now, that's irony."

Welles's voice tightened a notch. "She's been looking for you ever since the crash, Jay."

"And I've been looking for you."

"Well, you found me."

He tensed, waiting, but Jay only laughed again.

"Jesus, maybe we should hold a reunion or something. Whataya think?"

"I think you should do what you came to do." Welles dropped the brush into the grooming box and walked around the horse's rump. He stood toe to toe with Jay Barron. "Fight me. Beat my ass this time—or try to." He knotted his fists.

Jay gave him a considering look. "Yeah, there was a time when I'd have done just that. When it was all I thought about. Funny," he said, "how your perceptions change." He looked away. "Not too long ago I began to think better of killing you. Strange what a hundred and ten pounds of loyalty and devotion can do for a man."

His heart sank. His mind spun. Welles felt himself sliding, the rough boards scraping his shirt, his spine through the cloth. Then he was sitting on his haunches, his head tipped back against the wall of a stall.

"Quinn?" he managed. "You mean—?"

Jay looked at him for a long moment, then grinned, as he always had when Welles mentioned her, asked about her, gazed at her picture with hungry eyes.

"Where can I find her?"

His pulse kicked like one of Doug's unbroken horses. Welles wanted to warn her, but what good would it do? She'd always expected him to come back; she'd always believed. Welles had always thought the worst thing he could imagine was his past turning up. Then he'd met Quinn and thought the worst thing would be having to tell her the truth. Then he'd thought that, worse than the truth, was having her believe it—and hate him for it. Now he knew that wasn't the worst thing at all. The worst thing he could imagine was loving Quinn and having Jay Barron come back for her after twenty years.

"She's in the pasture working out a shot for the next Priceless ad."

"Thanks, Cochran. Or should I say Blackburn?"

Welles struggled to his feet, watching Jay Barron walk across the dirt yard to the gate. He wouldn't go after them, he told himself. He stood watching for some time—he couldn't have said how long—after Jay disappeared from sight, whistling. Welles wasn't a murderer or a liar now, but he was still a goddamn coward. His legs wouldn't carry him that far.

He couldn't take the risk. But with the thought, he was already taking one step, then another, moving out into the sunlight. Moving toward Quinn. She was his now. How could he not go to her?

Quinn squinted against the sun, holding up both hands as a frame for the mountains. Though she could have used Valerie's help, she was alone. The black and white backdrop still seemed best, but she needed a color accent. The jade again? Gleaming, milky-green diamonds sparkling in the light? Maybe they'd even use the necklace. The jade could be the unifying theme for the campaign. . . .

"I never could picture you anywhere but here. Certainly not in New York."

The low tone, the familiar deep voice, brought her head around. For a moment Quinn could only stare. Her heart pounded and her limbs went weak.

"I don't believe it," she said at last, shaking her head.

He stood for a moment, one hand on the gate, then closed it.

"Believe it," he said. "Come over here and convince yourself I'm real."

To her own surprise, Quinn stayed where she was, her blood running ice-cold with shock. The coffee-colored hair, the brown eyes. It couldn't be. She'd believed all these years, but he couldn't be. . . .

When once she would have moved, flown, raced to him over the few yards between them, now she couldn't. She had always been the one to give more, to go to him, Quinn realized, even before Vietnam; since then, she'd searched and yearned and settled for nothing at all— until Welles. He would have to come to her this time.

He walked slowly toward her through the pasture, picking his way around cow flops and large stones, the grin on his face the same that she had loved so many years ago.

"Oh, Jay." Her voice broke. She'd rehearsed this meeting a million times but all she could say was, "Jay."

"It's really me, beautiful." He took her hands in his, warm and calloused. "I always pictured you here in Doug Lloyd's field, cowgirl."

"I love it here. I'd forgotten how much."

She had a thousand questions but couldn't seem to ask one. She let Jay lead her to a shady spot beneath an aspen, urge her to sit down. "I've got a lot to say, a lot of miles to cover." But when he opened his arm to enfold her, she drew back.

"A lot of years," she murmured.

Jay studied her. "You mean we're strangers now."

Her gaze traveled over him, seeing the changes that time and experience and perhaps trouble had carved into his features. He was no longer the carefree Jay she'd known, had loved, just as she was no longer innocent, persistent, sassy Quinn. "We live different lives," she said.

Quinn haltingly sketched in her life with Andrew, then talked about her work and, briefly, Welles, but felt awkward, distanced. Jay told her about Vietnam and his life afterward, about his recent decision to retire from government service. "I'll do some teaching—training— at Quantico, but right now I'm on my way home," he finished, "to San Francisco to see Charles."

Quinn thought of Welles and his penchant for hamburgers and cowboy boots, for cheddar cheese and pecan pie—stored in the freezer in Zermatt.

"I'm glad, Jay, but I should warn you: Charles may be difficult."

"He always was, and I haven't exactly fit the family mold." He paused. "I've killed people, Quinn. Quite a few people. He won't understand. But it's time I made my peace."

Because she had so recently made her own, the questions tumbled out. Her shock had faded and Quinn felt more like herself. Jay tried to fill her in, but much of his life was classified.

"Hell," he finished, "Cochran could have saved me a lot of grief if he'd turned that knife half an inch to the right or left. He had a right to kill me." Jay got to his feet and helped her up. "I was a grandstander then, Quinn. A real hot dog. I used to make Cochran break out in a cold sweat when we flew. Poor kid," he murmured. "I should have been ashamed of myself. But he's got this funny streak of . . . I don't know what to call it."

"Honesty?" Quinn said.

Jay grinned. "He lied to get into the Navy. Christ, he was no different from a thousand other boys, but he never let himself off the hook. Drove me nuts."

Quinn smiled softly and he said, "You're crazy about him, aren't you?"

She nodded. "Yes. Yes, I am. Do you mind?"

"I wish you all the best, beautiful. If he doesn't take care of you, let me know." Jay paused. "I was never the guy for you," he said. "Cochran was. I always thought,

Put him on a white charger and he'd ride hell-for-leather from Saigon to Boulder after you."

"He never did," Quinn pointed out.

"Honesty." Jay shook his head. "At least I know my woman's safe from him." Both of them feeling more comfortable now, he told her about Helen, whom he was taking home to see Charles. "He won't approve, but the hell with him. He'll have to get used to us."

"Good luck." Quinn was still smiling. He had changed too. Certain those changes were for the better, she cradled his face in her hands and kissed him on the mouth. His lips felt warm, gentler than she remembered, but it could have been a brother's kiss, or a friend's. It affected her no more than that. Jay had never loved her, she sensed, as much as he loved Helen now.

Quinn had never loved Jay as much as she loved Welles.

Welles took care of her, as she needed to be cared for and so rarely had been; but the other night, when he'd told her about Jay, she had also taken care of him. That was love, she thought.

All these years, wondering about Jay, she'd made her own prison. Looking at Jay, she thought perhaps they all had.

The truth hit her hard, making Quinn's fingers tighten on Jay's cheeks until he took her hands away. Laughing, he picked her up and whirled her around in a circle, kissing her eyes and cheeks and mouth again. When he set her down, she was laughing too, through tears.

Quinn didn't know when she became aware of Welles, or sensed his presence, but she looked up to see him at the gate, one hand on the latch, the other at his stomach. As if he were holding himself together. His face was white as frost.

"Walk me to the car," Jay said. He would have looped

an arm around her waist but Quinn stepped back before he touched her.

"There's Welles." And she went to him without a backward glance. Up close, she saw that he had taken off his glasses. One temple piece, wrapped with tape, dangled from his shirt pocket.

His eyes looked soft and hazy and full of uncertainty.

Quinn took his hand. "You should have heard the stories." She waited until Jay joined them at the gate. "Jay's promised to come back soon with his bride and tell us more."

Welles blinked.

"Her name's Helen," Jay murmured. "One hundred and ten pounds of devotion and loyalty."

"You bastard."

"I couldn't help it, Cochran . . . Welles."

"I was on my way to break your nose when I saw you kissing Quinn."

"You asked for it."

Quinn looked from one man to the other, but neither seemed inclined to explain. With a shrug, she let her grin join theirs and the three of them walked Jay to his car. Helen was waiting at the hotel in Boulder, he said, and they wanted to get on the road to California. "I'm showing her the States." He paused. "There's one more thing before I go." He looked at Welles. "I want you to know the guilt all these years hasn't been just yours. When we plowed that Phantom into the jungle . . . the crash was my fault, Welles. I skimmed under the VC radar all right, but I didn't hold our altitude worth a damn. When those antiaircraft guns opened up, the old Slugger was a sitting duck. Fifty to a hundred feet below where she should have been."

Welles managed a smile. "From the vantage point of twenty years, it was a helluva ride."

"No shit." Jay shook hands with Welles, clapped him on the back, and then gave Quinn a last embrace.

"Keep in touch," she said.

He grinned in the open car window. "You too, beautiful. You have my address and our new phone number?"

A small burst of panic fluttered through Quinn. Patting down her pockets, she felt relief as her fingers closed over the scrap of paper he'd given her. When she looked up, her gaze met Welles's. His eyes were smiling. "I've got it. I know right where it is."

Gunning the engine, Jay took off, tapping the horn in farewell. Quinn stood in the drive, watching the sedan make whirlpools of dust in the air behind it. She stood there for a long moment. Then she turned into Welles's arms and leaned her head against his shoulder.

"By God, he *is* alive," he murmured. "You were right."

"So were you," she said, and Welles tipped her head back to look into her eyes. "The past is better left buried."

Quinn glanced over her shoulder for a last glimpse of Jay's car. The dust settled over them like Quinn's memories; the red sky to the west painted the driveway a burnished gold at their feet. The breeze ruffled Welles's dark hair, drifted through hers, and all but carried the words away on the wind. The words she had waited twenty years to say.

"Goodbye," Quinn whispered as the car turned onto the main road. "Goodbye, Jay."

Then she looked again at Welles.

"It's over," he said. "It's really over."

"Yes. Welcome home to you too." Quinn raised her face as he lowered his mouth to hers. "I love you, Welles Blackburn."

He held her close. "I love you, Quinn Tyler-Devlin."

For now, that was all either of them needed to know. The second kiss had them moving toward the house. "I think I've waited for you all my life," she told him.

AVAILABLE NOW

ORCHIDS IN MOONLIGHT by Patricia Hagan

Bestselling author Patricia Hagan weaves a mesmerizing tale set in the untamed West. Determined to leave Kansas and join her father in San Francisco, vivacious Jamie Chandler stowed away on the wagon train led by handsome Cord Austin—a man who didn't want any company. Cord was furious when he discovered her, but by then it was too late to turn back. It was also too late to turn back the passion between them.

TEARS OF JADE by Leigh Riker

Twenty years after Jay Barron was classified as MIA in Vietnam, Quinn Tyler is still haunted by the feeling that he is still alive. When a twist of fate brings her face-to-face with businessman Welles Blackburn, a man who looks like Jay, Quinn is consumed by her need for answers that could put her life back together again, or tear it apart forever.

FIREBRAND by Kathy Lynn Emerson

Her power to see into the past could have cost Ellen Allyn her life if she had not fled London and its superstitious inhabitants in 1632. Only handsome Jamie Mainwaring accepted Ellen's strange ability and appreciated her for herself. But was his love true, or did he simply intend to use her powers to help him find fortune in the New World?

CHARADE by Christina Hamlett

Obsessed with her father's mysterious death, Maggie Price investigates her father's last employer, Derek Channing. From the first day she arrives at Derek's private island fortress in the Puget Sound, Maggie can't deny her powerful attraction to the handsome millionaire. But she is troubled by questions he won't answer, and fears that he has buried something more sinister than she can imagine.

THE TRYSTING MOON by Deborah Satinwood

She was an Irish patriot whose heart beat for justice during the reign of George III. Never did Lark Ballinter dream that it would beat even faster for an enemy to her cause—the golden-haired aristocratic Lord Christopher Cavanaugh. A powerfully moving tale of love and loyalty.

CONQUERED BY HIS KISS by Donna Valentino

Norman Lady Maria de Courson had to strike a bargain with Saxon warrior Rothgar of Langwald in order to save her brother's newly granted manor from the rebellious villagers. But when their agreement was sweetened by their firelit passion in the frozen forest, they faced a love that held danger for them both.

COMING NEXT MONTH

A SEASON OF ANGELS by Debbie Macomber

From bestselling author Debbie Macomber comes a heartwarming and joyful story of three angels named Mercy, Goodness, and Shirley who must grant three prayers before Christmas. "*A Season of Angels* is charming and touching in turns. It would take a real Scrooge not to enjoy this story of three ditsy angels and answered prayers."—Elizabeth Lowell, bestselling author of *Untamed*.

MY FIRST DUCHESS by Susan Sizemore

Jamie Scott was an impoverished nobleman by day and a masked highwayman by night. With four sisters, a grandmother, and one dowager mother to support, Jamie seized the chance to marry a headstrong duchess with a full purse. Their marriage was one of convenience, until Jamie realized that he had fallen hopelessly in love with his wife. A delightful romp from the author of the award-winning *Wings of the Storm*.

PROMISE ME TOMORROW by Catriona Flynt

Norah Kelly was determined to make a new life for herself as a seamstress in Arizona Territory. When persistent cowboys came courting, Norah's five feet of copper-haired spunk and charm needed some protection. Sheriff Morgan Treyhan offered to marry her, if only to give them both some peace . . . until love stole upon them.

A BAD GIRL'S MONEY by Paula Paul

Alexis Runnels, the black sheep of a wealthy Texas family, joins forces with her father's business rival and finds a passion she doesn't bargain for. A heartrending tale from award-winning author Paula Paul that continues the saga begun in *Sweet Ivy's Gold*.

THE HEART REMEMBERS by Lenore Carroll

The first time Jess and Kip meet is in the 1960s at an Indian reservation in New Mexico. The chemistry is right, but the timing is wrong. Not until twenty-five years later do they realize what their hearts have known all along. A moving story of friendships, memories, and love.

TO LOVE AND TO CHERISH by Anne Hodgson

Dr. John Fauxley, the Earl of Manseth, vowed to protect Brianda Breedon at all costs. She didn't want a protector, but a man who would love and cherish her forever. From the rolling hills of the English countryside, to the glamorous drawing rooms of London, to the tranquil Scottish lochs, a sweeping historical romance that will send hearts soaring.

Harper Monogram **The Mark of Distinctive Women's Fiction**

ATTENTION: ORGANIZATIONS AND CORPORATIONS

Most HarperPaperbacks are available at special quantity discounts for bulk purchases for sales promotions, premiums, or fund-raising. For information, please call or write:
**Special Markets Department, HarperCollins Publishers,
10 East 53rd Street, New York, N.Y. 10022.
Telephone: (212) 207-7528. Fax: (212) 207-7222.**